The Doo Namdaron, Part Three.

Michael Porter

Copyright ? 2017 Michael Porter

All rights reserved.

ISBN:198367852X
ISBN-13:978-1983678523

DEDICATION

For my wonderful wife,
without whom none of this would have been possible.

"No matter how evil may assail you.
Remember, there is still love in this world."

CHAPTER TWENTY SIX

"Can you smell roses?" asked Gorgana, a huge smile on his face, the smoky torch was just not giving enough light to show the ground as he would have liked.

"No. Can you do anything about the light?" said Alverana. "I can track piles of horse dung in this light but reading the smaller signs is very difficult."

After a moments thought Gorgana spoke. "There may be something, let me ask a question or two."

Gorgana walked slowly back down the line, deep in thought, until he came to where Kevana and Worandana were.

"What's the hold up?" demanded Kevana.

"We have a junction with four exits and hard rock underfoot, Alverana is having extreme difficulty in reading the tracks in the wavering light of a torch."

"And?" asked Worandana, realising that there had to be some reason for Gorgana to have come back there.

"If I placed a stasis on the flame would that improve the quality of the light?"

"No. Flames rely on motion, without motion they have no life, and no light, once you make them static they just go out, and the energy of the flame is passed on to the man casting the spell, quite a few monks died trying to improve the reading lights in their cells. There is a way to enhance the flame, but that will burn the wood a lot quicker."

"We do have a restricted supply of torches, so that may not be a good idea."

"There may be another way."

"There is?"

"Perhaps, we could try a crystallisation and containment. That could improve the quality of the flame and not reduce its life, though it wont be able to move while the spells are in force."

"We'll give that a try, do you want to do it or shall I?"

"Can you?" asked Worandana.

"I think so?"

"The get on with it, if you have any problems call me."

"Right." Gorgana turned and walked back to the front of the line.

"Can he be trusted to do this?" Asked Kevana.

"Small risk, failure shouldn't cause any major harm, more damaged ego than anything else. He believes he can do it, and often belief is enough."

"Well?" Asked Alverana.

"Worandana thinks the quality of the flame can be improved by a couple of simple spells used in conjunction, it's the conjunction of the two that is going to cause some difficulty, but I believe I can do it. Nothing ventured, nothing gained. Give me the torch."

Alverana passed the torch over with a doubtful glance at Fabrana. Who was similarly sceptical.

Gorgana held the torch on both hands and spoke softly to himself, so softly that though the others were standing shoulder to shoulder with him, they couldn't de-cypher a single word, gradually a change came over the torch, the flame seemed to harden in some way, its motion became harsh and jagged, like it was flashing from one state to another, then it suddenly stopped, frozen inside a shape that wasn't really its own, like a globe of light, harsh yellow and red, unmoving and almost solid.

"Can you see what you need now?" Asked Gorgana.

"Perhaps, can you move it over here a bit?" Asked Alverana, pointing to one of the tunnel entrances.

"I'll try." Gorgana moved as slowly as he could all the time chanting to the torch, trying to hold its shape and size as steady as he could, until there was a sudden pop and the torch went completely out, they were plunged into such darkness that Fabrana gasped and reached for his sword.

"Relax." Said Alverana, hearing the sound of a sword being drawn. "The torch just blew out." A few sparks from his tinder box and the hot torch was rekindled.

"What happened?" He asked.

"I think that once the light is fixed and contained moving the torch breaks the containment and the thing just blows itself out."

"Isn't there any danger of a back blast from a spell like that falling apart so suddenly?"

"Yes, there was but on such a small scale I hardly felt it, something bigger then that would be another matter."

"Try again over here this time?"

Gorgana moved to the required spot, and on a nodded instruction from Alverana began the chanting again. The torch fixed in almost the same way, this time it seemed hotter, and whiter.

"This is definitely the way they went, I can see the smear of an iron shoe on this rock. Thanks." Gorgana nodded at the gratuity and ceased his chanting, the flame returned to normal, though a good portion of the torch had burned away. Slowly the procession resumed it's progress along the dark and twisted tunnels, Alverana's thoughts turned to the dangers of tunnels such as this, his watch on the surroundings never faltered, even though his mind was elsewhere, he usually travelled in this manner, no one else could tell that he was only half watching where he was going, relying on instinct to inform him when something was amiss. His instincts had never failed him, or at least never in any dangerous way, it felt to him that the higher the risks around him the closer his automatic awareness scrutinised every aspect of his vicinity. The path twisted and turned, each turn brought him closer to those that he was following, or if not closer then at least he wasn't loosing ground. The condition of the horse droppings that he was following told him that they were still a day behind, not any more but definitely not any less, it was getting to be more than a little tiresome, the fact that they weren't getting any nearer to their quarry. Alverana desperately wanted to speed things up, but in the confines of the cave system he couldn't take any chances, there were just too many potentials for danger, he had to go slowly, and carefully, even though the thieves had already walked this path, they could have set up another ambush, like the snow demon, this was one of the things that scared him the most, the fact that they could be setting up the snake, or whatever it is to attack him and his friends, it could be hiding anywhere, waiting for them to come within reach, after all that is how snakes get their food, they are ambush predators, patience is their greatest weapon. The cold blooded waiting was something that made him shiver every time he thought of it, snakes were a thing he hated with a passion. The tracks of the snake were now clear in the sandy patches, the curving scuff marks in the sand, both on top of the footprints, and below them. It seemed as if the snake was hunting the party ahead, but even with all his years of experience, he still couldn't avoid the thought of a huge snake waiting for him to come into range of it's strike. He knew something about snakes, he had made a point of studying the thing that frightened him most, in an effort to allay his own fears, an effort that was doomed to failure from the outset, his fear was irrational, and was not going to reduced by knowledge, however complete. Considering the size of the snake he was fairly sure that it couldn't be venomous, a snake that grew to this size had no need of venom to quell it's prey, only lots of prey, an excess of food over many years was the only way a snake could get to be this large. Questions started to rush through his head, even as his eyes and ears struggled against the dim light of the torch and the incessant echoes of the caverns. 'What had this snake been eating to achieve this enormity?' 'What could possibly have lived in these caves that gave it the sort of food supply it would have needed?' 'Had that food supply been exhausted?' He waved Gorgana to come close.

"What could a snake like this one eat?"

"Anything it damned well chooses."

"But what could it find around here?"

"This cave system could be very extensive, there could be a good supply of food for it somewhere."

"I have never heard of a cave with that rich a food supply."

"Then how can it exist, you do after all know everything there is the know." Snorted Gorgana.

"I have never said anything like that, it's just that I cannot envisage a life system that can generate enough food for a predator like this snake, at least not one that isn't fuelled by the sun. The sun makes the plants grow, the grazers eat the plants, the predators eat the grazers. That is the natural law of life. But there can be no plants down here, because there is no sun."

"Perhaps there is some other source of energy for the life system here."

"What could it be?"

"Heat?"

"How?"

"I don't know, but heat is a sort of energy like the sun, perhaps something uses heat like plants use sunlight."

"Some fungi grow in total darkness, don't they?"

"Yes, perhaps some of those use heat to make them grow."

"But where is the heat in this cold cave."

"It's not really cold in here, is it?" Asked Gorgana.

"Come to think of it, it's not. It's not the cold of a normal cave, if it were something like a snake, being cold blooded, couldn't ever have survived here. It's almost pleasantly warm. So there must be some form of heat around here somewhere."

"Perhaps there is some residual heat from a volcano nearby."

"Volcano's, that's just what we need right now, more things to worry about."

"Any volcano would be so long dead that it's never going to

erupt again."

"How can you say that? Only a few years ago, a volcano that had been dead for more years than anyone can remember, blew it self to pieces and killed hundreds of people, and that was a totally cold mountain, right up to the day it vanished."

"What do you mean vanished?"

"Vanished, gone, disappeared, destroyed, and taken the whole valley with it, and every living soul, every plant and animal. The place is now a vast expanse of ash and dust, and the mountain is a mere stump. Perhaps life will return one day, but not for many years I feel."

"Life almost always finds a way, it's sort of stubborn like that." Said Alverana.

"True, I suppose, but that place turned into a desert of ash overnight, the nearest sign that life had ever existed there was a whole days ride from the mountain, and that was just the toppled trees of a huge forest, lying down, all pointing away from the mountain, like a huge wind had blasted them over."

"I think that life will grow again there, far sooner than you would think, there is always the destroyed trees for it to use as fuel, the fungi that could not grow on the living wood will flourish on the dead, as they always do, and the cycle of life will start up all over again, it may take many years to get back the lushness that was there, but it will return. Sometimes I feel the ultimate fate of man is something similar, cities reduced to hunting places for forest animals, trees growing up through houses, and nature taking over all our plans and dreams."

"But for something like that to happen man would have to be dead, all men would have to be dead."

"I know, that is the hardest thing of all to understand. I dream of the jungle returning to take over the towns, and wonder what happened to all the people."

"Not even the gods could destroy all the people, they need some to be their worshippers, without the support of people they just fade away, every one knows that."

"Which can only mean that it is man that has destroyed himself."

"Perhaps this dream of yours is prophetic, that black bird we met said something about the destruction of all life being the only way it can be set free of this world, and that the thieves have the power to do just that, perhaps the outcome isn't quite as the bird would hope for, maybe only man is destroyed."

"Either way we are all dead."

"Perhaps this is a sign that we don't actually lose."

"Dead is close enough to losing for me, from the sound of things just staying alive is going to be difficult."

"These are all maybe's stacked on perhapses, piled on what ifs. All we can really do, is take life as it comes, and deal with what it sends us, each moment a new experience."

"I wouldn't mind a bit of a quiet patch now and again though."

"How long were you stationed in the fort, as honour guard for some weapon that may never emerge?"

"We were there almost a whole year, before all this started."

"Well that has to have been a very quiet time, doesn't it?"

"Yes it was quiet, nothing much happening, just drills and practices to keep our skills and swords sharp."

"Boring?"

"Definitely." Nodded Alverana, "Sometimes soul destroyingly

so."

"Bored now?"

"Definitely not."

"Which do you prefer?"

"Can't there be some middle ground? Somewhere between bored to death, and crawling through the dark being hunted by a snake."

"It seems that our lives seem to run to extremes, we have no middle ground." Gorgana shrugged and fell silent, his thoughts turning inwards, back to the sunny days of his youth, before he was taken in by the priests, that was a time of middle ground, hard work and a soft bed, good food and good friends, a time of innocence, a time of confidences, that had passed long ago. He wondered if the others remembered the time before the calling to the priesthood as fondly as he did. The soldiers joined because they were soldiers and as such needed an army to fight for, some of the clerics joined because they saw power in being a part of the priesthood, others joined because they wanted to help others find the god they served, but he was a little different from most, he joined because he had a thirst for knowledge, something that couldn't possibly be fulfilled in any farming community or even any small town, nothing less than the libraries of the monasteries could fill his need for knowledge. The price of this knowledge was the fact that he had to join the priests of Zandaar, a price he was more than willing to pay, though his belief in the god he served was not as many thought it was. He believed that Zandaar was indeed a god, but not necessarily the only one that deserved the service of the people, his research had taught him much about the other gods, the older ones and the newer, many of the things that he discovered in his rummaging through old books made Zandaar look unnecessarily cruel. Zandaar only dealt with the worshippers of other gods in one way, convert or die, that was the choice, inside his sphere of influence there were no other gods allowed, though the edict wasn't completely successful, some paid the necessary lip service to Zandaar, but still held on to their old beliefs, and old practises were merely driven underground. He realised that this is the main reason for the size of the military arm of Zandaar, the underground sects had to be winkled out into the open and destroyed, unlike the council of Zandaar, Gorgana thought that this was counterproductive, the more an army tries to destroy a religion the deeper underground it goes, and the more attractive it seems to the young, who are all rebels at heart, a rebellion grown from the natural discontent of adolescence. These religions should be absorbed into the body of the Zandaar religion and slowly changed until they are indistinguishable from the main religion. Gorgana knew enough to keep these opinions to himself, to even think this way was a risk, but then risk was nothing new to him, from his earliest days in the monastery, he knew that he was different, though he strove to hide it. The intellectual tests and magical tests were far too easy for him in the early days, but the religious tests, the knowledge of the book of Zandaar, was hard, he learned it as the others did, like a parrot speaking the words it heard, but he grasped the meanings behind it far quicker than any around him, he surpassed him teachers in very short order, something that singled him out for individual attention, even in the early months. Only his instant recall of the dogmas and teachings from the book saved him from disgrace and perhaps even death in those treacherous times. He saw that the religion of Zandaar had been misguided at some point in the past, deliberately or accidentally he couldn't tell, but it moved away from the underlying beliefs about two hundred years ago, it became more violent and more oppressive, only slowly at first, but much more quickly in the last fifty years or so, the members of the council seemed to be competing with one another to produce the most strict of religious instructions that they could find, something as simple as a hat to be worn on the religious festival, that suddenly became an important part of Zandaar belief, to be worn at all times, on pain of death, usually in some gruesome manner that no-one had ever thought of before. The council was driving the religion of Zandaar away from it's peaceful beginnings and into a path that could only lead into the darkness of self-destruction. Gorgana was certain of this, but there was nothing he could do about it, every extremity of the council only found more favour with Zandaar, every decision that they reached, only fuelled the gods vanity, the more that Gorgana thought about this the more he felt that he would be lucky stay alive in the gradually changing religion that he was using as a shield, a place to hide and learn. With a sudden flash he realised that he was going to have to leave the church of Zandaar, before it killed him for being different, or he betrayed himself, with the same result. The realisation was so sharp in his mind that his feet forgot that they should be walking, he stumbled into Alverana. A quick grab from the soldier made certain that Gorgana didn't fall, though it was a very close thing.

"Did your legs fall asleep?" Asked Alverana.

"No, but my thoughts distracted them a little, I think they forgot that they were feet, and they turned into clods of clay."

"Feet of clay?" An allusion to a story from the early days of the church, a man with feet of clay stumbles towards the light of the god.

"Perhaps." Said Gorgana, 'stumbling away from the fierce light of god, the light that burns more of the faithful every day.' He thought, wondering how he was going to deal with this sudden change of allegiance, it wasn't as such a great change as he was never really allied with Zandaar, or his teachings, he merely wanted to learn all he could about the world around him.

"Can you stand? Or do you want me to hold you up all day?"

"Sorry, " Gorgana answered taking his own weight on feet that certainly felt like clay just at that moment. "I'm very distracted for some reason, it feels like someone is walking through my mind with spiked boots, thoughts all mixed up and making absolutely no sense at all."

"An outside force?"

"I don't know, I've never felt like this before."

Alverana took him by the chin and stared deep into his eyes, the torch in his free hand held just high enough for the light to those blue eyes with yellows and reds. Gorgana felt that gaze cutting into his mind, burrowing like a mole through his head, pushing aside any defences that he erected in its path, tunnelling in, deeper and deeper, Gorgana became desperate, but knew that struggling would only make things worse, so he threw up a confusing image of swirling colours and disconnected thoughts, a maze of amazement. Alverana's piercing gaze struggled against the confusion that it saw, though he thought he was looking for something from the outside, all he saw was confusion on the inside.

"I'm not very good at this sort of thing, that's why I'm a soldier. Worandana will know what to do about this external force, why would it just pick on you?" Alverana released the monk and turned away, waving urgently for Worandana to come.

"What's the problem?" Asked the elderly priest.

"Gorgana suffered and attack of something akin to vertigo, and then complained about a confusion that seemed to come from outside, I could find nothing effecting his mind from the outside, but then I'm not skilled in this field."

"Has the feeling gone?" Demanded Worandana.

"Yes." Mumbled Gorgana, "It only lasted a moment, and then it was gone, it didn't feel like a specific attack, more a general, sort of broadcast thing. It's very difficult to describe, there just aren't the words for it."

"After it hit did it seem to focus, sort of target on your mind?"

"No, it was still just a general vague feeling of unsteadiness, like the ground was moving under my feet."

"You felt the ground move?"

"No. The feeling in my head was like the feeling you get from your feet when you stand on a wobbly plank, unstable, insecure, all those sorts of things, but nothing to do with actual feet, or ground. It's so hard to explain."

"Like the root of your world was being shaken beneath you?"

"Perhaps, but then no, like but different. Words just don't make themselves understood." Gorgana was getting more than a little distressed by the fact that Worandana was getting quite close to the root of the problem, Gorgana had suddenly decided to stop following Zandaar, and everything that the god stood for, so be discovered in this sort of apostasy could only result in death. "The more I try to focus on the thing, the more slippery it becomes, it seems to slide away from any approaching thought."

"Perhaps we are all getting just a little jumpy." Said Kevana, "this place is getting under our skins, and we are looking for malign reasons for everything, even the bored distraction of a usually sharp mind. This could simply be Gorgana falling asleep on his feet, the sort of daydream that we all experience in times of boredom, let's move on. We have a job to do. We have some people to kill."

Gorgana breathed a soft sigh, hoping that the spotlight of investigation would turn elsewhere. He turned away and started to walk slowly in the direction they had been taking, his eyes cast downwards to that none could see the relief in them. Kevana stared hard at Alverana, the questions in his eyes, Alverana shrugged he was uncertain as to what had happened to Gorgana, and wasn't going to incur the wrath of Kevana just to find out if this was something else from the cave or from inside Gorgana. Worandana's thoughts turned to the younger man, Gorgana's past was littered with small moments of discord, a wrong word here and there, in the wrong ear, never enough to warrant close investigation, but often just of the edge of heresy. These are the people he liked in his team, the ones that showed some signs of independent thought, and the creativity that is required in the strange circumstances that he believed lead to the expansion of knowledge, Worandana knew that this was the driving force of Gorgana's life, as it was his own, the decision is made, Gorgana will get some careful observation, his loyalty will be tested in subtle ways, but not just yet, let him relax for a while. Worandana nodded to himself and followed the bowed back of the man in front.

Alverana stepped slowly, his senses reaching forwards along dark tunnels, hoping for the clue that would tell him where that damned snake was, but nothing came, no matter how he focused, even the occasional sudden stop and holding of breath, only intensified the beating of his own heart in his ears. The hard rocks of the narrow places gave no clue that the preceding group had even passed this way, they must have been moving very slowly when they passed here, otherwise the sliding of the horses shoes would be leaving the tell tale shiny patches on the stones, this caused him to slow some more, they had known something that he wasn't feeling, perhaps the thing that had slowed them down had moved on, or maybe this was the place they had got to when they realised there was a huge snake down here. This was really starting to irritate the tracker. He stopped. Stood up straight and made the choice. Turning he passed the torch to the man behind him.

"Hold it high, so that I can see what is coming."

He slowly drew his sword, the harsh scraping of the blade caused all eyes to look in his direction.

"What is going on?" Demanded Kevana.

"I'm sick of creeping through the dark!" The quiet words rang like a shout down the tunnel, echoing the thoughts of many. "If

I'm to die today, it will be with my sword in my hand and a song of death in my heart, I'll skulk no more." He turned to face away from the others, raised his sword until the tip was almost touching the roof of the cavern, slowly he filled his lungs to the utmost, and howled "Zandaar." The shout echoed down the tunnel and a flash of light jumped from the upraised tip of his sword, a hot blue spark that echoed with the sound, a challenge to anything that was lurking in the deepest recesses of the cave.

Kevana turned to Worandana and smiled. "You better move your people to the back, things could get a little exciting now."

"Why?"

"Alverana is building up to a berserker rage, not a place for clerics to be, it's much better If his closest friends are around him when he finds the trigger."

"God's protect us." Muttered Petrovana as he shuffled past the retreating clerics, he took the torch and held it high so the light from it shone over Alverana's head, illuminating the tunnel with flickering and dancing light. Fabrana move to Alveranas right, bow strung and arrow ready, Briana to the left sword in right hand, poniard in left, Brianas sword is lighter and shorter than Alveranas huge two handed broadsword, slightly curved and razor sharp on the front edge, and for the first few inches on the back, a formidable weapon in his skilled hands. Petrovana's sword hung in his right hand, the left holding the torch, Kevana took up station behind them all, his right hand resting on the hilt of his sword, which remained in the scabbard. Kevava started to speak slowly the prayer of the warriors.

"We are the priests, we are the warriors, we are the flame, we are the scythe."

"We are the defenders of the faith."

"We are the arm of god in the world."

"We are the fire and the fist."

"Zandaar!"

The last word shouted by all, a blast of noise into the darkness, all their weapons outlined in blue light, the upright sword of Alverana a beacon of blue that outshone the flickering torch. As one they stepped forwards a steady march to a beat in their own heads, they seemed to be staring ahead, blankly almost, their eyes never moving from straight ahead. The clerics rushed to catch up, they had been caught unaware by the sudden motion.

"What is going on?" Asked Gorgana.

"Something rare." Said Worandana. "Sometimes groups of soldiers achieve a sort of unity that goes beyond the normal, they can think and act together as one, they become a single mind, with many bodies. These aren't quite there yet, but if battle is joined they will be."

"I've never heard or read of anything like this."

"You won't have, it's whispered of very rarely, and written of not at all. It is considered tantamount to heresy by the council, but that is only because they are afraid of it."

"Afraid?"

"Very afraid. It is said that such a group, should all its members attain that state of berserker rage, then the group could achieve anything, beat any opponent, even a god."

"They could turn against Zandaar, and destroy him?"

"So the council believe."

"Is their belief accurate?"

"Who can tell? There are no records, no attributable stories, no histories, not even any old legends, of anything even vaguely similar."

"Do you believe the council are right?"

"I've seen a single berserker take on a hundred men and win, I've seen a group such as this one take on a thousand men and kill more than half of them in a matter of minutes, who can say what a berserker group can do."

"What happens if they decide in the heat of battle that we are a threat?"

"You'll die before you know they have made the choice."

"Don't you find that more than a little frightening?"

"Do want to live forever?"

"No, but I don't want to die today."

"Not even in the defence of your god?"

"Our god! How could the death of someone such as me benefit our god?"

"That's for god to decide, isn't it?"

"I suppose so, but not today please, I can be of service tomorrow."

"You can be of service today."

"All this discussion means nothing." Interrupted Apostana, "They," he nodded forwards, "have decided that there will be battle today, and we had better be ready to support them, in any way we can."

"Don't get too close to them, they are a group entity, anything outside the group could easily be considered a threat, use fire and lightning, but sparingly, we have limited supplies, and I don't think we will be able to replenish those any time soon."

"So we just throw lightning and fire over their heads and pray for our lives?"

"That about sums it up, yes, however, be aware that though they are a group entity they don't need to remain together, they act as a group even when they are separated, that is biggest part of their impact. They will attack simultaneously from all angles. It's a very scary thing to watch even from a distance, there are no spoken orders, no calls for help, the only sound that can be heard is the prayer, softly spoken except for the last word, and that one is usually accompanied by the death of an enemy, or of many enemies. I have seen this only once, many years ago, I was on the edge of a major battle, offering healing aid to the injured. The battle was in it's third day, and the enemy had just received it's third batch of re-enforcements, our forces were going to be destroyed, there was no doubt, they were outnumbered 3 to 1 and by fresh troops. The general called the entire officer corps together and they all went into the group mind. Together they ran into the enemies lines, on a front 50 yards wide, it was like a farmer cutting wheat, they tore through the enemies heart, leaving a swathe with nothing standing, howling that single word they destroyed everything in their path. They died to a man, but the enemy paid a hundred to one or more. Once they were dead a dreadful silence descended on the field. Some of the more intelligent troupe leaders opened up our lines and showed the enemy five groups of well drilled soldiers all acting as one, as far as the enemy was concerned this was five times the mayhem they had just survived. They threw down their arms en-masse, the general and his officers saved the day and more lives than can be counted, on both sides."

"Surely there were so many witnesses that the stories must have got out?" Asked Gorgana.

"The officer corps all come through the priesthood, the common soldiery don't, all they saw was an act of bravery by the whole leadership, not something they are used to, but none the less, only brave men doing what they can to save the lives of their subordinates, in a hopeless situation."

"Are our new friends going to fight until they are all dead?" Whispered Apostana.

"No, in that battle it was purely weight of numbers that killed them all, they had no chance of survival from the beginning and they knew it, and still they went."

"I'm glad I'm not a soldier." Said Apostana.

"Would you not give your life for your friends?"

"Yes, for my friends, but for a whole group of people I don't even know, that would be a lot more difficult."

"Life is full of those sort of decisions. A man can only be judged by the choices he makes in times of stress, a decision made in a hurry is more likely to be closer to a man's feelings, than one made with plenty of time." Worandana was looking straight at Gorgana when he said this.

"I can see how that would work, but surely, the closer to the way one feels the truer the choice?" Replied Gorgana.

"Yes, but given time, other factors will be considered, things that can change the choice, perhaps to a better one, but not so true to the heart."

"But it is very important to be true to ones heart."

"Yes, but there are bigger issues, things more important than oneself."

"These things in themselves should be close to one heart, family, friends, god. All these are close to my heart."

"Yes, perhaps, but in the instant of choice, on the cusp of

decision, which order do those three come?"

Gorgana paused for a moment, he felt that he was being tested and that Worandana was learning more than he would have wished.

"My family are here, my friends are here, my god is here. There is no difference between them, all three come together as one, in any place where we are, for the brothers of Zandaar are my family, my friends, and our god is always with us."

"A text book answer with much consideration, in extremis you may choose otherwise." Worandana turned away, concentrating on the marching backs of the soldiers, he could feel the tension building amongst them, it was approaching a climax, one that would end in battle and death. The marching pace of the soldiers began to quicken, slowly at first then with increasing urgency, despite the un-evenness of the ground they held a marching step, Worandana waved his men forwards, they were beginning to get spaced out and too far behind the leading group.

Above the noise of the soldiers boots Worandana began to hear sounds of battle, shouts and the ring of swords, the sharp crackle of magical energies being somewhat extravagantly expended. He felt a sudden need to be where the action was, he soldiers felt it even more, the pace didn't quicken but the stride did lengthen somewhat, behind him he could hear Apostana's breathing becoming more laboured, 'They need more exercise.' he thought, not noticing that his own breathing was a little ragged. Soon voices could be heard, shouting commands and offering advice, the unmistakable sound of a heavy bow boomed occasionally, leaping shadows of blue fire danced up the tunnel towards them. The soldiers stopped so suddenly that Worandana almost collided with them. One more turn of the tunnel and he could tell that they would be in the open space where battle had been joined. He wondered briefly what the delay was, why were the soldiers just standing still and silent? What were they waiting for? Then they moved, as a unit, with every step their boot heels hit the ground at exactly the same moment, they marched round the turn and into the open space beyond, the last word of their prayer shouted from each set of lips "Zandaar". For an instant they stood again, then scattered, Fabrana stepped further right and his bow spoke its mournful song three times in quick succession, Worandana wondered what he was shooting at, the enemy were in plain view, some distance away at the other end of the large cavern, but Fabrana was shooting arrows upwards, towards the rocks that were falling from the roof of the cave. He saw the roiling fog that was clinging to the roof, occasionally there would be a glimpse of something moving in it, but he couldn't be sure. Apostana threw a lightening bolt upwards into the fog, perhaps hoping to hit something, perhaps just to shed some light, the result was neither of those, the bolt formed fully into the bright streak as it should, then disappeared into the fog, it struck something, the explosion of electrical energy illuminated a large part of the roof area, but only lit the fog, which blossomed like a flower around the point of impact, and the petals of this flower were fragments of stalactites. These exploded into smaller fragments when they reached the floor of the cave, scattering sharp stone shards over a large area, luckily for the monks none was seriously hurt, a few minor cuts where the only consequences, that and a quiet promise from Gorgana to explain 'something' to Apostana when there was a little time. The light coming from the other end of the cavern was quite intense, an old man was wielding a wooden staff that was hurling huge bolts of blue light at the head of a snake, the majority of the snake was hidden from view amongst the stalactites, standing close to the old man was a tall man with a heavy sword on his back, and the longest bow that Worandana had ever seen, the thump of the bow string was clearly audible over all the other noise in the cave, it was propelling arrows all the way to the feathers into the hide of the snake, it's head was beginning to look like that of a bird. Kevana noticed the sword, the black jewel in the pommel shone with a strange radiance, he knew it was the sword he was pursuing, rapidly the group of soldiers moved across the cavern, intent of the sword and it's capture. It must have been something about the way they were moving towards the snake that attracted it's attention, the head swung round, two hard black eyes swept them with passionless intensity, the coldness of the glance slowed the men not at all. Then from above their heads a huge length of snake, as thick as Alverana's body swept them all to the floor, its grey and brown mottled colours made it completely invisible against the rocks of it's surroundings, only it's motion made it obvious, Worandana and Gorgana threw fire bolts at the head as it came towards Fabrana's prostrate and motionless form, the head was engulfed momentarily in a fire ball that lit the whole cavern. Under the cover of this glare the other group of people disengaged and ran towards the only exit, where a soft light could be seen in the distance. As Worandana watched they escaped through the narrow opening, the man with the bow did something strange, he held his hand out towards the snake, for a moment Worandana was sure he saw a flock of arrows fly into the open hand, then the man reached over his head and drew the sword, Worandana was almost certain he could hear it moan as it was drawn, the man paused at the exit, grabbed the woman as she passed and signalled to the old man, the three stood in the exit, with a word the man struck the wall of the exit, the woman struck the other wall with an axe, and the old man loosed an enormous bolt of blue light at the apex of the opening. As the three retreated from view the opening collapsed in what to the priest appeared as extremely slow motion, blowing a plume of dust into the cave. Apostana and Kirukana joined the battle hurling lightning at the snakes head, the effect was no more than the fire, it stopped for an instant then with a shake came on again, Kevana faced the snake with his sword in his hand, Briana moved to the right, and pulled a handful of daggers from under his jacket, these he threw with force into the side of the snakes neck, every time the snake flinched away Kevana attracted it's attention with a wave of the sword. Petrovana moved to the fore waving the torch under the snakes nose, almost within biting range, an easy target that the snake couldn't resist, the flickering flames enticed it, as Petrovana ran away it followed, it skirted the fallen form of Alvernana, swinging it's head towards the flame.

Kevana retreated slowly not wishing to attract the snake again. Alverana suddenly leapt to his feet and ran to the side of the snake, climbing up the side, using daggers as stairs, he was on top before the snake was even aware that he had moved from the floor, taking his broadsword in both hands he plunged it point first into the snakes neck, just where head and neck came together, a shiver, then a spasm fled from the head to the tail, as Alverana stepped into empty air and fell to the ground the snake tried to curl up on itself, writhing into a huge knotted ball it hissed and coiled, then uncoiled and thrashed for a moment, then coiled into a ball, Alvernana rolled to his feet, and walked almost casually over to where Fabrana was starting to move, the monk staggered to his feet, and recovered his bow from where it had fallen. Kirukana hurled another lightening bolt at the snake.

"Stop." Shouted Kevana, over the noise. "It's dead, it just may take it a while to work it out." Waving to the men, he started walking towards the entrance, never taking his eyes off the snake, he waited until the others were all in the confines of the tunnel before he himself stood guard at the opening. Over his shoulder he asked "Anyone injured?"

"Bumps and bruises only, Fabrana's the worst, but nothing really damaged, he'll be sore for a few days, that's all, thanks to a thick skull. Alverana has twisted an ankle a little, but again nothing serious, he was just trying to look good jumping off that snake, fool." Said Briana.

"The only damage," retorted Alverana, "is that my sword is still in the snake, if it hadn't lifted up as I struck I'd have pinned the damned thing to the ground."

"Perhaps, but only a hands breadth of your sword has come through it." Answered Kevana, the noise of the snake was declining rapidly, the cavern was splattered with it blood, as was almost the whole length of the snake, it had made the wound from the sword even bigger with all the struggling, Kevana walked slowly towards it, cautiously, not wanting to get too close to a dying strike, then forked tongue flicked from side to side, ineffectually tasting the air, which reeked of the creatures own blood, even so that human noses could smell it, the cold black eyes were unchanged even in death, passionless puddles in a sea of blood. The quivering of it's length subsided, with a bubbling exhalation spewing blood from its mouth and the back of its head, it died.

"Well." Said Petrovana loudly, "We'll not go hungry, so long as you don't mind snake steaks, there's got to be enough here to feed an army."

"But nothing to cook it with." Said Gorgana.

"Raw snake steaks, it'll make a change from raw fish."

"You are a sick man."

"Maybe, but I won't be hungry."

CHAPTER TWENTY SEVEN

Jangor turned to Namdarin, Jayanne and Granger, all of whom were sitting on the grass coughing as if they would never stop.

"What happened in there?"

"We put a little something in their way." said Namdarin, laughing and coughing at the same time.

"What?"

"A mountain." spluttered Granger, "I'm too old for this sort of thing." he muttered further.

"How long will it hold them?"

"Who can tell, it should give us a few hours to get our breath's back, but nothing in this world is certain."

"That's for sure. We'll eat, then make tracks. Which way are we going?"

"East, that bird thing said there was a weapon that way that could help us, elven mindstone, or something wasn't it?"

"Mander." Shouted Jangor, "Make something to eat, let the horses eat for a while as well, we'll move on as soon as we've eaten."

Namdarin looked around for the first time since they had emerged from the darkness. The valley was broad and wide, the cave system exited through a large outcropping of grey rock that thrust upwards through the valley floor, not far away was a wide river, slow flowing and meandering across the valley, small clumps of trees were visible, there were none of the signs of cultivation but the valley somehow managed to give the impression that people lived here, or had lived here.

"Jangor. What do you make of this place?"

"It looks strange, feels odd, I can't quite work out why."

The smell of wood smoke indicated that a fire was already burning and Andel returning from the river with a large water skin that was so obviously full stopped conversation until Namdarin had washed the dust from his throat.

"Any signs of nearby habitation?" Asked Namdarin.

"I see nothing, but again this place makes me uneasy." Said Jangor.

"If there is anything it will be downstream." Said Kern.

"Why downstream?"

"The grass gets shorter that way, so cattle or sheep come this way to feed, but not too often."

"That's it." Said Namdarin. "The damned grass looks like a partially cut lawn, far too green to be just natural and wild."

It didn't take long for Mander to produce an edible broth, a chunky soup of vegetables and dried meat, rich with fat and herbs.

"We are going to need supplies soon," He said, to anyone who was listening. "This is almost the last of the meat, and there is very little grain left."

"We'll see if we can get something at the next village, which shouldn't be too far away." Said Jangor, then he turned to Namdarin. "How much rock did you pull down in the tunnel?"

"I don't know I wasn't wasting time looking back I was doing the best I could to keep my feet under me, there was a lot of noise and dust, it should be more than enough to hold them back for a while."

"Do you think they'll turn back rather than digging their way out at this end?"

"Not a chance of that, they want this sword too badly, they've invested far too much time and too many men to turn back now, or ever."

"Sooner or later we are going to have to deal with them, once and for all."

"Sooner or later, but not just now, from the glimpse I got they out number us by a few, not many but enough to make a difference."

"Do you have any idea where the weapon is we are now looking for?"

"I know nothing of the land this side of the mountains, I don't even remember seeing a map of it, we'll just have to ask around as we go."

"I don't like making too much contact with the locals, there is always the chance that they will learn something of us and pass that information on to our enemies."

"The risk we have to take." Namdarin shrugged, his thoughts turned inwards, he wasn't really sure if he wanted to hunt for the elvish weapon, he felt that Gyara had told them of it for it's own reasons, it wanted the weapon found for a reason, one that Namdarin was worried wasn't to anyone's advantage other than the birds. Gyara said the mind stone was only limited by the mind that wields it, a human, or elven, mind would be no problem, but what would happen if a god took this thing, what of limits then? The more he thought about it the less he liked it, but the overriding consideration was that any weapon could be very useful, as they neared their final target the odds against them would stack up, stack high and fast, every advantage was going to be needed as they got nearer to Zandaarkoon. Mentally he took a coin and tossed it, heads we get the weapon, tails we don't, heads he called.

"How far away is that village?" Asked Jangor of Kern.

"No more than a couple of hours, I don't see people walking more than an hour or two to feed their cattle, and this is obviously a place they wouldn't leave them overnight."

"Very true, we only have a couple of hours of light left so let's get moving." The fire was doused in a moment and everyone was on their feet, gear packed and mounted in only a couple of minutes, the horses had had enough to eat for a while but the temptation of fresh grass was too much for them, all the riders were pulling heads up away from the longer clumps of grass, that always seemed to grow just to one side of the path. As they headed south along the valley loosely following the river, the grass became shorter and shorter, and a bare path developed, leading straight south, gradually widening and deepening, over the tops of an approaching grove of trees there was a plume of smoke, which soon developed in several plumes from many chimneys. Following the path they came round the grove of trees and saw the village proper for the first time, it had a wooden wall about eight feet high all the way round, in front of the wall was a forest of sharpened stakes, each pointing outwards and about two feet high. The only visible opening in the wall was blocked by a rather rickety gate, just wide enough for a small cart to pass through. Kern waved a subtle hand single from his usual place in the lead. Stergin, Mander, and Andel, eased their swords in their scabbards and moved slowly into a line abreast, the covered the whole width of the path. Jangor moved in behind them, and slowly advanced until he was level with Kern.

"What's happening?"

"Someone by the gate saw us and ran off, like the devil himself was after him. I expect a reception committee of some sort to be assembled in fairly short order."

"Let's see what they've got, slowly as if we haven't a care in the world."

The slow walk towards the village continued, they watched as the gate swung slowly shut, and a group of men formed up on the other side, ill equipped and disorganised. Looking more than a little scared. Jangor heard the creaking a Namdarin stringing his bow, so he looked back quickly and shook his head, Namdarin frowned, and Jangor shook his head again, so Namdarin desisted, leaving the tactics to the experienced soldier. Through the gaps in the wall and gate they could all see a somewhat decrepit village, most of the space inside the wall was taken up with cattle pens, sheep, goats and cows, though the pens had no food in them it was certain that the cattle were let out every day and then returned to the pens for the night, and judging by the droppings in front of the gate they had only just been penned for the night. Looking closely at the force arrayed against them Jangor was certain that every able bodied man in the village was there, and one or two that were anything but able bodied, some far too old and some barely dry behind the ears. Jangor knew he could take the village by force if he wished, it would only take a few minutes, but the village would die, most of the men would die and the village would never recover from that. Jangor and Kern stopped their horses with the animal's noses almost resting against the wobbly gate. Jangor raised himself in his stirrups and Kern scowled at the men on the other side of the partition, Jangor swept the men with a hard, cold gaze, he paused briefly staring into the eyes of the only man with a bow, until the man's hands started to shake so badly that he dropped the bow, but didn't actually start to run. Jangor took a deep breath, filling his lungs until his chest was several sizes bigger than it normally was, then spoke in a calm voice, in the sort of tone that struck terror into the hearts of soldiers on the parade ground.

"We are short on supplies, and come in peace, we would like a place to sleep for the night, and this looks like a nice enough place to us." While he was speaking the men inside the wall, all looked in one direction, they were looking to their leader for instruction, Jangor followed their glances until he was looking straight into the eyes of the leader. The man had the build of a blacksmith, huge arms and chest like a barrel, the sunlight glistened in the sweat on his shaven head, he held a long spear with a rather ornate head, not the sort of thing that Jangor would have taken to battle. The man appeared to be thinking, it was a slow process, Kern moved his horse forwards half a step, horse rested its chin on top of the gate and snorted at the people, it seemed to them to be laughing in their faces. Namdarin came up alongside Jangor, the extra hands of Arndrol put him in plain view of all the villagers, the long bow showing above his right shoulder and the black pommel stone of his sword above his left, Arndrol didn't even have to lift his head to see over the gate. The headman looked at his forces and knew in his heart that they would never fight against these men, and running away they would die.

"If you come in peace, then come in peace, I am sure we can come to some sort of arrangement for supplies and sleeping quarters." His men breathed for the first time in what to them was an age. Most started to disperse immediately, not waiting for a command to do so, somehow this irritated Jangor, the headman stepped forward warily. "The gate opens outward gentlemen." The horses stepped backwards and allowed the headman to open the gate, Jangor dismounted and faced the headman.

"Jangor." He said holding his hand out, waiting for the other to do the same.

"Garin." Was the reply, their hands clasped and held firm, Garin was indeed a strong man, his grip was like Iron, and obviously the weapon he used to subdue everyone he met, Jangor stared coolly into his eyes, they were the same height but Garin was some considerable amount heavier, the muscles in the headman's forearm were standing prominently as he exerted all his force on Jangor's right hand.

"Lead on." Said Jangor without any hint in his voice that the man was even touching his hand let alone trying to crush it. Jangor made a mental note to teach this bully a lesson before they left. The grip broke and they turned to walk into the village, Kern and Mander stayed by the gate, until all the others had passed through, only then did they follow their friends into the village. The crowd of people was quite large, in fact Jangor was convinced that every person in the village had come to see the strangers, he was surprised that the arrival of a small group could cause such a stir. As they walked slowly along what could only be described as the main street, the cattle pens to their left were full, near to bursting in some cases, the beasts milling around and making all the noises that are associated with such places and the smells as well, luckily the light breeze was blowing most of the stink away from the houses. Houses that were in general in need of repair, mainly made of wood, that showed much damage from weather and the decay to which wood is prone. All in all, this was a particularly run down village, though it did seem to have everything that a village could need, the blacksmith's forge was blowing some dark smoke across the street, and filling the air with that characteristic hot metal smell. The clothing of the inhabitants wasn't in any better state than the buildings, tattered and torn, patched and mended, generally scruffy and ill kempt, the worst cases were the two people coming towards them, each holding the handle of a large handcart, their clothing was a nondescript brown colour, that looked in serious need of a wash, as did all the rest of them, the crowd parted to let them pass, no one talked to the shabby pair, most even turned away, as the hand cart slowly passed Jangor observed the contents, this was the manure cart, not doubt it had been full recently, when the cattle were out being fed, now it had been emptied, but the remains of it's cargo were clear for anyone with a sense of smell. Jangor knew there must be another gate, one that probably led to the fields that grew the vegetables for this village. As they approached the smithy the headman guided them around the back to where there was a fairly large corral, with just two shaggy looking horses.

"You can keep your animals here, and we'll talk about provisions in a little while, there is a small green area just that way, you could set up your tents it you wish, I'm afraid that we probably couldn't get you beds in one house, and the tavern such as it is, is far too small. If that's all right with you?"

"I'm sure that will be just fine." Said Jangor, he waved a few of his hand signals, and people started moving, the horses were taken to the open green area, and unloaded and tents set up, without a single word being spoken, Mander and Andel took the mounts back to the corral, though Arndrol was unhappy at the idea of being penned up with the two scraggy looking ponies that were now trying to hide in one corner. All the time the curious crowd followed them around but said nothing, the whole village was eerily silent, the only sounds those of the cattle and the odd stray dog yapping on the end of a leash. Jayanne stayed very near to Namdarin, the people were making her quite unsettled. The two of them were sitting on the ground in front of their tent, waiting for the headman to return with news of provisions and such when Mander walked back into their impromptu camp.

"I have found the tavern and the smith is right it is very small, it is across the other side of the green, perhaps the best place for it, it doesn't smell much better than the animal pens." He said.

"How's the beer?" Asked Namdarin, feeling more than a little thirst for something a little stronger than water.

"How would you expect beer to be in a place like this?"

"Looking at this place I would say that by the time you'd drunk a whole bucket full it must be tasting almost palatable."

"You'd be wrong. As far as I can tell the only good thing about this town is the beer, the man that makes it is an artist, it's nectar of the gods, you wouldn't credit that a shit hole like this could produce such a great beer, I never want to leave here."

"By the time half the daughters in this village are expecting your children and your money has run out you won't have much choice but to leave." Laughed Namdarin.

"That's right, you look on the gloomy side of everything as always. Are you coming for a beer?"

Namdarin looked at Jayanne for a moment and they stood up together. Namdarin settled his sword but looked at the bow, it was far too big to be taking into a bar, and would be of absolutely no use in there, but he was loathe to leave it behind, he put it in the tent and tied the flap down. Three of them walked across the green and around the upright stone in the centre, Namdarin paused for a moment to examine the rock, it was an upright, rough hewn rock, but the top which was only the length of his forearm on each side was perfectly smooth, like a very small altar, but at chest height, were most altars are about waist height. There were no markings or stains on the surface, but it still looked like a sacrificial stone of some sort. He shook his head and they carried on towards the tavern.

"What do they do for religion here?" Asked Namdarin.

"I haven't seen a church, or anyone that looks like clergy of any sort, and I've covered almost the entire village."

"Almost?"

"Only a fool would get downwind of the pig pens, that stench would permeate your clothes for days, I like to keep a few friends around me."

Namdarin and Jayanne both laughed as they walked down off the slightly raised green and across the track towards the front of the tavern, which was now clearly identified by the rough tables and chairs placed on its veranda. The building was in a little better state of repair than most of the others in the village, the front was painted a drab sort of green, but it was paint not rough wood. The windows had shutters on them that were open, letting light and warmth into the rooms, the large open veranda already had a few customers seated, each had a huge mug in front of them, the mugs looked like glazed stoneware, all the same dark brown colour.

"How many mugs have you had?" asked Namdarin.

"Only one." replied Mander. "Two or three of those would be more than enough for anyone, except perhaps Jangor and Kern."

"One?" asked Namdarin, doubtfully.

"Honest, only one. It was hard to walk away after that one, but only one."

"You had difficulty walking after only one?"

"No difficulty walking, it was just hard to leave knowing there is still beer in the barrel. I think we'll sit outside, it's really small inside." Namdarin nodded and they picked an empty table, the high backed chairs made it impossible for Namdarin to sit down while still wearing his scabbard, so he took it off, and propped it against the table so that the sword would be close to hand, Jayanne sat to his right, she placed her axe in a similar sort of position, Mander sat next to Jayanne, but he placed himself in such a way that his scabbard wasn't tangled in the chair, and wouldn't be fouled if he had to stand and draw at the same time, he didn't look in the least comfortable, but he did look ready. A serving girl wandered out through the wide front door of the tavern, she must have been all of thirteen years old, her dress was ragged around the hem, which would have been more suitable for a girl two or three years younger, it's length was almost immodest. Her knees and elbows were dirty, her face grubby, and her hair lank and greasy.

"Good afternoon, my dear." Said Mander, before the girl could even open her mouth. She looked up puzzled, this sort of thing just never happened here, most people just yelled orders at her until she got them right. Mander caught her blue eyes with his, he was amazed at the colour, her eyes were such a pale blue encircled with a darker band, he had never seen their like before, the speechless moment passed.

"We would of course like some of your fine beer, but we like food to go with the beer, how can you help us with this?" He stared straight into her eyes, and smiled, to Namdarin it seemed that his whole face lit up with that smile. She held his eyes with hers and smiled slowly back, a smile that revealed a set of perfectly white teeth, and illuminated her face far more than the failing sunlight that came from behind Mander's head.

"We have some chicken, if that's all right?" She said quietly.

"I'm sure that chicken will be fine, or anything served by your fair hand." Said Mander. She gave a short bow, and disappeared into the darkness of the building. Mander laughed softly to himself. Namdarin was looking around at the other clientele, and didn't see the girl return with the beers, at least not until the mug hit the table, the sound attracted his attention, he muttered a quick thank you.

"Thanks my dear." Said Mander. "Will the food be long, and can you spare a few moments in your busy day to chat to a lonely traveller?"

"The food will be ready soon, and I'll talk to you when I can." She tossed her long hair and turned away, swinging her hips as she went back inside. Mander smiled.

"You had better be careful." Said Namdarin. "She's very young."

"In some places that I have been she is young enough to have children of her own."

"We don't want to go upsetting any one here."

"Have no fear, all I like to do is spread a little love where ever I go."

"Be careful that is all you spread." At this point Namdarin picked up his mug of beer and had a taste. "This is wonderful. How can something this good be made in a place like this?" He shook his head, then drank some more.

"It's not easy," said a voice, "but I do the best I can."

"And you are?" asked Namdarin.

"My name is Garath. I make the beer."

"How do you do this here?"

"I think I'm just lucky, the barley they grow here is just great stuff, the hops that grow lower down the valley give it that bitterness, and the water here comes straight from the snow of the mountains, there is nothing purer in the world. This is a great place to make beer. It's a shame that the people here don't really appreciate what they have."

"I'm impressed, your beer is probably the best I've ever had, and I have travelled a lot more than the people here. Thank you master brewer for your efforts, this is truly excellent beer." said Namdarin.

"I thank you kind sir, you are one of the strangers that arrived earlier?"

"Yes. I am Namdarin, this is Jayanne and Mander."

"Pleased to meet you madam, and sir." said Garath. "We don't often get visitors here."

"Why is that?" asked Mander.

"We are a long way from anywhere. The valley has good soil and grows good crops, mix that with the large number of cattle it can support and you have a thriving community, but we don't need much from the outside, and anything that we have left to sell isn't really worth enough to transport out, people don't come here and the people here don't travel much. It's just the nature of the place." While Garath was talking Jangor came onto the veranda.

"I thought I'd find you in the nearest bar." he laughed, taking a seat at the table.

"This is Jangor." said Namdarin, "Jangor this is Garath, he makes probably the best beer in the world."

"Well if Namdarin says it is probably the best then I should probably taste it." He reached out and took Mander's mug and tried the beer. "Very good indeed, and nicely cool, which is unusual." Mander reached for his mug of beer. "Get your own." said Jangor.

"I had my own, then you turned up."

"Carin." shouted Garath, "More beer for the gentleman, and add another order of food for this table. Sorry gentlemen and lady, but I have a bar to run, perhaps we can chat later." He walked away from the table, collecting empty mugs and wiping tables as he went back into the darkness of the tavern.

"What to you think of this village?" asked Namdarin.

"It has a good water supply on the inside, good food stores, little fuel stored, but the wall is far too long and the gates are a joke, they wouldn't even stop an angry goat, this place cannot be defended with anything less than three hundred men, even then losses would be very high." Carin arrived with tray this time with four mugs on it. Her dress was somehow tidier, her knees and elbows were clean, her face had been washed, and her hair combed and tied back, her smile was as radiant as ever, and seemed to add a couple of years to her age. She served Mander first, standing very close to him as she did so, her hip brushed against his arm as she leaned over to serve the others.

"The food will only be a short while, I am sorry for the wait. Will there be any more coming tonight?" she asked turning that smile on Mander.

"There are a few others, they'll probably be round in a while, don't worry we'll have enough to keep you busy all night."

"Good." she said, turning away, as she did so Mander stroked her back gently, she looked back and smiled.

"Don't you ever stop?" asked Jangor.

"Not while I breathe."

"I don't want to have to fight my way out of this village, and I don't want any excess baggage when we do leave, understood?"

"Yes. Since when do I ever bring any excess baggage with me, I always leave it behind."

"Except for that one in Boradan."

"Ah. Yes. That one. You'll never let me forget that one, will you?"

"No. That cost us many days hard riding, and her family a lot of good horses."

"They didn't have to ride their horses to death, she'd have gone back in a couple of weeks anyway."

"But did you really have to take her away the night before her wedding?"

"She wanted it, not me."

"Garbage. Namdarin, can you do the horse thing and find out if those priests are still in the cave, I'd hate to go to sleep and wake up with their swords in our bellies."

"I'll go and have a little chat with Arndrol, and see what we can find, but I'm not sure that the horses will be able to reach one another through all that rock."

"Just give it a try."

"Right, I'll be back in a little while, don't let this pig eat all my food before I get back." he said, nodding towards Mander.

"Somehow I don't think that food is going to be in short supply tonight, but I'll keep an eye on the pig, though I think he's got his eye on something other than food."

"A man cannot really live on chicken alone." said Mander. Jangor just shook his head.

Namdarin walked back across the green as the sun was sinking towards the white frosted mountain tops behind him, he paused by the stone in the centre of the green, It looked even more like a sacrificial altar in the setting sun, Granger walked up while he was staring at it.

"What do you make of this stone?" he asked.

"I'm not sure." said the old man, "It looks very old, I think it was here before the village, it feels like it's roots go very deep and many years back in time. Notice how the sun approaches that notch in the mountain top as it sets, perhaps on a special day of the year the sun sets in the centre of that notch, it could be a calendar marker, or something like that."

"Perhaps, I have heard of such things before, but usually on a grander scale."

"Where are the others?"

"There's a tavern over there," He pointed in the general direction, "Where else are they going to be?"

"I'll see if I can cadge a beer or two."

"There's food as well."

"You know, suddenly I feel very hungry."

"See you soon." Namdarin continued his walk to the horse corral. Arndrol was enjoying a good meal of fresh grass, that someone had hung on the fence in a large net bag. Namdarin walked up to the horse and stroked his head.

"How are you my old friend?" The horse flicked an ear and blew a clump of grass into the air. Namdarin leant into the corral and put his head right up against the horse's, he made the mental contact with the herd mind in an instant, this was getting easier with practise. In a moment he had full contact with all the horses in the corral, and then reached out to the others, it was a struggle because the contact was very faint, but he reached them, they were huddled together in the dark, tied to the wall of the big carven, the men were busy, doing men things, the most prominent thought in the horses minds was the presence of a huge snake, not moving but still far to close for comfort, it was making the horses very nervous. Namdarin withdrew the contact and returned to the horses in the coral, they were now more than a little nervous, the ponies from the village were stamping and whinnying, disturbed by the idea of a snake that big. Namdarin calmed them down, and thanked Arndrol before breaking contact. Breathing a huge sigh, he turned back towards the tents, there were people there so he decided to find out who they were. Kern was stacking supplies in one of the tents, Andel and Stergin were helping out a little. They saw Namdarin walking towards them, "Where's everyone else, I thought they'd be here?" asked Stergin.

"There's a tavern with good beer. Where do you think they are?"

"Beer sounds good to me." says Andel. "Where is this tavern?"

"Across the green, I'm going back there now."

"What do you think of the village?" asked Namdarin.

"It's seems a little strange to me," replied Kern, "very isolated, insular, the people are not used to visitors at all."

"That's right, apparently it's too far from anywhere else to have much traffic with the outside, should be ideal for us."

"But how long can we stay here?"

"Long enough to get supplies, and a good nights sleep."

"So we'll be moving on in the morning."

"I think so."

As they approached the tavern Namdarin saw that two tables had been pulled together in preparation for their arrival, each table had a pile of roast chicken, potatoes and soft white loaves, with plates and gravy jugs in abundance. The headman had also arrived and was sitting next to Jayanne, her hand was resting on the haft of her axe, Namdarin's strayed to the hilt of his sword.

"Garin." said Jangor, "I believe that Namdarin would like to sit next to his betrothed, if that's all right with you?"

"Certainly," Said Garin, getting to his feet. "Apologies, I wasn't aware that the lady was betrothed."

"I'm sure it is a surprise to you." said Jangor, while Namdarin regained his seat.

"You have news for us?" asked Jangor.

"Yes. The others are still trapped in the cave, the horses are very disturbed by the presence of such a large snake, even if it is dead. They could be a while breaking out, I believe that's what they are attempting, but the horses aren't at all clear on what they are actually up to."

"You think we can sleep safely tonight."

"Almost certainly, I'll have a chat with Arndrol, and get him to keep an ear on their horses."

"Great, get some food down, and some more of this great beer. We'll rest here tonight and move on at first light." Jangor held up a mug of beer and drank a great draft, wiping the froth from his lips with the back of his hand he issued an enormous belch.

"Some people are just peasants." Said Mander, more to Carin than to anyone else, she smiled and laughed a little, before going back inside.

"How can you know what is going on in the caves?" asked Garin.

"Namdarin is a little strange," said Jangor, leaving Namdarin to his food. "He talks to his horse, that big grey," Garin nodded, "and the grey talks to other horses, even those far away, it's something to do with the herd mind of the horses, it's complex and simple all at the same time."

"Very strange. And you say the snake is dead, definitely dead."

"Oh yes, if the horses are even in the same place as that snake it drives them mad, to be actually looking at it, then they must be sure it is dead."

"How did you kill it?"

"We didn't, it was very much alive when we left the cave, and collapsed the entrance."

"You deliberately trapped people in the cave with the snake?"

"Yes, but then those people would have done worse for us, let's just say we don't see eye to eye about a few things."

"What sort of things?"

"It's a religious thing really, they want to convert us, and we don't want to be converted."

"We don't go in for religion much around here, but what is so wrong with joining a new religion, even if you don't believe in it?"

"No, you didn't quite understand, they don't want to convert us to their religion, they just want to convert us to being dead people."

"You've obviously done something to upset them."

"Yes." interrupted Namdarin. "They burned down my house with all my family inside, so I burned one of theirs, and then things started to get worse."

"Who are these religious people that believe in conversion by fire?"

"They are Zandaars, they wear only black, and preach absolute servitude to their living god."

"I think they have been here, some years ago a monk came and tried to convert people to a new religion, I didn't take too much notice, and nor did anyone else, I think he gave up and went away, we don't pay attention to religious people, mostly I think they are boring. I better go and check the gates and fences, the sun is almost down, and sometimes the gate keepers are asleep by now." This said he rose, and wandered off in the direction of the gate, he carried a mug of beer in his hand, his legs seemed a little unsteady.

"Strange people." said Kern, in between mouthfuls of chicken and beer.

"I agree." said Granger.

"And wrong." said Garath dropping into the empty seat.

"Wrong?" asked Jangor.

"Oh yes, very wrong. They have a religion they just don't realise it, they serve a god, they just don't know his name."

"Who is this nameless god they all serve?" asked Granger, suddenly very interested.

"Have you seen money change hands here?"

"No, not even when I collected the supplies from the store, and I don't mean store as in shop, I mean store as in warehouse. A building were everything is stored, a very strange way of doing business to me." said Kern.

"We don't use money here, we all trade in services, it's a very fair and simple system."

"How do you mean?" asked Granger.

"If you want, say a new axe," he reached towards Jayannes axe, her hand was there first, and a snarl on her lips. He raised his eyebrows, "Sorry my dear." He apologised before going on, "You could go and dig a barrow full of coal from the mountain and take it to the smith, you fill his forge and pump the bellows for an hour or two while he makes some horseshoes and he'll make you an axe head in a couple of days. Take the axe head and some glue you've made from horses hooves to the carpenter at the other end of the village and he'll put a nice hickory haft on it for you. Simple as that."

"That is nothing unusual, it happens all over the world, why is it different here?" asked Granger.

"Have you seen anyone pay for beer?"

"No, but that's not too unusual, many tavern owners keep a running total of their clients bills in their heads."

"Not me, I don't charge."

"Now that is unusual," said Mander, "I'll have another beer."

"Are you sure?"

"When I've finished this one of course."

"See you are getting the religion already."

"Are you saying that we are sitting in a church?" laughed Andel.

"Definitely."

"Hang on," said Mander, "If you don't charge, how can you afford the materials you need to make beer?"

"I don't pay for things either. I say to a man with a field, I need barley, he delivers barley, he drinks beer. I say to a man with a run full of chickens, I need chickens to feed my customers, he delivers chickens, he drinks beer. A very simple system, and it works. I think our isolation here helps."

"But what happens when people don't want to work for their beer."

"Oh, there are the odd ones who take unfair advantage of a system that relies so much on honesty, but it isn't long before the whole village realises who is not participating properly. These people soon become pariahs, they are shunned by all, no one talks to them, no one helps them, they very quickly get into a very bad place to be."

"Don't they turn to theft to get what they want?"

"Sadly that is true, but there are ways to deal with this sort of aberration."

"I see no stocks, or gibbet, how do you deal with thieves?" Asked Granger.

Jangor laughed out loud.

"What's funny?" demanded Granger. Jangor just kept on laughing.

"He knows." said Garath, "There is a way to get back into the good graces of the village, it is a hard road to walk, a lonely road to walk, but minimum food and services are provided to those that chose to walk it, but when sufficient time has been served, then a person can return to normal life, and most never go back again."

Jangor continued to laugh, and pointed to a small rickety table that was set up on the path in the open air, two jugs already in place, and two small piles of sandwiches. There was no one sitting at the table, two dirty figures were walking across the green towards the tavern. No one else noticed them or commented on them, the two sat at their table, to eat and drink their evening meal.

"Jangor," said Granger. "Share your knowledge, please."

"The ones that don't play by the rules get to shovel shit."

Every one of the strangers looked at the two eating with heads bowed, they were indeed the two seen earlier pushing the manure cart.

"They provide a useful service," said Garath, "they take the manure to the fields where it is used to help grow the food we all eat and the barley for the beer, and the corn for the spirit."

"No body mentioned spirit before." said Jangor.

"No body asked."

"Could we try some of your spirit?"

"Do you sing? do you dance?"

"We are soldiers, warriors, we sing the song of steel, we dance the dance of death."

Garath looked around the table. "There are enough of you, you have at least one storyteller amongst you, tell some tall tales for the customers tonight, and you shall have spirit, the like of which the gods themselves have never tasted."

Jangor nodded, looked straight at Mander. "You're up, you earn us our spirit."

Mander looked meaningfully at Carin, "Boss, I'm sort of busy."

"Yes you are, you're telling stories to interest the good people of this village. And I'm going to get totally legless on spirit, any other questions?"

"No, boss." Mander's head dropped, he knew better than to come between Jangor and a good spirit.

The sun sank below the mountains and a dark shadow progressed at a slow walking pace across the green in front of the tavern, two large braziers were lit, one at each end of the veranda, people started to arrive from all over the village, drinking beer and talking, no-one actually approached the strangers, it seemed that the presence of armed strangers in their midst was something they weren't used to. One man sat on the wall at the other end of the veranda, strumming softly on a guitar, he sang in a soft and gentle voice, after a couple of ballads he returned to just playing guitar, a woman in a long green dress stood next to the guitarist, and sang a couple of songs of her own. The bar was getting very full, the beer was flowing and a party atmosphere developed, soon the villagers were talking to Jangor and Mander, Namdarin and Jayanne were sitting very close, not touching but never beyond arms reach. Kern was sternly unapproachable, he had a mistrust of crowds, and Jangor knew that it wouldn't be long before Kern did his usual disappearing trick, for such a large man Jangor was surprised at the easy with which he just vanished in a crowd. Stergin and Andel, were sitting quietly, enjoying a rest in lively company. Garath came out onto the veranda and spoke to the crowd.

"We have some strangers amongst us, as you all can see, they come from far away and have tales to tell, will you listen?" The talking stopped in an instant, and people sat, or stood, waiting with some patience. Jangor nodded to Mander, who moved to the wall at one end of the veranda, it is just about waist high, he hitches up onto the wall and leans against one of the uprights that hold the roof in place. With his left arm around the post and a mug of beer in his right hand, he starts to speak, slowly at first, introducing himself, telling the people of the place he was born, and briefly of how he was chosen to be a soldier. His story of waking up in an army barrack room, with the mother and grandfather of all hangovers, a five year contract to be a soldier, signed in his own hand, which he had no memory of, brought more than the a few laughs. From that first laugh, he had them, he could have explained why grass was green and the audience would have been enthralled, but he was telling much more exciting tales, dead men who return to life, demons that run on four legs and hunt in the snows of the high mountains, monks that rain black fire on their foes, sword play to rescue maidens in distress, long before he started to get really fanciful Garath came out carrying a tray with some small stone flasks, and some very small glazed cups. He gave a flask and some cups to Jangor, passed the other flasks around the audience, and took a cup full to Mander, who paused in the middle of his latest tale of daring do, to take a taste of the spirit, his eyes shone, the fire of the fluid burned his throat, but in that extraordinary way that only a good liquor can. Mander thanked Garath and carried right on with the tale, Carin came out onto the veranda, and sat on the floor with her back to the wall and her arm around Mander's leg, he reached down and stroked her hair, without ever breaking the thread of the story, gradually the crowd began to thin as they got tired and returned to their homes and their beds.

"The people here go to bed early." Said Jangor to Garath, in a voice that only just bridged the gap between them.

"They are working people, they work hard all day from sunrise to sunset, then they come here and relax for an hour or two, it's only people like us that don't have work to do can stay up all night."

Mander's last tale ended in the usual heroic manner, and he slumped to the floor beside Carin, his arm around her shoulder and hers around his waist, he leaned close to her and whispered something in her ear, she laughed and kissed him softly at first then harder and deeper, she broke away and laughed, climbed to her feet and went inside. Jangor looked round, knowing that Kern had gone long ago, Stergin was deep in conversation with a woman in a long green dress, Andel was snoring at a table, blowing bubbles in spilt beer, his own spilt beer. Jayanne and Namdarin were resting against each other, her head on his shoulder, his head against hers, their eyes closed and their hands clasped, but they weren't sleeping. Carin came out with a flask and a mug of beer. She put the flask down between Jangor and Garath, and sat on the floor next to Mander passing him the mug as she did so. Mander's hand slid slowly up her leg and disappeared from view, she giggled and kissed him again. Garath poured more of the spirit for himself and Jangor. They raised their cups and toasted the stars, which for some reason seemed so much brighter than usual, the braziers at the ends of the veranda were dying down, due to lack of attention.

"This is a nice place to visit." Said Jangor.

"Thank you, I like it here, it can be hard work but it's a good life."

"I'm sorry if we are going to cause you any problems."

"What problems could you cause for us? You are good people, and you'll be gone tomorrow."

"We are good people, up to a point, but those that pursue us, they most certainly aren't. They could cause you some problems."

"How? They'll come from the north, as you did, and we'll tell them that you went south, which is the only way out of this valley, they probably won't even stay for a beer, they'll not want any spirit, and they'll never even know about the wine."

"Wine. Nobody said anything about wine."

"Wine is a good way to start the day, fear not, you'll taste it tomorrow."

"This place is just full of surprises, what do we have to do for the wine?"

"Don't worry about it, Mander's tales tonight will be the topic of conversation here for many a moon." He glanced round to where Mander was still sitting against the wall, only now Carin was sitting on his lap, facing him, her skirt hitched high up her thighs. "I'm sure his performance will meet all necessary requirements." He laughed softly.

"I hope that's not going to cause any problems." Said Jangor.

"She's neither married nor betrothed, and a little fresh blood is always welcome in a small place like this. Our community is too small to be self sustaining if you know what I mean."

"I understand, but she is a little young."

"Only in your eyes, take my word, she is no novice."

There was a sudden crash, Garath was amazed at what followed, Jayanne and Namdarin were on their feet and turning towards the sound, the sword in the man's hand and the axe swinging up in hers, Stergin was already putting his sword away by the time that Garath had turned, Mander was unmoved, but the speed of the two who had seemed for all the world to be asleep utterly amazed him. Andel came to rest on the floor, he didn't even wake up, just curled up into a foetal ball and continued with his sleeping. The woman in green stepped in close to Stergin and whispered something, Stergin threw a fast salute towards Jangor then turned away, with the woman on his arm, she was guiding him across the green, but not in the direction of their camp. Jangor replied with a clenched fist signal, and Stergin nodded. Jayanne and Namdarin waved to Jangor and set off in the direction of their tent, it seemed the party was over.

"What was the hand signal you gave that man?" Asked Garath.

"Sunrise, we move at sunrise, he'll be there, but Andel will probably still be asleep, you could always throw a bucket of water over him before the sun comes up."

"No problem, I'm always up by that time of day, it's something to do with the damned cockerel that lives behind the tavern, for some reason he doesn't wait for the sun to show itself."

"When did the rest of our party leave?"

"The old man with the staff, he left fairly early, but he did put his staff in the fire for a while, strangely it wasn't burned by the fire, and yet it looks like it's made out of plain wood. Very strange. The young man, who seems to be infatuated with the red head in your group, he left a short time ago, on the arm of a young girl, he was very drunk, I think his performance will be well below expectations tonight."

"What of Kern? The large man that was sitting at the end on the table."

"I don't remember him leaving at all. That in itself is remarkable, because I always know who is where and when, but he seems to have vanished at some point that I can't identify. Are you sure he left, perhaps he just faded away?"

"No he left, and I have no idea when, I try. Every time we are in a place like this, I know he is going to vanish, he doesn't deal with crowds well, so I try to watch him, but he always just slips away, and no-one ever knows when. He's a good man, but very quiet, I thought I knew him as well as any, but he has given me a real surprise in the last few days."

"Perhaps you do know him as well as any, but he decides how much people know."

"Very true, he is a good friend, and if he wants to keep his past secret, then that is his choice, I'll not question him."

"The best way, he strikes me as a man to have at your back."

"Oh, he's that and so much more."

"What can you tell me of your journey?"

"We are heading south."

"I know that but what else? What do you intend to do? Where are you going?"

"The people who are currently doing impressions of moles will soon be coming this way, and the less you know the less danger you are in, I wouldn't want to put this place at any risk, you have been so good to us."

"Moles?"

"They will be trying to tunnel their way out of the caves, they can't afford the time it would take to go back and round another way. All I can say is that they are likely to be unpleasant. If they try to leave one of their number behind to provide religious direction for your village, then you must wait until the main party is far away, then kill him, but kill him fast, if he knows that someone is going to kill him they will die first. Arrows are best but only if the killer is a good shot, a head shot is essential. If you give him time he can communicate with the others even at extremely long distances, he must be surprised and dead before he can do anything about it."

"I think I understand."

"Don't make any attempt to fight them, they have weapons you won't believe."

"You are really serious about this, aren't you?"

"Deadly, and I do mean deadly. The priests of Zandaar are the ones that burned Namdarin's house to ruins, I saw the ruins, not a pretty sight. One priest took over the whole of Jayanne's village, but Namdarin beat him eventually. They are serious people, who serve a living god, and will do anything at all in his name. I don't know enough about their political structure, but I don't think it's anything unusual for a theocracy, they always seem to tend towards the extreme. You and your people must be very careful of them, to some extent they can see what people around them are thinking, but my head feels so fuzzy now that I don't think they could find anything of interest in here."

"And, if they drink enough they wont even want to think."

"There is that too." They were distracted by the moans from Carin, she was still astride Mander, her hips rocking back and forth, her dress open at the front, her breasts swinging with her movements, Mander's eyes were shut, as he slid his hands from her hips up to her breasts, he rolled the nipples in his fingers, until they were hard and erect, then he squeezed them quite hard, she gasped with the pain and pleasure that mixed in her sweating body, her breathing came in short sharp gasps, rocking faster they moved together to a shuddering climax. She squealed and he groaned, with the final thrusts, they collapsed together and rested for a moment or two, her head on his shoulder and his arms around her waist. Once their breathing had returned to a more normal pace, she stood up and took his hand, pulled him slowly to his feet and the walked into the tavern, not bothering to cover themselves, the sweat glistened on her belly as they walked through the door.

"No novice." said Garath.

"Indeed."

"How far are you going to take this battle with the priests?"

"Namdarin intends to fight until he has killed them all or is dead." He laughed at the thought of the time they met Namdarin in the forest.

"Will you fight with him?"

"Perhaps, if there is an honourable way for me to back out, I may just take it, but Namdarin is in all the best ways right, it will be very difficult to walk away, especially knowing what that will do to his chances."

"You agree with his fight against these priests?"

"Yes, they are a law unto themselves, and they will impose their laws on the entire world, like it or no, they will."

"I like the way we live here, I don't want that changed by these priests, I hope you succeed, though I feel that your chances are small."

"There are things on our side, these priests and their god may just be in for a serious surprise."

"What sort of things work in your favour?"

"You wouldn't believe the things that have happened since we teamed up with Namdarin."

"Such as?

"Sorry, I'm not going to tell you, those priests may just see the memories in your head, and I want it to be another surprise for them."

"I understand, you need to get some sleep, and so do I. There will be breakfast available for travellers from before sunrise. See you then." Garath stood and went inside, leaving Jangor on his own, to listen to Andel's snores. Jangor picked up the flask that was left, it was more than half full, he left the veranda and headed across the green towards the tents, the light from the dying braziers faded to nothing in only a few paces, he was making his way by the light of the stars, which was barely enough to pick out shapes and silhouettes, he heard some noise off to the right, but this was a moan of pleasure not pain, he decided not to investigate, the people didn't want any attention, so he left them to their entertainment, the starlight was just enough to pick out the shape of Crathens buttocks moving to a rhythm that Jangor couldn't hear. Before long he could see Korn, his face was lit by the fire he had set between the tents, Jangor wasn't surprised that Kern was looking straight at him, the tracker had obviously heard him moving across the grass, even over the noise of the fire. As Jangor neared the camp, another face came into view, a woman with her head on Kern's shoulder, she was no girl, but certainly not beyond thirty years old. He staggered round the tents and sat down hard beside the fire.

"Has the whole world gone sex mad?" he asked of the fire.

"It always has been, you just don't always notice it." said Kern, in a tone softer than normal, nearly inaudible above the crackling of wood burning in the fire, a sudden pop and a spark sprang forth, drifting upwards on the heat plume burning fiercely, but fading quickly.

Jangor laughed and wobbled a little too close to the fire, Kern's upraised arm was all that stopped him from falling into the flames.

"Bed time for you." whispered Kern.

"Where is everyone?"

"Granger is snoring, Crathen is somewhere on the green, entertaining some girl, Namdarin and Jayanne are in their tent, Stergin checked in a little while ago, he said he'll be here before dawn, Mander and Andel I've not seen."

"Mander disappeared with some girl, and Andel is sleeping under a table."

"He still thinks he's a big drinker." laughed Kern.

"Yes." nodded Jangor. "I think I'll get some rest."

"I don't call becoming unconscious resting." snorted Kern.

"It's as close as I can get in this village, it's seems there is going to be noise all night."

"For some, that is the best sort of rest they can get."

"Night." said Jangor, he didn't bother to stand up, just crawled into his tent and was soon snoring, a loud rattling, snorting.

"He complains about noise." said Kern to his companion, she looked up into his eyes and smiled, the flickering fire lit the blue of her eyes. "You know we'll be gone in the morning?" he continued. She nodded and smiled again, her hand sliding inside his tunic, softly stroking the hairs of his chest, circling his nipple, she turned her head upwards, and reached towards his lips with hers, they kissed for a long time, their world shrunk around them until there was nothing other than themselves within it, his hand found her breast and held it, thumb and finger rolling the nipple until her breath caught in her throat, the nipple hard under his touch. Taking her by the hand he went into Stergin's tent, he had no wish to disturb Jangor, as he turned towards her again, her dress fell to the ground, revealing her naked body in the light filtering through the opening of the tent, the sight was such that he didn't bother to close the flap, it had been a long time for him and he wanted to savour every moment. He climbed out of his clothes in an instant. They fell together in a frantic joining, each seeking comfort in the other, hands hot on each others bodies, mouths searching and finding, the heat of their passion far exceeded that of the fire, had it been visible it would have lit up the entire expanse of the green with hot white light. Joining in the rising motion of passion they reached an intense climax together in minutes that seemed to be hours. Collapsing they rested.

CHAPTER TWENTY EIGHT

Once the snake's body had stopped it's twitching and writhing, though it was long dead by that time, Kevana and Alverana approached the point where the exit used to be, very cautiously they approached.

"What do you think?" Asked Kevana, as another rock skittered to land near their feet.

"It doesn't look good, they certainly pulled down a lot of rock here, there could be a way to tunnel over the top of the fall, but it's going to be slow and dangerous."

"Perhaps we can use the same sort of magic as we used at Granger's cave?"

"I think not, that was a totally different case, here the rocks are piled precariously on top of one another and we are going to be going underneath, the forces involved are a hundred times greater, and the risk many times more than that."

"Damn them, we nearly had them."

"Except for that huge snake in between us, and now this rock fall."

"I don't need reminding of the obvious."

Alverana shrugged and turned away, he went back to where the horses where, they seemed more than a little disturbed by the presence of the snake. He gathered them up and took them back to the entrance, where they could be further from the snake, he stroked their necks and whispered to them until they were more relaxed.

"Do you know any mining magic?" He asked of Gorgana.

"I know a miners digging song, something about 'swing that pick, break that rock.' Not the most inspiring of melodies, but fitting for miners, they are mainly deaf, the noise of picks and shovels, it makes their hearing fade. I can't think of anything that could be of constructive help just now, but I'll have a look through one of my books, I seem to remember something about holes in the ground."

"You do that, but don't come up with anything too stupid, Kevana is so mad right now he could do almost anything, including cutting the head off someone who says something as a joke."

"I see, I'll be careful what I say."

"But you'll have to be quick, light is going to be a serious problem soon, we don't have many candles and very few torches, so we need to get out of here before we run out of light."

"Understood, I'll search as fast as I can, and get one of the others to help, Worandana may know something." He waved the chief cleric over. "We need to get out of here very soon, any ideas?"

"Nothing that springs to mind, but I'll have a rummage around, see what is there." The old man sank to the floor, straight into a cross-legged posture, in a single fluid motion that spoke of years of practise, his hands rested on his knees, his eyes closed, his head fell forwards as if he were suddenly asleep or dead.

"Does he often do that?" Asked Alverana.

"Not too often, but occasionally he does it in the wrong company, we are used to him, others aren't, they think he's just died on the spot, their reactions can be quite amusing." Gorgana went to his horse to get a couple of books out, before he sat on the floor, flicking through two books at once.

Kevana came over, "What's happening here?"

"Research, one with book, one with memory, they'll find a way to get us out of here, have no fear."

"You suggest I'm afraid of something?" Kevana snapped.

"Only that they'll get too far away for us to catch, it is possible if we have to go all the way back to get out of here."

"You look round for another exit, there could be one."

Alverana, nodded and took a small candle, using it to plot the courses of all the drafts in the cavern, he found that the other exits were far too small for a man, even a small one.

"Are you getting anywhere?" Demanded Kevana.

"Not really," replied Alverana, "all the exits are too small, but it may be possible to open one up, there is one to the left of the original exit, it looks like a single large boulder has blocked an opening, there are four small passageways around the boulder, only big enough for air to flow at the moment, it shows promise, if we can find a way to move the boulder without actually bringing the whole mountain down on us."

"Anything from the clerics?"

"No, but they are looking, so who can tell."

"I want those damned thieves dead!"

"From this distance, I believe you have tried that once, with no success as I remember."

"We are a bigger group now, we should be able to kill them."

"They will be expecting something, it will be very difficult, and they learn something every time we try."

"Learning will do them no good if they are dead."

"I don't believe they can be killed in their dreams, they are too strong for that now."

"I don't care, I want them dead!"

"We'll have to see what Worandana thinks once he surfaces, he's deep into his trance just now. He may have something better once he comes round." He was trying to calm Kevana, the tension in commander's voice made everyone edgy.

"Do you think there are any more snakes like this one?" Asked Kevana, moving away from the subject.

"I think not. This one was something special, it may have been created by some magical force, so it is unlikely there is another, there may be smaller ones though, the natural ones that were here before this one was made. Unless they have all been eaten."

"Did you see any tracks of others?"

"No, just the large one, but then the small ones would be keeping out of its path."

"Well, let's hope the small ones don't realise the big one is dead."

"I'll agree with that thought."

Kevana walked away towards the place were the rocks were still moving occasionally, he sat on the floor as close a he dared to the rock fall. Focusing his mind slowly, turning it first inwards, then slowly outwards, he used the power of his mind to follow the path to the exit, it turned twice before there was clear sky above, he felt the open space above, and knew fear, the blue sky started to pull on his consciousness, trying to drag him up into the pure azure, he turned inwards again, focusing sharply on the path backwards to his body, returning he found something unusual, he encountered a slow intelligence, so slow and so cold that it barely registered against the background, the merest hint of colour before his mystic eyes, it came from a large rock. Turning towards this rock, he sharpened the focus and blotted everything else out of his view, the rock sprang into a clarity that he had never seen before, it was sharp, defined, intense, and far down the energy spectrum, way down in the red band, a sure sign of a slow mind, but normally not associated with a rock, not abnormal for a man, but a rock with a mind was so strange that he started to doubt his vision, a quick glance around the cave showed his own body glowing red, the others a selection greens and blues, high energy colours, two members of the party were high into the ultraviolet, real high energy personalities, the rock was still showing a deep, dull red. Kevana withdrew from the rock and returned to his body. The return was such a shock to his system, that he fell to the floor, gasping for breath, it seemed that he hadn't taken in a single lungful of air for some minutes.

"Are you alright?" asked Alverana.

"Yes." gasped Kevana. "I'll be fine, once I get this breathing thing sorted out, can't understand why I'm so short of breath, I've done this sort of thing so many times, and never had this much difficulty."

"Done what?"

"I had a quick look outside, the sun in the sky caused me the same problem it always does, but I managed to get back this way, and I found something very interesting."

"What did you find?"

"There is a large rock in this wall here, that has some form of consciousness, it's very low grade, way down in the far red, but it is there."

"This rock here?" asked Alverana, striking a rock in the wall.

"Yes that's the one, how did you know?"

"I think this is the one we are going to have to move to get out of here, there are small openings around it."

"And a passageway beyond. This rock has to be moved."

"All we have to do is lift a few tons of rock, with the whole weight of the mountain resting on top of it."

"Should be easy for men such as us." Laughed Kevana. Together they walked back to where the others were performing their research.

"A rock that thinks? How ridiculous. Is this some sort of prank?" stormed Gorgana.

"If you don't believe me, go try it for yourself, it's so far down in the red band that I almost missed it, though it did feel like it wanted something, strange that."

"Strange. It's preposterous." Gorgana stamped across the cavern, picking his way around the corpse of the snake. He stopped at arms length from the rock, staring intently, breathing the slow calming pattern that helped him to concentrate his mind, slowly the psychic colours started to become visible to his mind's eye, sure enough there was a core of the deepest red inside the boulder, if glowed with a sort of careless pulse, nothing sharp or steady, just soft fuzzy and variable. Slowly he tried to tune into the pulse of the light, it was so slow and so unstable he wasn't able to pull it into any form of focus, every time he thought that he had it, it sort of slithered away, almost as if it was hiding from him. He returned to the group saying, "I believe you are right, it seems to have a very low grade life, perhaps even intelligence, but I cannot focus on it, it is far to slow and variable for me. Maybe Worandana will be able to talk it into moving out of our way."

Worandana chose this moment to rouse from his trance, he heard the derision in Gorgana's voice.

"I may be able to, if it can catch on to an idea any quicker than some people around here. What are we talking about, by the way?"

"Kevana has found a rock with a sort of life, and it could be our way out of here."

Worandana looked at Kevana, who nodded and looked at the rock in question.

"This rock has life?"

"Yes." replied Gorgana. "It's so far down in the red, I've seen livelier trees."

"But it managed to generate a colour that was detectable by you?" Worandana nearly spat the words.

"It's very confused and impossible to focus on."

"Impossible for you, you mean." Worandana's voice rose with each word.

"If you think you can do better, please show us, oh master." The sarcasm was unmistakable. Kevana nodded to Alverana, the big man moved quietly behind Gorgana and Kevana stepped softly to Worandana's shoulder.

"Sarcasm is understandable in one whose work is so sloppy." Said Worandana, in the coldest of tones.

"Well how would you move it?" Demanded Gorgana, backing off somewhat, realising that confrontation wasn't what he really needed just now.

"I shall talk to it, it should be easy, if I can slow down to the red band."

"Easier said." Interrupted Gorgana.

"Many things are easy to say, some of us find them easy to do as well. May I continue?"

Gorgana nodded, but with no obvious apology.

"I shall convince it, by what ever means I can, to heat itself up, until it melts. Once this has happened, we will merely walk through the place it was. Does that meet your approval?"

"How can it melt it's self?"

"Rocks often hold deep inside themselves a strange energy, something that can be triggered to enormous outbursts, sometimes dangerously so, but a small risk."

"So you will tap it's internal power and melt it, what will that do to it's consciousness?"

"It's mind comes from the order of its shape, the shape will be gone and any order with it, it will cease to be."

"You plan to kill it!"

"It can have no life, so it can lose none."

"It has life, of some sort, but it has. You cannot arbitrarily destroy something so rare."

"Watch me. I'm going to get us out of this place by any means I can, if you have a problem with that then you can stay here in the dark."

"If it has a life, you can't just kill it, it could have untold knowledge, it could be a great source of history, it's a rock, it cannot die, it must have such a store of knowledge, you cannot destroy such a library, it would be like burning books!"

"And of course that is something you would never do."

"Of course not, I'd never destroy knowledge, it just isn't replaceable, once it's lost it's gone for ever."

"You'd be surprised just how hard it is to destroy knowledge."

"What do you mean?"

"Have you ever heard of a group called the Halvetics?"

"No, who were they?"

"A religious order, somewhat akin to our own, though they served a different god."

"What happened to them?"

"A god decided that they should be destroyed, every one of them was killed, every trace of them erased, even the records of the military actions against them were deleted."

"How can you know of them then?"

"I was the one that did most of the editing of the histories, I confused the tales, muddled the stories, and jumbled the records, in such a way that no one would ever find that they had even existed, and that was in your lifetime, wiping out a race is nothing new to me, this would be a little different though, sort of hands on, not just a literary removal, but a literal removal."

"You participated in the eradication of a whole people?"

Worandana merely nodded.

"How could you do such a thing?"

"I was told to, the task came to me, I performed it to the best of my ability, but my actions were of necessity flawed."

"How flawed? No one here knew of these people."

"From the things that I know, I could rebuild their history, put them back into the history books, though I couldn't remake any of their religious texts, they were just burned, without being read. Some of their magic I have incorporated into my own work, so even though no one knows of their existence, their influence still carries on in the world. Such flaws weren't expected of me, or perhaps they were, maybe the council knew that I would select the best parts of their knowledge and keep it alive, could be the reason they chose me for the task. Still I did a very good job of erasure on Halvetics, didn't I?"

"You certainly did, and now you're going to wipe out another race, only this one is totally unique. It's just not right."

"I care not, we have to move that rock, or we aren't getting out of here."

"I cannot stand by and watch you destroy this unique life form."

"You will not just stand by, you will help me in any way you can, I don't expect you to like it, I don't care if you like it or not, but you will help. Do I make myself very clear."

Gorgana, watched as Worandana reached inside his robe, right hand, so that meant a lightning bolt, Gorgana knew which side the old man kept his weapons, he sensed that the wrong word would make him very dead very quickly, the obvious answer was not to stand in the old man's way, but this felt wrong, all his life he had pursued knowledge where ever he could find it, here was an opportunity for research that was going to be thrown away, merely in the name of expediency.

"What you will." He said, knowing in his heart that this was wrong, but the necessity of staying alive was more important than the life of some rock, he turned away, and walked over to where the rock was, wondering what it could possibly have experienced in its long 'life'.

"Gorgana." Called Worandana, "You aren't going to do anything that I would regret, are you?"

"No. I wish I had time to communicate with this rock, but I don't and you wouldn't allow it anyway. If there is one there must be others, this cannot be the only conscious rock in the whole world, I'll find another to talk to, once this current mission is over."

"He's going to cause trouble." Whispered Kevana.

"More than likely," replied Worandana, "but not right now, we need him, he is volatile, but he also has a great deal of knowledge in his head, and power as well. I wouldn't like to guess on the outcome if it came to a showdown between the two of us. The only thing he really lacks is confidence. If he comes to believe in himself, then he will be capable of almost anything"

"He sounds dangerous, we can fix that in a moment."

"No, he is too valuable to us alive."

"Your choice, but you watch him, if I think he's becoming a threat, I'll have someone put an arrow in his head, before anyone can move."

"If you're going to do that, you better do it from behind, if he sees it coming an arrow may not be quick enough to reach the head before things get really bad."

"I'll bear that in mind."

"Be aware, if he does decide to become a problem for us, you are unlikely to notice until it is far too late, he is very intelligent, and no where near as naïve as he appears."

"He sounds more like a liability than ever."

"Admit his usefulness, his ideas have served us very well, his power has aided us every time we needed it, he is an asset."

"Agreed, but he is a risk."

"Agreed. We'll keep a close eye on him. I need to rest for a while before I start working on the rock." Worandana turned away and sat on the ground with his back to the wall, closed his eyes, and in a moment was snoring softly to himself. Kevana saw to the provision of food and drink for all the men and horses, though supplies were restricted, there was enough for all, some was set aside for Worandana, which he ate like a ravenous wolf as soon as he woke, then he drank a great deal of water.

"How are you going to approach this?" Asked Kevana.

"I'm going to make some sort of contact then see where I can go from there, it's something I've never tried before, something I've never even heard of before, so I have no information to go on."

"Good luck, this a probably our only way out of this place."

"That's right just keep piling on the pressure."

"Sorry, good luck."

Worandana walked slowly away, doing some stretching exercises, to loosen up his muscles, not that he had any intention of using them, just didn't want a cramp distracting him at a critical moment. He approached the rock very slowly, feeling for it with both hands and mind. He sat down on the ground resting both hands on the surface of the rock, he felt that it did indeed have some form of consciousness, very slow and very low energy, but there was something there. He closed his physical eyes, and focused his psychic eyes on the rock, the colour was very deep into the red, far deeper than any he had ever seen before, the simplest of consciousnesses are usually far more energetic than this one, it was only by extremely tight focus that he could even be sure it was there. 'If I didn't know it was there I would probably have missed it completely.' He thought. 'Yet Kevana saw it, perhaps he is more sensitive than I am? Or just more sensitive at that end of the band, he does seem to understand animals, and such far better than I, and they tend to be at the red end.' Worandana shut everything out of his mind, other than the rock in front of him, he tried to tune his mind to the deep red of the rock, he knew it was going to be very difficult, as his mind was one of those that was normally tuned into the ultraviolet, he had to tune across the whole spectrum of colours, as he pushed his mind down he felt it slow, his thoughts became like treacle, slower and slower, until he made some contact with the consciousness of the rock. The rock seemed to be thinking on something in its past. Worandana's probing thought gave it something of a surprise.

"Who are you to impinge upon my space?" demanded the rock.

"I am Worandana. Have you a name?"

"I need no name, for there is nothing else that thinks in my universe, now that the soft ones are gone, I am the only sentience here, and so I am the universe, how did you come into my space?"

"I have not come into your space, you exist in mine."

"Don't be ridiculous, you must have come into my space, there is nothing sentient other than me, unless you signify the return of the soft ones."

"I assure you there are many sentient beings in this universe, some hard, some soft, it is just that you are so different from them that they normally don't see you and you can't look for them."

"I see all there is to see, there can be nothing else."

"Your life runs to a much slower pace than the other sentient beings, they don't even know that you exist, a colleague of mine saw your light when he was looking for something else. He told me of you some time ago and I decided to investigate further."

"I thought I saw a flash of intelligence a moment before you contacted me, but I ignored it as some form of internal aberration."

"It was much more than a moment ago for us, we live at a far quicker pace than you, which is why communication is so difficult."

"Why would I want to communicate with you, you are such a fleeting thing?"

"Because our lives are so short, and run so quickly we tend to learn as much as we can, as quickly as we can, perhaps I can teach you something about the universe that you don't know."

"I remember it all, from the moment of my birth in the fires of a pit, to the present time, I haven't forgotten a single instant, can you say that?"

"No, we forget things, sometimes on purpose, our brains are finite they get cluttered with junk if we aren't careful. Please tell me of your birth?"

"I awoke in the bottom of a pit, it was large and burning, so hot as to be almost too much, it took a little time to cool, and soon thereafter the pit filled with soil and grit and I was buried for a while, this was no real problem it gave me plenty of time to think, the only distraction was the slowly changing forces around me."

"What forces are those?"

"There is the strong force, that pulls in one direction, but will occasionally get very confused, it tends to spin around, pulling in all different directions, until it finally chooses one, and stops moving around, the weak force is something else, it changes slowly getting stronger then weaker, it is getting weaker now, I expect it will disappear altogether in a while, then it will return in a new direction, it is a capricious force."

"These are indeed unusual thoughts that you have, though I think I can tell you something about the forces that you are feeling, the strong one we call gravity, it pulls towards the ground, the weak one could be the magnetic force that sailors use to guide them when they are out of sight of land, though I wasn't aware that it ever changed, is seems to have been the same for all time."

"If this magnetic force is the weak one then it does change, but very slowly, even by my sense of time. Perhaps it changes far too slowly for you to have noticed it. That aside, if the strong force that you call gravity always pulls in the one direction, how can I feel it moving?"

"I think it isn't the force that moves but you, as you are moved by a flowing river, or roll down a hill, then it would seem, from your perspective, that the force is moving around you, you cannot tell the difference because the force is the only point of reference that you have, unless you count the weak force. When the strong force is moving, does the weak force move with it?"

"Now that you mention it, it does. Strange that I didn't think of it."

"Not really, until you talked to me, you weren't even sure that there was anything outside your self."

"But I know of things outside, the soft ones, they used to talk to me, or more likely a few of them developed the skills so they could talk to me."

"What were these soft ones like?"

"They used to tell me of the world around them, I was sure they were mistaken, for they said the strangest things. Much of what they said made no sense to me at all, they talked about animals and food and weather. I didn't understand them, but occasionally they would give me something that felt good."

"What was that?"

"I don't really know, they said it was an 'offering', it tasted strong and warm and mineral in nature, I am mineral, but this was somewhat different."

"Did they call themselves the 'soft ones'?"

"No. That is the name I gave them, they each had names of their own, but these changed so quickly that I found it difficult to keep up."

"I thought you didn't forget anything."

"I don't, but it's very difficult to have a conversation with someone who changes their name every time they speak."

"Perhaps some one was chosen to speak to you, it could then be seen as some form of honour."

"They did seem to be people with experience, they had many things to say before the offering "

"Did they tell you of their experiences?"

"They talked of many things that I couldn't understand, but the offering was always good."

"Can you remember the last time they gave you an offering?"

"Of course, I don't forget anything."

"Tell me what the offering said."

"Why?"

"His words may tell me why they left you, though they mean little to you."

"There was the usual time when contact was very loose, it was sort of there, then gone. This went on for a little while, then I started to hear the real voice, it came from deep inside the soft one, not a lot different from your voice, but different perhaps only in clarity, it was fuzzy, sloppy, sort of disjointed. He started by talking about 'children', what ever they are. His children were suffering, they were starving, the cold was so deep that they couldn't find water, or food for the game. The ice was nearer again this winter, the grass was dying early in the summer, how could I have let this happen. All these things mean very little to me, but were of extreme importance to him. The associations that come along with the words are equally meaningless. What are children, game, food? I don't understand."

"Children are the future, they are the ones that come next." Worandana didn't want to talk about this too much, it would only add confusion.

"Why should some come next? Why can't the ones that are here stay?"

"Unlike you we people wear out quite quickly, we only last a few years, then we die."

"Many of the soft ones who spoke to me talked of this dying, it was something they didn't want, what is it?"

"It is the ending of life, thought stops, the body stops, but the body almost always wants to go on."

"If they want to go on, then why don't they?"

"They can't, the body or sometimes the mind is worn out, it cannot go another day, so it stops."

"This is a strange concept for me, I am as I have always been, I am here, why should I want to change. It's incomprehensible."

"People aren't like that, the only constant is change, they grow, they grow old, they die, that is the unbreakable law that we live by."

"Why live with it, why not change the law for a different one?"

"As yet we have found no way to do that, if we did, it would be a bad idea, the world would soon be full of people, and not enough food to go around, dying would continue, just the cause of it would change."

"Why would the world become full, there are only so many of you in it?"

"We continually replace the ones that die, so the numbers would just keep on going up if the dying suddenly stopped."

"How can you replace the ones that die?"

"It is part of the process of our lives, we make more of us, they start small, helpless and fragile, they grow bigger and get older, before long they are able to look after themselves, and then capable of creating more, the new ones are called children, they grew slowly to become adults. For us it is such a commonplace process that we don't even think about it, it just is."

"This is a very difficult for me, I don't understand, your lives are short, but you seem to live it extremely quickly, cramming every moment with action. You create these children, that you regard as your future, even though your future is short and already decided, you die. This seems pretty futile to me."

"What have you done recently?"

"What do you mean?"

"I am currently on a mission, we chase some thieves, when we catch them we are going to take back what the stole, and most probably kill them all. What have you done?"

"I think and I feel, sometimes I wish for the soft ones to come back, they gave me so much of themselves, they tasted good."

"They tasted good, is that all you can say about that which you call life, we wouldn't call that living, one of our worst punishments is to cage a person so they can meet no one and talk to no one, any subjected to this for an length of time go completely mad, your life is in itself insanity."

"But I have always been so, I have known nothing else, so this is my life as I have to deal with it, sometimes I feel that it is a little slow, but what else can I do?"

"Your life could be so much more, you could have given more to the soft ones, much more."

"But what could I have given them, I have no experience of their world other than what they gave to me, I had little help to give them."

"You could have done more than just take their lives."

"What do you mean, take their lives?"

"Every one of them that you heard was dying."

"They all died."

"But these were killed in order to talk to their god, the god of the rock."

"They were given as sacrifice, to me?"

"Of course, why else would they be bled to death whilst tied across the top of your form, the black blood stains must reach a long way inside the surface, that is why they 'taste' so good."

"I didn't realise, I had no idea. How can you be sure?"

"I have seen this sort of thing before, but never found the 'altar stone' to be alive before. But then I have never seen an altar stone so soaked in blood, they must have died in their hundreds, over the years."

"I do remember many of them, many of them, but why did they all die?"

"They die in worship of you, obviously, the first may have been an accident, the first one contacted you and told the others of you as he died."

"She. Now that I know more of your people I know that the first was a woman, she was worried about her children, as they all are, but she saying that it wasn't her fault. It seemed that someone died before their time and she was blamed for it."

"In the past it wasn't unusual for a woman to be declared a witch when someone in her care dies, a despicable practice, but then human history is sometimes like that."

"You are sure that the soft ones died in order to contact me?"

"I think there is little doubt that the first one died, using the flat top surface of your shape as a convenient place to slowly bleed her to death, perhaps that is how the one in her care died, who can tell? In her extremis with loss of blood her heart would slow, and her brain would follow it, until they were both running in a way that could feel you and be felt by you, much as I am now, though I'm not dying, I do this by trained control of my mind and my body."

"Are there others that can perform this sort of control?"

"Some, but not many, and none that would believe me if I told them."

"I want more of you to talk to, I need to know more of the world outside myself."

"At the moment all there is, is me. That will have to suffice for now, what did the first of the soft ones say once she felt your mind in this rock."

"She called me Astoroth, god of the underworld, I don't know what she meant by that, but those were her thoughts. She demanded that I kill those that had killed her, 'By the blood shed on your altar.' Her words. Can you explain them?"

"Perhaps, did she speak to the others, the ones that you couldn't feel."

"I'm not sure, so little of what she said made any sense at all, but she may have spoken to them, 'By my blood I have awakened Astoroth, and he shall destroy you all.' Her words again, could that have been what they heard?"

"That would certainly have been enough to arouse the superstition that this rock that is you was a sacred altar to the god Astoroth. They would then have assumed that some form of sacrifice was necessary to appease Astoroth, they probably started with something small, an animal, or some such, but if the imagined curse was unabated they would have progressed to sacrificing people, bleeding them on your altar, until they could talk to you and give their lives to save the people of their village."

"Do you see this as a bad thing?"

"How else can it be viewed, not only were the people killed to appease an imagined god, you even admit that they tasted good."

"But they did taste good, and there was a definite increase in my energy afterwards."

"So not only did they bleed to death, you fed on their blood."

"I don't think it was the blood as such, it was something else, something in their minds, an emotional thing I think, but these concepts are new and strange to me, I've never held a conversation with anyone that lasted this long, they have all died long before this time. You're not planning on dying any time soon, are you?"

"I don't intend to die for many years yet, though I do feel more than a little tired."

"They are all tired near the end, they start to get very excited, their hearts race and the blood comes quicker, then they die. Is your heart starting to race?"

"Now that you mention it, I am beginning to have a little problem holding my heart down to maintain this conversation. Perhaps this is because I am tired."

"Perhaps you are dying."

"Un-likely." Worandana paused and sent out a mental plea to his friends, he was in need of help. It seemed to be only a moment then a huge rush of energy filled his body, and sharpened his mind. "That feels much better."

"Where did that come from? That was an enormous boost to your energy level."

"So you can feel the energy in me, and no doubt you are feeding off it. This sort of energy is nothing compared to what you could get if you really tried."

"What do you mean?"

"There are other forms of energy that you could use."

"Where, how do I reach it?"

"There is an enormous store house of power directly below us, it is a way down, but you could reach it."

"What form is this energy and how to I reach it?"

"The energy is that which drives the whole world, it is at the source of the strong force, all you have to do it reach along the strong force, until you get to it."

"How do I reach this energy?"

"Just follow the strong force."

"But I can't move, I cannot follow the lines of the force."

"Perhaps if you change your state a little you could."

"But how?"

"Try concentrating some of your energy into a part of yourself, energise that portion and push it along the lines of force."

"That is going to take a lot of my energy."

"But think of the power you could gain, by taping the core of the world, there would be no power greater than yours."

"Do you believe I can do it?"

"I think you can do it, if you have the will, you can reach the core."

"Can you guide me?"

"I can try, there is no chance of me reaching the core, but I could show you the way."

"Then show me how it is done."

"Take all your spare energy and concentrate it into your outer skin, I'll add more of mine to help you." He sent another plea, and almost instantly received a huge donation of energy, which he passed on.

"Oh. That is very strong."

"But nothing compared to the core. Push the power into your shell, make it hot with power, then reach out towards the strong force, feel it and push towards it."

The surface of the rock burst into a bright display of fire and power, slowly it melted and flowed down into the cracks, shedding sparks and plumes of smoke.

"Can you feel the power?" Asked Worandana. "You must be near it now."

"I feel nothing."

"Push harder, more power, more energy, reach for it, it will be worthwhile."

"I am still feeling nothing, only that I am loosing something, and I'm not sure what."

Worandana reached out to his friends for more power and fed it straight to the rock saying, "Does that help? I can tap more to help you to reach your ultimate goal, you have to reach the core, or your life, such as it is, will never be fulfilled."

"More, I need more power, I am using up mine far faster than I ever have in the past, but it somehow feels good to be using power in this fashion."

"Using power like this is often its own reward. Keep pushing, you'll soon reach the core. Keep burning energy, push harder, focus on the power that you have, use it faster." Worandana was almost shouting these words with his mind, trying to keep the rock being from backing off and really thinking about what it was doing, gradually more and more of the huge rock melted and flowed down into the cracks in the floor of the cavern, every time he felt it running out of power he gave a big jolt of his own, each influx of energy melted more and more of the rock, Soon there was a clear path around the rock, not quite big enough for a horse, but very close, and the rock was loosing so much weight, that it must be movable, but he couldn't spare any of his attention to tell the others to prepare to move it.

"Keep pushing, you'll soon reach the place you need to be." Screamed Worandana with his mind, trying hard to broadcast for the others to pick up. He reached for another blast of power, but nothing came, his friends seemed to have deserted him, another layer of the rock flared to liquidity and poured into the floor. As it did so a strange surge of force twisted the world and the rock moved across the floor of the cavern on the liquid that used to be part of itself.

"What has happened? Where has the strong force gone, it has moved again."

Worandana said nothing.

"I know you are still there, I can feel your mind, why have you gone quiet."

"My purpose was to move you from my path, I need to get out of this cave and you were blocking the exit. With the help of my friends that purpose is now achieved, though I was actually hoping to reduce you in such a fashion that you ceased to exist. That is no longer necessary, nor worth the effort it would take now."

"Why would you want to destroy me?"

"Because you feed on dying people, you eat their essence as they pass from this existence, this is horrifying to us. You should be destroyed, but I think that is no longer a problem, you are so far away from any people and so much reduced now, that you will simply fade away, it may take many years, but it will happen."

"You have killed me then?"

"I think so. There is one man in my group who will be happy that you still have consciousness, it was probably him that moved you from my path, so that I wouldn't actually reduce you to nothing, but the result will be the same."

"I would speak with this man who has saved what little I have left."

"He may return some time in the future, but right now we have other things to do, but be certain, any that contact you will be warned that you suck power from any within range, hopefully that is something else that has been reduced today. None will come close enough to feed you again, and so you die." Worandana moved his mind forwards to it's more normal speed, shook his head slowly and tried to get to his feet.

Two strong hands picked him up by the elbows and carried him over to a fire that was waiting, he was wrapped in warm blankets and a cup of hot soup was placed to his lips, the mere act of swallowing seemed to take all his energy.

"Don't try to talk," said Kevana, "you've been working on that damned rock for a long time, probably much longer than you think, we've been feeding you our energy because there was no way to get food inside you, Gorgana was standing watch on you so he's in almost as bad a way as you are. I know you are going to be upset about the fact that the rock is still alive, if greatly reduced, we're sorry about that, but the energy drain was just too much to be sustained, we'd all have died before it was completely destroyed, so we decided to move it as soon as it was light enough. It took overything we had to shift that damned thing, but it's done now, so all you can do about it is moan."

Worandana tried to speak but his voice failed completely, a glare was all he was capable of, but such a glare.

"Seems you can't even moan yet," Said Kevana, patting his friend on the shoulder, "that will change soon enough. Rest now, we'll get moving as soon as some life returns to your limbs, hopefully that will happen before you get your voice back, I don't like the idea of all that screaming in this cave." He smiled, hoping to cheer his friend up, if only a little. Worandana nodded, then nodded towards the opposite side of the fire, where a pile of blankets seemed to have been thrown in a careless heap.

"That's Gorgana, he's very tired, but he'll be fine in a few hours, I've sent Alverana and Fabrana outside to look around and to get food and firewood, they've been back once already, it's late afternoon, the sun will be going down in a couple of hours, so I think we'll stay here until sunrise, then we'll go on. It's probably Gorgana's fault that you are still alive, keep drinking that soup. He kept a permanent watch over you after the first day, he had to be forced to sleep, I watched while he slept, but no more than an hour or two at a time, he's far better at watching than I am, he spotted that the rock was sucking out your energy, but he couldn't break in to tell you. He's a very skilled man, but I feel that his heart is elsewhere, if you know what I mean?"

"Yes." Croaked Worandana. "They used to say that about me."

"You see something of you in him."

"Perhaps, but I'm not at all certain that his loyalties lie with us. He's a very complex man, but as you say, skilled." With every word spoken Worandana's voice improved. "You said 'After the first day'. How many days was I talking to that rock?"

"It's hard to tell in here, with no sun to go by, but perhaps three, but not four. I'm really judging this by the growth of my beard, but it's now so long that it hard to tell how much its growing, I'm going to shave as soon as I get some real light to work with."

"So we have lost some days."

"Definitely."

"Yet you are still here?"

"You and Gorgana are in no condition to travel, a days rest will be better for you than racing to catch up. The horses need time to get some food inside them, just as we do. If we keep running ourselves into the ground, we'll never catch up. Rest until tomorrow, then eat, perhaps rest through tomorrow, I know that together we'll get them. If I were to rush off now, I'd only lose them again. We leave when you can travel, then the gods help them, because they are going to need some help from somewhere."

"We'll get them, but you are right about my need for rest, and presumably, Gorgana's. Where are the horses?"

"Picketed out in the valley, they have lots of good green grass, something they haven't seen for many days, they are happier than you." Laughed Kevana.

Worandana nodded and smiled, the thought of the horses in the sun, eating and more than likely rolling in the fresh grass. "What is the weather like?"

"It's like a warm spring day, we have come along way down the mountain, Alverana says that it should be fine tomorrow, if you are up to travelling."

"Given a night's rest, I'll be ready to travel, of course, much depends on what Alverana reports when he returns." he smiled, and looked at his friend, the flickering light of the fire chasing shadows across Kevana's face.

"Yes, if Alverana reports that they are camped half a day away, then I'm afraid that I will be forced to give chase immediately, but that is exceptionally unlikely, they haven't stopped moving for a single day, why should they do so now?"

"They certainly seem to have kept on the move. Have you given any thought as to where they are going, or are they just running from you?"

"I have to admit that I haven't thought of that." he paused for a long time before continuing. "They seem to have been running, every action has been away from us, but that could be because which ever way they turn, we follow. Generally eastwards. Though I cannot think why they would go east, the further east they go the more of us they will meet, they are running into our territory."

"It could be worse than that." muttered Worandana.

"How?"

"Where will they be once they have left the foothills of this range?"

"They'll have to cross the river, not going to be an easy task in anyone's book."

"What if they don't want to cross the river?"

"Then they have to go south."

"South to where?"

"There are many places they can go to on that river."

"South to where?"

"Zandaarkoon. Are they going to Zandaarkoon? Why? They couldn't hope to survive in our home city for more than a moment, there are just too many of us."

"But only we know they are there, and only we are searching for them. It could be time to report in, we could use some more help in this. If we leave it much longer it could be too late."

"If they turn south on the river, then we'll call for help."

"Agreed. If they turn south."

"Why Zandaarkoon?" muttered Kevana.

CHAPTER TWENTY NINE

The early morning cockerel squawked its pre-dawn greeting, long before that actual morning arrived, this brought the usual response from those around, hurling abuse and boots, until the damned bird stopped it's noise. Jangor crawled slowly out of his tent, groaning softly as he went, looking for something to drink, something without alcohol in it. A large jug was set just out of the reach of the heat from the fire, the mouth of the jug was just big enough, Jangor plunged his head into the jar and drank as much of the water as he could without actually breathing. He pulled his head from the jar, and shook it from side to side, scattering drops of water all about the camp, in no danger of waking anyone, as all those in the camp were all inside their tents.

"Rouse. Wake. On your feet!" he yelled. 'Why should they sleep when I feel like this?' he thought. Kern crawled from his tent into the half light.

"What's the noise?" he demanded.

"If I'm up, then everyone should be!" said Jangor, in a suitably loud voice, the sort of voice that strikes fear into new recruits on the parade ground.

"Just because you've got a hangover, why should everyone else suffer?"

"We need to be on the road as soon as possible, do you have a problem with that?"

"Sometimes I can really get to hate you when you've been drinking." replied the big man.

"It's nothing at all to do with the drink."

"Bollocks. Every time you get drunk, you take your hangover out on everyone else, it's your problem you deal with it!"

"But we still need to be moving very soon."

"That is as may be, but there is no need at all for you to be such an arse about it."

"Right, I'm the biggest bastard that ever lived. We still need to be moving."

"I am certain that the others will be ready to travel in plenty of time to keep you as happy as you could possibly be, though that isn't much today, not with the amount you drank last night."

"Are you suggesting that I was drunk last night?"

"No. Would I do such a thing? Who could even think a thing like that? Let alone imply it? Of course not. You have never been drunk in your entire life. You don't drink. You are the soul of sobriety, now can I go back to sleep for a while, or is there something else?"

"I'm not like that."

"Of course, you're not. Sleep?"

"If you must, but we have to be moving soon."

Kern made no verbal reply, but it very soon became obvious to Jangor that the scout wasn't on his own, the noises emanating from the tent weren't the sort that a man on his own would make. Jangor put his head back into the jug to avoid the climax of the activities in the tent.

When Jangor finally surfaced from the depths of the jug, or more accurately, drank the water down to a level where he could actually breathe, he looked around the camp to see a woman kissing Kern, she was most enthusiastic, not wanting to let him go in any way. She released his head, and picked up her dress with one hand, not stopping the kiss that was to be their goodbye. Suddenly she rose to her feet and turned away, walking slowly into the lightening sky of morning, not bothering to dress, just dragging the offending article along behind her, her hips swaying in the growing light of dawn.

"Sometimes." said Kern. "This life of ours has its rewards." He rolled onto his back and stared up at the lightening of the sky, a deep sigh passed his lips.

"Oh. Shut up and put some clothes on." said Jangor, flicking his head, and scattering drops of water about the camp, some sizzling where they dropped amongst the flames.

"Why? Does my nakedness embarrass you, because it doesn't embarrass me?"

"Somehow, I'm not in the least surprised that you aren't embarrassed, sometimes you have the morals of an alley cat."

"That's another strange saying. As far as I am aware, cats know little about our morals, and care even less. To be accused of having those sorts of morals is definitely no insult in my eyes, but then perhaps you aren't actually trying to be insulting?"

"Of course I'm trying to be insulting, I'm having a bad day and determined to share it."

"Well, in that case I'm not listening." Kern rolled over and returned to the tent, he knew that he would have to get out of bed soon, but wasn't going to rush.

Namdarin and Jayanne crawled out of their tent, and began to pack it away, no words were spoken between them but the looks were more than enough.

"Is everybody sex mad in this camp, or is it just me?" Asked Jangor in a loud voice.

"It's just you." Said Granger, from inside his tent. "Everyone else is just mad."

"I'm going to the tavern, just to get freshened up, you understand." said Jangor, climbing slowly to his feet and staggering across the green, in the general direction of the inn.

"What is his problem?" asked Namdarin when Granger's head showed through the flaps of his tent.

"I think he has a problem with his sex life." laughed Granger.

"What sex life?" asked Namdarin.

"That's the problem."

"I don't have a problem with his sex life, so why should he share it with me?"

"It's just the sort of nice guy he is, he likes to share everything."

"Well. Some things he should keep to himself." Namdarin's voice rose hoping to keep pace with the man now walking away. The dismantling of the camp proceeded at its usual pace, not hurried, but with enough speed to seem that everyone was trying there best to get it done as quickly as possible. The missing members of the group returned to the camp before the sun was truly clear of the mountains, actual sunrise came late in such a deep valley. Crathen looked a little sheepish when he walked into the camp.

"Are you all right?" asked Kern.

"I'm fine, just a little tired, why?"

"You look a little disturbed, or were you disturbed?" Kern winked, in an utterly innocent manner.

"I have no idea what you mean, I had a long talk with a young lady, her husband didn't seem to mind at all."

"You mean he just went to his bed and left you to it?"

"No." Crathen blushed and turned away.

"Don't worry about it, youngster." said Kern. "In some of these out of the way places they are more than a little lax about the sort of things that seem so important in the larger settlements."

"I don't know what you mean!" said Crathen, without looking at the older man, his tone bordering on the hysterical.

Kern turned away, the only thing he could think of that would defuse the argument that anyone could see was about to occur, Crathen had a real problem, but only because Jayanne was within earshot, If she had been elsewhere then he would have been very calm about his late night liaison. Crathen kept looking at Jayanne, then looking away, he was trying to see if she was paying any attention to him, it was fairly clear that she was not, though he kept trying to catch her looking at him, he would glance out of the corners of his eyes, using the very limit of his peripheral vision, hoping to see her staring at him, but it always seemed that she had just that very instant looked away. 'She must know that I am looking, and keeps her head turned away. She must be so much faster than I am, and so much more aware as to what is happening around her.' He thought, strengthening his own ego, she was obviously hiding her interest in him, from everyone, including herself, he would have to try harder to bring this to the fore. Kern dismantled his tent and packed everything away, knowing that Jangor was going to be of no help at all this morning, but his was a very minor consideration, the man was more than worth the minor inconvenience, and Kern was not going to let anything upset the warm feeling he had for the woman whose departing shape he would see for a long time whenever he closed his eyes and thought of those swaying hips.

"Why don't we all go and see just what Jangor is up to?" said Kern, once all the tents were down, and the packs were ready for loading onto the horses. As a group they walked slowly across the green towards the tavern, people were beginning to leave their houses and start about their daily tasks, the cattle were being herded out of the pens and out of the village through the northern gate, much noise they were making about this, both the cattle and the people. Some rather robust dogs were yapping at the heels of the cows, in a vain attempt to get them moving, the cows, as their part of the game, were going slow enough to keep the dogs just inside kicking range, as the occasional pained yelp confirmed. Namdarin and Jayanne walked hand in hand, their eyes turned to the ground in front of them, they spoke no words, though none were needed. Crathen walked alongside Jayanne, his head turned towards her all the time, hoping for a glance, but knowing in his heart that she was hiding her feelings for him, because she needed the protection of the group, she obviously didn't realise that he could provide whatever protection she could ever wish for. He would have to show her that she has nothing to fear so long as he is around. 'I'll make her see, she must know that I can be her protector where ever she may go.' His mind made up, he was certain that she would see before long that there was no one in the world who cold protect her like him. All too soon the green was traversed, and they stepped up onto the veranda of the tavern, Jangor was already there, a large goblet in his hand, and an expression of absolute pleasure on his face.

"What has made your day?" asked Kern. As Garath came out from the darkness with a tray in his hands, the tray contained enough goblets for them all and a small flagon.

"Would you care to find out for yourselves?" he asked, with a grin on his face.

"Looking at him, I am not entirely sure I want to take the risk." said Namdarin.

"Take it, it's worth it." mumbled Jangor.

"I suppose we don't really have any choice do we?" said Namdarin, reaching a little diffidently for a goblet, the others watched as he slowly tasted the contents, the same stupefied grin appeared on his face.

"This is just wonderful." said Namdarin. "A great vintage, pure fruit and glorious flavours, blackberries and apples, raspberries, flavours just too big to name. A superb wine, how can you make something this good?"

"There is a south facing slope, well drained, and with the best of soils, planted entirely with grapes, and no shortage of volunteers to tend them. The pressing and fermentation of such isn't too different from the beer makers art, the bottling is a small problem, but I soon discovered that standard size bottles are of absolutely no use in this place, a bottle is gallon sized here. And the year's production is many gallons. If I could find someone I could trust to transport the wine, then this place could make lots of money, but everyone that I know would simply drink it all as soon as they got outside the gates."

"I, for one," said Namdarin, "can understand that, this wine is the best I have ever tasted. If I survive my current quest, I'll certainly come back here and take half your production and sell it for you, for only a small percentage of course."

"You would be welcome, but so many have tried just that, and returned with only a hangover to show for their efforts, some even got as far as the river before they started to drink the stock."

"It would certainly be hard, but I think the world should know about this wine, and as soon as it does, the wine drinkers of the world would be camped on your doorstep."

"Why would that be?"

"Because this wine is that good. What do you use for yeast?"

"Only what occurs naturally on the grapes."

"That's even better, nothing better than what comes naturally."

"The only way."

"What do you think Jangor?" asked Namdarin.

"I don't care what makes this what it is, it is wondrous, and I should know, I've tasted wine from all over the world, and this is the best there is. Do we really have to leave here?"

"You can stay here if you wish." said Namdarin. "I am sure they can find some work to which you are suited. Though you may not think so, but the wine will be worth it, wont it?"

"Somehow I think the beauty of this will fade quite quickly, depending on the task I have to perform to get it."

"As with anything, beauty is relative, at the moment this is the best wine you have ever tasted, and well worth any task it takes to get it, but in a few weeks, this wine will be ordinary, and not worth the work."

"Sometimes Namdarin, you can be a really bad man. You know how to destroy a dream with a few words."

"Dreams are good, I should know, I had few of them myself, but somehow the Zandaars tore them all to pieces."

"Now you have a new set of dreams."

"No. I have a new set of nightmares, dreams that I wish could end, sooner the better. Dreams are like that."

"That is a sad thing to say."

"True none the less, time we were moving I believe."

"I suppose, can't we just stay for one more glass of this wonderful wine."

"No, one would lead to another, and the whole day would be lost."

"Right Everybody on their feet, it's time to hit the road." said Jangor pushing away from the table, and turning his goblet upside down upon the table. The others followed suit in a few moments, and they thanked Garath for his hospitality, before leaving the tavern, the walk across the green became a grim procession. The horses were saddled and packed in short order, and the group mounted and turned to the south. Walking the horses slowly towards the gate, they each looked around at the people and the place they were leaving, this could so easily have become home for all of them. The locals turned out to wave them on their way, not as many as their reception committee, but a few who didn't have anything better to do at the time. A woman, now dressed, ran up to Kern, who bent down in he saddle and kissed her quite firmly, when he released her, she turned with a flick of her long hair and strode resolutely away, her hips swinging defiantly. Kern laughed gently to himself and led the group out of the village, through the rickety south gate, and along the road between the carefully tended fields. The grain had all been harvested and stored, the straw was in the process of being burned off in some of the fields, teams of large horses pulled ploughs turning the ground over. Kern paused, watching a ploughing team making a turn at the end of a run.

"Problem?" asked Jangor.

"No, just curious. I've never seem teams pulling ploughs before, and now I see why they do."

"You've got me, please enlighten me."

"Each plough isn't a single blade, there are three blades to a plough, which is why it takes two horses to pull the thing, actually there are six blades to the plough. At the end of a run the ploughman turns the plough over, turns the team round and cut the next set of furrows the other way, because the blades curve the other way the sod turns over the same way as the last ones. Whoever had this idea was a genius, each plough is expensive to make, certainly, but rather than one horse making one furrow we now have two horses making three in the same time, and because of the turn over of the plough, there is no time wasted to make the next furrows, just turn the team round and flip the plough over, and off you go again. This must save them so much effort at this time of year, it must be at least four times as fast as a single horse making a single furrow."

"This is all very exciting, but can we get along please?"

"Of course, it's just that I've never seen this before, and the more I think about it, the more I am amazed that two horses can pull a three bladed plough. Just look at those furrows, they've been cut deep and turned over precisely."

"I find it very difficult to be excited about farming methods." said Jangor, shaking his head, and starting the horses moving again.

"But think of the effort that's been put into the design of that plough, think of the experimentation, getting the curve of the blade just right, the depth of the cut just so." Kern shook his head, and kicked his horse into motion. "It must have taken so much work, or a sudden flash of real genius. That is what I mean, it's not a new way to grind the edge of a sword, it's not a new weapon, it's a way to feed people. That's really something to be proud of, something to pass on to one's children."

"Neither of us have children, nor are we likely ever to do so, we are soldiers, if we can do something about the damned Zandaars we may prevent the deaths of many more people."

"But that's not the same as showing them how to feed themselves better."

"Once we've stopped the Zandaars, then you can go and teach them to farm better. Is that all right with you?"

"I suppose so." said Kern looking back at the ploughman making another turn. "But there has to be something special about the curve of that plough blade."

"Well, you can worry about that some other time, right now I need to know what is ahead of us, so get out there I find something that would interest me."

Kern kicked his horse hard, and pounded off along the path at a full gallop.

"Mander!" shouted Jangor. "Point, the rest of you keep a close eye out, we are in unknown territory here." Mander rode up ahead, until he was almost out of sight, and then settled down to the steady walking pace that the horses could easily maintain all day. Jangor and Granger rode side by side, with Namdarin and Jayanne behind them, Crathen came next, just behind and to Jayanne's right, whenever she looked out over the fields Crathen saw at least one of her green eyes. 'She's not checking the fields or the hedges, she's looking back to see where I am, she likes to be sure that I am here.' he thought. Andel and Stergin brought up the rear of the column, along with the pack horses, the two looked at each other and smiled.

"At least it should be relatively quiet at the back here." said Stergin.

"So long as these damned animals don't start arguing." laughed Andel.

"Or discussing farm implements in loud voices."

"I just wish that Crathen's horse would stop standing in the droppings of the other horses, it keeps flicking them this way."

Namdarin looked back, having heard this remark and said, "Consider yourselves lucky, if it was Arndrol doing that sort of thing, he never misses, and he's got really big hooves."

"True, but at least a person would be sure that he was doing it deliberately, it makes a difference when one is being covered in crap by a horse that not only doesn't know it's doing it, but he doesn't care either. Arndrol makes sure everyone understands that he knows what he is doing."

"Yes. He's considerate like that."

"Consideration I can do without." said Andel, casually flicking something off his shoulder. Jayanne turned and smiled, her big green eyes laughing as they always did. To Crathen's distress she turned the wrong way, she looked over her left shoulder, so he didn't get to see the smile or her eyes.

Before very long they passed beyond the cultivated fields of the village, out into open land, unaltered by human intervention. The path they followed was still fairly clear, but nothing like as well travelled as the paths around the fields. The open ground was so clear and smooth that they increased their pace to a fast trot, the horses could keep this going all day, if they hadn't been carrying people, but as they were they could hold this sort of pace for hours, whereas the people couldn't, trotting is easy for the horse, but hard on the rider, the constant rise and fall of the horses gait causes serious load on the riders knees. Once the knees get tired the backside starts to hit the saddle just a little too hard for comfort. There are times when the discomfort of the riders is a very minor consideration compared to the distance that can be covered by trotting all day and resting the dark hours of the night.

Kern came into view, his horse just standing waiting for them to catch up, as Mander drew level with him, Kern simply waved him on. Kern turned his horse into the direction they were going and trotted alongside Jangor.

"I see nothing at all unusual ahead, but that in itself, could be unusual for us."

"Perhaps, but what is ahead?" asked Jangor.

"A great deal of nothing, open expanses of emptiness, there is absolutely nothing to be seen for miles and miles. Garath was right when he said this place was out of the way. It's so far out of the way, that there isn't even a way to follow."

"No road, or path?"

"Nothing, at this pace in an hour we'll be without anything to guide us at all."

"Which way should we head then?"

"The river is to the east, so we head east, once we find the river the choices are easier, north or south, cross or not."

"Well head for the river then, go and help Mander, sometimes he can find his way with the help of a map, but without one he has absolutely no chance at all."

Kern kicked his horse and set off to catch up with Mander, who for some reason had already started to drift to the south. Soon they had turned east again, gradually following the slope downwards towards the river, there was little in the way of vegetation to slow them down, so a fairly consistent trot kept them moving along at a decent pace, small copses passed them by, Kern trying to stay far enough away from each without actually changing their course too much, he had no intention of finding out that there were soldiers hidden in any one of the small clumps of trees, especially not by being shot with an arrow. As the day progressed into afternoon, the ground began to flatten out, there was no gradient to follow, and the occasional dip in the ground usually contained a small stream, normally very slow moving, the growth of reeds along these streams slowly became more and more verdant. Kern turned to Mander saying. "How long is it since we saw some trees?"

"It's been a while now. The ground is certainly getting more and more boggy, we must be getting close to the river now."

"I don't think so, the river should have trees growing along its banks, I can see no trees on the horizon. These reeds are certainly getting bigger and bigger though."

"And closer together, I think we are heading into a swamp."

"That could be true. We'll wait for Jangor and see what he has to say."

The pair stopped, and waited a few minutes for the others to catch up.

"Problem?" demanded Jangor.

"I think there's a swamp ahead, which way do you want to turn?"

"Why should we turn?"

"Swamps are not good places to be travelling in."

"How far are we from the river?"

"I cannot tell. Normally a river has trees along its banks, but with so many reeds growing around us, I just can't see any trees, if there is a swamp on this side of the river, then there would be no trees, in which case we are likely to get well and truly stuck in the swamp."

"Which do you think?" asked Jangor, "North or south?"

"We are probably going south, so let's get to the river on the south side of this swamp."

"I agree, south it is."

They turned towards the sun, which was almost at its zenith, Kern moved his horse along at a quick trot, trying to keep to the higher ground and the dryer ground. It was only a short time when he realised that they had been too late in their decision to change course, the reeds were closing in, and getting taller, before long their horizon was only feet away and their pace had dropped to a walk.

"Do you still know which way to go?" asked Jangor.

"While I have sky above me I'll not get lost," said Kern, "but in this place I think it's going to get difficult, the height of these reeds mean I don't have much of the sky to see, or any warning of the things around us."

"What things?"

"That is entirely the problem, I have no idea, and I can only see a few feet, so I have no warning."

"Has anyone heard anything of this swamp?" Asked Jangor of the entire group.

"I think I have read something about this place." said Granger. "I think the source isn't very reliable, it was a tale of many years ago, a folk tale really."

"There is much fact in folk tales." said Kern.

"Yes, but I'm not sure it was applied to this swamp on this river, the tale told of a beast that hunted in the swamps, it seemed to have a liking for virgins."

"Don't they all." said Kern.

"I suppose they do, but this one had some special reason, the tale doesn't tell what it was, and the beast was killed by some knight, he stabbed it through the heart, and cut off its heads."

"Heads?" said Mander.

"Yes, it had two apparently."

"Anything useful in this tale of yours?" asked Jangor.

"Not really. It was mainly a warning about swamps and the things that live there, I think."

"Nothing useful then." said Jangor, "Kern, Mander, you take the lead, keep the pace as fast as is safe, and as southerly as possible. Stergin, bring those pack horses forwards, we'll try and keep them together in the middle, Namdarin, Jayanne, Crathen, take the right side, Granger and I will take the left, Stergin and Andel stay behind, try to keep these pack animals in a bunch, the riding horses shouldn't be a problem, but pack horses tend to bolt if one of them farts. Keep them tight, Move out!"

Kern and Mander rode side by side, but with a few feet between them, breasting a path through the reeds at a slow walk, the others followed, each flattening a patch of reeds for the ones behind to walk through. Stergin glanced behind once the column was moving again. 'Anyone following would have to be blind to loose this trail.' The path they had taken was twenty feet wide of flattened reeds, the ground under the reeds was wet but firm, though if a horse stood too long in one spot it did start to slowly sink into the reeds. The ridden horses were more prone to sinking than the pack horses, but the pack horses were more prone to panic, Jangor knew there could be no stopping until they had firm ground underfoot.

"Kern." he called. "Try to angle away from the river, we need to get to higher ground."

"I had thought of that, but I don't know where the river is, so how can I move away from it, I've turned a little west of south, but how much good that will do, we can only wait and see." Kern knew that moving away from the river should get them to higher ground, unless they had joined the swamp at its northern edge, this was the thought that was worrying him. The reeds grew higher and more tightly packed, constantly swaying in the breeze, making that rustling sound characteristic of marshlands everywhere. A continuous susurration, a soft noise that seemed to blanket out any other sound. Kern found it difficult to pick out the sound of his own horses footfalls, not that they were making much sound anyway, but he felt that he should have been able to hear them. The progress of the group slowed until they were only making a sedate walk, almost funerary. Slowly a new sound impinged of their ears, it grew gradually above the sound of the reeds, a high pitched howl, something of pain and anger echoing across the marshland. The sound was impossible to locate, it seemed to come from all around, its pitched changed in an unpredictable way, there was no discernible pattern, growing in volume all the time, as if it was getting nearer, but still it appeared to come from all around, almost as if the reed beds themselves were screaming in agony.

"What the hell is that noise?" yelled Andel.

"I've never heard its like anywhere." replied Granger, trying his best to make himself heard over the screaming. The horses were getting very restless, the pack animals were pushing against each other, either in an attempt to be on the inside of the group , or just to reassure them selves that they weren't alone. The sound rose until the people had to put their hands over their ears, it actually became physically painful to them. Suddenly it stopped. Not only the screaming, but the sounds of the whole wetland, the reeds stopped waving, the breezed failed completely, utter silence descended. Arndrol breathed deeply, then coughed and caught his bit between his teeth, Namdarin clenched hard with his knees and his sword came instantly to hand, Jayanne flicked the wrist that brought the haft of her axe to hand, and held her reins tight and low in the left.

"Swords." Yelled Jangor, taking his hint from Namdarin, and knowing that bows would be useless at the sort of range they had available.

"What is happening?" asked Stergin, softly.

"I don't think that anyone really knows," said Andel. "But Jangor trusts the instincts of that damned horse."

"Shut up fools." said Jangor. "Horses see and hear things that we don't and that horse is far better than most." Turning slowly he scanned their limited horizon, nothing but stationary green all around.

"Where? Arndrol where?" whispered Namdarin. The big horse looked around then turned slightly to his left, planted his fore hooves as firmly as he could and pointed both ears straight ahead. "Stand." said Namdarin softly into the horses right ear, then he released his feet from the stirrups and climbed up onto his saddle, slowly standing upright his head became higher than the reeds, but not by very much. Looking straight ahead he saw that the reeds were swaying some distance away, and that swaying was getting nearer, he couldn't tell what sort of thing was moving the reeds, it seemed to only affect a few reeds at a time, but they were spread along a sort of wavy line that was coming their way. He lifted his sword and pointed at the disturbance in the reeds.

"It comes, quite quickly."

"What comes?" asked Jangor.

"I can't tell." shrugged Namdarin, as Jayanne moved alongside him and Kern moved to the other side. Crathen, Stergin and Andel moved to herd the horses away from the thing that was coming, pushing the pack animals in the opposite direction to the one that Namdarin was pointing.

"Be ready." said Namdarin, not taking his eyes off the moving reeds. "It comes." he said dropping back down into his saddle, and flicking his feet into the stirrups, the clenching of the man's knees released the horse from its rigid pose, and it seemed to settle, lowering its whole body, ready to move in any direction. A large triangular green head appeared through the barrier of reeds, only feet from Namdarin, as the man prepared to swing his sword at it, it reared upwards, fully ten feet up in the air, it opened is mouth and issued the nolsome scream, that they had heard earlier, noisome in more ways than one, the snakes breath stank of open ditches and foetid sewers. Arndrol shied away from both the sound and the stench. Namdarin clenched his knees and drove the horse towards the snake, but not before Jayanne had moved in with a massive overhand blow from her axe, the snake sensed the blow and moved the section that she was aiming at out of the path of the axe, the head turned towards Jayanne, as Namdarin moved in and slashed at it, the sword just touched the snout as the head retracted, the others were coming to lend a hand as fast as the horses could be convinced to move. Crathen moved in to protect Jayanne's left side, Kern was trying to get close to where the snakes body was in contact with the ground but this section was moving so quickly that he couldn't get a good stroke in. The four of them clustered around its head, gave the snake more targets that it could deal with, it couldn't decide which one to bite. It reared backwards and closed its mouth, the hard black eyes were immobile in the head, so the head turned towards Kern, the muscles in the neck achieved that tension that only leads to a strike, the head flashed forwards and hit Kern directly in the middle of the chest, Namdarin's sword swung in a long arc, an arc that intersected the return path of the head, the blued edge of the sword met the back of the snakes head and almost completely severed it.

Namdarin was already moving to where Kern was lying on the crushed reeds.

"Where did it hit you?" he yelled over the screams of the snake, and the thrashing in the reeds.

"I'm fine, it just knocked me off my horse." Kern banged his fist against his chest, there was a barely audible clang. "Steel breastplate." He yelled. "How can that snake still be screaming without a head?"

Namdarin turned as another snake reared up above Jayanne. "Look out." He screamed scrambling towards her. She turned, and saw the strike coming, with a rapid backhand blow the axe flashed through the snakes head, separating it and deflecting the strike so that it missed her completely. Silence descended again, or at least the screaming stopped, just the thrashing in the reeds continued for a while.

Jangor was helping Kern to his feet, the big man was beginning to get his breath back, "Good work you two." he said to Namdarin and Jayanne, the former turned to his horse, the later nodded and hung her axe on her saddle horn, before getting down from the horse. Namdarin grabbed Arndrol's reins just below his chin, and wrenched them down, so that he could look straight into those big brown eyes.

"What's the matter with you?" he demanded. "You take the bit from me, then back away like some frightened foal." Arndrol snuffled softly, blowing steam into the man's face, his ears drooping.

"You could have got our friend Kern killed." he went on, the horses head sank, until its lower lip was resting on the man's wrist, the horse seemed to be trying to stare at the ground while shifting his weight from one foot to the other. Namdarin dropped the reins and cuffed the horse firmly on the nose, before turning his back on Arndrol and going to Kern.

"I didn't know you wore armour?" said Namdarin.

"I don't, often. But the sort of things that have been happening recently, I thought it might be time to get the thing out of my pack, it's heavy, but today it was worth the carrying."

"How big are those damned snakes?" shouted Jangor, to Crathen who had gone into the reeds to look.

"Snake." he called, as he returned to view.

"Two snakes." said Jangor.

"No." replied Crathen. "Two heads, one snake, the heads are about thirty paces apart, but definitely on the same body."

"I've never heard of a two headed snake."

"But you've now seen one and seen it killed."

"What did that folk tale say about heads?" ask Jangor, looking straight at Crangor.

"Stabbed through the heart and cut off its heads. It seems the knight in question wasn't completely successful. I believe that we have been successful."

"I don't think the damned thing's coming back to life from this, do you?"

"No. Can we get on now, I think I have had my fill of snakes for this lifetime."

"Seconded." said Stergin.

"Thirded." said Andel.

"Carried unanimously." said Jangor. "Mount up, let's get out of here, before that thing starts to stink even worse." He was right in that it was starting to get ripe, though it was most likely that the thrashing around had release some quantity of marsh gas. Kern led the way and turned even more towards the west, trying to get out of the reed beds and onto higher and dryer ground.

"Why is it always snakes?" asked Andel. "I hate snakes."

"It's not always snakes, it just seems to be recently." said Stergin. "Two snakes in a row, is becoming a bit of a pattern, we'll have to see what comes next."

"If it's another damned snake, I'm going somewhere on my own."

"And you'll probably put your boot on one morning and find a snake curled up in it." laughed Stergin.

"That's right, look on the bright side of everything." Andel turned back to the horse's tails that they were following, he made the clucking sound they used to hurry the horses along, it had all the usual effect, that is none at all. In disgust he snatched his whip from the saddle and snapped it loud over the horses rumps, that got them moving, and a rather disapproving stare from Jangor.

It was the middle of the afternoon before they finally forced their way out of the reed beds, they were able to turn southwards and pick up the pace, the rolling trot of the horses really started to eat up the miles, though they had no real idea where they were going, and wouldn't until they found some people to talk to, so a riverside settlement was their destination. Only a few hours later such a place came into view, or rather the smoke from such place came into view.

"That is either a village burning or a large town." said Kern, as they pulled the horses to a stop.

"That is certainly a lot a smoke." said Jangor. "I think we'd be better approaching such a large town in the morning, let's find somewhere to camp for the night." Kern directed them away from the river, up into a small valley, there was enough space to camp and feed the horses, and it had a stream for fresh water. They set up camp with the usual speed, it took less than an hour and there was food to eat and fresh water to drink.

"How are we going to make the approach to this town?" asked Crathen.

"I'll go in." said Jangor. "With Kern and Stergin, we'll have a quick look around, to see if anyone is looking for us, there are always people with this sort of information in big towns, temples are always a good place to look. The town patrol may know something, we'll find out if it is safe for us all to go in."

"What if they are looking for you?"

"It's unlikely that anyone is looking for us, at least not for just the three of us, and anyway blank shields are almost always welcome in any town."

"Blank shields?"

"Mercenaries, soldiers who fight for profit. Most towns seem to have a small fight brewing somewhere nearby, and they don't really want their own sons to die in it, so usually the fight just brews and waits until one side or the other has enough mercenaries to start fighting. Sometimes one can live in a place for months waiting for the time to be right, sometimes it's only days."

"So. What are you going to do?"

"We'll go into town and ask around, see if there is anyone around who remembers the last elven war, there has to be someone who knows, if it was anywhere around here, it could even be that there are places named after the people who died in it. Elves used to bury their dead in mounds, perhaps there is a place called 'Elf Kings Mound', we can only hope."

"The bird said that the burial place was across the river. So we will need to cross, there must be ferries and such, or perhaps a bridge?"

"That is something else we need to know, but it is more important to find out if we can cross safely as a group or if we must split up, or perhaps even make our way downstream and cross somewhere else. We shall find out all these things and more tomorrow, for now let's get some sleep, it's going to an early start for some." Jangor crawled into his tent, even though there was still more than an hour to dark, Kern followed.

"You lot sort out the watches for tonight, we need to be really fresh in the morning." Said Jangor from inside the tent. Namdarin and Jayanne stood up. "We are just going to have a look around." He said the anyone who was listening, Mander raised a hand in acknowledgement. "Don't go too far, and be careful." he said, before he laid back down on the soft green grass, and stared up at the blue sky, high clouds blowing fast from the mountains, without a care in the world, or so it seemed. The two walked slowly out of camp, upstream, following the river they were soon out of sight. They passed through a small group of stunted willow trees, the crowns of the trees no more than a few feet above their heads.

"Not feeling sleepy, I hope?" asked Namdarin.

"What?" replied Jayanne, looking more than a little confused.

"Willows, sleepy?"

"No." she smiled, remembering the sleeping willow. "That seems like years ago, so much has happened."

"Do you still think you did the right thing tagging along with me?"

"Of course, I could have stayed in my old home, I'm sure that Morgan and his mother would have taken me in, but I feel that I belong here, on the road, with you and the others."

"This is a very dangerous path to tread, one that could easily lead to your death, all our deaths."

"I am fully aware of the dangers, and I accept them, somehow this quest of ours gives me something important to do, someone important to be."

"I'm sure you would have no problem being someone important, without all the risks."

"How do you mean?"

"A beautiful woman like you, in any place you choose to settle, would be important to some man, or even many, in a matter of days."

"I don't want to important to some man, or many, I want to be important to me. Here I can do things, help, be an important member of the group, almost one of the men, I suppose."

"I can never see you as one of the men, and I am not on my own in this." he turned away briefly, then waved at a large flat rock, beside the stream, bathed in sunlight, together they sat, with their feet dangling over the edge of the rock, the surface of the stream passing very close beneath their toes. Namdarin reached down with one foot, and yelped at the temperature of the water.

"That is cold."

"It's probably snow melt, or something." she laughed, and placed her hand on his arm. He reached across and put his other hand on hers, turned towards her and smiled. There was a sudden noise, a cracking of a twig, from amongst the willows, Namdarin reached for his bow, only to find he had left it in the camp.

"What a time to leave my bow behind?" he said, reaching for the sword instead, he didn't draw it, but sat with his hand on the hilt and waited to see what was going to approach. Jayanne's axe was in her hand, but she made no other move. Together they waited, no further sounds came, other than the normal rustling of the willow trees, the sounds of the water in the stream, struggling on its way through the rocks.

"Must have been a twig falling or something." said Namdarin, relaxing again and pushing his sword away, not out of reach but a little further from his side.

"So long as it's not another snake." said Jayanne, smiling, her green eyes flashing in the descending sun. The sky above was starting to turn red as the sun fell behind the mountains, the rock was now in shadow, and the light was failing.

"How can it be so peaceful here?" Sse asked, thinking of all the troubles of the last few days.

"Peace can be found in the most surprising of places, almost anywhere, I think it very much depends upon the company." he smiled and leaned towards her. A smile flickered across her face, briefly, then she frowned, briefly, then the smile returned. Namdarin laughed gently. Reached out and held her hand.

"This is a beautiful place, isn't it?" he asked, his voice was soft and somehow a little rough.

"Yes it is." she said, not taking her eyes from his, the smile flashing momentarily across her face. Her voice was so quiet that he could barely hear it.

"It would be a nice place to build a house." he said, not looking anywhere but into her eyes.

"It's got fresh running water." she whispered leaning closer.

"Plenty of game around here." he muttered. His mind shutting out everything but her.

"Yes." she mouthed the syllable, but issued no sound, she leaned towards him and kissed him, softly at first, closing her eyes, then harder. His mouth accepted hers, and returned the passion, his tongue probing and hers responding. She fell backwards to lie upon the rock and he followed his mouth not breaking contact, his left hand reached up and touched her face, then followed the curve of her neck downwards, inside her jacket until it found her right breast, there it paused, holding firmly the soft warm flesh. Her breath caught in her throat, her eyes flashed open, she tried to back away, but had nowhere to go. He sensed the sudden withdrawal and released her, he moved his head away but only an inch, took his hand from inside her tunic and rested in on her belly. He kissed her softly on the lips, the chastest of kisses. He looked deep into her green eyes.

"You must know how I feel about you?" he whispered, then he kissed her again.

"But." he continued. "This must always be your decision, this is no one else's to make, only yours." he kissed her again, soft and light.

"No rush. Take whatever time you need." he kissed her again.

"No pressure. When ever you are ready." he kissed her.

"I can wait." he kissed her.

"We've got all our lives." he kissed her.

She kissed him, her arms flew around his neck and dragged him down into the kiss. Her tongue was urgent in his mouth, pushing and searching, his hand was inside her tunic again, holding the breast, and rubbing the nipple. Her back arched but she didn't pull away, her hands stroked his neck, and slid inside his jacket, she felt the coarse hairs of his chest, and the solid muscle underneath. She stroked his chest and squeezed his nipple, feeling his heart racing under her fingertips. He slid his hand out of her tunic and fumbled the buckle of her belt, his hand was shaking, the tremors making it very difficult to open the buckle, with a snap it was open. The laces of her trousers followed in a moment, his hand slid down inside her trousers, across the rough hair of her pubic mound and down into the soft dampness that was hidden there. Gently he rubbed her and teased her, circling, and tickling, pushing the tip of his finger into the wetness concealed within, then out again. Soon she was moaning and wriggling with the sensations his fingers were creating, she grabbed his hand and pushed it hard against her. His mouth left hers and moved to her exposed breast, taking the nipple between his teeth, he squeezed it gently, and flicked the end of it with his tongue. She pulled his head down to her breast, as if she was trying to smother him in the soft flesh. Pulling gently away he started to remove her trousers, she lifted her hips to help him, then reached for his head and kissed him some more, the urgency of her kisses driven every higher by the action of his fingers. He pulled his head away again, moved to kiss and lick her breasts, all the time his fingers were working on the centre of her womanliness. She moaned and moved in rhythm to his motions, her nipples hard against his tongue, and her hands on his chest. Moving slowly down her body, he tasted the salt in her navel, and followed the run of gradually lengthening red hair down to her mound. She pulled his head in hard to her groin, as his tongue worked on her opening, tasting her fluids and working around the hard nub at its top. For him it seemed to be only moments until the spasms shook her body and her hips jumped upwards against his face. He moved and kissed her on her lips, whilst slowly removing his trousers, he placed one leg in between hers, and then the other. He held his straining manhood at the entrance to her. He looked into her lovely green eyes, and spoke very softly. "Are you sure you want this?"

She kissed him and nodded. Pulling him towards her rising hips. They moved together in the rising heat of passion. Utterly oblivious to the world around them they moved as one to that peak of such intensity, that she almost screamed, and he did likewise, the shudder of release silenced them both. They stayed for a moment, his weight resting fully on her, but she was unperturbed by it, though it did restrict her breathing just a little. Slowly he rolled off, and laid beside her, waiting for his breathing to return to normal. He was staring up at the stars, that were slowly starting to appear in the sky above, not wanting to move but knowing that they had to, and soon. She trailed a hand across his chest, and spoke. "We better get back, or they will be coming looking for us."

"Let's get dressed first." he smiled at her. His breath hot on her cheek.

"Now." she said, pulling her pants and shoes on and straightening her jacket. He followed her lead, and they were soon walking back through the pitch dark willows, they arrived at the camp, and Granger said.

"I was beginning to worry about you two. But if anyone in this group could look after themselves it is definitely you." The two smiled at the old wizard and crawled into their tent.

CHAPTER THIRTY

Crathen walked into the camp some minutes later. He nodded to Granger and sat across the fire from the old man.

"I thought you had got lost too." he said.

"No." replied Crathen. "I was just walking and thinking, and the darkness just crept up on me."

"Did you think of anything exciting?"

"Not really, I am beginning to wonder if I am doing the right thing be tagging along with this crowd."

"You could do far worse, they do at least have a purpose in mind. Not something you can say about most groups of people these days."

"But is the purpose the right one?"

"Who can tell you that? That is for you to decide. Namdarin intends on removing a god from this world, a god who causes great pain and suffering to those around him. This god has killed Namdarin's entire people, not just his family, but everyone that meant anything at all to him. Namdarin survived by pure chance, and chance is going to pay a large part in his continued survival. That is probably true for all of us that follow him."

"But what if we don't want to follow him."

"You can always walk away. That is always your choice to make, Namdarin would expect anyone who wished to leave to do just that. He would help in any way that he can, with supplies and such, though he would be sad to see any of us leave."

"I don't think he would be sad to see me go"

"Of course he would, we all serve a useful purpose in this quest."

"What useful part have I served?"

"I'm sure you have done your share, as have we all, I seem to remember your quick reaction saving Jayanne's life, on at least one occasion."

"But how does that aid Namdarin's quest?"

"Everyone here has a part to play in what has happened and in what is to come. You have saved a life, and will have some part to play in the future. I think that Namdarin and Jayanne will play the most important parts in what it to come, but the rest of us will do our bits."

"Sometimes I think that we are all going to die, and that Namdarin doesn't care, just so long as he takes Zandaar with us."

"Namdarin is certain in his path, Zandaar must die, and Namdarin is willing to spend his own life to achieve that end."

"He is willing to spend all of our lives as well."

"True, but only if we are willing. If we aren't, then we can walk away. Any one of us, or indeed all of us, can walk away at any time. Surely you can see that."

"But how would my leaving affect his chances of success?"

"Who can tell? It could be that you are destined to leave before the quest is completed, it could be that your part in this is finished. It could be that you walk away this very night, and never return, meet some nice girl and settle down and live happily ever after, if you believe in happily ever afters."

"But I can't just leave, at least not on my own."

"Your choice, stay or go, no one else can make this decision for you."

"Why do you stay, this can't be easy for an old man such as yourself?"

"Be careful who you call old. It is true that all this traipsing around the world is hard for me, but for a change I am being useful, just sitting in my cave was realistically achieving nothing. Here I am helping in something worthwhile, or that I see to be worthwhile, whether it is or not, I hope to find out before I die."

"Or this quest kills you."

"That too is a possibility. But I hope to buy something when I spend my life. Can you understand that young man?"

"Not really."

"If I die, and by dying I save the lives of my friends, then I have bought something with my life. For all the soldiers in this group that is how they live, and die. I can think of no better inscription on a man's headstone than, 'He gave his life for his friends' can you?"

"I suppose you are right, but I cannot see me giving away my life for anyone here."

"Anyone? Are you sure?"

"Damn you, no I'm not sure."

"So there is someone here you'd die for?"

"I suppose."

"Let me guess, she doesn't even know you exist."

"She does!" Crathen almost shouted.

"Careful, you'll wake them up, and we're the ones on guard duty."

"But she does know." Crathen said in a more controlled fashion.

"She knows that you would die for her, are you sure?"

"Yes. But she is beholden to Namdarin, because he saved her and her village from the Zandaars, which is the only reason she puts up with his attentions."

"You have to be absolutely sure of that, if you are going to make anything of this."

"I am certain, that is the only reason she has anything to do with him, it is her sense of duty that makes her act that way."

"Duty can be a powerful force for some people, in those like Namdarin duty can rule their entire life."

"Jayanne doesn't have to be like that, she should stop pandering to him, just because he did her village a favour."

"It could be that she feels more than that."

"No. I've seen the look in her eyes, that faraway look whenever she looks my way. She would rather have me than him."

"I know little of women, it has been so many years since I was married, but it can be very difficult say what a woman is thinking from her looks. I would go so far as to say that it is impossible to tell what women are thinking, that is part of their charm."

"I am certain, but there is little I can do about it, I'll just have to help her in any way I can, until she sees the truth of her own feelings."

"I think that is a vain hope, but if it is the way you feel then, you go the way you feel is best."

"I can't stand the way he looks at her, sometimes I think he is going to rape her."

"I don't think so, that axe of hers is never more than an inch from her hand, I've heard the things she can do with it. She is in no danger of rape, not any more."

"But he a strong and powerful man."

"He is, that is very true, but I don't see him as a rapist, it's just not in his make up. He is far too honourable a man."

"I don't think so, he is capable of almost anything."

"He is a very capable sort of person, and as such has no need to resort to rape. You are just getting yourself upset over nothing, if you stopped dwelling on these thoughts they will soon pass."

"But I can't stop thinking about her. She loves me, not him, why can't she see that?"

"How can you be so certain of her feelings? Has she expressed this in words to you?"

"I am absolutely sure, and no she hasn't said anything in words, but a look, a glance is more than enough to tell me how she feels."

"I think you ought to step back a little, and look at these feelings in a clearer fashion, I think you could be in for a really big surprise."

"You don't think she cares for me at all, do you?"

"It's not that. It's just that I think she cares for you in much the same way as she does me, she sees me as a friend and a member of her group, someone to protect her, and someone to be protected."

"No! You are so wrong. Every look tells me, the way her eyes sparkle when she turns to me. All these things and more, she doesn't need the words to communicate her feelings for me."

"Talk to her. Tell her exactly how you feel. That is the only way to be sure. Do it tomorrow, try and catch her on her own, she usually goes for a short walk in the mornings, try and catch her then."

"But I am already sure. Why do I need to tell her?"

"Perhaps she just needs to hear you say it, then she'll be more open with you."

"Maybe I will tell her, then you'll see."

"It could be that you already have." Crathen frowned, and waited for Granger to continue. "They are only a few feet away, and in a tent, voices such as ours can travel a long way in the dark."

"No. It's been a long hard day for her, she'll be very tired, and sleepy just now."

"She didn't look all that sleepy when she came back into camp, she looked positively glowing."

"But she was tired, I am certain of that."

"Well you just have to tell her, and then you'll know, she doesn't seem to be the sort of person who would string a man along."

"No, she'd never do that sort of thing."

"You had better be careful how you talk to her, I know she does have a fair temper. She is capable of extreme violence, if the stories are true."

"I have nothing to fear from her."

"I pray you are right. If you upset her too much, that axe is always to hand, and she wields it quite proficiently."

"I know that, but she'll not attack me."

"Well, I think I'll go to bed, you can take the next watch, seeing as you're awake."

"Right. Good night."

Granger walked slowly over to his tent, leaving Crathen to his thoughts. Thoughts that turned to Jayanne, he thought about the morning, when he was going to tell her how he felt, his mind could come up with no reaction other than a total declaration of love, she would tell him how she had been waiting to be sure of his feelings, she would hold his hand and kiss him softly, then with gradually increasing passion, until they fall to the floor in each others arms.

"That is how it must be." He whispered, distracting himself from the thought by adding some more wood to the fire, it was in no real danger of dying out, but he needed the distraction. His thoughts turned the things he had watched from beneath the rustling branches of the willow trees. 'Why didn't I run to her aid then, when she needed me?' He found no answer within himself, at least not one he could live with, the only reason he could come up with was plain and simple cowardice. He should have rushed forwards and stopped her from being raped, in such a brutal manner. Punching his thigh he berated himself for the coward he appeared to be, in his mind he swore an oath, she would never suffer such an indignity, at least not unaided, he swore upon his own life, that he would save her from anything and everything that tried to do her harm. He had already proved himself, on more than one occasion, he had been right there to help her, when Namdarin had been too busy elsewhere. He would always be there for her. Once she has made her feelings clear, more to herself than to any of the others, then they could leave this group of doomed warriors, and set up on their own somewhere, he saw a small house in a clearing, surrounded by thick forest, living off the produce of the forest. He closed his eyes and tried to project himself into the dream, but sleep and the dream evaded him. The crackling of the fire, and the soft whispering of the trees, the sound of the horses, all these things only served to focus his mind on his surroundings 'Things are going to change very soon.' He thought stirring the fire with a long stick, producing a shower of sparks and a crackling that sounded like a roar in the quietness of the night. Something else attracted his attention, something more to do with the job in hand, two green eyes shone in the darkness of the trees, flickering as they moved behind the branches. When the eyes noticed him watching they stopped, very still, they stayed, never blinking, staring straight back at him. Crathen looked down for his bow, and picked it up, when he looked back into the trees he eyes were gone. But the wolf had only dropped to it's belly and turned it's head towards the forest floor, pointing it's head in this manner it had learned it could get very close indeed to the camps of men, without being seen. With the sort of stealth usually associated with felines it crept forwards, avoiding and twigs that might crack under its weight, and any leaves that may rustle with it's passing. Keeping the shadow of the man between itself and the fire, it approached quieter than any small rodent, its target was any food that may be lying around the fire, the fire that it had an intense fear of, but this fire was one that had been tamed by man. The grey muzzle drew level with the last of the trees, only open grass reached all the way to the camp, the heavy scent of horseflesh wafted from the left, but the lone wolf wasn't interested in chasing horses, big as he was a horse would be too much of a risk. Nose down and tail flat on the ground behind him, he waited, breathing as softly as he could, the wind was in the wrong direction to blow scents from the fire, so he waited. The man turned back to the fire, put down the thing in his hand, and settled down, the wolf could see the tension slowly fade from his shoulders. The man relaxed, gradually sinking into a state of torpor, the wolf raised itself, and slowly walked forwards, lifting each foot high, above the grass, no sighing came from the grass, despite his passage. Tension roared in his mind, his muscles trembling with the control needed to move so slowly when instinct said 'Run.' 'Attack.' But this wolf knew better, for these were men. Men with more food than they needed, and too sleepy to see him come, his tongue rolled free from his mouth tasting the air. A brief swirl in the breeze brought the scent of cooked meat to his nose, and its location to his brain, having the scent he could now pick out the pack that contained the food, it was across the fire, up on a rock, the pack was small enough to be carried with ease, but large enough to feed him for a few days. He had learned that man food was always rich in meat and fat, and had little of the low value stuff that made up the greater part of any kill. He paused in his advance, looking carefully around, his ears turning every way and hearing nothing unusual. Everything seemed to be fine, but the wolf stood still. He felt that something was anything but fine, he looked back the way he had come, there was no scent of anything following him, looking forwards again, the man appeared so relaxed that the wolf expected him to snore at any moment. To the right there was only darkness so thick that it was as a wall, to the left the horses, out of the pool of light shed by the fire, they were hidden from view. Only the occasional glint of an eye showed that they were there at all. Except for one, the horse was staring straight at the wolf, he could see both eyes shining in the light from the fire, the reflections dancing in the dark eyes. As he watched the horse seemed to appear out of the blackness, its outline lit by stars, its grey bulk appeared to grow out of the dark. It showed no alarm at the sight of it's natural enemy, it just stared, then with a flick of its powerful neck it yanked the peg from the ground, now it was free. The wolf was surprised that the horse still stood and watched, it should have turned and fled, but it didn't. Very slowly the horse walked forwards, one foot moving at a time, the soft thud of each hoof throbbed through the ground, the wolf could feel the impacts in his paws. This was something he had never seen before, a horse that would willingly walk towards a fully grown wolf. Watching carefully the wolf decided that the horse wasn't just walking towards him, it was trying to creep up on him, it was placing each foot as quietly as it could. The sight of this huge horse was getting to be too much for the wolf, with a lash of his tail, he made his run. Flashing from motionlessness to full flight in only two bounds, the third cleared the fire, and the dripping jaws latched onto the pack without even slowing down, Crathen saw the huge tail for only three more bounds, then it was gone. The man hadn't even moved, only when the wolf was gone from view did he actually jump to his feet. Arndrol reared high screaming at the departing wolf, and slammed his hooves into the ground. The effect on the camp was predictable, people came scrambling from their tents weapons in their hands, and murder in their eyes.

"What's happening?" Shouted Jangor, swinging slowly from side to side, sword tracking with his eyes.

"A wolf." Said Crathen.

"Where?"

"Gone."

"Gone? Make sense man!"

"A huge wolf, it ran through the camp, jumped the fire, grabbed a pack and ran on, in no time it was gone. Is that gone enough for you?"

"No! We've been attacked by wolves before, the only real gone that counts, is dead."

"But it didn't attack, it just stole some food and moved on. And did it move. I've never seen such a large animal move so fast."

"Kern, can you track it?"

"Not in the dark. I don't want to track anyway, a lone wolf is usually a very cunning animal, it needs to be just to stay alive, and this one walked through a camp and past a fire, just to steal some food. I don't want to be anywhere near an animal like that."

"Nor do I, but I want to be sure it is gone, and preferably not coming back."

"It didn't walk." Said Crathen. The others looked at him. "It ran, and jumped over the fire."

"So it's not afraid of fire." Said Kern. "I'm not tracking that one even in the light, if I see it's tracks, then I'm going the other way."

"I want double watches." Said Jangor. "At least one bowman on duty all night, I know that means that Namdarin and Crathen will have to take turns, but I want an arrow in that wolf's guts before it gets close again. Namdarin you're on duty, but put some clothes on it's going to get cold tonight." It was only now that Namdarin noticed his nakedness, Jayanne the same, they both retired quickly to their tent, in moments Namdarin returned putting on him clothes as he came.

"I'll take this watch." said Kern. "If it's going to come back, it's most likely to be sooner than later, I may have the senses to feel it before anyone can see it." Jangor just nodded and returned to his tent, Namdarin collected Arndrol, and took him to a place nearer the fire, where he could see and be seen. Kern checked the other horses to find that they were surprisingly undisturbed by the recent activity. Returning to the light from the fire, he found Namdarin standing with his bow strung and an arrow at the string.

"Don't you think you may be over reacting just a little?" he asked.

"If that wolf is as fast as Crathen suggests, I want to be ready for it."

"Crathen was probably more than half asleep. If you hold that bow for a while, the only thing you'll hit will be yourself in the face. Relax, you'll get plenty of warning. Personally, I think the thing is still running." Arndrol snorted and stamped his feet.

"He doesn't think so." said Namdarin, watching his old friend closely for any hint that he actually seen, or smelt something. The horse was fairly relaxed, his head down and this ears forwards, there was no sense of any specific focus of attention. Namdarin sat down on the rock where Crathen had been, and Arndrol walked up to put his chin on the man's shoulder.

"Watch out." said Kern softly. Namdarin tensed. "He's going to dribble horse spit all down your back." Kern laughed, Namdarin shook his head, putting the bow down across his knees, the arrow upright in the grass in front of him.

"Have you ever heard of a wolf raiding a camp like this?" asked Namdarin.

"No. But that doesn't mean it hasn't happened. It is completely out of character for a wolf to do this, even a lone and hungry wolf. Usually they scavenge campsites after the people have moved on, but this one seems to have a taste for cooked meat."

"Is that unusual?"

"I would say it's incredibly unlikely."

"Why?"

"Think about it. What is the only way a wolf could have developed the taste for cooked meat, and such a disregard for fire?"

"He'd have to be trained to eat cooked meat, and not be afraid of fire."

"And who could train him with cooked meat, and get him accustomed to fire?"

"It would have to be people."

"So this wolf has been, at sometime in it's past, a pet, a man's plaything."

"Who would want such a dangerous animal as a pet?"

"Some keep snakes, others poisonous spiders, and many keep dogs that have been bred to be far bigger than any wolf. I have heard of a breed of dog that can hide in a flock of sheep, and when the wolf attacks it meets something that doesn't run away, and has just as many teeth as he does. An interesting concept don't you think?"

"Certainly strange. I don't think I'd like to meet such a dog."

"They are trained, they are good with people and sheep, it's just wolves they don't like."

"In that case I'd like one just about now."

"Sorry, I don't have one. We'll just have to make do with our own resources."

"Sometimes you can be so helpful." The pair laughed softly, Kern wasn't looking anywhere but into the fire, Namdarin was slowly looking all around.

"Stop worrying." said Kern. "The horses will let us know, long before we can see the wolf."

"How can you be so sure?"

"If he approaches from across the river, the wind will bring his scent to the horses, if he approaches up wind, as he should, then he'll meet the horses first. Realistically, we could rely entirely on the horses and get some sleep."

"I have had to rely on Arndrol in the past, but I'd rather not."

"I understand." he paused and stirred the fire for a while. "That must be some wolf though."

"Just what are you thinking?" asked Namdarin, already convinced that he knew the answer.

"Well, it's a wolf that already knows people. Perhaps it's time it knew people again."

"You really want to add that wolf to this party?"

"Why not? They are very loyal to their pack. Good fighters. Excellent runners. Cheap to feed."

"And killers, don't forget that."

"Yes, but he had the opportunity tonight, and he didn't take it, he stole a pack of food rather than kill for it."

"Obviously scavenging is easier than killing, especially when it is an armed man that must be killed."

"Wolves do scavenge, as this one did, but normally they do prefer to kill."

"Normally they aren't alone, this one was alone." Namdarin looked round quickly. "Or at least I hope it was."

"Oh yes, it was alone. And it was a big, fit and healthy fully grown wolf, it wasn't badly fed, or in poor condition, so it is doing a good job of surviving on it's own, which is something most pack bred wolves don't do. Pack bred wolves will take any sort of loss of rank, rather than be chased away from the pack. This one has an independence that has to be respected."

"You aren't saying anything that is making me like the wolf any better than I did!"

"I think this wolf is a mighty fine animal."

"Yes, but I don't want to share a camp with it."

"You already have a very close affinity for the horses, why not expand that to include a different sort of animal?"

"You think I could reach it the way I do the horses?"

"I'm certain the horses know where it is, after all they gave no alarm until it was almost at the fireside. Have you ever known Arndrol let a wolf get that close?"

"No, he's usually very wary of any predator."

"So perhaps he saw something different in this wolf?"

"That is possible but extremely unlikely." Namdarin shook his head.

"So why don't you see what Arndrol thinks of the wolf, and if he can find it?"

"What if he can feel where this wolf is?"

"Perhaps we can communicate with it."

"You are certain you want this killer to walk into our camp as our friend?"

"You remember the snow demon? You communicated with it, and turned it into an almost friend, this wolf has been a friend to man before, it can be again."

"Why should it want to be a friend to us? It is running free and doing very well for itself. It needs no-one."

"It's history, all it's ancestors, they all ran in packs, it is bred into them, they need a pack to run with, we could be it's pack."

"If we let this wolf become part of our group then we will be trusting it with our lives, that is not an easy thing for people to do. Again it is all those ancestors of ours, the ones that hunted wolves for their fur, and because they are a danger to our livestock and our children. You will have a lot of work to do to overcome that particular obstacle."

"All this is speculation, if we can't actually contact the wolf, please try." Namdarin could tell from the determination in Kern's voice that he wasn't going to let this lie, at least not until Namdarin had tried to contact the wolf.

"I'll try, but there can be no assurances of success, it's not a horse, and there is a large town just a few miles away. All these things are going to muddy the water."

"Just try, I hate to see a beautiful animal like that lost and alone."

Namdarin stood and turned to Arndrol, he placed one arm across the horses shoulder and the other around its neck, resting his head against the curve of the horses neck, he muttered the gentle words that always calmed the big horse, softly the two grew closer together, the horse relaxing against the man, and the man relaxing against the horse. Namdarin's breathing slowed until it matched the pace of the horse's huge lungs, Namdarin focused slowly on the other horses in the group, their nearness and totally relaxed presence had a calming affect, letting the calm suffuse his thought Namdarin reached out, looking for other forms of life, not just members of the extended herd, the horses felt the difference, and it disturbed them. The comforting strength of the man's presence soon calmed them again, and the search proceeded, slowly spreading outwards Namdarin's thought searched for any form of life that could be intelligent enough to have an independence from instinct. He was specifically looking for an animal that had the taste or smell of cooked meat about it. Without warning he found it, sitting in a dense patch of woodland, the wolf was happily tearing into the pack of food, discarding the greased cloth wrappings, and feasting on the tender filling. Immediately it sensed his presence, the wolf laid its ears flat to its head, and growled deep in its throat. The agitation of the wolf made it hard for Namdarin to maintain contact, trying as best he could to make calming noises, when he had no ability to make noise of any variety. His efforts were rewarded by a gradual calming of the wolf. Namdarin tried to feel what the animal was feeling, seeking some common ground to establish communication. The wolf went back to enjoying the flavour of cooked meat. Namdarin could almost taste it in the intensity of the wolfs feelings, the scents and flavours had such power in the wolf's brain. Namdarin tried to get the wolf to think about the place the meat had come from. He sent pictures of a man and a camp, the wolf ignored them. Namdarin tried horses and tents, the wolf ignored them. He tried fire and meat, the explosion of strange reaction was so blinding that the man was forced to back away. As he did so the wolf jumped up from its meal, and stared at Namdarin, almost as if the man was actually there in body, not just in mind. Namdarin was startled by the reaction and almost lost the connection, focusing tightly on the deep throated resonance of the wolf's growl, was the only way he maintained the link, the growl was both frightening and enticing, for the man it symbolised all the power of the wolf, a point of contact. But the man had no idea how to use it, the wolf stood, it's meal between it's feet, the huge mane about it's neck erect and vibrating, the growl seemed to fill Namdarin's world with noise. He suddenly remembered another growl, a bigger and more frightening growl, one that a young woman had faced, and fought against. He pictured in his mind the white bear, standing its full height, and howling in pain. With his mind he imitated this image and sound and projected it at the wolf. The effect was stunning, the wolf dropped to it's belly and slid backwards from its stolen meal, as far as it was concerned the image of a man had turned into a rather angry and extremely large white bear. Namdarin let go of the bear image. The wolf was confused by the return of the man, It remained belly down, but it was no longer looking for a place to run to. Namdarin imagined another package of food, and dropped it to the ground in front of the wolf. Slowly he backed away, leaving the pack for the wolf. The wolf rose tentatively to its feet, it's ruffled mane relaxed, it stared at the image of the man, its head tilted first to one side then the other, big yellow eyes sharply focused. It could tell that the man wasn't actually there, it was an image, and so was the food, then another pack of food appeared in the man's hand, more images. The wolf stepped forwards, until its feet were either side of its meal, then it lay down with its chin on the food, clearly proclaiming possession. It didn't eat, but only watched the image of the man. Namdarin looked at the wolf lying calmly with its meal, those hard yellow eyes were very difficult to look away from, he imagined another pack of meat, and dropped it to the ground, stepped back and imagined another. There were now two images on the ground and one in his hand. The wolf was getting anxious for all the food it could see, even the though it knew that most of it was immaterial. It was twitching to get at the imagined packs.

"We have plenty of food, and we will share it. Come back to us." He said, as calmly as he could, then he turned away and broke the connection. Namdarin returned to the camp, to the comforting feeling of a horse, whose neck he was hanging on to.

"Thank you my old friend." He said patting the horse on the neck, before sitting down at the fire.

"Well?" Demanded Kern.

"That was hard work." Said Namdarin, breathing slowly.

"Did you reach the wolf?"

"Yes. It's not too far away, actually quite close, it was more than a little surprised to see me, but I think we came to an understanding, it's very hard to communicate with an animal that doesn't talk, but it got the idea that we have plenty of food, and that we are willing to share it. Perhaps it will be curious enough to come back, or at least stay close enough so I can contact it again."

"Wolves are very intelligent, if you have made it curious it will certainly stay nearby."

"Just how intelligent are wolves?"

"Very, the story is that dogs have been bred from wolves and some of them are very bright. So the intelligence is in there to start with, it just needs stimulating when they are young, and I believe that this one must have been with people from being only a cub."

"I certainly would like to attempt to train a full grown wolf."

"By the time they are fully grown they are beyond training, they are trained to the pack and all it's rules. The only way to train them is to become part of the pack, and work from the inside."

"That has to be very difficult."

"There are cases where a pack has adopted a human child, normally that child grows to be the leader of the pack, probably because of humans native intelligence, but any of these children recovered from the wolves are un-trainable, they respond only as wolves, it's sad."

"You have seen this?"

"Yes. There was a 'Wolf Girl' at a fair once, when I was younger. She had to be kept in a cage, she was incredibly violent, very strong and ran like a wolf on four feet."

"Poor child."

"Yes, I think it was cruel to keep her in a cage, she should have been out in the wilds, running with her pack."

"You think she should be free, but that wolf should be running with us? Isn't that a little contradictory?"

"Perhaps. She was much happier with her pack, and that lonely wolf would be happier with us. That is what counts."

"So why didn't you free her when you had the chance?"

"I would have, but her pack were destroyed, all of them."

"Why?"

"They wouldn't give her up, they fought for her to the death, every last one. But the people couldn't leave the pack to run wild. Because she was leading, they had a human mind guiding them, the sort of intelligence that wolves have never had, her pack was forty strong and growing rapidly, ranging far and wide. They would kill for a few days in one place, them just as the people were getting organised to hunt them down, they would run all night and be somewhere else for the next few days. Her tactics were excellent, the only problems came when the pups were new born, they couldn't run fast enough, so a den had to be found for the pups to grow in. She did well for about ten years, but her pack became so big that its territory just couldn't support it any more, they had to expand, and that brought them into conflict with a large town, these people were better organised, and had an actual militia that responded very quickly to the threat. They tracked the wolves to the den, then killed the cubs when the pack went off to hunt, then ambushed the whole pack when they returned. It was a massacre, but they kept the girl alive, she must have been about sixteen years old. When I saw her she was about twenty, and thoroughly broken by all the years in a cage. Very sad."

"Sad, I suppose, but I'm still not happy about inviting a wolf to dinner, not even as the main course."

"That wolf could be really useful. I'm going to be going into town tomorrow, with Jangor, if the wolf turns up, you'll have to look after him, is that all right?"

"I suppose so, but the others are going to be difficult about this, you know that?"

"You'll have to deal with that."

"Thanks, friend, I like a challenge."

"You'll manage, but I hate to say something like this, watch out for Crathen, he has certain problems with you."

"What do you mean?"

"You haven't noticed?"

"Noticed what?" Namdarin was starting to get irritated and his voice was rising.

"Quietly, please, he seems to be infatuated with Jayanne."

"What do you mean?"

"I can't be any more specific, he thinks Jayanne should be with him, not with you."

"Well that is something that is not going to happen."

"Just be careful around him, he is deadly serious, and I do mean deadly!"

"He's just a boy, I have nothing to worry about."

"A boy he may be, but he's looking for promotion to man any time about now."

"He can look elsewhere!"

"He's not going to, just be careful around him."

"Thanks for the warning."

"I'm sure that Jayanne can put him straight, if he ever gets to asking her."

"He could be doing just that very soon, the tension in the young man is clearly visible for any one to see, at least anyone who is looking."

Suddenly there was a sound from the horses, a stamping of feet, as the men looked towards the horses all the animals were looking in the same direction, away from the fire.

"There is something out there." said Namdarin, rather unnecessarily. The two got to their feet and walked over to calm the horses, Namdarin had an arrow ready, Kern had his long sword to hand. The horses calmed immediately, the mere presence of men usually did that.

"Could it be the wolf already?" asked Namdarin.

"How would I know, but I don't think it would some back in the dark, it would probably come in the day and have a good look before it approached. No this should be something else." There was a rustling from the trees, something was coming towards them, and it didn't seem at all bothered about the noise it was making.

"Well." whispered Namdarin. "It's not the wolf, that one got right into camp without alerting any one." The rustling got closer and louder, as if something had stumbled through a pile of twigs. A bush started waving like in a storm, Arndrol moved to herd the other horses out of the way, Namdarin's bow creaked as he drew it, the string easing slowly to half pressure, the bush was a few feet away, anything coming through would still give him plenty of time to pull and release. The bush waved again, even more wildly, Namdarin shifted his aim higher. Kern held his sword in a two handed grip, watching the bush for further signs. The tension built in the pair, until they could hardly stand still, Namdarin took a step towards the bush to shorten the distance. The bush swayed again, this time coming towards the man, he pulled the bow, kissed the string. A small nose poked its way out of the bush, a black head appeared, with two white stripes running backwards from just behind two small ears.

Kern laughed out loud, turning away and putting his sword back in it's scabbard. The animal dropped out of the tree to the ground, another just like it walked slowly out from under the bush, each had the same markings, two white stripes that reach from behind the ears to the tips of their bushy tails. Both animals peered short-sightedly about, then turned their attention to Namdarin, the one that had fallen out of the bush stepped forwards, and stood up on it's front legs waving it's tail forwards over its back at the man.

"Namdarin!" said Kern. "Step back now!" Namdarin did as he was told, though he maintained the bow at full stretch.

"What are those things?" he asked.

"Skunks. Their defence system is interesting, they have huge scent glands at the base of their tails, that can squirt an aromatic liquid, with some accuracy and over some distance."

"How can that be a defence system, a little perfume is no problem, surely?"

"The perfume they use has some special properties, it has been known to make a grown man throw up every meal he has eaten in the last month, it sticks to anything, and stinks like nothing else your have ever smelled, and I include week old corpses lying in the sun." Namdarin stepped away, until the skunks had quietened down.

"So what do we do about them?"

"We leave them alone and they leave us alone, that's the way it usually works."

"What if they don't want to leave us alone?"

"Don't worry about it they will."

"How can they stumble through the forest at night and not be attacked, they are much smaller than the wolf?"

"Any animal that attacks them will get sprayed, the stink is bad enough for humans, think what that would be like for a scent hunter. Have you ever seen an incautious dog trying to bite its own nose off? That was a funny sight, and no one would have anything to do with that dog for days, it stunk."

"So anything that attacks them only does so once."

"Exactly."

"Interesting defence system indeed." Namdarin laughed and retired to the camp fire, keeping one eye on the striped invaders, who rummaged around the edge of the trees before vanishing back into the safety of the forest.

"I think I'll turn in." said Kern. "I'll get Stergin up to keep you company, I need some rest. I'm going into town tomorrow."

"Do we really need a bowman to stand watch?"

"No. But Jangor thinks he's the boss, so you get to stay on duty, I wouldn't want to upset him."

Namdarin merely nodded and waited for his next companion for the rest of his shift.

CHAPTER THIRTY ONE

The next morning Jangor rose early, long before the sun was above the horizon. In the cold pre-dawn light, he was issuing commands in his usual peremptory fashion.

"Kern and I are going into town, we need to find some things out, the rest of you have your own tasks, I want all of our equipment checked, tents patched, weapons cleaned and sharpened. You all have plenty to keep you busy for at least a whole day, I hope to be back long before that."

"I thought I was coming?" asked Stergin.

"I've changed my mind, low profile, two men better than three. You get a lazy day here."

"Thanks." snapped Stergin, sarcastically. Kern and Jangor mounted their horses and left the camp, Kern exchanged a few quiet words with Namdarin before they left. Jangor kicked his horse into a fast trot.

"What were you talking to Namdarin about?" he asked, the movement of the horse beneath him gave his voice an unusual rhythm.

"He made contact that lone wolf last night, I think that wolf could be trained to be with people again." replied Kern.

"A dangerous course, someone could get hurt."

"Perhaps, but can you think of a better guard than a full grown wolf?"

"It would make a great guard, but can we trust it?"

"There is the rub, the trust has to go both ways, he must trust us, as we trust him. It has it's risks, but it has huge potential benefits."

"There are benefits, he could be a night time guard, and a food hunter, properly trained he could be a real asset, who is going to give a hard time to a group of people who have a snarling wolf at their side."

"It may come to nothing, Namdarin was able to give it the impression that we were willing to share food with it. In a pack that is normal, perhaps the wolf will want to be a member of our pack."

"We are going to have to be careful when we get to town, we may already be targets, so let's not push too hard, right?"

"No problem, boss. You do the talking, I'll do the usual, frown, growl, and be generally menacing." laughed Kern.

"Can you ever take anything seriously?"

"Yes, but most people don't like it when I get serious, a lot of the time they end up dead when things get serious."

"Right, you leave the talking to me, we'll find out what we can, then leave as quick as may be."

They were riding through the rolling hills, mainly open pasture land, scattered with cattle and sheep, the occasional herder waved or shouted to them, the responded to the waves and ignored the shouts, not wanting to get into conversation with every shepherd along the way. Jangor knew that conversation with shepherds can take hours and reveal no information other than the death rates of newborn lambs. Soon they were riding along lanes in between fields, crops were grown, and being cut even as they rode through. Kern saw carts taking cut grain to the threshing places, each cart pulled by a single bony horse.

"Their horses aren't in very good condition." said Kern.

"They don't waste food on horses that only pull carts, it's only riding horses and war horses that get fed, the others are only one stumble away from being dog food."

"Or wolf food." laughed Kern.

"You are really hung up on this idea of a wolf running with us, aren't you?"

"Definitely."

"Is there something else I should know? Something from your past perhaps?"

"What do you mean?"

"Could it be something to do with Gyara?"

"There is a prophecy, it concerns a wolf that saves a world, it's more of a fairy tale, not so much a prophecy, but sometimes the two things are so much akin."

"And you want to be a part of this fairy tale?"

"It is one way to go. In the battles ahead I feel that we need all the help we can get. Is that a problem?"

"No. But I'd like to know in advance before you try anything like this."

"Right. I'll try to remember that. Though sometimes these things don't come to mind until after the event. I only remembered the fairy tale after I went to bed last night, after Namdarin had contacted the wolf."

"What do you think of this talent of his?"

"One cannot doubt the efficacy of it, he can reach horses over many miles, but to make the leap to a predator, that is something else."

"Definitely. But do you trust this talent?"

"It hasn't led us wrong yet, until it does I'll trust it, though it only supplies low grade information, useful but not immediate information. The whole process is too slow to be of any real use, if Namdarin could tell us what the horses were doing moment by moment then it could be considered as a real advantage, as it is, it only keeps us ahead of those following."

"Is that not enough for you?"

"No. I'd like to have control of their horses, even though they are riding them. That would be really useful."

"Now that would be something, we'll have to talk to Namdarin about that when we get back." Jangor said as they rode through the last of the fields, the hedges that ran along the road, stopped and the open ground in front of the town wall was before them, an expanse of flat ground that stopped at the depression that might have been a moat at some time in it's past, but was little more than a reed filled bog now.

Following the wall they came to the gate, which was guarded by two men, both in uniform, red tunics over breastplates, light armour on arms and legs, steel helmets, with bright green plumes. Jangor and Kern stopped a few yards short of the guards and regarded the gate, for this was unlike any they had seen before. The gate was narrow, barely bigger than a cart, only ten feet high and made entirely of stone. The single piece of stone was pivoted at one end and supported at the moving end by three huge rollers that ran on curved tracks across the roadway. Once the gate was shut it would make a perfect fit with the contours of the wall, from what Jangor could see, it should be an almost seamless joint.

"What is your business here?" Demanded one of the guards, disturbing Jangor's inspection of the gate.

"We are blank shields, looking for work, from the look of that gate we have found the work we need."

"We have little need for more soldiers, our militia is full, there are more than enough younger sons in this town to provide the meat we need for the grinder."

"Meat is easy to find, but it's the bone and gristle that you need in a fight, have you enough of that?" Retorted Jangor, not in the least upset by the lack of concern for the lives of the soldiery.

"Sometimes there is a lack of backbone in the youngsters, they do tend to talk a good fight but their bowels turn to water when they meet one."

"You interested in a little 'friendly' wager?" asked Jangor.

"What sort of wager?" responded the guard, more than a little suspiciously.

"I'll fight the champion of your watch, if I win, then you introduce me to the captain of the guard."

"And if you lose?"

"There is only one way to lose in this game, isn't there?"

"Then what is in it for us, if you win you get what you want, if you lose we get to see another man die, that is nothing new to us?

"I have a good horse, some good armour, and an excellent sword, call them the spoils of victory."

"I could of course call out the guard and have you killed, if for nothing other than your insolence."

"Then I'm sure my large friend here would be obliged to hunt you down, one by one and gut you like the cowards that you are." Kern smiled, as if enjoying the thought.

"I could get someone to stick arrows in the pair of you right now, then what would you do?"

"I begin to tire of this idle chatter, you obviously have no one worth fighting anyway." Jangor turned his horse and started to walk away. Kern chuckled and slowly followed.

"Hold!" yelled the sergeant, seeing good money riding away. "Our champion will be right out to meet you." He waved at a man standing nearby, who ran off to the right hand side of the gate. Jangor stopped his horse and slid from the saddle.

"Don't you think you're a bit old for all this?" muttered Kern.

"I think I'm about to find out, I haven't had a good fight for far too long."

Jangor was looking towards Kern, not at the gate, Kern saw the man walking slowly towards them.

"It's not going to be a good fight, but it is going to be very messy." He said, nodding towards the gate. Jangor turned and looked at the man coming through the gate, he didn't need to bend to get through but not by much. The man's arms looked to be about six inches too long for his body, and that was more than big enough to start with.

"He must be seven feet tall." said Jangor.

"And the rest." answered Kern. "Watch his reach, you could try to run him around a bit, or just dig yourself a grave."

"I'm so glad you are concerned for me."

"You picked this fight, I'd have done this differently."

"Now you tell me."

"I am Brank. Who challenges me?" said the giant, with a voice that sounded like a bucket of gravel thrown down some stone cellar steps. He beat a ham sized fist against his hard leather breastplate, the whole chest boomed like a gong.

"He's impressive." whispered Kern. "I think I'll go over there and see how the betting is going, I might put some money on him if the odds are good enough."

"There you go with all the support again." replied Jangor, a small grin on his face.

Kern moved away to join the rest of the guard, who had formed up to watch the stranger get minced by Brank. It was the sort of event that didn't happen very often any more, no one wanted to challenge the giant, at least not after what happened to the last two that did challenge him.

"Morning gentlemen." said Kern. "What do you feed that monster on?"

"Anything he damned well wants, and today it looks like it's going to be your friend." said the sergeant.

"Care to make a friendly wager on that?"

"How much of a wager?"

"Twenty gold sounds good to me." The sergeant was amazed few people ever bet against Brank, and certainly none ever bet that high.

"I don't have that sort of cash on me, but I can get it very quickly. Deal?"

"Upon your word as a gentleman." said Kern, then he held out his hand for the shake that seals the deal. The soldier paused, no one had ever trusted his word so highly, he thought again about the risk he was taking, this man seemed very confident in his friends abilities, and there was no way that the sergeant could get twenty gold pieces, not in a month. Brank would win, there could be no doubt, so he took the bet, for good or ill. Kern had sensed his concern.

"Upon your word." he said as their hands clasped briefly. Still holding onto the hand he shouted. "Jangor. This man has bet twenty gold. Put that animal out of it's misery then we can go and get drunk." Only once that statement was made did Kern drop the sergeant's hand and whisper "Upon your word." He saw the fear in the man's eyes and knew that the winnings could be difficult to collect.

Jangor continued his circling of his huge opponent. Brank's sword was huge to match his arms, it came at Jangor's head in a flashing arc, surprisingly quickly for something so heavy. Jangor stepped back out of the way, the tip slashing the air only a fraction from Jangor's nose, even as the sword went past him Jangor was moving forwards again, spinning in towards his opponent, Jangor caught Brank on the chin with a solid blow from the elbow, then he spun away, as Brank recovered his sword, which had been over extended to his left. Brank spat blood onto the ground between them.

"You shouldn't put your tongue out when you concentrate on a stroke, especially if you leave yourself so open." said Jangor, in his best drill sergeants voice. Again Brank slashed at empty air, as Jangor side stepped and slapped him in the belly with the flat of his sword, not that the edge of his sword would have made much impression in the hard leather armour.

"Even on the backhand you over extend, and leave yourself open to a faster opponent." shouted Jangor, trying to be heard over the encouraging shouts of Branks colleagues. Even Brank was beginning to get the feeling that things were not going his way. Jangor saw the decision in the giants eyes, before is was even made, and drew his belt knife with his left hand and waited. The sudden lunge with those long arms had never failed Brank in the past, but this time, he wasn't dealing with someone too terrified to act, Jangor used the flat of his sword to push the lunge wide to his left, and stabbed the back of Branks hand with his belt knife before dancing away again.

"The lunge can be a good tactic, but not often against a faster opponent, who isn't tired yet, you should always tire him before leaving your self open like this." Shouted Jangor, above the roar of the crowd. Brank stood looking at the back of his hand, dripping blood from a wound that had been calculated to do only that, cause pain and bleeding. He spat blood onto the ground and roared. He swung a massive blow at Jangor's head, Jangor stepped inside and down, slashed at the sword just above the hilt, as it passed over his head. The combination of shock, blood and pain, the shear mass of Branks sword, and the timing of Jangor's stroke spun the sword from the giants hand, the point of Jangor's sword appeared under Branks chin, lifting his head as he tried to move away from the sharp steel.

"Yield, and live." said Jangor.

"Kill him." yelled the crowd.

"Yield and live." repeated Jangor. Brank struggled with the term 'yield', it was not something he was used to, but eventually he remembered it's meaning.

"I surrender." he muttered.

"I accept." said Jangor, who then held his hand out for the giant to shake. Their eyes locked for a moment then Brank looked down, and took the hand offered.

"Well friend." said Kern. "Looks like he gets an introduction and I get twenty gold pieces. Upon your word." The sergeant looked for support from his friends, but they were fading away, returning to the barrack room on the inside of the wall, it was only a moment until he was standing outside the wall with Kern, Jangor and Brank.

"Has this gentleman kept to his word?" asked Jangor.

"Not yet." said Kern. "But he did give his word, so can trust him, can't we?"

"Trust him." laughed Brank. "Trust him with money." He held onto his belly as it was going to burst.

"I feel that I have made a mistake." said Kern.

"So it would seem." said Jangor, looking at the staggering form of Brank.

"It appears he is no gentleman, no man of his word, if he were I could challenge him to a duel. As he's not I think I'll just gut him like the robber he is." Kern's knife appeared in his fist as if by magic, and he thrust it towards the sergeants belly. The sergeant jumped backwards and screamed. Clutching his stomach, he realised that there was actually no injury.

"But you need him yet." said Kern looking at Jangor.

"Yes. Once he has provided all the service that I want, then you can have him." Jangor turned to the sergeant. "You are going to be useful, aren't you?"

"Of course. There is much I can do for you. I'll send word to the captain immediately." He made to scamper off towards the gate. Kern grabbed him by the collar as he went past.

"If you even consider running out on your deal with us, I'll hunt you down like a dog. Is that perfectly understood?"

"Believe him." said Jangor. "He is the best tracker in the world, you could never hide from him."

"Have no fear, I shall be right back, once I have sent a messenger to the captain. It doesn't do to drop in unannounced." This time he managed to get beyond Kern's reach.

"How did a worm like that get to be sergeant in the guard?" asked Jangor.

"His sister is married to the captain." said Brank.

"I see." replied Jangor. "Keeping the jobs in the family, so to speak."

"Not really. From what I heard, which admittedly may not be entirely true, he was hanging around his sisters skirt tails like a love sick puppy, she begged her husband to get him a job, he tried, so very hard he tried. But the man is such a maggot that no one would take him, the captain knew that to put him in the army as a common soldier would get him killed in short order. So realistically he had no choice but to put him in as a sergeant. A task that he is barely capable of." Both Jangor and Kern were staring up at Brank, their mouths hanging open.

"What is the problem?" asked the giant.

"I am sorry, Brank." Said Jangor. "Not wishing to cause any offence, but that last speech was so completely outside the character that we had expected, that we were utterly amazed."

"I am not as I appear." said Brank.

"No one is totally that." replied Kern.

"Only the gods see us as we truly are." said Brank.

"Only the true god sees truly." answered Kern.

"Am I missing something?" asked Jangor.

"I believe we both follow the same god." said Kern.

"It has been some years since I've been to the temple, but some things one doesn't forget." said Brank.

"It has been more than a few years for me." said Kern, holding out a hand for Brank to shake.

"Brother." said Brank, taking the offered hand.

"Brother." said Kern. "Just how much can we trust that sergeant?"

"Not much, he's a worm of a man, if that's not an insult to worms."

"I hope he finds some way to pay me the money he bet, otherwise I shall have to kill him. I am a man of my word."

"Knowing this I am sure the no one will go out of their way to help him." laughed Brank. "There are even a few who would quietly rob him, just to make certain he cannot pay up."

"Is there a surgeon nearby, you should get that hand looked at, the cut shouldn't be deep, but it is better to be safe." said Jangor.

"Follow me." said Brank, starting towards the gate. "I don't trust the local doctors, I usually do all my own patching, it's not that it happens too often. Normally people don't fight me, and the ones that do tend to die before they can hurt me." He stopped, and stared for a moment into Jangor's eyes. "You had no intention of killing me, did you?"

"No." laughed Jangor. "There is no better introduction to a group of soldiers than beating their champion. Had you been a less," He paused and looked the big man up and down, "formidable opponent, then that small injury wouldn't have been necessary."

"You are a leader of men." said Brank.

"I have been for many years. Now I am looking for information, who should I talk to?"

"That would depend entirely on the type of information you are after." They passed under the arch of the gate, Brank ducked his head, even though it wasn't actually necessary, the gate itself was an impressive structure, its massive weight was supported on rollers, it pivoted at the left hand side, and when closed huge metal bars locked it firmly into the wall, on both sides, above and into the ground below. "Is it architectural information you want, I am sure there is a warlord or two who would pay a great deal on money to find out how to break the gates."

"No, I'm just interested in the design, these are some imposing gates. I'd say it would be as easy to break the wall as the gate, once it is shut. I would stop it closing then it should be relatively easy to sack this town."

"How would you stop the gate from closing?"

"The rollers are the weak point, jam them or break them, either way the gate stays open."

"That is the way I would do it." said Brank, nodding. "But how would you accomplish this?"

"It wouldn't actually take all that much, a few small metal pyramids, sprinkled on the tracks, that should be enough to jam the rollers, once the roller hits a pyramid the whole weight of the gate would be lifted, stopping any forward motion until the track is cleared."

"There is a way to stop that working." said Brank.

"Do tell." laughed Jangor.

"If they were to fit stiff bristled brushes in front of the rollers, then the tracks would be swept every time the gate closes, not as now, someone sweeps the track if the gate jams."

"Have you mentioned this to anyone?"

"No. They don't pay me enough to do their thinking for them." Brank waved them through the door to the barrack room, it was just behind the guard house by the gate. A quick glance was all that Jangor needed, barracks are much the same all over the world, cots, footlockers, weapon racks, all the usual stuff. Brank walked the length of the room, at the far end there were two small rooms, Brank walked into the one to the left.

"Aren't these rooms for the non-commissioned ranks?" asked Jangor.

"Normally yes." said Brank, opening a small cupboard and taking out a sewing kit, and a flask. "But, the sergeant is the captains brother in law, and the corporals just kept having, erm, accidents. Besides this is the only bed in the place that is big enough for me."

"When did the corporals stop having accidents?" laughed Jangor.

"When people stopped wanting to be corporal, they quickly learned that the additional pay was nothing like enough to cover the doctors bills." He winced as he poured the spirit from the flask over the wound in the back of his hand. It was only superficial but it was bleeding quite copiously. Brank wrapped a cloth around the hand, and poured four measures of spirit into small cups, he gave a cup to each of the men and took one for himself. Raising his cup, he spoke softly. "Do you want to live for ever?" A soldiers toast. "No." Was the answer, and three cups were drained in a moment.

"That's good spirit." said Jangor, though he was struggling a little with his paralysed vocal cords. Brank nodded and refilled the three empty cups. From the sewing kit he took a small spool of thread and a curved needle, and dropped them into the forth cup. Carefully he wiped the wound on his hand, then removed the spool and needle, cutting a short length of thread, he threaded the needle. Holding the needle carefully in his left hand he attempted to stitch the cut.

"Damn." cursed Brank. "Have you any idea how hard it is to sew the back of your right hand, when you are right handed?" He passed the needle to Jangor. "You did it, you fix it." He chuckled.

"I'd love to, but my old eyes aren't up to that sort of close up work any more." said Jangor passing the needle on to Kern.

"And mine are any better?" asked Kern.

"It doesn't have to be pretty." said Brank. "Just make your minds up before I bleed to death, please." Taking up his cup, he sipped, and held his hand for Kern to sew. Kern raised his eyebrows, but bent to the task. Brank barely flinched when the needle slide through the leather like skin of his hand, Kern made the stitch small, and tied a tiny knot in it, then cut the thread. He slid his fingers along the thread, and held it up to the light streaming in through the open shutters.

"What is this thread, I've never seen it's like before?"

"It's something special I have made for just this purpose, as is the needle." Said Brank. "It's the same as the strings on a fiddle, but much thinner. Any other thread tends to stick in the wound, and can do more harm than good, but this, once it's been dipped in spirit, is soft and pliable, and causes no real problems. For a really bad injury I just leave the stitches in until the body absorbs them." Kern continued with his sewing, it only took seven tiny stitches to seal the wound, Brank looked at the work closely and nodded, then wrapped it in a new bandage.

"A good job. Thanks, I'd have made a complete mess of it." At this point the sergeant came into the small room, which was already crowded.

"The captain will see you in a few minutes, he's supposed to be on his way here right now."

"That will be just fine." said Jangor. There was a long pause, the sergeant seemed unsure of what to say or do, he shuffled from one foot to the other.

"Was there something else?" asked Jangor.

"Well. Er. No, not really." stammered the sergeant.

"Dismissed." snapped Jangor, turning his back on the sergeant, who seemed glad of the opportunity to leave. Brank refilled the cups and they drank again.

"I had better not drink too much of this." commented Jangor. "It's far too early in the morning to be getting drunk."

"That doesn't usually make that much difference to you." said Kern.

"I know." replied Jangor. "But I want to at least remember some of today." The three laughed.

"What is it like working in this town?" asked Kern.

"Relatively easy, at least for me." said Brank. "I don't have too much to do, other than the occasional menacing duties, I'm left pretty much to myself. I'm not expected to attend any of the ceremonial garbage that so many enjoy, I look a little out of place, being so much taller than any one else."

"Who does the training of the men?" asked Jangor, sipping slowly at his cup.

"There is an old sword-master, and an even older horse-master, but they don't show until much later in the day. They are after all old men."

"Are they any good?"

"Oh yes, in their time they were of the best in the land, but time has dulled their skill, but not their knowledge, they still know how to do it, it's just that their bodies aren't up to all that punishment any more. It is sort of sad, really sad sometimes."

"It is sad what time does to us all." agreed Jangor.

"But these two certainly deserve the honorific master. They are very good teachers, though there are those that don't like the lessons they teach."

"They teach the hard way?"

"Sometimes very hard." laughed Brank, thinking of a time when a certain sergeant got pitched off his horse for the fifth time in one day.

"It is better to learn the hard lessons on a practice field. There is only one lesson to learn on the battlefield, and that is how to die." said Jangor.

"A lesson I'd rather not learn just yet." said Brank. The sergeant came back into the room, saying. "The captain will see you now, in the guard room by the gate."

"Right." said Jangor. "Lead the way." They all followed the sergeant out into the street, there was more traffic now, carts moving in and out of the gate, people on foot, and the occasional horseman. The guard room by the gate was a small structure, more of an administration centre than anything else. The sergeant led them into the office at the back, the captain was a fairly young man, for a captain of the guard. He stood as Jangor followed the sergeant into the room, waved a hand at some chairs, indicating that they should sit down.

"You can go now, Jackis. Close the door on your way out. I'm called Harvang, captain for my sins. Why are you still here?" The last at the sergeant, who turned and almost ran from the room, the door slammed hard after him.

"I'm Jangor, this is Kern."

"And that is a somewhat damaged Brank. I hope you didn't hurt him too much."

"I'll be just fine." said Brank. "It makes a change to have someone worth fighting."

"If you can beat Brank, I'd be more than happy to sign you up right now, the pay isn't very good, but food and lodging are provided, some of the men have some interesting sidelines, they think I don't know about them, and I probably don't know them all, but so long as they cause no trouble I'm fairly easy to please."

"Actually we came seeking information, not employment. But I have found that sometimes it can be very difficult to get past the man who sees himself as the guardian of the town, the one on the gate."

"Sometimes it can be very expensive as well. I know what that scoundrel charges strangers."

"I don't wish to tell you your job, but perhaps you should do something about him."

"I wish that I could, but he is my wife's brother."

"We have been made aware of his relationship to you, it is a great shame that one cannot pick ones relatives."

"For certain." sighed Harvang.

"It could be that your problem will be solved for you fairly soon." said Jangor.

"How?"

"Your sergeant bet twenty gold on Brank, presumably a bet that he has never lost in the past. Now it seems he is unable to pay Kern here the money he owes. Kern has informed him that while he is of some use to me he will stay alive, at such time as his usefulness ceases, so does his life."

"I can never condone murder, not even in this case, I am sure it will be a fair fight?"

"I am sure it will be fair, Kern against Jackis, and me against all his friends."

"Hey." interrupted Brank. "If there's going to be a chance to kill some of Jackis' cronies, then I want some, you've got to save one or two for me."

"Don't worry." said Jangor. "If the man has enough friends to bloody more than one knife, I'll be amazed."

"I'd be astounded." said Harvang. "In the case of such a fracas in my town, I would be forced to investigate thoroughly. If this was to happen just before you leave town, then there would be several days of local investigations, and you could be sure that any pursuit would almost certainly go in entirely the wrong direction. What say you Brank?"

"I'd say that the pursuing team, would not only be many days late in departure, but would have very clear instructions to return with exactly no prisoners, after a suitable time spent tramping around the countryside, questioning the sheep as they go. Do we have a professional sheep questioner, captain?"

"There is one man who is thought to have some connections with sheep, though I don't think he actually talks to them, ah, but he's likely to be dead by the time the search is underway." laughed Harvang, and Brank.

"Isn't it nice to have friends?" asked Kern, softly.

"We have a saying." said Harvang. "A man gets the friends he truly deserves."

"And Jackis has many friends?" asked Jangor.

"The sort of friends he deserves, the kind of people who will empty his pockets as he is bleeding in some gutter. But how may I help you and speed you on your way, the quicker the better, because that will give the worm no time to steal the gold he needs."

"Fine." said Jangor. "We have heard of a great treasure buried with an elven king, somewhere near here, we have been told it could be of use to us. Can you tell us of any elven graves nearby?"

"Not as far as I am aware, but then I'm not much of a historian. Brank, you spend far too much time listening to the old story tellers, do you know anything?"

"I'm not sure, there is some talk of an old battle, a long way to the east, it's difficult to remember. There was an elven king, with a powerful sword, there was something special about the sword." Brank looked down at the ground, holding his head in his hands. "It was so long ago, I was only young the last time I heard the tale." Somehow his voice seemed to change. "The elven lords came down out of the north, their troops blackened the plains with their numbers. The peoples of the plains stood behind their king, their banners fluttering in the breeze, many coloured, and many shaped, like the playthings of happy children. The five elven lords rode huge white horses, and wore white helms upon their heads, they rode in line abreast with their king in front, tall and thin though he was, he was of pure elven blood. Almond shaped eyes, with deepest amethyst irises, slightly pointed and elongated ears, and hands more fitted to a lute than the broadsword that swung at his back. Without a word the elven army stopped its march, and stood, stock still upon the slope above the army of humans. The elven lords continued to walk slowly forwards, only paces from the human lines they stopped.

"Return to us that which you have stolen." said the elven king, in a voice though quiet, it reached far into the crowded humans.

"We have stolen nothing from you." shouted the human king.

"You and those under you have stolen our lives, they cut down the forests that we depend on, this cannot be allowed to continue."

"We have cut nothing that belongs to you, take your army back into the trees, where you belong."

"We will not. We will take back the land that you have taken, and we will grow the trees again, you shall never have them again."

"You will all die today." screamed the human king, and drew a mighty broadsword from its holder on his saddle. A huge groan came from the elvish army, not a noise from any throat, but the sound of a thousand bows drawn to their prodigious limits. One of the elves in the kings escort raised his left hand, palm towards his enemies, and fingers widely spread. The human escort drew their swords and advanced towards the elves, even though this final parley was under the flags of truce. The elf lord clenched his fist and a thousand bows sang their deadly song, the very air turned black with the arrows that filled it, these were not the usual arrows of the elves, these had huge metal tips and small black feathers, no hint of green was to be seen. The arrows fell upon the humans like the very scythe of death himself. All around the elven lords the humans fell, but none of the elves were in any danger. Again the elven bows spoke and again the sky went black, but the human horsemen were already moving, heavy cavalry came down upon the elves from both flanks and stormed towards them, from their places of concealment. The elven kings party retreated as fast as their fleet footed horses could go, they raced for their lines of troops. The Elf king arrived at the front lines only feet ahead of the charging cavalry which had appeared almost by magic through huge breaks in the humans front lines, as his party passed through the front line the elven pikemen raised their long poles. The wide bladed heads of these poles, with their long cross pieces impaled the horses in the front of the charge, but the sheer mass of horseflesh behind them made it impossible for them to fall. The line held, but only briefly, locally at first then across the whole front the line of pikes went down, crushed by the sheer weight of armoured horsemen. The elven second line of swordsmen came into play as their king tried to rally them, the elves use little in the way of armour, and their thin light swords were of no use against the broadswords of the heavy cavalry, but the elves had speed in their favour, moving as fast as only elves can, those razor sharp swords took many lives, finding eye holes in helmets, joints in armour and holes in the chain mail of the horses. They fought step by step back towards the forest they had left so short a time ago. From the middle of the elven army came the king his great sword drawn, he was surrounded by a bright green light, which some say came from the sword itself, but others say it came from everywhere. Every where the king went the enemy soldiers fell, it is even said that they stepped towards him waiting to be killed, and kill that great sword did, until its green glow was tainted black with the blood of his enemies. The King reached the eaves of the forest, and turned, pushing the human cavalry back with the ferocity of his attack, he slowly managed to open up a path for the elves to retreat through. Less than half of his army made it back into the forest, the rest were trampled under the hooves of the human cavalry. Once sheltered from the cavalry by the huge trunks of the trees, the elven bowmen came into their own again, no huge flights of arrow, the thickness of the trees wouldn't allow such a tactic, but a terrible retaliation, for the horsemen attacking the forest knew, that for every bow they heard released, a man died. In only a few minutes there was nothing standing within a hundred paces of the forest, except for a few empty horses, the twitching of corpses the only movement to be seen. The elven king walked slowly from beneath the trees, his broadsword swinging slowly in his hand, he stopped as he came into the sunlight, the green glow of his sword wasn't suppressed by the sun, if anything it enhanced the light until the valley was flooded with the sort of green light that shines through a canopy of trees. The king rested the point of his sword in the blood soaked grass, and stared out over the battle field, a human bowman stepped forwards and shot an arrow at him. The king ignored the arrow as it dropped to the ground a full twenty paces short of its mark. Three elven bowmen didn't ignore the arrow, their bows thrummed as they released, the human bowman suddenly had three new black feathered ornaments, one in his head, the others in his chest. The human army fell back from the forest edge. The carrion pickers, that follow any army moved forwards and started to despoil the dead, picking over the corpses, and finishing those not quite dead. The elven king spoke an angry word, and the bows answered. More corpses fell to the ground. Small groups of elves left the cover of the trees, and flanked by groups of archers they recovered their dead, unlike the humans they didn't despoil or dishonour the enemy dead, they merely ignored them. The human army fell back, trying to keep out of range of those dreadful bows. The human king was utterly defeated, though the battle was without doubt his, he could do anything about the remaining elves, his heavy cavalry was just about destroyed, the light cavalry he had left, could never close with the elves, they would be shot from their saddles long before they reached their foe. Nothing short of a prairie fire would have moved the foot soldiers towards the elves. He knew that no amount of praying was going to make the damp grass burn. So he stood screaming orders at his generals, orders that none made any move to obey. It took a long time for the elves to complete the dreadful task of removing their dead from the field, the sun was past it's zenith before the last party of elves withdrew from view, only the king remained, standing solitary guard over the edge of the forest. He raised his sword over his head, and turning into the darkness under the trees, he extinguished its light."

"That is some story." said Jangor.

"But it is the truth, this tale has come down from my family, my great grandsire was actually there at the time, he was a young man at arms, he took a blow to the head, probably from an elven arrow, and lay on the field until the elves had all gone. When they were recovering the dead, he saw them really close. He said there was no hatred in their eyes, only sadness. They knew he was alive, but left him alone. Without that kindly act I would never have been born."

"Have you any idea what happened to the elf king and his sword?"

"He left the field that day, alive though injured, and I have heard nothing of him since."

"Do you know where these elves were based?"

"No, but I can show you where the battle was."

"That's as good a place as any to start." said Jangor.

"We know much more than we did when we came in here." Said Kern.

"I suppose this means you'll be leaving immediately?" asked Harvang, a wicked smile on his lips.

"I'm not sure." replied Jangor. "There could be someone else in town who can tell us more about where this elven king was buried."

"It is unlikely, Brank here spends every moment of off duty time in the taverns, drinking and listening to the old men telling their tales."

"That's more listening than drinking." said Brank.

"So there are no more tales of the elven king?" asked Jangor.

"No, but plenty of the human king of the time." answered Brank. "I think I may know someone who can help you, he's an old man who usually frequents the Blue Parrot, down near the river. We could go there and see him. With your permission captain?"

"See what I mean." said Harvang. "Now he wants to go carousing while on duty."

"But at least he is polite enough to ask." laughed Jangor.

"Go ahead, but take Jackis with you. He might enjoy your company." Harvang laughed out loud.

"Sometimes people tell me I am a bad man." said Jangor, smiling at the captain.

"Sometimes you are." said Kern.

"I think I'm quite nice compared to this man here." said Jangor waving one hand in the direction of the captain. Laughing they left the room and collected Jackis, who had been loitering outside, Jangor hoped that he had been listening at the keyhole, not that the door was actually shut.

"Lead on." said Jangor, Brank set off along the street with the gate behind him, it was slightly downhill as they walked towards the centre of the town, the houses seemed to lean into the street, the upper floors being slightly larger than the lower ones, some of the houses had more than two stories, but not many. The design of the houses led to alleys that were as black as night even in the full light of day.

"Don't you feel a little closed in?" asked Kern.

"Sometimes." said Brank, "But I got used to after the first five years."

"But you've only been here three years." said Jackis.

Jangor and Kern laughed aloud, for they already knew what Brank had meant.

"What is so funny?" demanded the sergeant.

"Not so much funny as tragic, how can a man with your obvious intelligence have remained a sergeant for so long? Is there no justice in the world?" laughed Jangor.

The confused look on Jackis face only made them laugh more. Their walk took them down towards the river, the dark street suddenly opened out onto a large square, there were a few trees scattered about and places for people to sit, and talk.

"Most days this is the market place, but there are two days a week when it is left open like this, I think it's a nice place when it's not full of screaming traders after your coin." said Brank. "The place we want is beside the river, it's not too bad in the winter, but in the summer the river does smell bad sometimes."

"I hope the water people use doesn't come from that river?" said Kern.

"No. There are some good springs and wells inside the walls, most of the water used comes from them."

"Most?"

"There are some people who can't afford the best of water, they have to get theirs from the river."

"How can people not afford water, it's a natural resource?"

"That may be true elsewhere, but here, the water belongs to the owners of the wells, so they sell the access to it. It's only fair, it costs a great deal of money to sink a well, and even more to pump the water up everyday."

"Looking at it like that it seems fair, but it's not something I've every heard of before. Strange indeed." Kern paused for a moment before continuing. "What about the water that falls out of the sky, does that belong to anyone?"

"That's a strange thought. One you should keep to yourself, the governing council may just decide that it belongs to them and charge people for using rainwater."

"People actually collect the rain here?"

"Oh yes! It's more than good enough for bathing and washing clothes, and if your roof doesn't have birds nesting on it, then quite often it tastes better than the water from the wells. Most people use it for such, see how the gutters around the roofs all run into the houses, there the water is collected in cisterns. It's much cheaper than water from the wells."

"This is a very strange place to live." said Kern.

"I like it." said Brank. "The people are mostly nice, with the same sort exceptions as anywhere." This said with a pointed stare at Jackis. Kern laughed.

"Where is this tavern we are looking for?" asked Jangor.

"Across the square, it has a sort of garden at the back, which looks over the river. It's a nice place to sit and think."

"You mean drink!" said Jackis.

"Kern. How much longer is this man going to be useful to you?"

"That has yet to be decided. We might be leaving town today, or tomorrow, by then he will be of no use to me at all. Unless he manages to pay the gold he owes."

"And if he fails to pay up?"

"Then there will be a different sort of accounting, one that involves payment in blood."

"That may not be as easy as you think."

"We'll find out soon enough, wont we?"

"True enough." said Brank, turning into a wide street. "There is the blue parrot."

"It is the one with the small parrot on the veranda, by any chance?" laughed Jangor.

"It is indeed." said Brank. "Subtle, don't you think?"

"How could anyone think that a twelve foot high, bright blue, wooden parrot, is subtle?"

"For some around here, that is the height of understatement."

Jangor just shook his head in disgust, and followed the big man up the steps, he tapped on the parrot as he walked past it, just to be sure it was wood. Not only was it wood, it was hollow, and wobbled when touched. The inside of the place was no better than the parrot on the doorstep. The décor attempted to remind clients of a ship at sea, or and idealised view of a ship at sea, but the effect was as laughable as the parrot outside. The barman obviously recognised Brank, and came over before they had even selected a place to sit.

"Brank, my friend." he said in the deepest voice that any of them had ever heard. "You are welcome, as always, as are the strangers, but that one is not welcome here." A fat and greasy finger pointed at Jackis.

"I am sorry, but the captain told me to come here and not to let the sergeant out of my sight. Somehow the captain doesn't trust him to pay his debts."

"No one trusts him, he is a liar and a thief, a swindler and a robber."

"I am sure that he will behave nicely." said Kern, his hand on the hilt of his dagger, and a stern look for Jackis.

"Of course." said Jackis. "The fact is I am none of those things, I am merely an honest man who has been misrepresented."

"Garbage. You were using loaded dice, at least two pairs, switching depending on what you wanted the throw. You were lucky to get out alive."

"I'll make sure he behaves himself." said Brank. "Has Andreas been in yet?"

"Not yet, but he shouldn't be long, he's usually in around this time."

"Good. I'll have my usual, and your best beer for my friends." He looked to Jangor who nodded. "Oh. And water for the dog." Jackis was the only one looking for a canine.

"Are you sure the captain said you could drink this early?"

"He said it with his own fair lips, and I'm not going to argue with a man that tells me to go to a tavern at any time of the day, especially if he happens to be paying my wages at the time." Brank turned and walked out of the small rear door, the door had a small round window, not unlike a porthole. He held the door for his friends to follow him, out into a quiet courtyard, with a couple of large trees, that supplied shade from the morning sun, a lawn sloped gently down to the riverbank, where sluggish brown water flowed.

They all sat at a table near to one of the trees, the rough furniture looked like it had never been inside, the weather beaten table top was softened by slow decay, and the stools were more than a little wobbly.

"Not a very nice place you frequent." sneered Jackis, picking at the table top with a fingernail, releasing a large splinter of wood from its captivity.

"This place is nice enough to know not to allow you in. The only reason you are here is so that you be readily available when the time comes to pay your debt to the gentlemen." At this point a serving girl came over with a loaded tray. A huge flagon rested in the middle of the tray, and a trio of large mugs. Brank reached up and took the flagon, a huge smile on his face, the girl served the drinks to the others, leaving Jackis to the last, and making sure he understood that with any provocation at all, he would end up wearing his water, rather than drinking it.

"The service here is terrible." said Jackis, but only once the drink was safely in his hand. Brank nudged him quite hard and he spilled a good deal of it. Brank lifted his flagon, and with a practised action lifted the lid and drank a huge draft, as the flagon came away from his lips, his thumb released the lever and the lid fell back into place, a swift hand wiped the residue from his lips, but not before Kern had noticed it's colour. Briefly Brank had a small white moustache.

"When can we expect this Andreas to turn up?" asked Jangor.

"He should be here any time, or may not come today, in the mean time enjoy your beer, I'm told it's quite good."

"What do you mean told, you drink here all the time?" said Jackis.

Kern took a taste of the beer before him, then looked at Jangor with raised eyebrows. Jangor tasted his, and returned he look, then both men laughed out loud.

"What is so funny?" asked Brank.

"We know where this brew came from, and have both been trying to think of a way to go back for some more. Now we can drink it here." Said Jangor. "Do you think we should tell the rest?" He continued. They both shook their heads and raised their mugs in salute.

"The rest?" asked Brank.

"We are a small group of travellers looking for something. We passed through the place where this beer is brewed. It's better there, but here it is more than good enough. I wonder how far it would travel?" Said Jangor.

"Beer doesn't travel well, the movement of a cart disturbs it, and the changing temperature is bad for it, it's far better to move it in the winter, when the weather is cooler." replied Brank.

"You would know all about beer." sneered Jackis, merely sniffing at his water, before placing the mug back on the table, untasted.

"But do you know about any monks in black robes hereabouts?" asked Jangor.

"I don't have much truck with gods." said Brank. "But I have heard something about a new monastery set up recently in the hills to the south. They come to town occasionally, to trade and such, but they don't seem to be looking for converts. They have an odd bearing about them."

"Military by any chance?"

"Now you mention it, they could be, their deference to the leader is more instant than I would have expected from clerics. You could be right." Brank nodded.

"So we could have the militant arm of the Zandaars nearby." muttered Jangor.

"Are they friends of yours?" asked Jackis, sensing something that could be of use to him.

"Not exactly, but that is none of your business, you have more pressing matters on your mind at the moment." Jangor glanced at Kern, who merely stared at the sergeant. Jackis swallowed hard, but said nothing more.

"Could these military monks become a problem?" asked Brank, taking another huge draft from his flagon, and wiping his lips very quickly.

"It is possible, they do tend to take the things they want, if they want your town, they will take it, and I don't think your wall and gates will hinder them all that much."

"Do you think they would do that?"

"Not really, they don't usually behave the way an army would, they take things carefully, slowly, most of the time these religions take over before anyone has noticed, just make sure they stay outside, if they start to set up inside the wall, then I'd find a new place to live if I were you, they don't take kindly to opposition."

"I will mention this to the captain when we get back, he will probably have some questions for you, you know what captains are like, seriously nosey people." Brank threw back his head and laughed loudly, taking another huge drink, he slammed his flagon down on to the table top, causing all the other mugs to jump from the quivering surface. The serving girl walked through the door, and came over to the table, took Branks flagon and went away again.

Jangor looked questioningly at Brank.

"The flagon makes a characteristic sound when it is empty, and she knows that I want more, it's simply a matter of training."

"So many things are just that." laughed Kern. "But to train a woman to respond like that must have taken a great deal of time, and effort."

"Not really, I just had to explain things to her employer once, and I managed to get involved in one small drunken fight. After that things calmed down quite quickly."

"And permanently, no doubt!" said Kern. Brank just nodded slowly, understanding that both Kern and Jangor knew exactly what was going on in this establishment. Out came the girl with another tray, the flagon and more beer. Jangor smiled at her, and received a minor smile in return. She turned away with a swirl that swung her skirt in a wide circle, showing plenty of well curved leg, she walked slowly away swinging her hips in a wide arc. She turned again as she reached the door.

"I think Andreas just walked in, I'll send him out here." she said, her voice a different than it had been, somehow softer and richer. She turned back in through the door.

"That girl knows how to make an exit." muttered Kern, shaking his head. "Mander would have been straight in after her."

"Yes, he would." said Jangor, "but I think he would have met his match there, she's far too good, she knows exactly what she is doing, and she wouldn't have made that sort of performance for Mander. Kern, my friend, I think these city folk are far to complex for us poor country yokels." Kern nodded in agreement.

"Garbage!" said Brank. "You two can hold your own anywhere, even in the courts of kings. Jangor, you give no rank, but general is how you act, Kern, you have no rank, but need none. You are both the sort of people who others look to when things go badly. I would follow your lead, rather than this scumbag." He nodded towards Jackis. An old man walked slowly through the door, and came over to their table.

"Morning Andreas." said Brank. "Please meet, Jangor and Kern." He waved to each in turn. Jackis decided to take advantage of the distraction, with a lightning hand he snatched Kern's dagger from his belt, and spun out of his chair, before any of them could move he was behind Andreas, Kern's dagger held to the old man's wrinkled neck, a thin line of blood ran down inside the man's open collar.

"I'm leaving here." whispered Jackis, "If any of you even move this man dies, is that clearly understood."

"Andreas, my friend." said Brank. "Your call." Brank held his hands flat on the table, but the tension in his arms made all the cups shake. Andreas never took his eyes from the cold blue of Brank's. Jackis tried to walk backwards towards the door but the old man was not for moving at all.

"I've lived a long life, kill this dog turd for me my friend." he spoke softly, anger shaking his voice.

All three of the seated men moved in the same moment, Brank sprang to his feet and a long knife appeared in his hand and vanished in a flashing of bright steel, Kern fell from his stool and struck Jackis' elbow on the way down, causing the knife to move away from the old man's neck, Jangor spun into action drawing his knife and driving it straight into Jackis' kidneys with a single motion. Jackis fell over backwards leaving Andreas, standing if a little wobbly. Kern picked himself up and kicked his dagger from the fallen man's twitching hand. Jangor wiped his knife on the sergeants jacket, and pulled Branks knife from the ruins of an eye socket.

"Good throw." he said returning the knife to Brank.

"Andreas." said Brank. "Are you injured?" The blood from the cut was flowing quite freely.

"A scratch only. Don't fret about me, think about yourself for a change, today's work is going to cause you no end of trouble. That turd was the captain's brother in law!" Andreas' voice was shaking with more than old age.

"Have no fear for me, he was dead already, he made a bet he couldn't pay, and these gentlemen were going to kill him on their way out of town anyway."

The landlord came running out of the door, looking from the men standing to the man lying down, his mouth open and moving though no sounds were coming out.

"Sorry friend," said Brank, "but these things do happen occasionally."

"I suppose it's good thing it happened when there is no one in, are you going to clean this mess up, or do you want me to take care of it?"

"No. Just leave it there, I'll get some men to come back for it later, as you say, there is no one in, so the stink isn't going to put any one off their beer."

"At least prop him up against a tree, so he just looks like he's drunk, not dead."

"Agreed. I think I feel the need to celebrate the passing of a dear friend, beer please landlord."

"Not the usual?"

"No. Beer. My friends say that your beer is very good. So I think I'll try it."

"But not too many, right?"

"Of course." Brank turned to set the table upright again, and help Andreas to a seat, while Jangor and Kern moved the quickly cooling body of the sergeant over to one of the trees.

CHAPTER THIRTY TWO

The serving girl appeared at the door, and came through with a tray of large mugs, she obviously had some difficulty crossing the short grass of the lawn, she couldn't take her eyes off the feet of the man propped against a tree, the feet being the only part visible. Jangor came to her aid, he took the tray from her, and balancing it with unexpected skill on one hand, he patted her gently on the shoulder.

"Don't worry about it, he can't cause any harm any more."

"Right, but I still don't think you should just leave him there."

"He's not going to run off. We'll sort it all out later, have no fear."

"It's still not right to leave him there." she struggled a small smile.

"I know, but we are a little busy at the moment." he smiled gently and rested his hand on the bare skin of her arm, his eyes held hers for a short time. She smiled a little wider and went back inside. Jangor walked over to the table, and slid the tray onto its surface, without rocking a single one of the four mugs. Taking the last stool at the table, Jangor passed out the beer, and flipped the tray onto the grass beside his feet.

"To a recently departed friend." he said raising his mug, in a toast.

"I don't think I could drink to that." said Andreas, one hand on the wound to his throat.

"Right." Jangor thought for a moment. "To a thoroughly stepped on dog turd."

Three other mugs raised and touched over the centre of the table.

"Now." said Andreas. "Why are you all here in the middle of the day? I know that captain Harvang wouldn't have let you come here during the day, even with the turd as escort?"

"We came to see you my friend, these gentlemen are interested in some of the history that you know so well. And we were escorting him, not the other way around. The captain thought he might try to run out on his debt, as indeed proved to be the case. The captain wanted me to be here to help these men find Jackis again if he actually managed to run away."

"The captain is a wise man. Sometimes he sees to the very heart of the matter."

"This matter had no heart, at least none worth talking of."

"Agreed. Now what do you gentlemen want to know?"

"We need to know about the war between elves and men, where the elves sort of won, we are looking for the burial place of the elven king."

"Why do you want to find his grave?"

"It is believed that there is something buried with him that belongs to a man we know."

"So you are just grave robbers!"

"No. We are just recovering something that is needed to help us win a war."

"It makes no difference really, it is said that the elven kings grave is protected by those that died for him."

"Yes. We heard his resting place is well defended, but we need to get the stone from him, if he wishes it or no."

"I can't tell you where he is buried, but I can put you on the road there I think. What do you know already?"

"We know about the battle where the human king lost, and the elves returned to their forests, Brank says that you know what happened after that."

"I do indeed. This is all about the human king, and his defeat at the hands of the elven king, for that is how he saw it. He came to a bad end, it seems he upset far too many people by his determination to destroy the elves. The elves it seems just faded back into the forest, very little news is ever heard of them, but the king, he made a real fool of himself, he kept sending troops into the forests, to hunt down the elves that had embarrassed him so. His embarrassment only grew as the troops always failed to return. It was about a year after the battle, and he commanded a general and five battalions on a raid into the forest. The general said that he needed light horse troops, not the heavy cavalry. Heavy horses are almost useless amongst the trees. After some heated discussion the general left at the head of his troops. They crossed the plains and marched towards the forest, by the time they arrived at the forest edge, the five battalions were only four, the very next morning they were only three. With half his foot soldiers gone, the general knew that he had no chance at all against the elves, he had little chance with his force intact, but depleted as it was he was bound to lose against any serious opposition. He stripped the cavalry of some of their horses and turned them into scouts. It was surprising how fast those big horses could run when they weren't carrying all that iron or those huge cavalry soldiers. The general sent these horse soldiers into the forest carrying flags of truce, hoping that the elves would honour such after the perfidy of the king. The scouts were given very specific instructions, they were to travel one behind the other, at the limit of visibility, if anything untoward happens to the man in front turn and gallop back as fast as possible. The general was determined to lose no more men than he absolutely had to. Three groups of scouts were sent, three men to each team, ambushing a string of men like this should be far too difficult, they were told. They rode out of the camp, more than a little nervous, the general hoped that this would make them a little more careful. The waiting was hard on the general, he paced, he shouted orders, he demanded instant reports from the lookouts, everywhere he went in the camp he spread disquiet, and disorder, until a brave captain pointed out to him that he would do the men much more good by staying in his tent and waiting as calmly as he could for the news from the scouts. The general's huge intake of breathe made the captain wonder where he had put his old sergeants stripes, the explosion of the breath was an anticlimax, the general sighed and nodded, walking meekly to his tent, and demanding a wineskin on the way. Soldiers scrambled to provide the wine, he had more than enough wine to quieten a platoon by the time the flap on his tent fell into place, it was only then that the captain breathed again.

It was before the end of the first day that the scouts started to return, each group had the same story. The elves had stopped them and told them to turn back or they would all die. To be sure this point was understood the elves showed themselves to be beside each of the scouts, all three in each group would have been dead in a moment. The general had hoped that the elves would talk to the scouts, but it was clear they would not. He made the decision that he would have to go into the forest himself and talk to the elves, not a prospect that he enjoyed, but it could wait until the morning. The camp settled into the normal pattern for a peaceful site, guards were posted but not to any great degree, the whole place settled into a sort of lassitude, drink flowed slowly, and food was eaten in a leisurely fashion. Musical instruments appeared at almost every fire, soft ballads were sung, and sleep descended like a blanket over the entire place. The general and his captains discussed briefly the tactics for the morning, the final consensus was that they would ride into the forest, horns blasting out a warning, or invitation, depending on the point of view of those hearing them. The captains dispersed to their own tents and the general went to an uneasy sleep.

The sun rose to find the general and his staff already awake, the general was not in the best of moods, hangovers tend to do that to a man. The scouts were dispatched as outriders, but they didn't even make it as far as the outer perimeter of the camp. Horns blew an alarm, and the camp woke with a start, soldiers scrambled for weapons, all eyes turned to the intruders. A group of elves on white horses, standing quietly under the eaves of the forest.

"Stand down." Yelled the general. He had no wish for the situation to escalate, he didn't take his eyes off the elves, but used hand signals to summon the captains to him. Grooms brought horses for the general and his captains, without any instruction. The general and his men mounted and walked slowly toward the elves. All the soldiers in the camp stood to attention as the general passed, an eerie silence descended on the entire camp The procession moved at a sedate pace towards the forest. The elves didn't move, other than to arrange their group to match that of the approaching group. The horses came very close together before any word was spoken.

"Hail." Said the leader of the elves.

"Hail." Said the general.

"I am Braid."

"I am called Marko."

"What do you want in our forests?"

"I have been sent by my king, his purpose is to destroy your entire race."

"You say this as if it is not your purpose?"

"It is not. I bear no ill will for the elven kind. I have no wish to cause you or yours any harm."

"Even though you have been commanded by your king?"

"Kings can be changed, they tend to do that on a regular basis, and there is always some other fool to take over."

"What is your purpose then?"

"I intend to help your race survive this difficult time, at least until a new king can be found, one who is a little more rational. This war between our peoples is costly to both sides. A cost I have no wish to pay."

"The war, such as it is, is costly. How will you achieve this purpose?"

"I am not entirely sure, in fact I have no real idea, have you any thoughts that we could discus, perhaps over breakfast?"

"You think that we will walk into your camp, and eat with you? Would you do the same, come into the forest, where we can talk in peace?"

"Perhaps not. But food could be brought here where we both feel sort of safe, would that be acceptable?"

"Yes." Replied the elf after only a moment of thought. As the general turned to tell a captain to go and make the arrangements an elf turned and galloped into the forest. No words were exchanged between the elves, but the departing rider knew what he was to do. Only a few words and the captain left in a similar manner, dust blowing from the heels of his horse. An uneasy silence descended on the group, horses started to fidget, stepping from side to side, General Marko felt that he had to say something but couldn't think of anything to say, so he slowly swung out of his saddle, and passed the reins to a captain, the man so indicated was handed the reins of all the horses, and he walked them slowly away, passing them to a perimeter guard, a few whispered words and the captain returned to the group under the trees. By the time he had returned, all the elves had dismounted, and the two leaders were facing each other, not speaking, sizing each other up, almost like the prelude to a duel.

General Marko moved with the solid steady action of a trained warrior, Braid moved with a fluid grace, like a skilled dancer, though the dance he knew was the dance of steel and death. No words were spoken, no sudden or aggressive moves were made, but the tension of the situation rose quickly. General Marko was keenly aware of the barrier of trees only paces away, where a hundred elven bowmen could easily be hidden. Braid could see the human bowmen, the stood in small groups, not formed in ranks, but each held his bow, in a state of nervous readiness. One frightened young man pulled an arrow from his quiver, until a passing sergeant slapped it from his hand, a few very quiet words were exchanged before the youngster picked up the arrow and returned it to its usual resting place, his head hung in shame.

People started to move towards the meeting, carrying chairs and tables, food and wine were on the way from the field kitchens. Marko coughed, and Braid's deep green eyes locked onto his.

"Those are some fine horses that you ride, how do they deal with the trees in the forests, I'd have thought forests would seriously hinder them?" Asked Marko, not actually all that interested, he just wanted to get conversation started, and the elf didn't appear ready to open any form of dialogue.

"We train them from being foals, before they are full grown they can follow a deer trail at a full gallop." He turned to his horse and pointed to the equipment hanging from the saddle. "Notice how nothing sticks out to the front, all the equipment is tight to the horses shoulders and points backwards, nothing to get snagged on passing trees. It does take some practice to draw the longsword on the backhand, but that too is only a matter of training."

"I see no bridles or reins to guide your mounts?"

"Again training, and when moving at speed in the forest I usually find that the horse knows best which way to go. How can your horses move at all with all that iron all over them?"

"Our horses are heavier than yours, not as fast, but stronger, they are suited to open fields, not forests, their weight gives them an advantage against a lighter enemy."

"But only if the enemy stands and waits to be hit."

"True, but foot soldiers generally can't run as fast as even the heaviest horse."

"We have learned much about war from your king. He has spent many lives teaching us."

"That is something I want to stop, he is just wasting too many men trying to wipe you out. Something that I don't believe could be achieved, and certainly shouldn't be attempted."

"We can at least agree on that, but how can we both convince your king to stop this stupidity?"

"It is not going to be easy, have you any thoughts?"

"I have no knowledge of the man himself, you have that, don't you?"

"Yes." sighed Marko. "He has an utterly irrational hatred of your people, something to do with the spectacular defeat he suffered a few years ago."

"I don't count that as a victory." said Braid, his voice cold and flat, free from any emotion at all.

"Why is that?"

"We lost far too any good men, on that day. I said goodbye to many friends."

"We lost many, but not as many as you did, but still you left the field with your honour intact, the same could not be said for our king. He was totally dismayed by the fact that so many of you survived, and the fact that he could do nothing at all about your withdrawal."

"Our king did well that day, his bravery was all that won the day for us."

"Indeed, he was sorely injured, and still managed to rally his men, and remove all the dead. An inspiring performance. I know he was hurt, did he survive?"

"He still lives, but will not venture far from our city."

"You have a city?" Surprise made Marko's voice raise more than a little.

"Yes, not a city as yours are, but a city for us, none the less."

"That must be something to see. There have been many who have passed through your forests and found almost no traces of your existence, let alone a whole city."

"It is a beautiful place, and your kind could probably walk straight though it without even seeing it. Our home is not like your towns, it exists in the trees, without damaging them, it is a part of the forest, perhaps you should come and see."

"That I would like, but we have more pressing matters to discus, don't we?"

"If we can find a way forward that doesn't involve war, then I will invite you to my home and show you a real city."

"Agreed, but first we need to find some form of accommodation that will satisfy us both. If I go home and tell the king I have killed all the elves, then he will demand an immediate invasion of your forest, so that is out of the question, if I go home with my force intact he will never believe I was beaten in a battle. We have to find a solution that will keep him from sending any more troops until we have found a replacement."

"You need to loose some of your troops, and return with a beaten force, something that he will believe. How about some of your men moving into the forest and living here for a while, just until the replacement is found?"

"That would work, those that stay would need to be volunteers, I should be able to do that, my force is already quite reduced, it seems that many of them didn't like the idea of fighting in your forest. I can't understand why." Marko laughed, trying to ease the tension.

"We could provide a place for your men to stay, I know many places in the forest where they would feel quite at home. How many men do we need to hide?"

"With the losses I've already taken, no more than three hundred. Can you handle that many?"

"Your people think you know the forest, and all your explorations have only ever scratched the edges. I could hide ten times that many and not even notice the invasion." Braid shook his head slowly from side to side. "How long would these men have to stay?"

"A few months, not as long as a year definitely, if no viable replacement can be found for the king, he has a nephew, only a babe in arms, he'll make an excellent candidate, and he will be totally controlled by the royal council of advisors, none of them want a war."

"Surely a lot of people stand between this nephew and the throne?"

"None that will be missed, at least not missed by the survivors."

"Sometime you can be real savages."

"I couldn't ever argue with that, some are more savage than others."

"Some of my people are the same, though our rulers do tend to be much more calm than the general populace."

"Most of ours are, they see the necessity, but every once in a while the stupidity of the royal line comes to the fore, then it is time for a new branch of the line to take over, such a time is now."

"You can take care of that when you get home. In the meantime you will have to convince your men to move into the forest, and stay until they are recalled. Soldiers aren't the most sensible of people when they get bored, they can get rowdy and create problems. I don't want to make any trouble for my people."

"I will make sure enough of the officer core volunteer as well, and they wont have time to get bored, I will make sure they are kept busy, they will have to feed themselves and make shelters for themselves, then there will be training and such, they will be fully occupied. They will probably return home far better soldiers than they are now, without ever having to fight in earnest."

"That is even more disturbing, they go home better able to return and fight."

"I have no wish to fight in this forest, and even more important I have no wish to fight your people ever, we should be able to live together in peace, you have your forest, and my people prefer the open ground. We are basically farmers, though we have grown a little big for the farms that we have. But we will just have to find somewhere else to expand, there is another valley we could move into, it only has a few people and a fair sized forest of its own."

"Do any elves live in that forest, I know of none, but sometimes we can be more than a little insular?"

"I don't think there are any elves in the valleys to the west, but when it comes to forest craft your people are the best, it could be that they are just staying out of sight."

"Perhaps, if you come across any in the future, then I would like to know, there are old tales of tribes that moved away, I am interested in what happened to them. History is a hobby of mine."

"You can be sure that I will contact you or your people if I find any elven kind any where else, it should help us to reach an understanding if they have someone of their own kind to talk to, translation can be so difficult sometimes."

"That may not be such a good idea, we are a long lived race, and grudges can be held for more years than you could imagine."

"Different tribes don't get on then?"

"That is one way of putting it, sometimes just knowledge that the other tribe it still breathing can set off a war, usually over something from too many years ago."

"Isn't that a little stupid for a race that is without doubt on the decline?"

"Stupid it may be, but it is the way of elves. Yes we are a declining race, too few are born and too many die, many die without progeny. I think we will soon pass from this world."

"That will be a sad day."

"Not true for all of your kind."

"But a sad day for me, and for those that believe elven kind are a force for good in this crazy world."

"We have little to do with your kind, how can they think this?"

"It is the fact that your folk seem to able to live outside the human world, or alongside it perhaps, without being changed by it. Where we are dragged along by all the changes around us."

"We don't tend to change quickly, as a folk we are suspicious of change, whereas your people seem to actively encourage it, they pursue it, they embrace it, we do not."

"You use steel swords, and your bows are no longer made from a single piece of wood, these are changes that you have accepted."

"A wooden dagger is no match for a steel sword, your bows far out ranged ours, until we Improved on your designs, these changes were a matter of survival, though there were some who died rather than change the weapons that they had grown up with."

"You remember wooden weapons?" Shock shook Marko's voice, just the thought of living so many years made his voice quaver.

"Not I." Assured Braid. "Nor any that are alive now, well, there may be a few, but they are very old, I do remember the old swords that men used to carry, short and heavy, with very thick blades, bronze I believe you called the metal."

"No human alive remembers using a bronze sword, they have been out of use for more than a hundred years. I have seen one or two hanging on peoples walls, just as decoration, not as something to be used in battle. You remember these swords?"

"When I was very young, there were many amongst my people, but steel was replacing them as I became of age to join the guard."

"Guard, are you not an army then?"

"No. We are the guardians of the people, and of the forest that is our home. We have no army, nor need of one. If the guard do not suffice, then the people will all fight, we are just the first line."

"All your people would fight?"

"All."

"All, even women and children, to the death?"

"All the people will fight until we are victorious or are no more, that is the way we are."

"By all the gods that there are, I hope never to have to kill women and children. That is no work for a soldier." Marko shuddered at the thought.

"They would give you no choice."

"Your people are very strange to us."

"As are you to us."

"Can we ever come to some common ground?"

"We both have the will to survive, isn't that enough?"

"I hope it is enough, we must never go to war again, for there can only be one outcome." Marko spoke these words slowly and softly.

"Numbers alone will be the judge in such a war, and we are far too few, you people can spend lives like the wheat of your fields, and replace the lost in only a few years, we will never recover from the last war we had. We lost so many that there are many families without fathers, and more families that wont ever be, we can never win if it came to all out war between your race and mine."

"I for my part, would have nothing to do with a war like that."

"But there will be some of your race that would fight given the instruction or the motivation."

"That is always true. Perhaps we can avoid such a thing, if we do this right. I shall talk to my soldiers, perhaps I can convince enough of them to go along with my plan to hide them in the forest."

"There may be another way." Said Braid, slowly, staring straight into Marko's eyes.

"Speak, what is your thought?"

"Only those around this table know of your plan, but you intend to tell the whole of your army. If one man who goes back tells of those who remain here, then your king will know you have deceived him, and you will die, then someone else will come here to kill us."

"That is a risk, but one I have to take."

"There is another way to hold troops here, and then go back to your king to tell him whatever you want until you can arrange his replacement."

"How?"

"We depart this table with a storm of angry words, elven horsemen are seen leaving the forest, only to be intercepted by you own horse, then they are chased back into the forest. None of your men really want to go into the forest. An order to prevent elven forces from leaving the forest would take most of your force, occasional forays would keep you soldiers busy for days, weeks, months, even years, if you wish. With almost no chance of anyone being killed."

Marko laughed softy to himself, shaking his head. "You could tie up a force twice the size that I have, and keep them here for years. Carefully worded orders, some form of communication between the officers and the elves would be essential, so that you will know where the holes are in the perimeter. The more I think about it the better I like it. I say we break for a while, and meet again at midday, that will give us time to sort out the details. Is that all right with you?"

"I agree. With a small demonstration of bad feeling."

"How do you mean?"

"The usual sort of thing, table thumping, and storming off."

"Fine. Do you want to start?"

Braid leapt to his feet, kicking his stool away in the process, he slammed both hands down on the makeshift table, making all the pots and plates jump and rattle.

"Did that get their attention?" He asked calmly, as the other elves followed his lead.

Marko jumped up likewise, knocking some of the pots onto the ground. "That will be just fine. See you about midday then?" Braid barely nodded and turned away with a swirl of long hair and stamped off to where the horses were held by his men, with a single fluid motion he threw himself onto the horses back and galloped off into the forest, is seconds not an elf could be seen. Only the sound of hoof beats echoed through the strangely quiet forest.

"What did I tell you?" asked Brank, laughing at Jangor and Kern, who were both sitting on the edges of their stools. "Can this man tell a story? Or can he tell a story?"

"Story." said Jangor, softly. "I am not interested in stories I want history, I want to know what happened all those years ago. Not fanciful tales."

"Oh, this it true." replied Andreas. "This is how my father and his father used to tell of those times, I have no doubt at all as to the truth of this tale."

"How can you be so sure?" demanded Jangor.

"Because my grandfather was one of the captains who was there, he was one of those who passed back and forth between the forces of men, and those of the elves."

"But that is far too long ago " said Kern. "Unless?"

"Yes?" asked Andreas, a small smile on his lips.

"Unless?" asked Jangor.

"Unless, his father and grandfather lived a very long time for men." answered Kern.

"And?" demanded Jangor, getting more than a little angry at the confusion of the others words. Kern turned towards Andreas.

"How old are you?" A simple question, asked in a shaky voice.

"I have seen a hundred and thirty summers."

"Never." said Jangor. A cold stare from Kern caused the older man to look at the table, a little ashamed of his outburst.

"How old is your father?" Kern's voice even shakier this time.

"He was one hundred and seventy one when he died two years ago."

"No one lives that long!" stormed Jangor, again the stares and the lowered eyes.

"How about your grandfather?"

"He was only seventy when he died, he only lasted a few years after grandmother died. Really he just gave up."

"Take off your hat." said Kern.

"This is getting us no where." snapped Jangor as Andreas slowly removed his cap.

"What in all the god's are you two talking about?" demanded Jangor, his face reddened with temper.

"This man's grandmother was an elf, he has the narrower head, and a little of the pointed aspect to the ears, he has at least a quarter elven blood in his veins."

"Is this true?" asked Jangor, quietly.

Andreas merely nodded.

"Ha." said Brank. "I knew there was something different about you, old man, but I had no idea it was this strange. Ha, it takes strangers to see it, I think your little secret may just get out now, and I'm going to change my bet on that pool, I'm not betting on you dying this century."

"What pool?" asked Andreas.

"The watch have bet on how much longer you are going to live, I gave you another ten years, thinking that you were actually lying about your age."

"I have never hidden anything about my age, or my heritage!" said Andreas.

"I had always thought the races were completely separate." said Kern.

"That is usually true, elven kind aren't as prolific as us, they breed much more slowly, and mixed race relationships tend not to last long enough for progeny to occur. But in the case of my grandparents this was not the case. He was a young captain of Marko, and she the daughter of Braid. They grew to like each other over a period of years, the dummy stand off at the forest lasted ten years, it's seems the king was more difficult to replace than was first thought. Actually he was just hard to kill."

"Did your father have any brothers or sisters?" asked Kern.

"No. Grandmother died in childbirth, it would have been a daughter, but she died as well, a dreadful day for the whole family, that is when grandfather gave up."

"How did Braid deal with all this?"

"The elves were a little distressed by the whole thing, I don't think they actually cut her off, but they certainly didn't see her for many years at a time. They only met when grandfather went to the forest. He took her there after she died, so that she could return to her people. He returned a broken man. He only lived for his stories then."

"I am not surprised she died in childbirth, elves aren't designed to give birth to human babies, or even those of mixed blood. Elvish heads are narrower, and longer, where human heads are more rounded, an elf woman's pelvis is not shaped to pass such a large head. She was lucky to survive the first birth." said Kern.

"How do you know so much about this sort of thing?" asked Andreas.

"I haven't actually thought about it until now, but, have you ever seen a fat elf?"

"No, but that doesn't mean anything."

"Not on it's own, but it is a place to start. Even old elves have a thin appearance, they are all narrow across the hips, their tall thin faces tend to pull the eye away from the rest of them. Even in their later years they don't get fat, humans do, old men get big bellies, especially those that drink too much." Andreas laughed. "Old women put weight on their backsides and hips, especially after childbirth. Elvish women don't do that they stay narrow at the hip all their lives. It is logical to assume that a short fat human type baby would be a hell of a squeeze for elvish hips. It can be hard enough for human woman sometimes, many of them die in childbirth."

"This is getting away from our purpose." said Jangor. "Interesting as it is, I want to know about the elf king's burial place."

"Oh." said Andreas. "That's easy, he didn't die."

"What?" shouted Jangor. "That was centuries ago, even elves don't live that long, do they?"

"Of course they don't. He didn't die, but they buried him anyway. Along with twelve of the best elvish warriors of the time."

"Thirteen of them buried alive, that's ridiculous!" said Jangor.

"Not really alive."

"Sorry." said Jangor. "Dead or alive, no other choices as far as I know."

"Then your knowledge is at fault. For elves there is another state that can be invoked at times of extra ordinary stress. They sleep, a very deep sleep, waking can only be triggered by a specific event. They can sleep this way for thousands of years, some think they can sleep forever. The sleeping warriors on the edge of time."

"Have you any idea why they chose such a drastic step?" asked Kern.

"I think they did it to protect the king and his sword. It is said that they will awaken and fight on the side of good, when the chosen one comes and takes the sword from the king. But I think that is bullshit, they will wake and fight at some time in the future. Perhaps they already have, it has been more than a few years since I had any contact at all with my 'relatives'."

"Do you know where they buried the king?" asked Jangor.

"Yes, it's a special place, a huge barrow west of their city, about a days walk from the city gate. It is easy to find there is a well travelled path that leads straight to it. It seems that some people still like to go and talk to the king, sort of keeping him up to date, even though he cannot hear them. Elves are strange."

"Is it defended?"

"Why should it be? Thirteen of the best warriors in the elven kingdom await anyone who disturbs their peace. No-one in their right mind would go there to do them harm."

"Then we are definitely mad. Because go there we must."

"I'll none of that. You find your own way, and die your own way."

"All I need to know now, is how to find the city?"

"That will be a more difficult task, elves do not take kindly to intrusions into their forest, for such it is, even though their numbers are greatly reduced, it is still their forest."

"Perhaps, our tame magician can help us?" suggested Jangor.

"How?" asked Kern.

"I don't know. Magician things, any spell that can make men, or elves, sleep for a thousand years has got to give off some form of power, or maybe it draws power from its surroundings. Granger and our friend should be able to track that sort of power usage." Kern nodded slowly, Jangor was probably right, but he wanted a flesh and blood guide, someone he could trust, at least to some extent.

"Who is this friend of yours?" asked Andreas.

"His name we will not speak, it seems he has enemies everywhere these days." laughed Jangor.

Andreas rose slowly to his feet. "I thank you gentlemen for my life this day." he said. "You have given me much to think on. I wish you luck with your quest, I think, whatever it may be. Please try not to hurt my elven kin, they have been hurt enough by men over the years." With a nod he turned and walked slowly away, somehow he appeared smaller as he stepped through the door, his head bowed in thought.

"A strange old man." said Jangor. "I like him." He turned to Brank. "I think our business here is finished. We know as much as we are likely to find in this town, do you want to leave the sergeant here, or shall we take him with us?"

"I think we ought to take him, it's not right to leave him here, someone might trip over him and hurt themselves. He shouldn't leak too much, I'll carry him, if you gentlemen will help me get him up onto my shoulder." Jangor and Kern helped to lift the cold sergeant up onto Branks wide shoulder, and together they walked through the bar and into the street. Jangor was amazed at how little attention they actually attracted, most people just glanced at them then turned away. Ono shopkeeper came running from his store, and lifted the head of Jackis as they passed. The shopkeeper laughed loudly and returned to his store, not saying a single word, just laughing until his shoulders shook.

"Can you manage that weight?" asked Jangor as the small group neared the halfway point on their journey to the gatehouse.

"Jackis was always a lightweight, no matter what his opinions were. I can cope quite easily, I can even see this as a training aid, to help the soldiers."

"Carrying heavy weights is always good for building muscle, good exercise for soldiers." agreed Jangor.

"No, you missed the point." said Brank. "If they get to carry the dead home, then they wont kill too many, or get too many of ours killed, more intellectual than physical training."

"Sometimes you look at things in a way that no one else ever would." laughed Jangor.

"This is true, but then I do like to be different." They turned the last corner towards the gate house, there was Captain Harvang, staring straight at them, a storm cloud upon his brow.

"I think tales of us got here first." muttered Brank. "Let me deal with this." Squaring his shoulders as much as he could with the load they were carrying, Brank almost marched up to the

Captain. He stopped and snapped into a close approximation of attention.

"My Captian. I regret to inform you that your brother in law was exceptionally stupid."

Harvang breathed deeply then sighed hugely. "Tell me something I don't know. How extra specially stupid was he?"

"He held a knife to an old man's throat, and threatened to kill him if we didn't let him leave."

"Who was the old man?"

"Aldreas."

"An old man indeed, he has seen more summers than any I know, how did the fool die?"

"He did better than most men, he managed to die twice. No, he was killed twice."

"How can any man be killed twice?"

"Jangor stabbed him in the kidneys just as my knife took him through the eye and into what passed for his brain. Both strikes would have taken his life, hence he died twice."

"Brank, you sometimes cause more trouble than you are worth."

"That is a whole heap of trouble, my captain." Jangor noted certain people moving around the scene, like soldiers getting ready to fight, a click of his tongue brought Kern to attention, Kern glanced round and felt the odds starting pile up against them.

"Put the fool down." Said the captain, then he waved two soldiers, who had been standing idly by, they came and the captain spoke softly. "Move that out of the sun before it starts to stink up the place." He turned back to Brank and the others who were now standing shoulder to shoulder. "What am I going to do with you and your new friends?"

"What is there to do? He threatened the life of an old friend and died for it. Even Kern will consider his debt paid in full, wont you friend?" Brank patted Kern on the shoulder with his left hand, casually letting his right hand fall onto his sword hilt.

"Of course." Said Kern, pushing Brank in return, creating enough space between them to get his own sword clear. Jangor swept the growing crowd with a quick glance, a few familiar things jumped into his brain as he did so, jumbled images that didn't quite make any sense, a horse, a cloak, an old man, they were scattered all around but felt like they should be together somehow.

"Murderers." Screamed a voice from behind the captain. "Murderers!" Screamed the woman again.

"Shit." muttered Brank, "Jackis sister and the captains wife."

"Husband." She howled. "Arrest them, hang them, kill them!"

"Why? They only defended an old man from your brother."

"My brother never threatened anyone in his life."

"That is indeed true, my love, he usually liked to sneak up behind them when they were asleep, even then he preferred the assurance that they had consumed some drug of his making."

"Liar! He was an honourable man, he would never have hurt anyone. These men lie, just like you. I want them dead, I want them dead now!"

"How much of this is for show?" whispered Jangor.

"I don't know, it could be she is after something other than our heads, she's supposed to be the most cunning of witches." returned Brank.

"She would certainly be beautiful, if she'd only shut her mouth. That voice really sets the teeth on edge."

"She does have a certain penetrative quality."

"My love." Said Captain Harvang, closing the distance to his wife, and enfolding her in his arms. "You know very well, it was only a matter of time before your brother stepped over the line, these men are honourable, of this I am certain. Your brother was not, he was a liar and a thief, a swindler and a trickster. I would not have more men die today."

"I only want the three killers of my brother dead, what care I for your men, they are soldiers and are meant to die, one of your men has died, my brother. I want them dead." She struggled in his arms and turned towards one of her friends, a large man, a member of the guard. He nodded and stepped forwards, towards the group of three.

"Will." Shouted Harvang. "Stand down."

"Sir." replied Will. "In some ways your wife is right, these men have killed one of ours, they should answer."

"I want no more to die today."

"Then let them be arrested and tried before a judge." More members of the guard began to move forwards. Harvang knew that he was loosing control of the situation but could think of nothing to calm it. Jangor saw a shape move through the crowd, Jangors hand flew to Branks wrist, then out of the corner of his eye he saw another moving towards them. Kern whispered. "Granger." The tall man walked slowly across the open ground drawing a huge sword as he came, the sword seemed light as a feather in his grip, nothing Brank could do would get his own sword clear in time, he stared at Jangor, and realised that this man was a friend, and presumably so was the woman in the white fur cape, and the old man coming up from behind.

Namdarin turned to Harvang, sword hanging casually in his hand.

"I am Namdarin of the house of Namdaron, these men travel under my protection. We have no time to wait for the deliberations of your courts. We will leave here today."

Granger lifted his staff above his head, held it horizontally, twice blue lightning leapt from the ends and struck the walls of buildings, causing no damage, but the thunder echoing through the courtyard rattled the teeth of everyone there. Once the flashes has died, the sun seemed to go a little dim, and the temperature around the isolated group started the drop, a chill reached out into the hearts of the crowd.

"Jangor." Shouted Harvang. "Who are these people?"

"These are a part of the group I am travelling with. These are very serious people. I suggest that you stand down, because you are now outnumbered. If Kern, Brank and I all sit on our hands you are still outnumbered. Please for the love of which ever gods you worship hinder us not."

Will took another step forwards, and some of his friends followed if a little slowly.

"I challenge!" yelled Namdarin. "I challenge any man to single combat."

"To what end?" demanded Harvang.

"If I win, we walk."

"And if you lose?"

"That is something I hadn't considered to be a possibility."

"I accept." Shouted Will, striding forwards.

"Allow me." said Jayanne. Namdarin nodded. She turned to face the tall man.

"You would fight in his place?" asked Will.

"Are you afraid?" countered Jayanne.

"Of a woman!" Will laughed heartily.

"Jayanne." shouted Jangor, slowly, almost insolently she turned. "His sword has a long reach, and he is wearing steel plate."

"And?" Her monosyllabic question.

"One clean stroke, do not play with this one, just kill him!"

She turned away with a snap of her head that flung her hair out in a halo, a shrug of her shoulders and the white cape fell to the ground, slowly, she walked towards the swordsman, her smile playing on her lips, her hips swaying with every stride. Jangor just shook his head.

"Is she any good?" asked Brank.

"She's good, that axe is better, but pray she doesn't get hurt."

"Why?"

"If she gets hurt, then Namdarin's anger will tear this whole city apart. I suggest you lie down and pretend to be dead, that way you may survive."

All eyes turned to Jayanne and Will, they faced each other, Will seemed a little uncertain as to what to do, but eventually the eyes of his colleagues gave him no choice, he had to attack. With a lightening stroke he tried to cut Jayannes right arm, but the flat of the axe took the slashing sword and showered a few sparks, but that was all. Will tried a huge overhand blow, that had the same effect, that is none, the axe was just there, directly in the path of the sword. He switched rapidly cutting left then right, high then low, then he lunged straight for her belly, this was the first time she actually moved her feet, she simply stepped aside and slapped the sword down with the flat of the axe. Will retreated quickly, feeling the truly exposed patch at the back of his neck. 'I was so far over stretched then, she could have taken my head.' He thought, beginning to worry about the outcome of this fight for the first time. Will renewed the attack with increased ferocity, every cut and every lunge was blocked by the flat of the axe, until he was sweating profusely despite the coldness of the air around them. He disengaged momentarily then swung a mighty blow, this one with all his weight behind it, this one didn't find the flat of the axe, it found the edge. With a flash the sword shattered, Will jumped backwards, waiting for Jayanne's counter attack, but it didn't come, she was looking at the fleshy part of her left upper arm, a fragment of the sword had cut her, bright red blood was flowing freely down her arm. Slowly she raised the axe and placed the flat against the wound, the blood flow stopped, the blood stains vanished. When she lowered it again there was no sign of the injury. Gasps came from the crowd, and a sword was thrown to Will's feet.

"Leave that sword on the ground." Shouted Jangor.

"Pick it up, you coward." Shouted Harvang's wife. Jayanne spared her a quick glance of contempt as Will bent to collect the sword. As soon as his hand closed on the grip he attacked, a rising slash at Jayanne's legs, not that she was at all surprised. The same could not be said for Will. He was more than surprised by her counter attack, he didn't even see it, the axe torn through his breastplate with barely a sound. His sword arm dropped and hung limply at his side, Jayanne turned and walked back to her friends.

"Come back and fight." Shouted Jackis' sister. Jayanne slowly bent to pick up her white fur cape, and Will fell, his legs and hips fell towards the front, his torso and head toppled towards the back, blood soaked into the soft ground. A dreadful silence fell on the crowd.

"Are you a man of your word?" Asked Namdarin, looking straight into the eyes of Harvang. Harvang waved to the soldiers and a path to the gate opened, not a single word was spoken. Even Harvang's wife was silent. Namdarin whistled softly and a large white horse stamped through the crowd, with several others in tow. While Namdarin and he others mounted Brank walked over to Harvang. He stood to attention and saluted.

"Captain. May I trouble you for a horse in lieu of wages, I feel it would be better if I left this place." Harvang snapped his fingers and a nearby soldier ran off.

"You are right, it could be dangerous for you here, but no more than with these people, I am sorry that we must part like this I had hoped to see you retire."

"Retirement is not for the likes of us, is it?"

"I suppose, but the group you have taken up with are going to some battle soon, I hope that you will survive. If you do, come back and tell us all about it, I think it could be a tale you could live off for a long and easy retirement." Harvang held out his hand, Brank shook it solemnly, stepped back, saluted one last time then mounted the horse that was standing behind him. Namdarin nodded to Brank, and the ex-guardsman led the way out of the city. Jayanne walked her horse very close to Harvang and his wife.

"You killed a man today." She said in a cold voice. "Not me, you. And to what purpose?" Not waiting for an answer she followed the others. Namdarin was the last to leave the courtyard, Arndrol just had to make an exit, rising up on his hind legs, and pawing the air, Arndrol screamed in defiance at the whole city. Somewhere a wolf howled in answer.

"Brank, my friend I wish you all the luck there is, and I feel that you will need it." Whispered Harvang, hoping to see his friend again one day.

CHAPTER THIRTY THREE

"Kern, south and pick up the pace." Shouted Namdarin as soon as they had cleared the gate, they all turned to follow Kern at a fast trot, still in view of the city walls they didn't deviate from the southerly direction.

"Jangor." Asked Namdarin. "What in all the hells was going on in that town?"

"We ran into a little trouble with the locals."

"Somehow I noticed that."

"Someone bet twenty gold pieces with Kern on the outcome of a fight, and lost, he didn't have the gold and so forfeited his life. His sister and the captains wife saw things a little differently."

"Why would Kern be betting on a fight?"

"It just sort of happened."

"You mean you challenged someone and then won."

"Pretty much the way it happened, yes."

"Let me guess, the man you beat in the fight is the newest member of our group?"

"How could you know that?"

"It is the most logical way for a new member to join this crazy group. But did you find the things we need to know?"

"Yes. The elven king is buried near their city in the great forest and he has the mind stone with him. Erm."

"I feel an enormous but coming here."

"But, he isn't actually dead, nor are the twelve other warriors with him, they merely sleep awaiting the time that the world needs them, or so the story goes."

"So, we have to find a city no men have ever seen, or at least no have ever returned from, steal the mind stone from the buried king who isn't actually dead, and fight our way past twelve equally undead warriors, only to find the entire race of elves have risen against us. Does that about sum things up?"

"That sounds about right to me." Nodded Jangor.

"It's never like this in the old tales, beat the dragon, marry the princess, live happily every after. I think my life has taken a wrong turn somewhere." muttered Namdarin.

"It could still turn out like the old tales, at least you are still breathing."

"That doesn't really make me feel any better."

"Perhaps I didn't mean to." laughed Jangor, kicking his horse and heading up to the front of the line. Namdarin watched him go, then turned to check their trail, as far as he could tell there was no-one following, but they could be hanging back, just on the edge of visibility, he had no wish to trailed by anyone, so he decided to lay a trap for anyone behind them. Looking far ahead he saw that the track they were following entered a dark wood, lots of old trees, and plenty of undergrowth around the edges, 'That will do. We'll wait just inside, and see if any follow.' He thought. Quickly he caught up with Granger.

"Granger. You keep an eye on the trail behind us, I need to talk to Jangor."

Granger merely nodded, he looked tired, slumped in his saddle.

"Do you feel all right?" asked Namdarin.

"Today I feel old, that is all, old and tired."

"Try and stay awake, there is no one behind to pick you up." laughed Namdarin.

"Be off, you young pup. I can stay awake longer than you, it's just the riding all day that takes the energy out of me."

"You are fooling no one, old man. The sun is much darker around you, like you are in a permanent half shadow, and the air is so cold it makes people shiver. You are sucking energy out of the surroundings at an alarming rate. What do you do with it all?"

"I am merely charging my staff, that lightning in the town cost a great deal of energy. Now I recharge."

"Fine, but keep an eye out for a while." Granger nodded slowly, his eyes not quite closed as he slumped in the saddle again.

Namdarin set off towards the front he passed Jayanne and smiled at her, she smiled back, her green eyes speaking much more than words ever could. He was tempted to ride alongside her for a while, but there were things that needed doing, so he rode on. Her smile only faded a little as he rode past. As he caught up with Brank he realised just how small the horse he was riding actually was. Branks feet were hanging well below the beast's belly, and Brank was obviously no horseman.

"Hello." said Namdarin.

"Afternoon."

"Harvang was right you know, you probably aren't very safe travelling with us."

"After killing Jackis, I'm safer out of that town."

"We haven't been introduced, I'm Namdarin."

"Brank."

"We are going to have to find you a bigger horse, that one is far too small for you."

"Bigger means further from the ground, I'm not happy this high up, a taller horse would be far worse."

"Sometimes we have to move in a hurry, that pony couldn't hurry if its tail was on fire. You are a big man, you need a big horse."

"One like yours you mean?"

"Perhaps, but I'd go for something a little easier to ride if I were you, this one can be a bit of a handful sometimes."

"But he does as he is told, comes to a whistle, I've seen him do that."

"He does have a few nasty habits though, he tends to bite, and he likes to pick up strays as we travel "

"Biting I can do with out, but what is wrong with the strays."

"He likes to break into stables to collect them."

"I can see that would cause problems. What are you people actually doing together? I know you are looking for the elven kings burial place, presumably to steal something of value."

"It is true that we seek the jewel from the hilt of his sword, it is a weapon of great power, and we have need of such things. Gyara said it would help us in our quest."

"You have talked to Gyara?"

"The black bird appeared to us, it said that the elven mindstone could help us."

"What is your quest?"

"When I introduced myself to Harvang I wasn't entirely truthful. The house of Namdaron is no more, the priests of Zandaar burned it down, and everyone in it. I now intend to do the same to them. I am going to burn down their house, with their god in it. Now do you see the extent of the danger you are in?"

"I see that you are going to need every good soldier you can find, and that the rewards could be immeasurable."

"I haven't made mention of reward, in fact it isn't even something I have ever considered, I'm going to burn the bastards that killed my family, that is all I seek."

"The you will have great riches to spend, this priesthood cannot be poor, none of them are."

"Again you seem to misunderstand. I'm not going to destroy the priesthood, I'm going to kill their god. I somehow think that survival in that sort of situation is exceptionally unlikely, don't you?"

"Perhaps, but the unlikely does happen occasionally. So let's just wait and see shall we, I'm not dead until I hear the soil on the coffin lid, then I'm sure I'm dead."

"So you plan to stay with us for a while then?"

"If you'll have me of course?"

"We'll see about that as well. I must talk to Jangor."

Namdarin moved forwards until he was alongside Jangor.

"How about an ambush for any that may be following, those trees look like a good place?"

"Strange that isn't it?"

"What is?"

"I had the same idea as soon as I saw them, and that was a long tIme ago, but then anyone following will suspect the same thing wont they?"

"So what did you think of then?"

"We'll just ride through, and if anyone is following us, they will be very careful of an ambush and they'll loose half day, and have no idea which way we went. Does that sound all right with you?"

"I think I'll stop thinking about these things, it makes my head hurt." laughed Namdarin.

"Anyway." asked Jangor. "What were you doing in town? Not that your help wasn't welcome, but you were supposed to be at the camp."

"We got a little bored, and it seemed that it was taking you far too long to get the information, so we decided to see if you were all right, the others were told not to come after us until the sun went down, so we have lots of time to get back to camp."

"Just how big an army do you actually have?" asked Brank.

Jangor lifted up in his saddle and looked back at Brank. "What you see here and four more, if you call that an army, then an army we be." He turned back to Namdarin. "Are there any horses behind us?" Namdarin leant against Arndrol's neck, he cheek resting against the rough hair of the horse. After a few moments he sat up again.

"No horses nearby, but there is another presence, four legs, but shorter than a horse."

"Large pointy teeth and a bushy tail."

"Yes, I think you know who I mean."

"Kern, it seems you may just get your wish, that damned wolf is around somewhere close, and is determined to make friends or a meal of us!"

"I am sure he just wants to be friends." declared Kern

"I have never trusted dogs, not since Sandoo. And I'll never trust a wolf at all." said Jangor, angrily. He snapped his reins and dropped back, until Granger had caught him up, then he walked his horse alongside the old magician for a while.

"What happened at Sandoo?" asked Nadmarin.

"That was a long time ago, we were in the employ of a minor warlord, he was trying to expand, he wanted to be a major warlord, as they all seem to. He decided to hit a tribe of nomadic sheep herders for some tax revenue, the usual sort of thing, pay us your gold and we stop killing your sheep. These sheep herders were very successful because they suffered almost no predation from wolves, they had a secret weapon hiding in the sheep. Once our employer had irritated them enough they gathered the herd together, and drove it straight at us. Now sheep aren't very bright, but they do understand that men can hurt them so as they got too close they just veered away. Tripping over themselves in the hurry to get away from the men in armour. I would say that about one sheep in twenty wasn't actually a sheep, they were sheep sized dogs, big white and angry, they had been trained to attack both men and wolves. We lost a quarter of our men on their first attack, once the sheep had all escaped the dogs rounded them up and collected them on a nearby hillside. Where they all settled down as if nothing had happened. The herders appeared over the top of the hill and sat on the ground watching their sheep, and us. The warlord gathered us together and formed us up into ranks, his intention was that we should march up the hill and take on the sheep and the dogs, this time we wouldn't be surprised. Before we had properly formed the herders had started whistling frantically, and the dogs were rushing around the sheep, packing them into a tighter and tighter group. It was clear that if that group came down the hill at us they would have no where to go but straight over the top, we would be trampled by sheep. At this point the warlord decided that expansion may be easier in another direction, so we turned round and marched quickly out of the sheep herders valley. Since then Jangor has had this thing about dogs." Kern laughed aloud. Namdarin joined in.

As they approached the small forest Namdarin lifted himself in his saddle and had a long look behind, he saw no one following them, but as he turned to settle back down he saw a flash of grey and black vanish through the undergrowth into the forest. He turned to Kern. "Did you see that?"

Kern nodded but said nothing, the wolf was indeed nearby, very nearby, less than fifty paces from them as they entered the coolness of the forest. Namdarin turned and looked back to where Jayanne was outlined against the bright sunlight, her hair shining redly in the golden light. Her face was in darkness but he could swear that he saw her eyes flash green. 'Some trick of the light, a reflection off something, perhaps the blade of her axe.' He thought. The darkness of the forest deepened as they moved further in, the trees had no branches near to the ground, they were all competing for the sunlight, reaching upwards towards the life giving rays. The small needle like leaves of the trees formed a thick brown mat that covered everything and provided no cover for any of the larger animals that usually inhabited a forest. The mere density of the tree trunks meant the vision was limited to only fifty paces in places, this made Jangor nervous, so he and Granger moved forwards until the group was much closer together, he didn't want them to get separated in this dense wood.

"Kern." He said loudly. "Is there any chance of changing direction without leaving any traces in this place?"

Kern looked at the ground, then shook his head, the leaf litter was too thick and too easily disturbed, every hoof print was clearly visible. "A man on a galloping horse could follow the trail we are leaving through here."

"We are just going to have to hope that no-one is really interested." Said Namdarin.

"After your demonstration today." Said Brank. "I don't think any one person would dare, and a platoon of men would have serious doubts. You have nothing to fear from the people in the city."

"That lady with the raucous voice could stir up plenty of trouble for us." Said Kern.

"She's probably beating her husband into buying her some present to help her get over the death of her brother. Or she is arranging his funeral. Most likely the former I believe." laughed Brank, he laughed so hard that he suddenly had to snatch at his horses mane to prevent himself falling from the saddle. His laughing stopped quite suddenly at that point, but the rest took it up, though they were laughing at him.

"Let us hope that what you say is true." said Jangor. "Turn north and see if we can make it to camp without being seen." Kern nodded and made the turn, taking them northwards through the forest. Brank moved up to the front of the line, which was moving slower now, for the urgency of escaping the view of the city was gone.

"Kern." He said. "Turn a little east there is a valley that heads north, it is deep enough to conceal us from prying eyes."

Kern simply nodded and turned in the direction indicated.

"The woman?" asked Brank. "How long has she been practising with that axe. She's very good."

"Jayanne never picked up a battle axe, until she found that one, and that was only a few weeks ago." Said Namdarin quietly.

"You are making fun of me now, no one gets to be that good in a few weeks."

"Look at her forearms. Have you ever seen a good axe man with forearms that thin?"

"No, but that axe moves with such blinding speed, how can she do that?"

"The answer is simple. She doesn't. The axe does what she wants it to do, probably because she is the one that feeds it."

"You saw it remove the blood from her arm, and heal the wound. You saw what it did to Will, have you ever seen anyone cut in half with an axe, who did not bleed all over everything in sight? That axe feeds on blood and life, every time she kills with it, both her and the axe get stronger. Try not to upset her, because that axe may soon be able to strike without her hand on it." said Namdarin

"If you are trying to frighten me, It Is working." whispered Brank. "How can you stand to have such a powerful weapon in your midst, doesn't it frighten you?"

"My sword is a little unusual, as is my bow, you have witnessed the power of Granger's staff. The axe feels quite at home here, amongst friends."

"I think that Harvang may have been right about you lot. This is a dangerous place to be."

"When we left your city, who was in danger, us or your ex-colleagues in the guard?"

"They were, but mainly because they didn't realise the strength of the force that faced them, there will be forces that know how dangerous you are."

"There already is such a force, they are trying to follow us and prevent me from reaching my goal."

"Will they be catching up with us any time soon?"

"I hope not, we sort of buried them in a mountain, but then they are powerful and resourceful people, so I don't suppose they'll stay buried for very long."

"What sort of people survive being buried alive?"

"They were in a huge cavern, with an enormous snake and we collapsed the exit. So, if they have killed the snake, and not actually been buried in the cave in, then they are alive. If they are alive they will find a way out."

"That is a whole lot of ifs."

"Yes, but none that they cannot deal with. Resourceful people."

"Aren't you frightened? Going up against this sort of thing?"

"Of course, but I want to hurt them more than they have hurt me. That is going to take some doing."

"But you believe that you and your friends can do this thing?"

"Any man can kill a god, that is the way I look at it, belief is how they live and belief is how Zandaar will die."

"You think that your belief can defeat the belief of all those followers of Zandaar?"

"I have seen the way their god feeds, no man can follow such a one, unless he can see no other way, I will show them another way."

"You want them to follow you, or do you want to become their god?"

"I don't want followers, and I cannot ever be a god, that sort of responsibility is just too much for a man."

"If you take away their god, they will follow you, such is the nature of men, and priests especially, most of them seem to hide behind the service of god, it protects them from the realities of the world."

"That is exactly what I don't want."

"What is it you do want, after you have killed this god?"

"I hadn't really looked that far ahead, somehow I think the being too close to a dying god is likely to be fatal."

"Well perhaps you should consider a course of action that is survivable, it is all well and good wanting revenge on the people who have hurt you, but is it really necessary to throw away your life in the process?"

"If a viable alternative presents itself then obviously I'll take it, but surviving is not something I consider essential."

"What about the survival of your friends? Can you send them to their death?"

"They are soldiers, just as you are, they know the risks, and could have left me on many occasions before now."

"Jayanne is not a soldier, she is a woman."

"You noticed that did you? But she most definitely is a warrior, and I feel she has some large part to play in what is coming, Granger said as much. You ask an awful lot of questions for a simple soldier."

"I need to know who I am dealing with before I commit to this cause of yours, you have some very good people on your side, and I begin to understand why they are here."

"You are willing to join us?"

"Perhaps, it seems that Kern and I share a sort of religious connection, we both served the same god for a while, if he is with you then maybe I should be. I'll have to talk to him." Namdarin nodded and shortened his reins, Arndrol slowed a little and let Jayanne catch up.

"How are you?" He asked.

"I'm fine, full of life so to speak."

"You did fine work on the soldier, did it feel easy to you?"

"The axe works well, it seems to know in advance where to be in order to block the attack, but that final blow was hard for me, I really didn't want to kill that man, but I had taken the challenge and knew I had no choice. The axe seemed to want to kill him more slowly, it almost tried to attack several times, but I held it back. Jangor was right, a single stroke was a far better way to end that fight."

"Better for everyone. Will didn't even know he was dead until it was too late."

"The axe wanted to carve little bits off him first, it is thirsty for blood. I am a little frightened of it."

"You mustn't be that, it will know and use your fear against you. You must be confident at all times, you must be in control. Also, there is nothing as disheartening for an enemy as a look of total confidence on the face of an opponent."

"I'll try not to fear it, but it isn't going to be easy, it gets more powerful every time I use it."

"It is going to be a very useful weapon for us, and it will give you tremendous power, but you have to control it." He reached out with his right hand and held her left, her green eyes lit at the contact, and she clasped his hand firmly. They walked their horses side by side for a while, holding hands and saying nothing, not even looking at each other. Each made happy by the nearness of the other.

"Kern." said Brank. "Why are you with this group, they seem to be intent on dying for Namdarin's cause?"

"The first time I met Namdarin, I sensed something strange about him. The next time I met him I knew there was something strange about him. After that we parted for a while, and then met again, this time we had been sent to collect the head of a robber. Namdarin already had that pretty much in hand by the time we got there. It seemed that we were fated to be together, so who am I to question fate?"

"So you believe it is fate that binds you to his cause?"

"That and something else."

"What else?"

"Some days ago we met someone. There was a tree, a very specially shaped tree, in an open expanse of lifeless stone."

"A tree of the goddess?"

"Yes."

"You performed a summoning?"

"And she came."

"In what shape?"

"She came as the black crow." Kern reached into his pocket and produced a single glossy black feather.

"Praise be. The crow is not a shape of good omen. What did she say?"

"She said that we need the elven kings green stone from his sword, so that is why we search for it."

"What did she say of Zandaar?"

"She said that it was time he left this world, and moved on, as most of the other old gods had. His time is done, and he should know that."

"Well, my brother. It appears we have been assigned a holy quest, our god has told you what you must do, so we must both obey."

"I am not so certain, there was something in what she said that didn't quite ring true."

"Gyara would never lie, not to one of her own."

"I am hardly one of her own, any more than you are, but I sensed something else in her, a plan that was hidden from us."

"How do you mean?"

"I just felt that she wasn't telling us the whole truth, there was something missing, something she should have told us, it is difficult to explain."

"She is a god, if she chose to hide something from you, then you would never know it, she is Gyara."

"Perhaps this is one of those occasions when free choice is necessary, by denying us the information she may guide us the way she wants us to go, even though it isn't in our interests to go that way. I have been present at summonings before and I have never felt that she was hiding anything. It felt very strange, almost as if she was trying not to lie to us."

"Perhaps it was the black crow shape that disturbed you so."

"Maybe, but I feel that something is wrong."

"Still I think this is a holy quest and I must go along with you, we must find this Zandaar and explain to him that it's time to leave."

"It may not be that easy, there will be many obstacles in our path, not least of which are the priests of Zandaar."

"Then we will just have to find a way to discourage them from stopping us." laughed Brank.

"How far are we from the valley you mentioned?" asked Kern.

"I'm not entirely sure, I don't come out here very often, and I am usually on foot, I don't like horses and they feel the same about me."

"We'll turn north now, and see how things go." Kern turned more northerly and soon they left the forest, the absence of the thick canopy meant that they soon became very hot in the full light of the sun. Both horses and people started to sweat. Jayanne shrugged her bearskin cape from her shoulders and it draped across her horses rump, much to the horses obvious disgust. The horse tried beating the offending item with it's tail, and the a couple of experimental kicks of its hind legs. This did nothing to dislodge the cloak, but came close to pitching Jayanne from her saddle. She snatched hard at the reins and gave the horse a disapproving stare, then she reached behind her self and rolled the cape up until it was only resting of the back of the saddle, and not on the horse at all.

The small valley they were in had steep sides and a flattened bottom, there were pools of stagnant water scattered about the valley, each with it's attendant cloud of flying and biting insects.

"Damn." Shouted Jangor, beating at an insect that had sneaked inside his clothes and was having a large meal. "I thought it was winter."

"It is winter." said Brank. "But it's been a very mild one and spring isn't too far away now."

"But it was the depth of winter, when we entered the mountains."

"That is the other side of the mountains, it's is normally a lot warmer on this side, spring comes earlier and summer is much longer."

"How do you deal with the damned insects?"

"I stay away from them, they don't like to stray too far from their ponds, and a good wind will certainly keep them down."

"So why don't they stay away from me?"

"They must think you are very tasty, I can't understand why." laughed Brank.

Jangor said nothing that anyone else could hear, but it was obvious that he was cursing the flies, it was a long and complicated curse, that affected the flies not at all.

The sun was half way down to the horizon when they came within sight of their camp. Crathen was the first to notice their approach, he sent up a shout that roused the others. Andel turned to the fire and started some food cooking, Mander, Stergin and Crathen stood at the edge of the camp.

"You have been a long time." said Crathen as they started to dismount. Mander and Stergin gathered the horses and led them off to the place the other horses were, an open patch of good, green grass. The horses set to eating with gusto, they hadn't had much of a chance to eat on the way back.

"We had to come back the long way." said Kern.

"Who's he?" asked Crathen, pointing vaguely in the direction of Brank.

"I am Brank. Is that a problem?" He drew himself up to his full height and looked down on Crathen, stepping in close to make the difference in height more perceptible.

"No problem, it's just that you are a stranger."

"Only to you, only to you." Brank turned away, and smiled at Jangor.

"Well?" demanded Andel. "Are you going to tell us why you have been so long?"

"We had a little trouble in town, someone made a bet he couldn't pay then made an even worse mistake, by threatening an old man, in an attempt to save his own miserable life. He failed. He was the brother of the captain of the guards wife. It made getting out of town a little tricky, and the need to avoid being followed all the more vital. Is that enough information or do you want a word by word and blow by blow account?"

"I presume the guard turned out to stop you. How did you get away with no-one even injured?"

"Namdarin issued a challenge to single combat, one man stepped forward, more goaded into stepping forward by the captain's wife, Jayanne begged an opportunity to be our champion. Namdarin stepped aside for her, and she won, with one stroke she halved the man. The captain kept good to his word and we walked out, bringing Brank with us, and the information that we need. Any more questions? Or are you just going to make us something to eat?"

"Food. Right, I'm on it." Andel turned back to the fire, and the meat that was cooking there, he added some water and vegetables to a pot and set them in the flames as well.

Crathen walked over to where Jayanne was sitting cross legged on the grass near to her tent.

"Was your fight as easy as Jangor made it sound?" He sat beside her.

"I had a little help, it wasn't so hard, actual fighting was easy, it's the killing that is hard."

"Who helped you? I thought this was single combat."

She didn't answer, at least not with words, she merely hefted the axe, that was as usual only and inch from her right hand. Crathen flinched away from it, somehow it frightened him.

"How did that help?"

"It is light and fast in combat, it strikes true, and it loves to kill. I don't." She laid the axe across her knees and stared at it. "Sometimes this thing frightens me." she whispered.

"Then get rid of it. Use a sword, or a bow, this axe is evil, I can feel it."

Her right hand snapped to the haft, the wooden handle slapped into her palm, Crathen shuffled backwards, trying to get to his feet.

"See." he whispered, as if trying to stop the axe from hearing him. "It is angry that you want to get rid of it, and it knows how we feel about it."

"It is an axe, it knows nothing of anger, but I do know how you feel about it, the others aren't so frightened of it. Or do you want it for yourself."

"I'd not have that axe as a gift, it is wicked. I am trying to look after you, I want you to be safe. This thing gets you into situations that are very dangerous."

"All our situations are dangerous now. Until we can complete our task."

"And then what?"

"I am not even going to think about that, I don't see much chance for any of us surviving the final conflict. Do you?"

"Namdarin has that sword and the bow, surely he will be strong enough to finish the task on his own, so long as we can get him into the city?"

"You would toss him over the city wall and consider your part done?"

"Not quite like that, but near enough."

"When Namdarin comes to face Zandaar I will be at his side, I will fight to the death for the things I believe in."

"Even unto your own death?"

"Namdarin means more to this world than any one else, don't you see that? The Zandaars are going to take over the whole world, a piece at a time. Their god will rule the whole thing, is that what you want?"

"No, but would it necessarily be a bad thing, to have one god co-ordinating all the peoples of the world. He could bring an order and stability that has never existed before."

"Zandaar is greedy, he needs to expand, he wants to grow. When there is no where left to expand to, then that greed needs must turn in on itself, he will destroy the world. He'll not bring stability, but stagnation. The world will die a slow and painful death, by his whim. If you think he is right then you should leave, express these thoughts to Namdarin and he will probably kill you on the spot. But the death he would give you would be far quicker than any that the Zandaars would think up."

"I would not be that stupid." He climbed slowly to his feet and walked off to where the horses were, he needed some time alone with his thoughts.

Namdarin, Jangor and Brank were gathered around the fire, waiting a little impatiently for the food to be ready.

"Where is this great forest of the elves?" Asked Namdarin.

"East and south, a good few days ride, or a couple of weeks marching."

"We don't walk, we ride." Said Jangor. "Speaking of which we'll have to find you a better horse, that pony is more suited to a little girl."

"I don't want a better horse. Horses to suit me are far too tall. I don't like heights, you know?"

"I know, but don't care. We will not be slowed down by your tiny little pony, you'll have to get used to a proper sized horse. You may even get to like it."

"How can anyone get to like a horse that stands the height of a man?"

"That is part of the joy, the risk, the excitement, the pleasure. You'll understand eventually."

"Or die falling."

"Or die falling." laughed Jangor.

"What are the trails like between here and the forest?" Asked Namdarin.

"Not exactly roads, but not a problem unless there is a lot of rain, then the mud tends to slow things down a lot."

"Does it rain much this time of year?"

"Not usually, but sometimes it rains early, and sometimes it barely rains all year."

"How far out of our way will we have to go to get around that town?"

"Not too far, I know a trail through the hills to the north that almost no one ever uses, far safer than going south then east, too many fields and people that way."

Jangor and Namdarin shared a glance, Namdarin nodded.

"Right." said Jangor, he decisions all made. "First light we move." He raised his voice a little so that everyone could hear. "I want this camp set for a fast departure, Andel, find a pack horse for Brank, something that will be able to keep up if we have to move. It's time he learned to ride anyway. Kern, check our trial, I want to know if anyone has followed us. Stergin, head towards town, make sure there is no one coming this way, I don't want us to be disturbed during the night. And someone do something about that damned wolf." He pointed upstream, there sitting on top of a pile of boulders was a large wolf, black and mottled grey, its huge grey tail wrapped around its front feet, it sat majestically watching them all. Huge yellow eyes missing nothing. It seemed perfectly relaxed, yet alert. Kern snatched a piece of meat from his pocket and tossed it in the direction of the wolf, it landed on the ground a few feet in front of the wolf. The yellow eyes followed the object as it sailed through the air and fixed on it when it landed. After a moments consideration the wolf looked back at the people, and jumped down from it's vantage point, approached the meat, sniffed suspiciously before taking up the piece and swallowing it whole. Again he sat, tail wrapped around his front feet.

"That was not exactly what I had in mind." said Jangor.

"He seems quite friendly to me." said Kern, tossing another chunk towards the wolf. The same result, the wolf a few feet nearer. Again Kern threw a piece of meat, again the wolf moved closer. Andel drew his knife from his belt, he reached down to the roast beside the fire to cut another piece for the wolf, when he looked up the yellow eyes were focus straight on his, no longer relaxed the wolf was crouched, muscles tensed and twitching, was it going to pounce or run, Andel was unsure so he simply froze. For what appeared to be an age no one moved. Kern took the meat from Andel and threw it to the wolf, this time it landed almost at his feet. The wolf stepped forwards snatched the meat, turned and ran off into the trees, tail streaming like a flag blowing in a breeze behind him.

"Well." said Kern. "He certainly knows about weapons and men, there can be no doubt of that. He's nervous of strangers, but that is to expected, we will have to earn his trust, that is going to take some time."

"You are mad." said Jangor.

"Why?"

"You want him to trust us, but I will never trust a wolf. Have you forgotten how we were attacked by a pack only a few days ago?"

"They were wild, this one has been tame, it knows people, it sees them differently, not just as food, but as possible friends. He'll not survive long in the wild, he needs us."

"He seems to be a big strong individual, why should survival be a problem."

"The first time he meets a pack he will die. A big wolf like that is always going to be a threat to the resident top male, and as such will be attacked by the whole pack, and killed. His only hope is to pick up a stray female and start a pack of his own, and that is going to be just as difficult."

"Why worry about him, it's only an animal?"

"Do you worry about your horse? Better yet ask Namdarin the same question. You've seen the bond between him and Arndrol. This may be only a wolf, but he could be as good a friend as Arndrol."

"Horses are different, they carry us and everything we need, they are useful, a wolf is not."

"But a wolf could be very useful. In time you will see." Kern turned back to the fire, and helped Andel with the food that was nearly ready.

"Brank." said Jangor. "What skills have you?"

"Well, I thought I was good with a sword until I met you, I am not as good with an axe, I wouldn't have liked to go against Jayanne in an axe fight. I can use a bow, but am no marksman, and I couldn't ride to save my life."

"Anything outside the warrior life that you are good at?"

"I can tell a tale, and I don't drink too much, if at all."

"Yes, I had noticed that, though it seems that none of your friends knew."

"Perhaps they were just too polite to mention it."

"No. Your captain was convinced that you spent all your off duty time in the blue parrot drinking and telling tales. Now there's an interesting question, if you weren't drinking all that dreadful beer, then what were you spending your money on?"

"Perhaps I was saving it."

"Oh yes, I really see that happening, soldiers are renowned for their saving plans. Try again?"

"Right." Brank sighed. "On the south side of town, in one of the poorer districts there is a place, a school, more like an orphanage, for the poorest of children, the homeless and destitute. Run by an honest churchman, I used to help him feed the children, and buy them clothes."

"I could almost believe that story except for the honest churchman, that I will not believe."

"Believe it, he would give his last morsel of food to a hungry child, he is a good man, I helped him when ever I could."

Jangor could tell that Brank wasn't lying, in fact Brank was so obviously willing to fight for the churchman's honour that Jangor had no choice but to believe him. Jangor nodded. "You are indeed a good man, how can some one so good end up a soldier?"

"I am big and lazy. Soldiering is easy for me, because I have little to do, mostly just the threat that Brank might wake up is enough to calm the most boisterous of rowdies. The high walls and strong gates means that no one from the outside is likely to threaten the city. That is until Namdarin turned up." Brank paused, then laughed loudly.

"What is so funny?" demanded Jangor.

"I just had the funniest thought, after all the excitement of today, something that they are all going to talk about for generations to come. Think what sort of security measures are in place at each of the gates, locked gates of course, even though it is still daylight, I am betting that the gates are closed and locked. The guard will be pounding a beat, all round the walls, all night. Lamps and torches will be lit at every point along the wall, saddled horses will be waiting in the courtyards, should the alarm be raised. It will be weeks before things settle down again, if they ever do."

"I thought you decide that just the two of you were going in to town, so as to create the minimum amount of disturbance?" asked Namdarin, with a huge grin.

"Yes." muttered Jangor.

"Your discrete information gathering mission collected two corpses, and a town in the highest state of alert in its entire history, along with the information. No real disturbance there at all." laughed Namdarin, rocking slowly and holding his sides.

Jangor just stared at the ground.

"Next time, let's just ride up to the town, set fire to it, and see if anyone wants to talk to us." said Namdarin, Brank was reduced to a strange girlish giggling, he was struggling to breathe.

"You were the one that threatened them all." said Jangor.

"If we hadn't been there, then you would now be in some dreary dungeon, or dead."

"Probably, there were a lot of them, many would have died but the three of us stood little chance, six against a city, now that is far better odds."

"Obviously, six was enough, they let us go."

"Only at the cost of another corpse."

"That was their choice, not mine."

"But did it have to be Jayanne that killed him?"

"She wanted it, and to have a young woman kill one of their soldiers, especially in such a spectacular way, impressed on them the fate that they all faced. It was the most bloodless way to do it. She put on quite a show."

"Yes, she put the fear of the gods into them all, but it was still more than a little brutal."

"Have you forgotten the first time you met her? Now that was brutal."

"I don't think I shall ever forget that meeting. She was frightening to look on."

"Such brutality is nothing new to her."

"But there was a cold bloodedness about the whole situation today, that first time was in the hot blood of battle, today was cold, I felt fingers of ice running up my spine."

"That was just Granger recharging his staff, he can certainly pull some heat out of the air."

"Yes he can, but it was more than just the dropping temperature, there was something else in that chill."

Kern turned from the fire, and spoke softly. "Something is wrong."

"What do you mean?" demanded Jangor.

"I don't know, but something is wrong, I can feel it. I am being watched, but by no-one I can see." He turned around quickly, as if trying to catch someone looking at him.

"I feel it." said Brank, standing with his eyes closed. "Something evil, something bad is watching."

"It's that damned wolf!" said Jangor. A distant howl told him otherwise, the wolf was a long way off and running for it's life.

Granger joined the group, the merest sparks of blue fire emanating from his staff. "I feel something strange. Something comes."

"What is it?" shouted Jangor, there was a sort of roaring in the air, like a huge wind but not a blade of grass was stirring. Namdarin ran over to Arndrol, the horse was very disturbed by something, hopping from one front foot to the other, tossing his head, and lashing his tail from side to side. Namdarin calmed him with a single pat, and place his head against the horses. With practised ease he made the connection to the herd mind, but all he could feel was a sense of danger, the horses wanted to follow the wolf, they wanted to run for their lives, something frightening was coming, though it had no name and no form to speak of, they could sense its approach. Namdarin broke the link and stepped back, drawing the sword of Xeron as he did so, with a single flashing stroke he cut the rope that held the horses. In an instant they were gone, the pounding of their hooves was barely noticeable over the soundless noise that filled all their minds.

"Why?" yelled Jangor, attempting to communicate above the noise.

"They are un-ridable, something frightens them too much, Arndrol will bring them back, but they are better away from here until we have dealt with this thing, whatever it is."

"Form a circle around the fire facing outwards, if this thing is an animal it may be afraid of fire. Weapons ready." They all formed a loose circle with the fire to their backs.

"Jayanne." shouted Jangor, "Two places to your left, Granger one to your right, I want your weapons balance around this circle, we are making our last stand here, let's make it a good one." Even before the places had been switched, the noise had thickened into a spiralling column of darkness, a twisting mass of night that obscured vision but revealed nothing of itself. Granger placed the end of his staff within the fire, and it rose up to a height of two men, a column of hot yellow fire to counter the darkness. The darkness flinched but thickened more and came slowly towards the group. It was heading straight at Namdarin.

"Step right!" yelled Jangor. "And again."

Two steps right, put Jangor right in the path of the swirling mass, it paused and moved towards Namdarin again. "Three steps right." yelled Jangor. This put him directly in it's path, he lashed out with his sword, and cut nothing only air. Again the spinning mass moved around the circle towards Namdarin, it seemed that it didn't want to touch anyone else.

"Step right." yelled Jangor. "Jayanne your turn, see what that axe can do to it." Quickly the circle moved around until Jayanne was in line with the darkness. She struck a sweeping blow that would have cut a man clean in two, but she impacted nothing.

"Anything?" asked Jangor.

"The axe stole the tiniest amount of power from it, but nothing like enough to affect it."

"Step right. Granger you try." Granger brought his staff to bear on the thing, he let loose a bolt of blue fire that was so intense it was almost dark itself. The bolt struck the thing and disappeared. The circle of friends was now moving continuously, each person stepping to the right, the grey vortex was following them around, trying to get to Namdarin.

"Namdarin, you'll have to try the sword on it, see if you can stop it, or at least affect it in some way, but keep the circle moving it must not catch up." Slowly the thing followed Namdarin around the circle, gradually it caught him up, as it neared it suddenly moved faster as if it had just sensed it's prey for the very first time, Namdarin slashed at it with the great sword, and had exactly the same effect as all the others, that is none. The circle kept moving but the thing had scented it target, and was homing in, until Crathen stumbled, he tripped over some unevenness hidden in the grass, Namdarin reached out to catch him, just as Crathen reached out to be caught, but caught he was by the darkness, it enveloped him in an instant, he screamed, the scream of a damned soul being sucked into the hottest of hells. The scream changed, not in intensity, but in quality, something about it was different. The spinning blackness faded gradually from sight, as the scream faded slowly from their ears.

Once the vortex had faded completely it was replaced by a different sort of darkness, a black cloaked figure lay on the grass, a strange staff beside him, he was struggling to breathe, and was obviously in some pain, Jangor stared open mouthed at the man who had replaced Crathen, Namdarin did not stare, he moved, before the man was able to get his black shod feet under him, the sword of Xeron had it's very tip resting in the hollow of his throat, and the weight of the sword would be more than enough to sink that tip into the grass.

"Hold." shouted Jangor.

"Why?" whispered Namdarin.

"This man had something to do with the taking of Crathen, then he will certainly have something to do with his return, if not then he is yours to kill as slowly as you wish."

"I see the logic, but I don't like it." Again a hoarse panting whisper.

"Logic is enough, he can be useful in other ways."

"Yes, we could feed him to the wolf, he's going to be hungry soon, that last man only lasted a couple of days." Said Kern. The man on the ground became quite agitated at the thought of a wolf, but movement of any sort would have killed him at this point.

"Zandaar, your life is mine, I will take it the instant I feel like it, any thought of doing anything other than your very best to help us and you will die, slow or fast I care not, I will end all of your kind, is that very clear."

The man on the ground nodded with the only part of his body he could safely move, his eyes. Namdarin lifted the sword until the weight was no longer pressing on the man's throat, the point was still there, but now he could at least speak.

"I am Gorgana, or was, call me Gregor. I am so glad to meet you, who ever you are."

CHAPTER THIRTY FOUR

Worandana slept through the night and through the next morning, not even rousing to eat. Gorgana was in much the same state. The reports showed that their prey had merely rested then moved on, heading along the valley towards a village that seemed to block the valley completely, its rickety walls spread from the scrubby forest on one side to the rocks of the other side, the small river that ran down the valley flowed right through the middle of the village. Alverana watched the walls carefully, observing without being observed. His reports told the warrior priest all he needed to know. While they were all gathered for the evening meal Kevana spoke to them.

"We set off early tomorrow, everyone should be fit for a little ride by then. We go to this village and see where the thieves went. We aren't in any real hurry, some of us aren't up to a fast ride just yet, but once we know where they are going, then we will be able to pick up the pace, I want to catch them before they get where ever it is they are going. So rest up, tomorrow things get back to normal, if a little warmer than they have been of late."

"It is certainly a lot warmer on this side of the mountains." said Fabrana.

"You're not complaining are you?" asked Petrovana.

"No. Just noting, it's such a difference, that is all."

"At least the hunting is better on this side." said Apostana, taking a large bite out of a haunch of the deer that Fabrana had killed that morning.

"Any idea what we will find in that village?" asked Briana.

"It looks like a very average farming community, no major buildings, the wall is a joke, it is barely enough to stop the animals running off at night. Strange that, they bring all the animals in at night, they are all corralled inside the wall." said Alverana.

"Why would they do that?" asked Apostana.

"They must fear for their animals, they feel safer with them in the village."

"They think there is something out here that will eat their cows?"

"Probably."

"If they think it could take a cow, then it could probably take one of our horses, or one of us. Perhaps we should set guards, and make a bigger fire?"

"Not necessary." said Kevana. "I think that the thing they are frightened of, will not be bothering them again, unless they get on the downwind side of it, it was definitely getting a little ripe by the time we left its little cave."

"I actually had forgotten about that damned snake." said Apostana.

Alverana laughed out loud.

"What is so funny?" demanded Apostana.

"Nothing much, I just realised why their wall is so weak, it doesn't need to be strong, it has a fence of outward pointing sharpened stakes all the way around it, I thought they were a little strange, they are barely high enough to bother a man, and a horse could certainly walk through them with a little care, but that snake, he couldn't risk them, they'd rip open his belly. I too had forgotten the snake." He laughed even more, and all the others joined in.

"Right." said Kevana. "Every one get some rest, we ride early in the morning."

"Guards?" asked Alverana.

"I think not, we shouldn't need them, and some of us are so rested that they aren't going to be sleeping much anyway." Alverana nodded, he understood. Kevana wanted guards but not the clerics, he wanted guards he could trust. Alverana prodded Pertovana indicating that he should be next. Alverana wandered out of the camp and found a comfortable tree to rest against. "It makes a change to be out in the open again, and not huddled round a fire." he said to himself, and sighed. Leaning back he looked up through the branches of the tree, and saw the first of the stars coming into view, they appeared even brighter than normal, perhaps because of the long absence. Counting backwards, he couldn't even be sure how many nights it had been since he had seen the stars above. Listening intently he could hear the sounds of the night creatures starting to move around, the dried up leaves around the trunks of the trees rustled as they were disturbed, small rodents and insects starting their nightly foraging for food, the night was even warm enough for snakes to be hunting, the thought made him shiver, but not with cold. A sharp rustling at the base of a tree to his left attracted his attention, something was scratching around in the leaves, perhaps a rat, it certainly seemed undisturbed by the noise it was making. Alverana felt something move above him, he didn't really hear it, but he felt the air change as it passed. He looked up straight into the moon shaped face, the face was lit by starlight only, but the whiteness of it made it quite visible. A round disc of a face, on a neck that allowed almost complete revolution, and revolve it did. The thing in the leaves had also felt its presence, it had completely stopped moving, a deep silence descended. The owl in the tree moved its head slowly from side to side, waiting patiently. There was the tiniest of rustling from the leaves and the owls head targeted instantly, focused on the sound, Alverana could barely hear the noise from the leaves, but it was more than enough for the owl. As he watched the owl leaned forwards and fell out of the tree, spread its wide soft wings and dropped towards the base of the tree, at the last moment before it collided with the ground, its feet, with their great talons, snapped forwards, and plunged into the leaf litter, there was a brief squeak, a tiny struggle and then nothing. The owl beat its wings and lifted out of the leaves, it had a mouse in it's claws, a dead mouse. It flew up to the tree above Alverana, and settled on a branch above his head, slowly it separated the leaves from the mouse, before swallowing the latter whole, Alverana watched in fascination as the mouse's tail slowly disappeared from view. The owl sat for while, it's head still, except for the occasional glance down at the man. Suddenly on a silent breath of wind the owl spread those wide wings and vanished into the night.

"Just beautiful." whispered Alverana. 'I wonder how long it will be before men come here and cut down the trees, and leave you with no where to live, poor owl.' He thought. Long night watch duties always gave him time to think, not always a good thing for a soldier. His mind turned towards home base, the people there would be waiting for their return, wondering where they all where, they were more than a few days late now. There would be parties out searching for them, but they would find nothing, no tracks would be found, the blizzard had taken care of those, a few dead horses here and there, that would give the searchers the idea that they may be dead. It would be until they went to see Melandius, then they would have a report of them being alive. At least some of them alive. There were more than a few died before they got to Melandius' house, and took new horses, then the weather improved, but the path they took, none would follow, unless forced. Kevana would be unhappy, that was certain, he needed their position to remain secret from the other Zandaars, so that none would find out about their failure to collect the sword. He stood, and leant backwards against the tree. 'Enough thinking, time for some lurking.' He laughed very quietly to himself, and crept through the trees, circling the camp site, he was moving so soundlessly that the owl would have had to listen for his heartbeat, when he was half way to the mountainside he came upon a deer, it's dappled colours would have hidden it from view, but here amongst the trees the light was so low that colours were impossible to see, there were only shades of dark and light. Alverana was close enough to touch the deer before it realised he was there, it looked up and saw him, it turned and walked slowly away, sensing that it was in no danger, at least not at this time. Alverana turned his attention to the place the deer had been foraging, there amongst the leaf litter were a handful of large mushrooms, they glowed with a soft internal light, Avlerana decided they might be good for breakfast, but he wasn't going to try one until he had seen it in daylight. He collected them up and stuffed them in a bag. Once the light was extinguished he immediately saw another group of glowing mushrooms a little way off. Moving a quietly as ever, he went towards the glow, and collected another bunch of mushrooms. So it went, every time he picked a clump of mushrooms and put them in his bag, another glow was visible. Suddenly he noticed that his bag was full to the brim with softly glowing mushrooms, far more than they could eat in one sitting, looking round he realised that he was completely lost. It was too dark to see his trail, not that he had been leaving much, other than mushroom stalks. The trees were too thick for him to see the stars, the wind was none existent. There was no moonlight to guide him. Slowly a deer walked from behind a small bush, it stood and stared at him for a while.

"Good evening madam." said Alverana. "Are you the deer I saw earlier, I have far too many mushrooms for us to eat, but I will give you some if you can tell me which way I came from?" He laughed softly even as he asked, but still he reached into the bag and pulled out a large mushroom, which he held on the flat of his hand. Gingerly the deer approached, he felt its soft breath and the hairs on its chin as they crossed his hand, the deer gently picked up the mushroom and started to eat it, never taking it's eyes off the man, and not relaxing for an instant. There was a sound in the trees, some distance away, and the deer was gone, a white flash of its rump as it vanished between the trees. Alverana turned towards the noise, he knew that the racket he was hearing could only be made by Petrovana trying to be quiet. Alverana headed towards the noise, now with little attempt to be quiet, there was no point, Petrovana was making so much noise that he couldn't have heard the deer running past him. Alverana placed himself in Petrovana's path and hid behind a tree. He stepped into sight when Petrovana was only a foot away.

"I wish you wouldn't do that." snapped Petrovana. "Have you seen anything?"

"I had lunch with an owl, collected a bag of mushrooms, and chatted to a deer, but other than that nothing much is going on out here, especially now that you have been creeping around in the dark."

"We all don't have your talent for sneaking around."

"I wasn't sneaking, I was lurking, at least that's what Kevana calls it."

"Sneaking, lurking, what's the difference?"

"Not much, depending on your point of view, but I think Kevana needs to contact some of our people, if only to let our families know we are still alive, after all we have been missing for more than a few days."

"I don't have any family to worry about, only an old mother who wishes I was dead."

"I don't even have that, but I don't want people to think that we are dead, at least not until it is true. Why does your mother wish you dead?"

"She says I should have followed the family trade, and not joined the priesthood."

"I have to ask, trade?"

"My family come from a long line of morticians, I have an aversion to dead bodies, the rest of them have no problem, but I just can't deal with it."

"So you joined the militant arm of the priesthood, that is obviously not going to bring you into contact with any dead bodies, at least not many that you haven't made dead yourself." laughed Alverana.

"I have no problem with those, it's the ones that have been dead for a few days, and have to be presented for family to look at. Why do people do that? I can't stand the thought of looking at a friend who has been dead for a while. I would rather remember them as they lived."

"I agree. But some families insist on this, something about final farewell's and all that. Personally I think these traditions were enacted by the cruellest of people. I saw one case some years ago, more years than I care to think of really. Our army had taken a castle, by force, not magic. One captain had fallen from the top of the wall, into the courtyard, we followed his wishes as well as we could, we scraped most of him up and put it in a box, not really a coffin, but a sturdy box. It was a four day march back to our base, in the heat of the summer. His 'body' was laid in state for all the family to see, I have no idea how the morticians did it, but he looked almost human."

"That was the sort of thing that my family specialised in, truly horrible. When I die, light me a fire, and tell mother I died well, she shouldn't spit on you too much." laughed Petrovana.

"I'll go and get some sleep." said Alverana. "You keep an eye open, there could be something really exciting out here, just waiting for the chance to say hello."

"Thanks!" snorted Petrovana. "Excitement is something I really don't need right now. I want to sit and watch the stars, until it is Fabrana's turn. I wonder why Kevana didn't want those clerics on guard duty?"

"Probably because they are scared of their own shadows, and shadows look so much bigger and more frightening in the dark." laughed Alverana, walking away towards the light of the fire. He threw a few logs on it before crawling into his tent, sleep came before he was even settled.

As usual, Alverana was the first to wake, before the predawn light was properly developed, he crawled from the comfort of his tent, and threw some logs on the fire, the embers threw streamers of sparks high up into the air, a glowing column of yellow and orange lights. He moved the remains of the deer closer to the fire to warm for the others breakfast. Slicing himself a goodly portion of the meat he went to the horses and began packing away what gear he could, he too felt the need to be moving today. 'Something in the air?' He thought, but the air seemed exactly as it normally did. 'Perhaps it is just that there is open sky over my head, something I have been missing for some days.' Nodding to himself he decided that it was merely the prospect of riding though green fields that had him excited to be moving. Moving backwards and forward between his tent and the horses, he soon started to loose interest in keeping quiet, before long the noise of his work awoke the others, Gorgana was one of the first, he went straight to the fire, and cut himself a large portion of breakfast, which he fell upon like a man who hadn't eaten in days.

"Hungry?" laughed Alverana.

"Muumbm." Gorgana's response was unintelligible, something to do with the food he was still eating. Alverana laughed even louder, using his jollity as an excuse to wake the more sleepy members of the party. Kevana crawled from his tent, just as Worandana did the same.

"How are you feeling today?" asked Kevana.

"Very tired, and extra-ordinarily hungry, but I'll manage, so long as there is something to eat."

"There is something to eat, but I'd hurry if I were you, and keep moving or Gorgana might just consider you a between meal snack." laughed Alverana, pointing at Gorgana, who was pushing more food into his mouth.

"I've always said that Gorgana has a big mouth," said Fabrana, "but it seems to be just a little on the small side for him at the moment." Gorgana's response only managed to dispel some fragments of food from his mouth, nothing audible emerged. More laughter ensued, until Alverana and Fabrana turned to start the dismantling of the tents. In fairly short order the camp was packed away, the fire put out and monks mounted on their respective horses, though two had to be helped into their seats, still not strong enough to manage it on their own. A few hand signals from Kevana and they were ready, Alverana took the lead, Petrovana, and Fabrana to either side of him. Kevana indicated a slow walk for the mornings pace, he didn't want to tire the invalids too much on their first day back in the saddle, they didn't have far to go anyway, the village was fairly close.

They had not been travelling long, when they saw a large group of cattle walking slowly towards them, there were two boys with the cattle and four large brown dogs. The dogs were patrolling around the cattle, keeping them in a tight group and keeping them moving at a steady walk, it seemed they were going somewhere special. Occasionally one of the boys would whistle or shout some command to the dogs, and one dog, or two, would go and herd a cow back into the group, or chase one that was lagging behind, the dogs seemed specially skilled at biting the heels of the cows, so much so that the cows didn't waste energy trying to kick a dog that it knew was no longer there, such a nip would cause a cow to run for a few paces, and then walk quickly for some time before it slowed down again. It was a constant battle for the dogs to keep them moving, but the dogs looked on it as a game, and looked as if they actually enjoyed it. As the herd grew close to the monks one of the boys came over to talk to them, two dogs came with him, each sat panting at his side, even sitting the dogs were quite tall, the boy had to lift his hand to stroke their heads, which he did before speaking.

"Good morning sirs. Would you be so kind as to tell me who you are and what you are doing so close to our village? We don't get many visitors around here, we are a bit out of the way, if you know what I mean." Worandana walked his horse to stand in front of the boy, then he threw back his hood, knowing the boy would see a very old man, someone who couldn't possibly cause him harm.

"We are priests of Zandaar, we are travelling, from one place to another."

"Your attire, sir, tells of your servitude to your god, and the fact that you are mounted tells that you are travelling. Is it possible you tell me something I don't already know?" Kevana smothered a laugh.

"You, young man are impertinent and rude!"

"You, old man, are haughty and secretive!" Kevana laughed out loud, and dropped lightly to the ground, casually tossing his reins to Briana. He walked up to the boy, and his companions, he dropped to one knee, so as not to tower intimidatingly over the boy.

"Are your dogs friendly?" he asked.

"As friendly as I wish them to be."

"Well trained then?"

"They have to be to run with the cattle, can't have an angry dog biting the cows for real now, can we?

"I suppose not. And they defend the cows as well?"

"Certainly, though there isn't much in the way of threats around here."

"Surely there must be wolves and such?"

"Wolves have never been a problem."

"You have a different problem then?"

"Yes."

"What sort of problem?"

"There are snakes here."

"I can assure you that the snake you fear is dead, I could even take you to the place where it lies, if you want?"

"I had heard it was dead, but I didn't think it very likely."

"Somehow they know we killed it. I wonder what," whispered Kirukana. He was stopped in the middle of the sentence by a sharp stare from Kevana, which caused the man to pull up his hood even further and look at the ground.

"It was a hard battle, but we won, and had to rest for a few days before we could continue. Now we are fit enough to travel, we go eastwards towards the great river."

"You will have to pass through our village to do that."

"Yes, we had realised that. Is that going to be a problem? We would go around if we could."

"The people have been warned not to trust you, but I don't think they will make any difficulty to your passing through."

"We are also in need of supplies, and shoes for our horses, we can of course pay for these with gold."

"The smith is always willing to take gold for his work, and the supplies should be purchasable at a reasonable price. We don't see gold very much, we don't see much of anything."

"Will you accompany us, young man? People always seem a little scared of groups of strangers, whereas your presence will allay some of that fear."

The boy thought for a while, before speaking. These men didn't seem as bad as he had been told they were, but then they weren't being completely truthful about something. "I'll have to make sure my friend can cope with the cattle first."

"No hurry." said Kevana as the boy turned away, one dog at his heels the other watched the men for a few moments before following. Worandana turned to Kirukana. "Have you no idea when to keep that big mouth of yours shut?" he hissed.

"I am sorry." muttered Kirukana.

"Don't fret about it." said Kevana. "It's just not something you have any experience of, there is a certain flow to that sort of talk, and anything that disrupts the flow gives a moment for people to think about what they are saying, often they let things slip when they aren't really thinking about it. Just learn from this."

"He must be getting soft in his old age." whispered Alverana to Fabrana.

"Definitely. I've seem him threaten to separate heads for that sort of interruption."

"Do you remember that time in."

"Shut up the pair of you, you are not helping. Anyway the boy isn't going to guide us into town with a headless corpse twitching on the ground now is he?"

"I suppose you could look at it that way." said Alverana smiling under his hood, and listening to Kirukana trying manfully to swallow, while he still could.

They didn't have to wait long for the boy to return, with only one dog in tow, he left the other to help with the cattle.

"Thank you, young man." said Kevana. "It is so much better have guide in a strange place. My name is Kevana, what is yours?"

"I am called Paulo, and my dog is Jim."

"We have a spare horse, if you want to ride, rather than walking?"

"I'll walk. I don't know how to ride."

"Fine, then we can walk and talk together. Lead on."

Paulo set off towards the village, Kevana walked beside him, or would have if Jim hadn't insisted on being between them.

"A nice day for a walk in the countryside, don't you think?" asked Kevana.

"I walk in the fields every day, so it's nothing special for me, though it does make a change to have a reasonable excuse for not following those cows around all day."

"Who is it that decides that you have to do this job every day?"

"The cows belong to my family, there are other jobs, but this is the one I am best suited to, my dogs are the best trained, and to tell you the truth the dogs do most of the work, and all they ask is a pat on the head and a bowl of food."

"So the head of your family decides what you do, but who tells him what must be done?"

"I don't know if anyone does, we all live in the same place, so we all know what needs doing, so every thing gets done. Sometimes the heads of the families get together, but that usually turns out just to be an excuse for a party."

"Do you have many parties?"

"Not really, only one or two a month, I suppose if they happen too often, then they would get boring."

"Are these parties in celebration of special holidays?"

"Not really, we usually have a big party as the days start to get longer, we celebrate the departure of winter. We celebrate the longest day of the year, that is one of the bigger celebrations, with singing and dancing and dressing up. It is a good time."

"Who decides when these times are?"

"No one. They just are." Paulo frowned, wondering why this man was asking so many very silly questions, what was he really after?

"But someone must tell you when to prepare for the celebrations?"

"The winter one can be difficult to judge, but it is a general feeling in the whole village, it may not be on exactly the right day, but what does that matter? Everyone is feeling like a party, so we have one. The longest day is easy to see for all, when the sun sets on the stone in the middle of the green then it is the longest day. For weeks it is obvious that the day is approaching, as the sun gets closer and closer, until it finally touches, then we know that tomorrow is the day. You are fishing for something, what is it?"

"I was wondering which god you worship, what sort of temples you have, things like that?"

"Gods and temples are all right for city folk, but what need have we for them? Our crops grow, our cattle multiply. We need no gods to make these things happen, all we need is the sun and the rain, they are enough."

"But the help of a god can improve the sun and the rain, it can make things even better."

"From what I have heard, gods mean priests, and priests are just lazy people who don't want to work, so they steal from all those around them. We'll have none of that."

"Heathens!" muttered Kirukana. Kevana turned a hard stare on the cleric. Fabrana chuckled softly, and turned to Kirukana whispering. "Keep trying, it's only a matter of time, at this rate, he'll have your head before the day is out." Kirukana choked and pulled his hood forwards, muttering soft prayers.

"So you have no religious leaders?"

"And we need none. We are almost completely self sufficient, we buy metals for tools that is all, everything else we grow or make ourselves."

"For a small village that must be a rather precarious way of living, all it would take is one disaster and you would all die."

"We live or die together, in my lifetime we have had the occasional problem, the elders come together and decide on the action to be taken, and the village does what needs to be done."

"What if there was a better way to do things that your elders weren't aware of?"

"That would have no real effect, I am sure there are many ways to do things, if one way works, then why worry about the others?"

"But the other ways could mean that the problem never arises again."

"Be that as it may, but we have survived in this place for many generations now, and we will continue. It was the feeling of my grandfather, and he spoke of it often, that our village would only be destroyed by something from outside, some strange people, or some strange idea. He was very wary of strangers. I like to have strangers visit us, they bring new tales and fresh blood to the village. The sad thing is most travellers are men, there aren't that many girls visit us."

Kevana felt the hairs on the back of his neck rise, as if someone was staring at him. He knew what that feeling meant, so he opened his mind and thought of Worandana. 'What is this fascination with blood?' Came the thought after a moments effort. 'I think it is something simple, but I'll ask.' Was Kevana's silent reply.

"This village needs fresh blood?"

"Of course, we aren't stupid, and have no intention of being so, we are too small, we need fresh blood or inbreeding will destroy our village. Don't you know about this sort of thing?"

"We have little to do with that side of life, but I have seen all sorts of strange things caused by inbreeding in animals. That is how the different shapes and sizes of dogs occur you know."

"Of course I know, we have two distinct breeds of cattle here now, one for beef and the other for milk. Why do you think country people are stupid?"

"I don't think you are stupid, but I have to admit that I did not expect such a conversation from a simple cow herder, you have proved to be anything other than simple. Is there a school in your village?"

"Not as such, but though we are simple people we still have plenty of time to share our knowledge, the elders aren't really fit for hard work in the fields so they do what they are good at, they talk, and some of us listen, not all. My grandfather himself helped to breed the dogs we use for herding the cows, it wasn't an easy balance to achieve, aggression and intelligence don't often come together."

"No, usually the presence of one precludes the other."

"Precludes. A new word. The meaning is obvious from the usage. I shall try and remember that one."

"Be careful Kevana." said Alverana. "The boy is learning from you already, don't you go giving any secrets away." he laughed softly.

"I care nothing for your secrets." laughed Paulo. "But, there may be others later, who will quiz you more intently, especially once they have lowered your defences."

"I'll never give away any of our secrets." said Kirukana, loudly, trying to recover some of the standing he had lost today. Paulo stopped and turned, he stared at Kirukana for a few moments.

"You are a young man, you may be surprised how low your defences will get in my little village." he laughed and started walking again.

"You certainly seem to have a great deal of confidence in your home." said Kevana.

"I do, I think my grandfather didn't truly understand the resilience of the people, he was just too frightened of change."

"You are not?"

"I'm not frightened of change, so long as it is for the better. So much change is just change for changes sake, that isn't enough of a reason. For things to really change, all the people must be behind it, at least that is the way it is in our village, in a city, or big town, then change is decided by the people in charge. We don't have that problem here. Here the people are in charge."

"But if your village gets too big, then a group of men will have to be put in charge, won't they."

"Men and women. Both are in charge now, so both will be in the controlling group. There are no women in your group, why?"

"There are no women in our order, it was decided many years ago that women would be a distraction from the pure study of the truth."

"They can be a distraction, but without women your order is doomed to die."

"Don't be absurd." said Kirukana. "Our god will not let our order die, we will go on forever, as will Zandaar." Kevana turned and frowned.

"Without the efforts of your mother, you would not be here." said Paulo. "The same is true for all men. Without women you cease to be, if they turn away from you today, then you are the last generation."

"That could never happen, they would not be allowed to do such a thing."

"They would be forced to obey the will of your god, interesting. I'd like to see him try and force my mother."

"Kirukana." said Kevana. "Please shut up, you are completely out of your depth here, this young man knows more about the world than you do, despite all the time and effort that has been invested in your education. Worandana, perhaps your selection of this man was an error."

"Perhaps, but he does have his uses, he has strengths, debate is not one of them though. Perhaps he would have been better with the militant arm of the church. What do you think?"

"No." said Kevana. "He has a talent for rubbing people the wrong way, he would have been invalided out after some tragic training accident very early in his career."

"I thought that sort of thing had been stopped."

"In the main yes, but military training, like military action is a dangerous thing, and accidents still happen, not as many, but still some."

"Kirukana." said Worandana. "Would you like a transfer to the militant section?"

"No, thank you. An honour though it would be I think I am better suited to a more cloistered lifestyle."

"I agree." replied Worandana. "A cloistered and contemplative lifestyle is better for you. So contemplate carefully before you open that mouth again." Kirukana merely nodded. Their slow approach to the gate had given the villagers plenty of time to assemble.

Kevana saw the waiting group and barely managed to restrain a laugh, they were a disorderly bunch, and obviously frightened. He paused while Paulo walked up to the gate and talked to the biggest man, obviously the leader.

"Hello Garin." he said.

"Who are these people you bring to the gate?"

"They are priests of Zandaar, they wish to stay a little while, they need supplies and horses shod."

"We have been warned of them, I hope you have done nothing to upset them."

"No more than they deserved, they seem to be a lively bunch, spirited almost."

"Your mouth is going to get you into some serious trouble one of these days."

"What sort of serious trouble ever happens around here, the odd lame cow, a sick horse, it is always interesting to meet new people."

"But can we trust them?"

"There are two sorts of men in the group you see, some are priests in the normal sense of the word, and the others are warriors. If you look carefully you can tell which are which. Between them they could ride through this gate and burn the whole place to the ground and kill everyone in it, probably without breaking into a sweat. They have offered me no harm, only some stimulating conversation. I say we let them in, and treat them fairly, they are probably no danger to us." Paulo stepped to the side and waved Kevana forward.

"Good day to you." said Garin. "Paulo says you come in peace and are in need of supplies, is this the case?"

"It is indeed, we need supplies and shoes for horses and then we will be on our way. We can of course pay for these services in gold."

"Gold is always welcome, but sometimes the price is too high."

"I don't understand."

"Sometimes people with gold in their purses think the have bought more than they have paid for, they believe themselves entitled to extras that were not in the agreement."

"All we seek is some food, some help for our horses, an evenings rest, and we will be on our way as the sun comes up."

Garin looked them over very carefully. They didn't look as warlike as he last lot of visitors, there was only one that carried weapon on display, a single bow could do little harm, but the long black cloaks could easily have hidden an arsenal. Even so he knew he had little choice, his small village force couldn't hope to stand against these men.

"Be welcome gentlemen. Come inside, but please be aware, we have no gods here and we wish none. If you try to convert the people here you will fail."

"Thank you for the invitation, we have no wish to acquire converts on our travels, we have a specific thing we are after."

Garin opened the gate and let them in, Kevana stayed on foot, and walked alongside the smith until the reached the corral behind the smithy, here tents were erected and a small fire laid, on the remains of an old one.

"Kevana." said Alverana. "Do you think this is where the thieves camped?"

"Almost certainly, why would they have visitors camping anywhere they wanted, they'd want them in a certain place so they could be watched." Turning to the others. "Fabrana, Pertovana. Check this place out, let me know how it looks. Gorgana take Worandana for a slow walk around the village, let me know how it feels. Alverana and I will talk to the smith."

Worandana knew exactly what Kevana meant, so he took his long staff from the saddle of his horse, threw his hood back, so that it draped across his shoulders and down his back, a few clumps of white hair barely covered any of his shining head. Gorgana followed suit, only he had a full head of hair, a rich brown colour unfaded by any hint of grey. Leaning heavily on his staff in the right hand and with Gorgana at his left Worandana set off at a stately pace for such an old man.

"I didn't know he was that old." said Apostana, to no one in particular.

"He is as old as he wishes to be." said Kirukana. "At the moment he is a smiling old man taking a tour of the village, that is what he wants the villagers to see, so that is what they see. We all know he is not as old and infirm as he currently looks. But the villagers will find it hard to see him as any sort of threat." They returned to their tasks of sorting through the gear.

CHAPTER THIRTY FIVE

Kevana went to see the smith, the forge was hot and there where iron rods in it heating, they were showing soft reds in the middle but still black on the ends.

"Garin." the smith looked up.

"I'm not sure how many shoes we will need, have you had chance to look yet?"

"Not yet, but some are obvious. Is that black stallion yours?"

"Yes, why?"

"He kicks his front left into the ground, the toe of that shoe is almost worn through, the others are fine, you really should train him not to do it, it will be expensive in shoes over the horses useful life."

"I know what you mean, sometimes he'll wear that shoe out in a few days."

"I have a special sort of metal that may solve your little problem, it's a little more expensive, but it should be worth it."

"What does it do, this new metal."

"It's harder than your average shoe, so it lasts longer, and if he kicks it against a rock or a stone, which I think he must do just for fun, it will give him a big surprise. This metal emits the most wonderful sparks when struck against stone."

"Interesting. Replace all his shoes with the new metal then. That should be impressive galloping through a town at night."

"Yes, but be careful with stabling, those sparks could set fire to any straw that is around."

"I'll keep that in mind. You mentioned price, how much?"

"Four of the special shoes are going to cost you a whole gold piece, for each of the other horses say a silver piece."

"We have fourteen horses, that is a lot of money. That's almost four gold crowns, let's call two and a half gold."

"Three and a half.

"Three, and you change all the shoes."

"Deal." They shook hands to cement the agreement.

"What is this special metal?" asked Kern.

"It's something very rare, it is an alloy of ordinary iron and the remains of a thunderbolt. I found a large one some years ago, and have been working on it for sometime. It is very hard to work with and sometimes the results can be a little off, but over all it is certainly an improvement."

"Where did you find this thunderbolt?"

"That is one thing I won't tell, it is smaller every year, but it should last me a few years yet, anyone with enough horses could take it all away in one trip. No, I'll not tell." laughed Garin. "I'll go and look at your horses and find out just how bad a deal I have made today." he continued, turning to leave the forge, and herding the others out with widespread arms, perhaps he was only worried about their safety, perhaps not.

Kevana allowed himself to be gently guided from the heat of the smithy, actually quite glad to be leaving, he always found the heat so oppressive, that and the smell, hot metal, hot coal, steam, all blended together into something that was far stronger than it's component parts. Once out into the sunlight, the two turned to the south, planning on checking out the gates on that side of the village. They had only gone a few hundred paces when they met Fabrana and Petrovana.

"This place is a joke." said Petrovana.

"What do you mean?" asked Kevana.

"The walls couldn't keep out a tired donkey, one good sneeze and the whole thing would collapse. Their barrier of stakes on the outside, is now completely useless, they may have discouraged the snake, but nothing else would be stopped by them. The gates are bound with rope, the beams and hinges are rotten, they could easily fall on someone and kill them. It would take a lot of men to defend this place, even against a small force. Defend it with a hundred soldiers and we could take it in a few days. It's only advantage is that it has wells and stored food on the inside, and if attacked at night, the animals should be relatively safe. Basically any small robber baron could take this place in a day, but it wouldn't be worth it, it has nothing of value. The place is broken down and broke."

"You don't sound very impressed with our hosts. Do you agree with him Fabrana?"

"Certainly, the only thing of wonder in this place is the fact that it actually exists at all, it should have died many times over, but the people here just keep on going."

"How do they manage that?"

"I have no idea, there must be some force that binds them all together, but what it is I have no idea, there is no central religious guidance, no obvious leaders, nothing to explain it. I am confused."

"Well perhaps Worandana will fare better when it comes to these people. I'm going to take a tour, you two go and help the smith, he's got some new metal that is harder than normal steel, he claims it is from a thunderbolt."

"That's ridiculous."

"Of course it is, but humour him you may find something of interest there."

Kevana and Alverana continued their tour of the village, the condition of the walls and the gates should have been of no surprise to them, but it was, despite the warnings.

"A minor invasion of mice could bring that gate down." Said Alverana standing in front of the gate, he shook his head and turned away. Kevana followed him along the inside of the wall, they passed the south well, there were a few people gathered at the well, they all smiled at the visitors, though none actually approached. Alverana went over to the well, he inspected the mechanism, a simple drum and ratchet, with a large bucket on a rope. He moved the lever into neutral position and the drum turned slowly lowering the bucket, once it stopped he moved the lever and started winding the handle, the ratchet made a soft clicking as it engaged in the cog on the drum, he let go of the handle to test the mechanism, the handle dropped backwards only a fraction of a turn before the ratchet stopped it. He started winding again with almost no effort, the bucket came into view full almost to the brim, he checked the quality of the water before he drank some, he looked round at the people who seemed to be a little amused by his actions. Alverana nodded to them and left without speaking. There was some gentle laughter as he turned away.

"What was all that about?" demanded Kevana.

"I wanted to find out how good their well was, and what they were all doing there."

"And?"

"The well equipment is very good, excellent even, the drag on the drum is just enough to slow the falling bucket, so the handle wont spin too fast and hurt someone, and the ratchet is just perfect, smooth, easy to operate, and only drops a fraction of a turn."

"What does all this mean then?"

"It means that someone has invested a great deal of time and effort is the well head equipment, and the water is probably the best I have tasted in a long time, but what are the people drinking?"

"They drink the water, obviously."

"No they don't. They laughed at me because I was drinking it, they were getting water for animals to drink not people. That water is more than good enough for people, so why don't they drink it?"

"I've no idea, ask them, not me."

"You ask them I don't want to appear any more stupid than I already have."

"And you don't mind me looking stupid."

"Of course not, I could easily cope with you looking stupid."

"Let's just keep walking, they may have a fountain of intelligence, that would stop us both looking stupid." Kevana laughed, and they continued their patrol around the village. They walked around the green and approached the tavern from the south, Alverana stood in front of the building and looked at it carefully.

"A problem?" asked Kevana.

"Not as such. If you stand where I am, and look away from this place, all the paths are coming straight towards here, they radiate from precisely this spot. Even the paths across the green, they all lead right here."

"I can't see any paths on the green, the grass is too thick."

"There are depressions where people have walked for many years, they lead here. Whatever is it about this village that is strange is here."

"No. Taverns are always like that, they are the centre of life here, people meet and talk, drink and eat, they make all the important decisions here."

"A village this size should have at least two taverns, not just one."

"How do you know there is only one?"

"I just do, I'd wager a fortune on it."

"I'll not take any of that, not if you are so sure."

"Shall we step inside and see what is so special about this place?"

"Why not? The afternoon progresses, let's just take a short look."

They walk up the steps on to the veranda, and take some seats at a table. A young girl came over.

"Good afternoon, strangers." she said, her voice soft and gentle. "What can I get for you?"

"What have you got?"

"We have beer, and we have food."

"We'll try the beer, what sort of food are you serving today?"

"At the moment we have chicken, and the mutton stew will be ready in a while."

"Just beer for now, then." said Kevana, looking around at the local people, who were all drinking beer.

"I'll be only a moment." she turned and went inside.

"Some of our brethren may not be too happy with us being here, or drinking beer." said Alverana.

"They can think what they want, we are soldiers and soldiers like a beer or two."

"I was just saying this could cause us problems." The serving girl came out and placed two tankards on the table. Both men pick up their drinks, and offering a silent toast, took a large draft each. They stared at each other, eyes wide. Each waiting for the other to speak. Finally it was Kevana that broke the silence.

"This is good beer."

"Now I understand why the people at the well were laughing at me, I am drinking water when beer like this is just around the corner. This is something special." whispered Alverana.

"Very special."

"We will have to tell the others about it, won't we?"

"Of course, in a place like this they'll be here before long anyway. After all this is the only tavern in the village."

"And now you understand why."

"Definitely, no one else could make beer like this. It has to be the work of a talented brewer."

"It is indeed, if I do say so myself." said a voice from the doorway.

"It is a truly great beer. And you are?"

"I am Garath." said the man walking slowly into the light and coming to sit at their table. "I am the humble owner of this establishment, or is that the owner of this humble establishment, sometimes I am a little unclear."

"The establishment is irrelevant, and the beer is anything but humble." said Kevana.

"Thank you. Your are?"

"Sorry, manners fled on a tide of ale. I am Kevana and this is Alverana."

"You are followers of Zandaar?"

"Truly we are, but today we follow someone else as well. We are pursuing some people that stole something belonging to our god. We aim to get it back. They came through here in the last few days?" asked Kevana.

"They did, and they know you are chasing, they went south. They also seemed to be looking for something."

"In this valley south is the only way out. What were they looking for?"

"I have no idea, something of mystical value to them, I think."

"Did they say anything about where they were going?"

"No. Very specifically, no."

"Specifically?"

"Yes. They thought it might be dangerous for us to know something that you may want, they said south and nothing more."

"We do have ways to find out the things we need to know."

"They said that as well, hence it was better for us that we didn't have any information to give you."

"I see, better for you or better for them?"

"Both really, I have given you truthful answers to every question you have asked, anyone in this village will do the same, the problem is we don't have anything to tell you that you don't already know."

"We could always test you to find out if you are actually telling the truth."

"But could you test everyone? You are working to a tight schedule, you really can't afford to waste days interrogating every person in this village, now can you?"

"Our method is time consuming and tiring, it could even take us weeks to test everyone here. Much depends on the strength of the minds we are dealing with, and judging by the young man that guided us here, they grow quite strong hereabouts."

"That would be Paulo, some say he is deliberately confrontational, but I think he just enjoys the sound of his own voice."

"We could find a place for such a one, if we had taken him in when he was younger, he has too many bad habits to break now, but then that would be a suitable challenge for some robust member of our clergy."

"You think of send such a man here, that would indeed be a challenge, for the strongest of men only."

"Actually I had thought of leaving one of our number here, to serve this community in Zandaars name."

"We have been told you might do that."

"What were you advised to do?"

"Resist, politely of course. You have one amongst you that you feel is up to the challenge?"

"Probably not, but I'd sure like to be rid of him, and I am certain that the people here will not want him around either."

"So why leave him?"

"I was only dreaming out loud. The more time I spend with this particular man, the more I come to believe I will have to do something about him, leaving him behind would make that decision someone else's, but if he comes with us, I think I'm going to have to kill him before long."

"This is not a good way to feel about one of your own, perhaps he should be persuaded to take a different path in life."

"He is totally beyond persuasion, he has a depth of belief that cannot be denied."

"Sounds to me like you have created a stick to beat yourselves with."

"In far too many ways you are right."

"I am sorry gentlemen, but I must leave you, I have things that need my attention, please enjoy the beer, and try the food, it really is quite good. I shall no doubt see you later." Garath levered himself to his feet and returned to the dark of the tavern.

"An interesting conversation." said Alverana.

"Yes. I'm not sure which of us learned the most there."

"I am."

"You are?"

"Certainly, you learned almost nothing about the ones we are chasing, and he learned a lot about us."

"I learned much by what he didn't say."

"What do you mean?"

"I don't for one minute believe that their resistance to a member of our order would be polite, at least not for one moment longer than it would take to arrange a fast death, and a plausible story. Looking around this place, I'd say that the priest concerned would be pig food in less than an hour, and a well documented departure to the north posted within two. I still like the idea."

"You couldn't in all honesty do that to one of ours."

"I know, but I can dream can't I?" Alverana looked sharply over Kevana's shoulder, two black robed shapes were walking slowly towards them.

"Worandana." he muttered. "Should we leave?"

"Too late now, he's seen us. We'll just wait for him here. Service!" He shouted the last. The girl came through the door as if she had been waiting in the dark for him to call her.

"Yes gentlemen?" she asked softly, a small smile on her lips.

"Another beer for each of us, and another for a friend who is almost here, and a drink of water for an old man, if you please."

"Certainly, only be a moment." she turned away with such speed that her dress flared upwards and revealed even more leg than it did before.

"Nice looking girl." said Alverana.

"Hush fool." spat Kevana, glancing over his shoulder.

"They are too far away to hear, and the wind is blowing in the wrong direction, stop worrying."

Carin brought the drinks out and put them onto the table just before Worandana arrived at the veranda. She turned to go back inside, and swept Gorgana with an intense look, and totally ignored the other man, after a moments pause she went inside.

Worandana wobbled slowly over to the table, and sank slowly into the chair, and then released Gorgana's arm, so that he could take his seat. For a moment Kevana ignored Worandana and passed a cup to Gorgana.

"Try that, you won't believe it." Out of the corner of his eye, he could see the tension in Worandana's face building towards an explosion. So he turned to the old man and missed the expression on Gorgana's face.

"We are here, in the cultural centre of this place, they have no church, they have no town hall, they have a bar as the place where people meet, so we are here. Problem?" Worandana's arguments were destroyed by this simple statement. This was obvious from his face so Kevana turned to Gorgana.

"Well?"

"It's beer. Its all right I suppose."

"Peasant. Have you no appreciation of the brewers art form?"

"I am sorry Kevana, but the study of beer has taken up exactly none of my time, however if you have a wine to offer, then you could expect a more extensive opinion."

"I am glad to hear that." said Worandana. "We leave the beer for the lower orders."

"Lower orders indeed." snapped Kevana, he knew he was going to have trouble, Worandana's opinion of beers is well known. A dark shape appeared behind the two newest arrivals, two large hands descended to the table, and released a small round shaped glass each.

"Be you gent's connoisseurs? Then try my humble offering." Said Garath.

"Thank you sir." said Grogana. "But the glasses themselves are works of art, no inclusions, no voids, a beautiful clarity. Are they made here?"

"Sadly no, we have no glass blower here, but I have a friend I buy them from in the nearest city, he does some excellent work, and will exchange enough glasses for a bottle of the stuff that is in them."

"A skilled glass blower will give you a glass for the contents?"

"Exactly."

Gorgana stood and took his glass from the veranda out into the sunlight. He held it up to the light, and swirled the contents. Then returned to his seat, sniffing the glass all the way.

"Sir. This is an excellent wine, colour a rich deep red, the smell is full of fruits and the acidic edges of lemons. From the way it hugs the side of the glass, it is quite strong as well." Garath only nodded. Gorgana took a small sip of the rich wine, and washed it around his mouth.

"Stop making a performance of it and drink the stuff!" snapped Kevana.

"Peasant." whispered Worandana. All eyes turned to Gorgana. The look on his face told it all. He swallowed.

"This is a truly great wine, it has all the characteristics of an excellent vintage, if anything it is the best I have ever tasted. You sir are an artist."

"Thank you." said Garath. "I think it's a little too tannic, but that could just be personal preference I suppose."

"The tannins make and excellent finish for such a well flavoured wine, I taste blackberries and blackcurrants, so strongly that they almost explode in the brain, yet there is a hint of vanilla under that, and something a little oily, I can't quite place it. A powerful and yet well balanced wine. You could make a great deal of money selling this."

"I have no need of money, I am a rich man."

"You don't live like a rich man, you work hard and long hours, serving beer to peasants, how can you be rich?"

"I have all the friends that a man can ever have, and a place to call mine. What more can a man need?"

"But you could make a fortune."

"I could, but I'd end up watching the beer and wine being made by someone else, and my life controlled by the price someone else will pay for my work. Rich perhaps but poor in other ways."

"I suppose. Don't you want to sit and watch while someone else does all the work?"

"Where is the fun in watching someone else do something that is best done alone?"

"But you could end up doing almost nothing."

"Where is the pleasure in doing nothing? Only a priest would come up with an idea like that."

"You don't see that as a good idea?"

"Of course not. There can be no reward for doing nothing. What is worth not working for?"

"I can think of many things?"

"Yes I am sure you can."

"You don't agree."

"Of course not. Anything worth having is worth working for. Something given for nothing has no value."

"That is a refreshing point of view and so rare these days, it seems that everyone wants something for nothing."

"Not around here."

"Right. All this aside, how much do you want for a bottle or two of this wine?"

"What have you to offer?"

"I have gold, not much but I have some."

"Gold I have no use for. Can you cut barley for beer, or grow vines for wine?"

"Of course not."

"Then you have nothing I want." Garath turned and went inside.

"Strange man." said Gorgana to Worandana.

"Not really, he lives in this place, and this is as strange as anyone could wish to see."

"Perhaps." said Kevana. "But it looks like a good place to live. They have no real problems with people or living, almost idyllic. Don't you think?"

"I agree." said Worandana, much to Kevana's surprise. "Taken in isolation from the rest of the world, then this is an idyll, but once the rest of the world gets involved, then things will change very quickly."

"I think you are right." Said Gorgana. "Outside influence is the only thing that can destroy this place. I have never seen people so innocent in their beliefs. It is a good thing to see. The barman could see nothing that gold could give him that he didn't have or didn't want."

"We will have to send someone to convert these people to the teachings of Zandaar, as soon as we get the chance." said Worandana.

"Why?" demanded Gorgana.

"Because they worship no god, and must be converted, that is part of the articles of our faith."

"But they have no need of gods here, and have proved it beyond any man's doubt."

"That is irrelevant, we are tasked with converting the heathen to the true god."

"They have no need of gods, ours or anyone's."

"Not important. We are avowed to convert the world to the service of Zandaar, that is what we must do." Said Worandana.

"If you try and convert these people, they will almost certainly rebel. I wouldn't relish the task, and can think of none that would."

"I am sure a team of five or six could convert this village to Zandaar."

"Five or six, may be able to do the job, but any less would only die." said Kevana.

"What do you mean?" demanded Worandana.

"I was talking to the brewer earlier, before you arrived, and it seems he has been warned about us, any priest sent here, or left here, to convert these people is living on borrowed time. I had been thinking about leaving Kirukana, that would give him a challenge he would survive or not, perhaps it might give him a different perspective on life, or he would die. Either way I'm not overly bothered."

"You mean they would kill a priest?"

"They would, to preserve their lifestyle, they certainly would, wouldn't you?"

"I suppose, but they need converting."

"No they don't." said Gorgana. "They have a thriving community here, something that has stood the test of time, why should we change it?"

"Because that is what we have sworn to do, we must convert the heathens to the worship of Zandaar."

"Even if they don't want it and don't need it?"

"Of course. There can be no exceptions, all must bow down to Zandaar."

"To send a team into this place would destroy utterly their way of life. Could you live with that?"

"What is your problem Gorgana? We live to serve Zandaar, and to convert others to such service. Why do you have such a problem with this fact?"

"I don't think these people need to be converted, their life is without conflict, they have almost no crime here, would you bring crime to them?"

"What do you mean?"

"Along with your team of conversion specialists would come a whole new batch of crimes for them to worry about, failure to observe this feast day, failure to attend services, failure to hand over their respective tithing. All these new crimes would come to them. Can you see this brewer handing over half of his production of wine to some priest?"

"He would have no choice."

"He would and I think he'd take it. Kevana is right, these people would fight to defend their way of life, probably to their last collective breath. Convert them then."

"Then the conversion would be complete."

"That is ridiculous, you'd kill them all to convert them to Zandaar?"

"What else can we do with those that refuse the only living god?"

"We could just leave them to live their lives without our interference."

"But we serve Zandaar, and he wants the whole world to serve him."

"Perhaps he is wrong?" asked Gorgana, knowing as soon as the words left his lips he had said far too much. This was the limit and he had stepped over it.

"You would question our god?" demanded Worandana.

"Only as tool for theological debate." he answered quickly.

"Good. No one can question the word of Zandaar, he is the only living god."

"Certainly, there can be no other."

"Glad you see it that way. Have you any idea where the nearest monastery is?"

"Perhaps the nearest city has one?"

"We shall have to find out, and get a team dispatched here as soon as possible."

"If that is the will of Zandaar." said Gorgana, in the most obedient tone he could.

"It is, and don't you forget it." Worandana was more than a little disturbed that someone could even suggest that Zandaar could be wrong, even in the slightest. Questioning the council was acceptable as they were only men, but to question the god was just too much. This man would have to be watched closely, he may be turning away from his faith. Turning to Kevana. "We really should be moving from here before you and your men get hooked on the beer and wine available in the bar. That is of course if you have collected enough information from these people." Kevana nodded and called for Garath.

"How much do we owe for the beer and wine?" he asked when the brewer appeared.

"Nothing. It is always nice to have visitors."

"Nothing?"

"Nothing at all, just take good word of us with you and we will be happy." Gorgana snorted, but said nothing, knowing that Worandana's eyes were on him.

"That we shall do. I can recommend this sort of hospitality to everyone." said Kevana. "Shall we return to our camp, and find out what is happening?" He asked, already climbing to his feet, Gorgana stood and helped Worandana up, then they all left the veranda and walked slowly across the green towards the camp.

"Did you find anything of interest?" asked Kevana.

"Nothing, this place is completely without any power or place of worship, they are in serious need of guidance."

"If you say so, but I agree with Gorgana, they should be left alone, any team coming here is going to lose some members, they will be killed by these kind people."

"Perhaps we'll just send a military force and wipe them out."

"What is it about these folk that offends you so?"

"They don't serve our god, and so should be converted."

"I don't think it's exactly that, it more that they don't serve any god, and seem to be doing quite well, and they are happy, they are smiling, and they don't care that you disapprove." laughed Kevana.

"They are disgustingly happy." agreed Gorgana, not actually laughing.

"Such frivolity has to be stopped." said Kevana.

"Enough." snapped Worandana. "We can't have an example like this for people to see, it could undermine the whole of our church, people would stop believing. That could be the end of everything."

"How many people see this?" demanded Kevana. "In the last year they have probably only had two groups of visitors, us and the ones before us, of course there are the ones from outside who trade with them, but that is all. I can really see news of this place coursing through the whole region and people turning away from Zandaar in their droves. This place is no risk to Zandaar, it should be left in peace."

"That is not the teaching of Zandaar. All the world must be converted before Zandaar can safely rule, you know the words in the book of Zandaar."

"I know them by heart, and still believe these people deserve to be left alone."

Worandana stopped, as if shocked into stillness. Slowly he looked at the ground, then he looked around.

"Gorgana. Can you feel it?" he whispered.

"Feel what?"

"Power."

"Where?"

"Beneath our feet."

Gorgana closed his eyes for a moment, then they snapped wide open

"Yes, I feel it, I wasn't looking for it, so I missed it. How did you feel it?"

"I felt it in the staff first."

"I see."

"Fetch the brethren, all of them, now!"

Gorgana left at a run, only to be followed by Worandana's shout. "Don't forget the books!"

"What have you found?" asked Kevana.

"Power, a huge amount of power, the like of which I have never felt, even in the presence of god. This is utterly beyond anything I have heard of. We should be able to use it. We should be able to achieve something important with all that power. But first I have to find it's centre."

"That's obvious, and there it is." He pointed to the single standing stone. Worandana forgot his age and ran to the upright stone. Once there he paced slowly around it, searching its sides for any symbols or markings, finding nothing other than signs of age. Tentatively he touched it, only risking a fingertip, he traced his finger around the surface, feeling for any sign that sight may have overlooked. He gingerly placed his hand on the side of the stone, and felt for its power, his touch was light, and his senses sharp, slowly the power resolved before him, it was a huge storehouse, a warehouse of energy, trapped, contained, stored. He needed a trigger to release it and a conduit to carry it, then he knew he could use it.

"Well?" demanded Kevana. "What sort of power is it?"

"It seems to be simply stored, awaiting the proper trigger to release it."

"And once you have found the trigger what do you intend to do with all that power?"

"Even that needs to be decided, there are many things we could do, but this will be a single attempt, once that energy is released I don't think we'll be able to put it back into it's bottle, it has to be used."

"They we have to be sure we are doing the right thing before we start."

"Definitely, but whatever we decide, that much power is going to be very difficult to control, we are going to need something to channel it, something to shape it to our purpose."

"What do you suggest?"

"The usual thing is a sword or a staff, something with intrinsic strength of its own, but we don't have anything like that."

"I have a sword."

"Not good enough, it needs to be something that was designed with the intent to perform this sort of task, any sword will not do."

"Your staff, it has been designed to work alongside you in certain aspects."

"Yes, but it is far too feeble, it would never carry the sort of load that is going to come out of that stone."

"What would it need to strengthen it?"

"It would have to be braced with precious metals, silver is best, it is physically stronger that gold."

"How about our silver flames? We could form them around the staff to strengthen it."

"We could, but that would use up most of the silver we have, I'd much rather find some other way."

"The blacksmith has some very special metal, he calls it the remains of a thunderbolt. Could that be used?"

"What other properties does this metal have?"

"He uses it for horse shoes, it sparks when the horses strike the shoe against stones, and it is harder wearing than normal iron shoes."

"We both know that is no thunderbolt, but it does seem to be meteoric in nature. We could try that." He paused for a long moment before continuing. "Yes. That should do nicely, make shoes for both ends of the staff, and bind it with wires drawn from the new metal. Then we should have a tool that could shape the power in this stone." Worandana turned at the sound of approaching foot steps. Gorgana was returning, his arms full of books, the others following him, at a distance.

"Brethren, brethren." called Worandana. "Gather round, we have work to do." he tossed the staff to Kevana. "Take this to the smith and explain what we need, but not why."

"He guards this metal of his quite jealously, this is going to be expensive."

Worandana reached inside his robe and withdrew a small pouch. He tossed this after the staff. "Try not to spend it all." Kevana snatched the pouch out of the air, and set of towards the smithy, signalling for Alverana to follow him, he knew that the first part of this task would mainly involve the skills of the clerics. It would only be later that the soldiers would be needed.

"Brethren." said Worandana. "This stone holds an enormous reservoir of power, we need to find the trigger that will release the power, I have Kevana getting something to channel it. I want to know how to set the power free, but in a controllable manner, I sense that if it was released without control it would make a smoking ruin of this whole area."

"That would be no loss." said Kirukana, speaking more freely than he had been, perhaps Kevana's absence had something to do with this.

"It would kill us too, and that most certainly would be a loss."

"It that case." smiled Kirukana. "Care is definitely indicated."

"I want each of you to feel this power source, I want to find out as much as possible, before we start to tamper with it." said Worandana, he stepped away from the stone and allowed the others to approach it. Gorgana didn't go near the stone, he walked away from it, slowly, Worandana stared at him as he stared at the grass, not really seeing it, but more seeing what was underneath, gradually Gorgana's steps became smaller and smaller, as if he was reaching some sort of boundary.

"Well?" asked Worandana.

"It seems to go very deep indeed. I can still feel the restraining force here, but it is a long way down." Looking back at the stone he was a good thirty paces away, slowly he started to walk around the perimeter. The path he followed wasn't circular, it was very irregular, between the stone and the mountains the pattern of force was very shallow and reached fifty paces from the stone before it vanished.

"Worandana." shouted Gorgana. "It is shallow here, and it suddenly stops, it doesn't go out of range, it just stops, I can feel the edge of the formation."

"What does it feel like?"

"I think it's some sort of rock, it feels jagged and disjointed here."

"So, we have some crystal or rock formation set up to hold energy?"

"I think so. But where does it get it's energy from?"

"Every answer brings another question."

"Always the way. And another. Who and why?"

"That's two questions."

"Yes, but the answer to one should give the answer to the other."

"Any one else with anything to add?" asked Worandana.

"It leaks." said Kirukana.

"Leaks?"

"Yes, it's energy is bleeding away very slowly, it radiates a sort of field, that is what you felt first, now another question, does it radiate because it is fully charged or does it just leak?"

"The feel of this rock makes me think that it charges suddenly in bursts, the rock has a glazed feel to it, sort of heat blasted." said Apostana.

"So." said Worandana. "We have a natural formation that has been changed to charge in bursts with power from some source, as yet unknown, for some purpose unknown, by some person unknown. We are doing well." He waved to Gorgana, who immediately stopped his patrol of the perimeter, and returned to the stone. "We'll try a group probe of the thing." The four men stood around the stone, forming a circle, each holding the hands of those next to him, Gorgana started a slow, soft, low pitched chant, which the others took up, gradually their minds came together and focused on the object between them, they touched it as gently as they could, as if they were trying to reach a living mind. The contact felt somehow slippery to the touch, like it was trying to avoid them, it kept turning away from them, but surrounded it had no where to go. Slowly before their minds eye an image started to form, a large crystalline shape, a green and slowly rotating form, its internal light pulsing with a slow and steady beat, they felt the enormous power that it had collect over a distance in time that they could not comprehend, it stretched back for a thousand years and more, slowly filling it's reservoir, and even slower it had expanded, gradually it changed the nature of the rocks around itself, turning them into more of itself, this expansion process took a great deal of time, and even more energy, but energy was not something it was short of. It had been a millennium since any being had tapped into the power it held, at least to any serious extent, and then it had been an accident, a fatal and destructive accident. Occasionally small amounts of power were tapped, but very small, and in the general scheme of things they were negligible. Suddenly Worandana felt one of them moving away, he followed slowly bringing all four away from the stone, back to consciousness of the outside world.

"Who broke away?" he asked as the hands dropped tiredly to their sides.

"Me." said Gorgana.

"Why?"

"I know how to tap that power, we simply have to tune the conduit to the frequency of its pulses and the energy will flow, then all we have to do is survive the blast."

"I agree, but what do we do with this power, it has to be something constructive, and something quite difficult."

"Something that is going to use a lot of energy, something risky."

"Certainly. Any thoughts?"

"Not at the moment, I'm a little tired."

"We all are, we'll rest and think about it."

They turned away from the stone to see a boy standing only a few paces away, with a dog obediently at his side.

"Are you having fun playing around our stone?" asked the boy, laughing loudly. "Only young children dance round that thing."

"Do you know what it is?" asked Gorgana.

"Of course, even the youngest of us know of the lightning stone."

"Why do you call it the lightning stone?"

"Because it likes lightning. I thought monks were supposed to be clever people?"

"We know of many things, but we have never before met a lightning stone."

"It's fun to watch but that is all, though looking at the sky I don't think there is going to be anything to watch today."

"Why is the sky so important?"

"You need clouds to get a thunderstorm, don't you even know anything about the weather?"

"We know weather and it's prediction, but I would agree with you, there will be no thunderstorms today, the day just isn't hot enough."

"Why does the day need to be hot?"

"Heat causes large bodies of air to move upwards, they form clouds and in extreme cases thunderstorms. But there are no clouds rising around here today."

"I am sure that it you hold hands around the lightning stone and talk about it for a while there will be more than enough hot air to make a storm or two." laughed the boy, turning away and walking back towards the main street of the village.

"That boy is beginning to irritate me." snapped Kirukana.

"He seems to be far too sharp for his own good." agreed Gorgana.

"But in some ways he is right." said Apostana. The others stare. "Well, you do talk too much some times."

Before the clerics had returned to their camp Kevana was approaching.

"Did the smith agree?" demanded Worandana. Kevana handed him his purse, but said nothing.

"Ye gods." said Worandana. "That was certainly expensive."

"Yes, but he does have some preformed wire, so that makes the process so much quicker. The staff will be shod at both ends with heavy pieces of metal, and spiral bound, both left and right handed, each place where the spirals cross will be soldered with silver."

"Could he not solder it with the new metal?"

"No, It's going to hard enough to solder with silver, without actually setting the wood on fire, the new metal is just too hard for that sort of thing."

"When will it be ready?"

"Tomorrow afternoon."

"Good. That gives us some time to think about what we are going to do with all that energy."

"There is a lot?"

"More than any one has ever seen in one place."

"Where does it come from?"

"According to the local know it all, they call it the lightning stone, it seems it attracts lightning, so that is were it gets it's charge, but it appears to have been here a long time, before the village was here certainly."

"So who built this thing?"

"We have no idea, but Gorgana has come up with a way of getting it to release its energy."

"Safely?"

"Who can say, we can but try."

"What can we do?"

"Rest to start with, and think." Worandana started walking back to the camp again, food was already being prepared, and he was feeling more than a little hungry.

"Could we just reach those thieves and burn them all?" asked Kevana.

"That would be fairly simple, the power available would make the search a matter of instants and setting fire to them and everything around would be easily accomplished."

"No. Without the thieves the sword would be more difficult to find, and could be taken by others, or damaged. No that wouldn't do at all." They sat beside the camp fire, and took the mugs of soup offered. Kevana drank but didn't taste the soup, his mind was elsewhere, and his taste buds were dreaming of beer.

"Could we just snatch the sword from them?" asked Alverana.

"That should be possible." answered Gorgana.

"No." said Kevana. "I want the thieves."

"Could we bring them here, or send us to them?" said Apostana.

"I have seen small objects and small living things moved over short distances." said Gorgana.

"Good." said Kevana. "We bring them all here and kill them."

"It took a hundred priests half a day to generate an energy pulse that moved a mouse ten paces, and two of them died."

"Two out of three is acceptable, we'll still have some left to kill."

"No, two priests died and one mouse moved across a room."

"Why did they even try it?"

"Someone said it could be done, and someone else said it couldn't."

"So it was merely a matter of pride?"

"It could be so. It was the last attempt in a long line of failures."

"No further attempts? I suppose volunteers were difficult to get."

"Certainly."

"Could we use the power of that stone to just bring one person here?"

"That is possible, I think, I'll check my books for the records of the other trials, they could give us some clue."

"How much of a risk would it be?" asked Worandana.

"That is very difficult to say, there are so many factors to be taken into account. It could be that a lack of power could cause a failure and that would be bad, it could be that the stone contains too much power, and that could be bad, it could be that the conduit fails, that could be very bad, and worst is that the stone might just decide to take rather than give."

"So what have we to worry about?" laughed Kirukana, scornfully.

"Those are just the biggest and most likely problems." said Gorgana. "There are bound to be many others that I haven't even thought of yet."

"But." said Kevana. "We could bring one of their number here, the one holding the sword."

"Oh yes. That is certainly a possibility."

"Then do your studying, find out what we have to do, tomorrow evening we get that sword back here, and the man that stole it. I am going to have a beer!" Kevana rose and stalked across the green towards the tavern, his intention was to celebrate in advance the recovery of the sword. Alverana looked a question at Worandana, who merely nodded. Alverana followed Kevana, hoping that it wasn't going to be too difficult keeping his friend out of trouble.

CHAPTER THIRTY SIX

"How can you sanction carousing when there is a serious task to perform tomorrow?" demanded Kirukana, staring hard at Worandana.

"For a man of action such as he is, the occasional drink is essential. However if you feel strongly enough about it, why don't you go and stop him. I'm sure we can manage tomorrow without you."

"Yes." said Fabrana. "You go and stand in his way, he probably won't even break stride to cut you down, you are after all so popular with him today." Fabrana chuckled softly as he returned to his soup. His intention had been to wait until the light had gone before going to try the beer, but he now decided to catch up with his leader as soon as his tasks were all finished. As it turned out he wasn't on his own. Gorgana had gone to see the smith and returned with a lantern and a pole to hang it from, the others performed all the tasks necessary in the camp and slowly set off to the tavern. Until only Worandana, Gorgana and Kirukana were left, huddled around the fire, pouring over the books. They discussed to relative nature of the chants they were going to use, and the forms of incantations that would support the staff that was to be the conduit.

"It's the failure of the staff that worries me the most." said Gorgana.

"And me." said Worandana. "It could be fatal for the one holding it, or everyone involved, or it could just stop working."

"How can we tell which it is going to do?" asked Kirukana.

"There is no way of knowing, it is one of those things that comes with experience." said Worandana. "And we just don't have that much experience of these things."

"I have used a focusing tool in the past." said Gorgana. "It was long ago, and it was only focusing a small amount of energy."

"Why were you doing that?" asked Kirukana. "While it isn't actually proscribed by the council, it is most certainly frowned on."

"I wanted to make a small change to something, that would have necessitated starting from scratch, several days work, so I asked a couple of friends to help me, we generated an energy pulse in the usual way, but I focused it through one piece of metal, and sort of melted two pieces of metal into one, the join could be seen, but it looked so strange that I doubt anyone could tell how it had been done. Even to this day there are probably only the three of us that know it has been done."

"Think about it Kirukana." said Worandana. "The blacksmith is making a tool to focus energy even as we speak, and tomorrow we are going to use it. Hopefully to good ends. It could be that when the council hear about this, and just what we have accomplished then such use of a tool may be banned, but until such time we are at liberty to try."

"You are the leader, you say what we must do, but you must also take responsibility for any judgement of the council."

"Have no fear Kirukana, your standing in the eyes of the council cannot be affected by anything that I decide to do, though I am certain that if things go well for us, then you will be amongst the first to claim the credit."

"That is not what I mean?" said Kirukana.

"Of course it is. Do you think I am a fool? You engineered your place on my team, either to forward your own desires, or to spy for the council. I have never been sure exactly which."

"You cannot mean that."

"Yes I can. You are a good priest, you have a strength that is useful, you seem to have the power of god behind everything you try to do, but you seem to miss the target a lot. I can't quite understand how you manage it, but your strength I can use, only so long as I am directing it. When acting on your own, you seem to lose focus, or miss the target or sometimes both. It is one of the things you could learn from Gorgana here, his focus is always excellent, and I have never known him to miss anything."

"Thank you." said Gorgana. "One tries."

"He is even more suspect than you!" snapped Kirukana.

"You really haven't had a good day, have you?" asked Worandana, coldly.

"That is just what I have heard, in Zandaarkoon."

"Kirukana you have made too many mistakes today, don't compound these with more lies. You let temper and vanity get the better of you. Now I know you are working for the council, and that they plan to bring me down. But you can still be of use to me, we have need of the power that comes with your belief in your own righteousness. You believe and that is enough for you. This brings you a power that is undeniable, but your control tends to slip. You lose focus for some reason that I can't quite understand. Any ideas Gorgana?"

"None that spring to mind, I shall have to give this some thought, if we can find some way to help Kirukana with the focusing problem, then he would certainly be amongst the most powerful of us."

"And if he can do that, by sticking to the council's approved doctrine, he is certain of a seat on the council, and perhaps even a good chance of leading it."

"I am here you know!" snapped Kirukana.

"There is the temper issue though." said Gorgana, totally ignoring Kirukana's outburst.

"Do you think he will ever be able to control that?" asked Worandana, now looking at Kirukana.

"Perhaps." said Gorgana. "If he can keep his temper in check then the rest may come naturally. It could be his temper that is spoiling his concentration." he then turned to Kirukana.

"Well Kirukana? What do you think?" asked Worandana.

"I think I am more than worthy of a seat on the council, and people like you who work outside the accepted doctrines should be controlled."

"Without people like us, the accepted doctrines would never grow, the power of the priesthood would stagnate, then die." said Worandana.

"It would have died years ago." said Gorgana. "If you had studied your histories properly, you would know this."

"What do you mean?"

"Two hundred years ago, the council was even more hide bound that it is now. And some fool decided that steel for swords was a bad idea, at least for some, and as such not allowed. Someone else decided the steel for any weapon was a bad idea, the total banning of steel took less than two years, except for the priesthood of course. We were allowed to have steel for swords, and steel for arrowheads, but the ordinary people were not. This gave the priests a distinct advantage, conversions followed, expansion ran amok. The militant orders couldn't keep up, they were spread so thinly that they became utterly ineffective. A group of barbarians came down out of the north, nomads with fast horses and long steel swords. They carved their way through the general population, like shit through a goose. They were eventually stopped at the very walls of Zandaarkoon. The council cancelled its edict about steel weapons and the barbarians were defeated, by sheer numbers in the end. Without the actions of a few wild priests, like us, your grand sires would have been slaves to barbarians."

"I wasn't aware that a council edict could be overturned." said Kirukana.

"Yes it can, but it takes a unanimous vote of the whole council to do it, and some members of the council didn't want to admit they were wrong."

"It must have taken a long time to get them off the council so the vote went the right way."

"Actually it took very little time indeed, after the first vote was counted, the motion was called to a second vote, and any council member that voted against died with a bronze dagger in his head. Elections took only moments. The priests taking over were the ones with an empty dagger sheath at their sides. The next vote was unanimous. Steel weapons were handed out to the peasantry and a counter-attack launched. The casualties were horrendous, but the barbarians took to their horses and went looking for easier meat."

"I have never heard such rubbish, there is no reference to any of this in the histories!"

"Not in the approved histories, no. But in some of the others, more difficult to find, the information is there, first hand accounts, names, dates, places. It all tallies, I have checked it all out."

"It cant be true, the council wouldn't countenance such action."

"The surviving members of the council only wish to carry on surviving. They saw no way to achieve this when some members wouldn't listen to reason. These sorts of changes have gone on all through the history of man."

"You are saying this could happen again, soon?"

"No. Those were very special circumstances, there is no threat big enough to cause so violent a change of leadership. At least not at the moment."

"If such a threat came along, could it happen again?"

"Oh yes, without a doubt. Ask yourself 'How many factions are there within the council?'"

Kirukana's eyes widened, he even went so far as to look over his shoulder, to see if anyone was listening.

"The next question is. Are you in the strongest faction, the most conservative, or the most radical?"

"I really don't know how to answer those questions at all, I have never even thought of it in those terms before. My patron tells me what he wants me to do, and I do it. So far it has been a very profitable relationship, members of the council meet with me, when I am in town, they tell of the plans that are in progress, and give me my tasks for the next few weeks."

"You have been attached to my group for a whole year now, and we haven't been anywhere near Zandaarkoon in that time. Your information is months out of date, you could even be working for someone who is already dead."

"I admit that it is a few weeks since I have had any contact, but I don't think that my patron is dead."

"A few weeks, they have contacted you while we have been on the road?"

"Yes, a few are powerful senders and I am a very good receiver, as you know."

"Of course, receiving needs a powerful internal focus, something you have in plenty, that is where your power comes from as well."

"Now you know I am working for the council, what are you going to do about it?"

"Well, realistically I find it hard to trust you, but equally I have no choice, nor do you. We are a long way from any sort of authority and we must act together to stay alive."

"Agreed. So we carry on as if this information hadn't actually come to light."

"Yes, I don't think the others need to know. Do you Gorgana?"

"I think it would be a bad idea to tell Kevana, that is for certain." Kirukana's eyes went wide at the thought of Kevana's reaction.

"No." said Worandana. "Kevana is almost certain to over react, without thinking, he's like that, and you are not his most favourite person at the moment."

"I shall have to be very careful around that man." said Kirukana.

"I think that you should definitely consider thinking before you open your mouth, some of the things you have said recently have created more than a little suspicion in that quarter." Kirukana merely nodded.

"To get back to tomorrow's work. Kirukana do you want to wield the staff when we tap that stone?"

"You would trust me?"

"Do you want to wield the staff?"

"No. As you say my external focus does tend to drift, and someone could get hurt."

"Good." said Worandana. "Gorgana?"

"Not particularly. It could be like catching hold of the tail of a dragon, the only way to stay alive is not to let go. I'd rather not."

"Equally good. However wrong. You have experience of working with a tool, and you know the forms we will be using, and you concentration is normally excellent. I have more confidence in your abilities to perform this than I have in my own. The task is yours. I am going to get some rest, I advise you all to do the same, I would like someone to go to the tavern and tell the others, Gorgana you better do it, but gently."

"Agreed." said Gorgana, both men rose from their seats and went in opposite directions, leaving Kirukana to himself. Kirukana sat staring into the fire, watching the flames, and thinking about his life, his choices, and his future. Gorgana walked slowly to the tavern, pausing for a while beside the stone, it's slightly darkened and pitted surface giving no clue to the power held within, only his trained senses could feel all that energy, sitting beneath his feet, waiting for release, almost eager for release. Resting both hands on the flattened top, he felt the power with his mind, slowly he tuned his mind to it, gently, with as delicate a touch as he could manage he reached towards that power, there was an instant of contact and he withdrew. He felt like lightning was coursing through him, he felt elated beyond anything in his experience, tingles ran up and down his arms and his legs, until he felt like his knees were going to give way. Stepping back from the stone, he felt the power subside, suddenly he wanted more, more power, more energy, just more.

"I'll have to be careful of this sort of thing it seems to be addictive. Probably the most addictive thing in the world, pure power and energy. I wonder if that is what it feels like to be a god. Zandaar has plenty of power, and a huge city to draw on at need. This power store may hold more than the whole city of Zandaarkoon, with this it may be possible to defeat a god, but one would need a conduit to carry all this energy." He whispered to himself, amazed that he could even consider the destruction of any god, let alone the one he served. He turned away from the stone, disturbed by the ideas it engendered within him. Slowly he continued his walk to the tavern, as he walked into the range of the twin braziers, he remembered his book, it was tucked unobtrusively into his belt. Stepping onto the veranda he was noticed by the others.

"Gorgana." said Kevana. "Join us please." Alverana kicked a chair out for the younger man to sit on, which he did.

"Carin." shouted Petrovana. "Another beer please, my dear."

The girl appeared in moments and placed a mug of beer in front of the new arrival.

"I have been sent." started Gorgana.

"I know." said Kevana. "We have work to do tomorrow and Worandana would like us to have clear heads when we are ready to perform."

"That is true."

"We will be fine, we've had very little to drink and a beer or two does help one sleep."

"I'll give it a try, but I much prefer a good wine."

"Wine is far more likely to give you a thickhead in the morning and you wouldn't want that, now would you?"

"I suppose not, a beer or two can't hurt. I have given the message if you choose to ignore it, there is nothing that I can do is there?"

"Very true. My rank is the same as Worandana's, and I see that you need the therapeutic quality of beer. So drink up. Has everything been sorted out to Worandana's satisfaction?"

"Yes, it's all decided. And I am chosen as the sacrificial goat."

"What do you mean?"

"I get to wield the staff and the power it releases."

"A most singular honour."

"Indeed, and both a responsibility and a peril."

"I am sure that Worandana has every confidence in your abilities."

"I am probably the best person for the task, but the amount of power in that stone is truly terrifying, the thought of it turns my bowels to water."

"All you have to do is control it, direct it, and convince it to do what we want of it."

"That sounds so easy."

"From my point of view it is simple. All you have to do is focus on the task, and not let anything get in the way, and fear is the thing most likely to do that to any man."

"Have you ever tried this sort of thing? The focus required is beyond most peoples understanding."

"How do you mean?"

"You think it is easy. Let's try an experiment, I'll pick something simple for you not to think about, this is not life threatening, this is just an avoidance test. Do you understand.?"

"I think so, you tell us what we mustn't think about and then we see how long we can do it for. Seems simple enough."

"There is no test other than a man's honesty, I have no way to know what you are thinking, you have to own up when you fail this test. Understood?"

"Sounds easy, we'll all do it." Kevana's eyes scanned those around the table and forced nods from each.

"Fine." said Gorgana. "My next statement will start with a word, a thing you mustn't think about, and when you do you raise your hand, is that agreed?" Slowly he looked around the table, getting nods from everyone.

"Chair." he said. "This beer is actually quite nice, it takes a little getting used to, but it is far better than most of the others I have tried, it has a clean taste and a sharp aftertaste, good hops used to give it, just the right amount of bitterness." All through this short sentence hands were being raised, until only Kevana was left, Gorgana leant back in his chair and sighed, then slid the chair slowly across the floor. Kevana's hand raised.

"See." said Gorgana. "Once you know of something you mustn't think about it becomes very difficult to do it."

"That was very hard." said Kevana.

"What were you using to help you focus?" asked Gorgana.

"I was singing a song in my mind, it worked until I heard your chair move, then I just couldn't help my self I had to think about a chair."

"You ask me not to think about failure, when such failure could kill us all."

"But your mind will be very busy at that time, you cannot afford to think of anything other than the task in hand."

"True, but right now failure is very large in my mind. There are just too many ways this thing can go wrong."

"And when it goes right, you will have beaten them all."

"Would that I could see it that way."

"I have confidence in you, you will be fine tomorrow."

"I hope so, I wish I could persuade Worandana to try something else, but he is determined. I think he sees this as a chance to perform something really different, and you see it as a chance to get that sword back, neither of you are going to walk away from this opportunity."

"Zandaar wants this sword, and I am going to place it in his hand. Worandana wants the glory of tapping an ancient energy source, which will give him a chance to thumb his nose at the council and all their restrictions."

"You two are both the same, the council will not be happy with either of you if you succeed. They don't like anyone to do well unless they are working exactly as the council decide."

"We do tend to make up our own rules as we pass through this world, but we always get the job done."

"The way the council are beginning to think is moving away from such freedom. They are only interested in total obedience, nothing less will do."

"I can only do what I do." said Kevana, slowly he pulled his chair backwards and rose. With a wave he gathered all the others, they all rose to leave the tavern.

"I think I'll stay a while." said Gorgana. "I have much to think about."

"Don't get too drunk." said Kevana. "If you think the council are getting restrictive in their thinking you have no idea. You try going against Worandana, then you'll know what restraint is, because he'll show exactly none."

"I understand. I need some time alone, call it meditation."

"I'll tell him you're meditating on tomorrows challenge." said Kevana turning away.

"Can't I meditate some more?" asked Petrovana. A look was all the answer he got, in a few moments Gorgana was only black robed priest on the veranda. Staring into the depths of his mug he swirled the dark liquid around before he sipped it. He was thinking about the risks that he was to face tomorrow, and though the others were involved the primary risk would be his, his failure could damn them all to an instant death. Through this reverie he suddenly felt a presence by his shoulder. Turning that way he saw the serving girl, she had a bottle in her hand.

"The master asks if you would prefer a glass or two of wine?" Her voice was soft and light.

"I would certainly prefer some of that good wine, but I must decline, I must stick to beer, if I was to start drinking wine now, I probably wouldn't stop until the next winter came around. Beer I can cope with, I can put the mug down and walk away. How about you, which do you prefer?"

"I am like you I prefer the wine, except when the sun is really hot, then a cool beer goes down much better."

"That is very true, but when the weather is hot, how can you keep the beer cool?"

"The cellars are deep, that way they are less affected by the temperature on the outside, and there is water running down the walls, which help to keep things cool."

"What is it like living in a quiet little town like this?"

"Quiet. Sometimes too quiet." She looked around the veranda at the rest of the customers then decided she was going to have a break from serving and sat down next to Gorgana.

"Must be very peaceful."

"We can go for years without seeing a single stranger, and then two whole groups come through in a matter of days."

"Did the thieves cause you any problems?"

"They were perfect guests, and great company."

"They are violent and desperate men."

"Funny, that is exactly how they described you."

"You met them?"

"Of course, I was serving beer and food as always, they were here drinking and eating and telling tales. It was a night that will be remembered here for many a year."

"Can you describe them to me?"

"If you wish. They had two leaders, one an old soldier, and one an ex lord. Both had hard eyes, eyes used to giving commands, and very unused to those commands being disobeyed. The soldier told one of his men that he was to entertain the gathered company with tales from their travels, Mander was unhappy to be chosen for this task, but after a brief protest he started with his stories. Some were funny, others sad, but all were worth listening to. For a soldier he was a surprisingly gentle man."

"What of the other leader?"

"He was a little aloof, but he drank with the others, and stayed very close to his lady, I think they are very much in love, even if they don't know it. One of the men got so drunk that he fell out of his chair, the lord and his lady moved like the fastest of lightning bolts, they were on their feet in an instant, his sword in his hand, and her axe fair humming as it swung up. That is when the party broke up, after all they had to leave early the next day."

"You have seen the man and he was holding the sword?"

"The blade was a funny sort of colour and the pommel was a large black jewel. Is that the sword you mean?"

"I believe it is, and he was actually holding it?"

"Haven't I already said that?"

"Sorry my dear, but I was told that no man could hold it."

"Oh, he could hold it, it looked like part of him, it looked like he had been using it for years. Who ever told you the no man could hold it was wrong."

"That is hard to believe, but believe I must. What sort of man is this lord?"

"He seemed honest enough, a little separate from the others, even though he was sitting with them."

"These others, what were they like?"

"Soldiers for the most part, not barbarians, if you know what I mean, they were nice. The old man was nice too, if a little strange."

"How strange?"

"He seemed to be watching everything at once, were ever you were his eyes were on you. I asked some of the other people, because I thought he was just staring at me, but he wasn't he was looking at every one and everything that was happening. He put his wooden walking staff in that fire over there, and it didn't burn, it just sat there bathed in flames, and it didn't burn. Is that strange enough for you?"

"That sounds strange enough to me. What did these people do here?"

"What to any normal people do in a tavern, they drink and eat and enjoy themselves. They did seem to be very happy that you were trapped in the mountain, it helped them to relax for a time."

"That shall end soon enough. We have to get that sword back."

"Is that piece of metal worth all this risk, he wont want to give it up?"

"He'll have to, our god wants it. He wont stop until he gets it."

"If he wants it so badly, then he should come and get it for himself."

"He has sent us to get it for him."

"Why?"

"I am not entirely sure, but this thing is powerful, so he wants it where he can control it."

"And once he has it he can control you and the rest of us?"

"He already controls us, and he doesn't know about you yet."

"So he will control us as soon as he finds out?"

"No. Why should he bother with a tiny little town so far away?"

"How does his empire expand?"

"It just does, slowly step by step."

"Each step arranged by men in black robes, how many tiny little towns have been swallowed by you and yours?"

"Lots. I suppose they all get swallowed up eventually."

"And what happens to the people?"

"They become part of the biggest religion in the world."

"Whether they like it or not?"

"Perhaps."

"New rules to follow, new laws to obey, new restrictions on thoughts and actions, new crimes and new punishments."

"It doesn't always happen like that."

"You lie. Your kind always lie, they offer a better future, but only for themselves. Worship our god and everything will be fine. There will be no more droughts, no more famines. These are the things you promise, and when the droughts and famine come again, then it is our fault, we have not observed all the new rules diligently enough, we have had the wrong thoughts, plotted against our god, and so he has punished us. Now we must work even harder to appease him, we must please him or the droughts will never end, we must give up our sons to his priesthood, and our daughters to his soldiers, until there is no one left. This is the way new gods come to town. We want none of yours here!"

"I can understand the way you feel, but there is little I can do about it. I think that my leader wants to send a priest here, the sort that specialises in conversion, and I think he will succeed. There are some of us more worldly than you would know, they are the ones that win over entire towns, I know of one who took over an entire city in a matter of weeks."

"We would not be an easy place to convert."

"Perhaps, but there is usually a way, a way that doesn't involve bloodshed, or any violence at all."

"It's only after you own the place that people start to die."

"No. We are only here to help, our priests bring you nearer to god, and to everything that comes from him."

"I have no need for anything from your god. I have enough here."

"But you cannot know the joy of the pure service to a power such as Zandaar."

"I know enough of joy thank you. And so do those you are chasing."

"What do you mean?"

"They are people who have a real joy for living, they know how to do it in style."

"But they are soldiers they live to kill."

"No, they kill to make a living, and they only kill when they need to, they don't sneak up on people in their dreams and kill them in their sleep."

"Who would do such a thing?"

"Your kind. That is one of your favourite techniques for taking over a town, isn't it? Kill the opposition while they sleep?"

"Where did you hear such a tale? Oh. I know. That lord told you. Didn't he?"

"He warned us that you can do these things."

"It is true that some of our people are called upon to remove certain hindrances, but this happens very rarely, not something as a matter of everyday action. Where a soldier would stick a knife between someone's ribs, we make him face his own fears, not many people can do that and survive."

"I know one who can, and has done."

"Who?"

"The man with the sword, the one you chase. He was killed by one of your priests, but he came back from the dead, and then turned his own methods against the priest."

"That cannot be, no man can come back from the dead."

"Namdarin can, and those with him witnessed him perform the feat."

"Namdarin. Yes, the man we are chasing appeared to have died, died in a fire, but he then got up and walked away. So what you say is true, and we have been after the same killer all along."

"What are you talking about now? You're not making much sense? Have you drunk too much beer?"

"No. The man we were originally after destroyed a whole monastery, single handed, he killed every man there, most of them while they slept, but the abbot managed to set the black fire upon him, though he died as he performed the task. Namdarin got up and walked away. But he came back, some days later, and killed a lone investigator. He tortured the monk before he killed him. When it comes to barbarism there are few to match him. Then we met Kevana, and set off after his thief, now we know for sure that the thief and the murderer are one and the same."

"Think about what this man has accomplished." She smiled, and leaned closer.

"He has destroyed a monastery, and every one in it, then he killed a priest, turning his own methods against him, somewhere in the middle he died twice, then he takes a weapon from it's protected hiding place, after killing the guardian, that isn't actually clear, but a possibility. Then he goes to Melandius and kills the minstrel, in his sleep behind a locked door. He makes a deal with the snow demons and wins free passage for himself and his friends, gets passed the snake and brings the cave down on the rest of us. There may have been other 'adventures' for them in the mean time."

"Quite a list."

"Your point is?"

"You are going to try to kill this man, and his friends, I think you need more men, and that you had better be absolutely certain that he stays dead, because I think he will be without any form of control if you kill his friends."

"You think he is under control at the moment?"

"He is a kind and thoughtful man, he cares for those around him. If Jayanne was to be killed then the barbarian underneath would be freed."

"How do you know?"

"According to the tales that have been told in this place, your brothers burned his house and his family, your bad fortune was that he was out hunting at the time. The barbarian came out for a while, and killed a few of yours, then he met Jayanne and the others, the barbarian went back into hiding. If you release him again then there will be no stopping him, and it seems even death has lost its power over this man."

"I see. We shall have to be very careful with this man, when we meet him."

"You think you are actually going to catch him?"

"I am sure of it, and sooner than he thinks. Though I am not sure that his death would serve any purpose, unless of course such is decided by Zandaar himself."

"You would take this man before your god to be killed?"

"I am certain that Zandaar can force death to take this man on a more permanent basis than he has of late."

"Have you thought that may be what Namdarin intends?" said a new voice, Paulo came up to the table and sat beside Gorgana.

"How long have you been listening?" asked Gorgana.

"Long enough. Well?"

"Why would Namdarin want to be brought before Zandaar, it is certain death for him?"

"You see it as certain death, only because you cannot see any other outcome. Perhaps Namdarin sees with better eyes than you."

"What do you think he could see?"

"Maybe the certain death goes the other way, perhaps your god dies. Namdarin would certainly like to kill him, he has the best of reasons."

"I cannot imagine such a thing happening."

"Oh, well. If it exceeds your imagination then it cannot possibly happen. Can it?"

"An interesting thought, but not one I would favour. Why should Namdarin be successful? Zandaar has brought peace to more towns and cities than a man can visit in a lifetime."

"True." said Paulo. "But what has changed since he brought peace?"

"What do you mean?"

"How have the peaceful people grown? How have they advanced? What new things have they learned?"

"The common people have no need of learning, they have no need to change, they are happy with their lives as they are."

"We are happy here, but your people are going to try to turn us into slaves of Zandaar."

"Followers of Zandaar are not slaves, their lives are their own to do with as they will."

"Only within carefully defined boundaries, try to bring something new to the people and you'll end up imprisoned or dead."

"How can you say such a thing, you know so little about us?"

"I know enough, I can see more than most. I have heard the way you speak of us, you have nothing but contempt for us and our little town. Your soldiers are simple plain speaking men, they are not going to be our problem, it is the clerics amongst you that are going to cause us the most pain."

"Worandana is a good man, and tries to bring many new beliefs and practises into every day use, he wants to expand the knowledge of man. Just as I do."

"No. He wants to expand the knowledge of Worandana, for him knowledge and power are the same. Kirukana on the other hand is utterly different. He hates the fact that others may know more than him, he wants to burn our town to the ground, I have seen it in his eyes. Only Kevana keeps him in check, and that may not last."

"You have nothing to fear from Kirukana, Worandana has just put him on a very tight leash. He will be no problem for you. Why would we burn down your town?"

"Because we are unlikely to bow to your god, some of us are very independently minded."

"I had noticed that, actually. It is sort of difficult to miss when a certain young man keeps throwing it in our faces."

"I wonder who you mean?" laughed Paulo, he stood and waved a quick good bye, before turning away and walking off into the deepening gloom.

"It certainly gets dark quickly here." said Gorgana.

"It's a thing called night, it happens regularly in these parts, I couldn't say about the rest of the world, as I haven't been there, but the stories I hear seem to say that it happens everywhere."

"It does indeed, but I haven't witness such a rapid descent of night for many a year, not since I was far to the south, there night seemed to rush in, like someone had thrown a blanket over the world."

"What were you doing in the south?" asked Carin leaning towards Gorgana, he glanced briefly at her dress, seeing the creamy mounds of her breasts pressing against the thin fabric, and for the first time, he noticed a subtle musky aroma, that seemed to emanate from her cleavage.

"Err." He stammered. She laughed softly as he stared into her eyes, a view no less disturbing than the previous one.

"We were looking for the ruins of an old temple, in the desert to the south. Worandana had found a reference to it in an old book, and he wanted to see if there was anything left, anything that could be of use. So we crossed the southern sea, a short voyage of only five days, but five days I will never forget. I am not a good sailor and the weather was dreadful, huge waves, and howling winds. On the fourth day the captain said that we would be putting into port, but he couldn't actually say which one, as soon as he found a safe place to lay up out of those gales, that is exactly what he did. Worandana complained that this was no port, it was a cove with a beach. The captain said that his ship was not moving again until the winds changed, as far as he was concerned this is a good a port as any. He sent men ashore to fill the water chests at a river that could be seen flowing across the beach. Hunting parties went ashore to gather fresh meat and vegetables. It looked like the captain was setting up for a long wait, so Worandana ordered the horses brought out and boats lowered so we could all go ashore. As we crossed the beach I looked back at the ship, it seemed so calm in that little cove, the sun was flashing on the waves, it looked like an ideal place to rest for a while, but Worandana wanted to be on the move, he knew that we had to get across a large stretch of desert and back again before the summer came to it's full heat. We followed the river upstream, only a short distance back from the beach it came down a steep cataract, not a waterfall as such, but pretty close to one. It was hard going for the horses, but we made it to the top of the escarpment, the river was running in a shallow gorge, we were a hundred feet or so above the flow. Open grassland all around, after those days on the ship, it was a wonderful sight. There was a herd of wild horses in the distance, they seemed undisturbed by our presence, but they were a long way off yet. Worandana set a course across the green, it wasn't what I was expecting to see, it looked so fresh, I thought we were going to a desert, this was far from a desert, though we still had a long way to go. As we crossed the plain of grass, it was quite long in places, the day began to get really warm, the sun beat down like a hammer on the head."

"Black robes probably didn't help too much." laughed Carin lightly. Gorgana smiled and continued.

"By the time the sun reached it's height we were desperate for shade and water. Worandana turned towards the river. The banks were high, but there were paths down, the river had mud and sand and rocky beaches almost like a sea shore. It was hard to find shade under the high banks but we managed it for a while, the horses stayed in the water and kept as cool as they could. Worandana had said that we would rest for an hour, but that quickly passed with no lessening of the heat. We stayed by the river for three hours, each of us removed as much clothing as we could, our skin was not used to sunlight so we had to keep at least one robe on, and those were liberally soaked in water before we mounted the horses. It felt very strange to be so undressed, we spend all our lives wrapped up in layers and layers of black, it was a liberating feeling to be wearing only a thin black sleeping robe. Crossing the plain of grass was a little easier when wearing so little, but the sun was still a heavy weight upon our heads, the horses weren't doing any better than us, the wild ones were fine, they weren't carrying any weight. The stallion came close to have a look at these strange shaped horses that were crossing his territory, but he didn't like the smell of men that was all about them, so he pawed the air screaming, then galloped off back to his herd, and began moving them away from us. We were about half way to the mountains ahead of us when the sun went down. It seemed to grow in size as it approached the horizon, huge and deep red by the time it's lower edge touched. Impressive though the sight was a sudden movement to the east attracted my attention, there was something huge and dark out there in the distance moving, and moving towards us, at an incredible rate. It looked like a dark tide, rushing across the grassland, coming straight at us. I called to Worandana and pointed at the approaching menace, he just laughed at me. Then I realised that the approaching hoard was merely a shadow, when the shadow reached us, the sun was gone. There was a brief and intense sunset, and the stars started to show. It took only a few minutes and the day had fled entirely, night had come. We were stumbling across the plain in almost total darkness. Starlight is not enough to ride by, but the horses of course see much better than us, so it is better to let them find their own way. The two major moons rose at the same time, this made riding so much easier, but the loss of the suns heat was noticeable, slowly at first, then with gathering speed the temperature started to fall, until we were shivering with cold, and dragging our robes from our packs. Those were some seriously uncomfortable days, scorching hot during the day and freezing at night."

"But did you find what you were looking for?"

"Yes, we crossed the mountains, and went down into the sand of the desert, horses are not the best thing for crossing soft sandy desert. Did you know that the desert peoples use a different sort of beast for transport in the sandy places?"

"No, what is it like?" She was leaning even closer to him now, her breath was actually warm on his face. He wrenched his eyes away from hers, and mumbled a little before getting his mind clear enough to describe the beast in question.

"It is like a horse in that it has four legs, but that is where the similarities end." He glanced briefly into her eyes, and noticed two jugs of beer arrive as he looked away. Using this interruption he took a huge draft on his beer, finished the first one, and then started on the second, the cool liquid felt somehow warm going down, his neck started to feel a little hot where the collar of his robe was rubbing against it.

"Go on." She said, putting her jug of beer down.

"They have feet more like a cat, not clawed, but with wide spaced toes, for spreading their weight over a much bigger area, so they don't tend to sink into the sand. Their faces are different, they have huge eyelashes to keep the sand out of their eyes, and nostrils that can be closed. The strangest thing about them is their walk, they move both legs on one side at the same time, they sway quite alarmingly from side to side. Trotting and galloping are much the same as for a horse, but these aren't designed for speed, they are designed to walk all day in the hot sun, I was told that they don't actually drink water, except perhaps once in every five days, but I just didn't believe that. How can any animal live without water for so long in a place that hot."

"Perhaps they store it somewhere in their bodies?"

"They are a strange shape, but to store enough water for five days travel, that can't be done. Our horses were in a bad way by the time we found someone to guide us to the waterhole. Well he didn't actually guide us, we merely followed his tracks."

"In that case you were lucky he was going to a waterhole, not coming from one."

"I never thought of that at the time, we didn't know that there animals could go long between water holes."

"Very lucky none the less." She put her hand on his arm, briefly, he felt the heat of her body for a moment, then it was gone, she had picked up her mug and taken another drink. Somehow he missed the touch of her hand.

"I suppose." he said, pausing to have another drink. "There were quite a few of those strange animals and their riders at the waterhole, it took Worandana a while to find one that could actually understand what he was saying. It was quite funny to watch him trying to communicate in sign language that we needed a guide to take us to a place that had a name that they wouldn't understand." He laughed loudly at the memory, Carin joined him in the merriment, and placed her hand on his arm, this time it stayed, he took a drink, this time with his left hand, not wanting to disturb her small hand from its resting place. He stared into her eyes for a long moment, then went on with the story.

"Our guide turned out to be a fourth son of some minor noble, he didn't actually have to work for a living, but he preferred to be away from home and the bickering that went on there. He had picked up the language of the southern traders when he was in a port some days away, it appears that he spent most of his time there getting drunk and a very small portion trading salt to the desert people. The latter more than paid for the former, he was actually far better off as a trader than he ever would have been as a fourth son. He had heard of the ruins we were looking for and though he didn't actually know where they were, he did know which people to ask about them. The next day he came to our camp, long before the sun was up, he was still drunk, Worandana was very upset about such an early start, but Naseem, that was he name, I had forgotten it until just now." He smiled at her and she returned the smile quite warmly, her hand tightened briefly on his arm.

"Yes. Naseem insisted on an early start, it is essential to get moving before the day gets too hot. All our water bags had been filled so off we went, Naseem led the way, he had two of the desert beasts, he seemed to switch from one to the other without a moments thought, and with a fluid grace that was surprising for a man so drunk. He set a fair pace, our horses were having to trot to keep up, those desert animals have such long legs, they barely seem to be moving but a shorter horse has problems keeping up."

"They must have been something special to watch."

"Not really, they are ugly, not just their shape, or the way that they move, but their temperament, that was the ugliest of all. Sorry that isn't entirely true, the ugliest thing about them was the smell, they plain stink."

"Horses aren't exactly odour free you know." She laughed softly, sniffing delicately.

"I am sorry if my smell offends, but there are precious few opportunities for bathing on the road." He pulled away from her, but her hand clasped his arm tightly.

"So why do you miss out on an opportunity when it comes your way?"

"You have a bath in this place?"

"We have a bath, and hot water to fill it, would you like to try it for size?"

"At the moment more than anything in the world. I suddenly stink of horse sweat." he laughed. She stood slowly, taking her drink in her right hand, and keeping hold of his hand with the other one. He stood and smiled. Carin nodded towards the table, where his mug of beer lay, laughing he reached out and took it. Carin led him through the darkened interior of the tavern, and out of the back door, across a small cobbled courtyard, and into a low roofed building at the back of the tavern. She walked through the heavy wooden door, into a small room, lit by three bright lamps, there was a large fire burning in a hearth on one wall, but the room was dominated by the huge tub in the middle of the floor, Gorgana was open mouthed with amazement, he had never seen a bath so big, leaning over he looked inside.

"It's huge." He said. "How do you heat enough water for this thing?"

"There is a metal tank in the chimney, the fire heats it." She said, she let go of his hand and checking that the bath was sealed she went over to the fireplace, and pulled a lever downwards. Gorgana heard a rushing of water and water started to pour out of a pipe at the edge of the bath, and run down a sluice into the bottom. Curls of steam drifted from the sluice and from the depths of the tub. Carin laughed at the look on his face, then she pulled on the second lever, more water ran into the bath from the other sluice this time.

"That one is cold water from a tank on the roof. The hot water on its own would boil you alive, and we wouldn't want that now would we?"

"Definitely not, but how did you come by such a thing as this?"

"Simple really, the tub itself is a variation on a beer barrel, the heating and the plumbing are part of the brewing process, nothing magical about it, just a little thought and some skill to build." She guided him to the bench by the wall, the wall had a series of hooks fastened to it, clothing hooks. She turned and leaned into the tub, swirling the water with her hand, checking the temperature, and giving Gorgana a long and close view of her body, barely hidden by the thin material of her dress. She looked back at him over her shoulder and caught him staring at her behind, he snatched his eyes away and grabbed his beer hiding his face in the raised mug, Carin laughed and went over to the wall, raised the levers, and spoke softly. "Your bath is ready, it shouldn't be too hot for you, though you look a little hot right now, or is it the heat from the fire, making your face red."

He said nothing but drank some more of his beer, finally realising that the mug was empty.

"You get in the bath, I'll go and get us some more beer." She turned and went out of the door, leaving him to his thoughts. He was more than a little disturbed by what was happening, he was certain that Worandana would have some harsh words to say if he knew exactly where Gorgana was. 'Harsh words.' He thought. 'More than harsh, perhaps. If this is supposed to be wrong why does it feel so good. The slightly fuzzy feeling of good beer, not as good as a really good wine, but still it feels good. The company of a woman, even if she is little more than a girl. How can this be wrong? This hurts no one.' Slowly he removed his clothes, looking at his body he realised for the first time that he was loosing weight, his clothing was getting loose, he was loosing fat, and gaining muscle. 'Not too bad for an old man.' He thought. He walked around the bath tub and climbed up the steps set into the end, reaching down he felt the luxury of hot water on his hand, and slowly lowered himself into it, the tub appeared even bigger when he was in it, he could stretch out his legs and barely reach the end, it was possible to lie full length in this bath, and there was more than enough room for at least one more person. As he lay in the water he had his head resting on a step at the end of the bath, and his feet resting on a similar step at the other. 'If I was to sit on the step then there would be enough space for four people to sit in this bath, very friendly.' He had never heard of communal bathing before, never even thought of it, but it did strike him as an interesting idea. He was musing on these ideas when the door opened, in walked Carin, a large jug in one hand and a smile on her face.

"Is the water warm enough?"

"Yes. It's wonderful, I can't think how long it is since I had a real bath."

"I really like the feel of hot water, it's far better than a quick dip in a river, especially round here, most of the rivers are really cold even in the height of summer." She said filling two mugs from the jug. Perching on the edge of the bath, she handed one to Gorgana, and took a sip from the other. She merely glanced at his naked form in the water, and he fought the urge to cover himself, it felt very strange to him to be naked in a room with a woman, it was in fact something he had exactly no experience of.

"There are some people in the world who believe that bathing is bad for a person, they say it makes you ill."

"How can that be?"

"In some ways they are right, if you bathe in dirty water, then there is a good chance that you will get ill, even the cleanest of mountain streams can have a dead sheep in it just a hundred paces up stream, and then you could be exposed to whatever illness it was that killed the sheep."

"Well I don't think you have anything to fear in the water here, it comes from a well, a deep and clean well."

"That's a thought. How does the water get up into the tanks?"

"The brewer has a wind powered pump, it works very well when it is windy, sometimes he has to deliberately stop it pumping, if it's too windy then the pump will work itself to death."

"It's certainly the biggest bath tub I've ever seen." He sat up and took another drink.

"It's the only bath tub I have ever seen." She said. "Are they usually smaller?"

"Oh yes. Much smaller, they are normally a tight squeeze for one person, not like this one."

"Where's the fun in that?"

"Bathing isn't supposed to be fun."

"Why not?"

"You know, that is a question I have never thought to ask."

"Perhaps you should ask more questions, Paulo says that the only way to find out anything is to ask, and he just never stops."

"I had noticed that, but he does appear to know a lot."

"I don't think he knows all that much but he thinks about things a lot, he is a very serious young man."

"Do you think he is too serious?"

"Yes, I think he should have more fun, perhaps you are the same in many ways."

"You could be right there, we monks do tend to take everything too seriously."

"Especially yourselves."

"How do you mean?"

"You all seem to think that you are so much better than the rest of us ordinary people, or do you call us 'commoners'?"

"Perhaps we do tend to look down on ordinary folk, but I would never call you in the least bit common."

"And you must find it awfully hard to look down on me, when you are lying naked in a bath and I am fully clothed above you."

"I was just beginning to get used to the idea of being naked in the same room as a woman, and you have to go and mention it, I'm sure I'm going to blush."

"If you blush anywhere I'll see it." She laughed. "Let's even things up a little shall we?" She stood slowly, and faced him, she reached behind her head and did something to the fastenings of her dress, then with a simple shrug of the shoulders it fell to the ground. He gasped at the sight of her naked body, her small breasts with the upturned nipples, her soft flat belly, her long legs. She smiled at his reaction, it being all that she had hoped it would be. She took a slp from her mug, then walked around the tub and climbed in next to Gorgana. She sat down with her thigh resting against his, and her shoulder against his upper arm, her hand on his hip.

"That's better." She said. "Now I am lower than you and you can look down on me."

"Actually I much preferred looking up at you."

"Why?"

"For some reason your nearness makes me very nervous."

"You don't have to be nervous of me, I'm not going to eat you, well not too much." She laughed aloud, and drank more beer. He drank more to hide his embarrassment than for thirst, his mind was on other things, things he knew he shouldn't be thinking. She turned towards him, her left breast brushed against his arm, and she looked up into his eyes.

"Are you sure you'd rather I was out there?" she whispered, and smiled.

"Er, no, not really, I don't think so." His stuttering reply, his body frozen solid, he was suddenly more frightened than ever.

She laughed again and drank, she put her mug on the side of the bath, and then moved away from him, his breathing eased and his tension lessened, but only for a moment, she was suddenly at the other end of the bath, facing away from him, on hands and knees, reaching for something that was resting on a ledge built into the bath side. His view of her backside, and her femininity took his breath away completely. She turned her head around and caught him staring.

"Do you like the view?"

"Er." He snatched his eyes away, like a guilty schoolboy. "Er. Well. Yes."

"I have been told that I have a very nice ass."

"Er. Er. Very nice indeed. I'm sure."

"What do you really think?"

"It's very pretty, that's for sure."

"And how many ladies asses have you seen?"

"Including yours?"

"Including mine."

"Including yours, er, one."

"So how can you judge?" She sat back down next to him, this time with the soap in her hand.

"Part of my studies has included anatomy, but the real thing is very different from the pictures in the books."

"You have studied anatomy? That I find surprising, I'd have thought your studies were entirely devoted to your god."

"Yes, and no, by studying people we learn to help them, by helping them we can get them to trust us, and we can bring them to the service of our god, that is why so many of my brothers turn out to be physicians. They travel across the lands treating the sick, and helping the injured."

"But that is all a propaganda exercise to increase your following."

"That as well, by bringing these people into the fold we help them, and remove many of the causes of conflict, we help prevent wars, and famine."

"That is a little irrelevant considering your current position."

"What do you mean?"

"While you are discussing religion, your bath is getting cold." She laughed.

"Perhaps the heat of our discourse would warm the water." He laughed.

"Perhaps the heat of something." She smiled, reaching out she drank some more beer. He did the same. While his back was half turned towards her, she started to rub it gently with the soap, small circles around his shoulder blades to start with. He put his mug down and turned away from her, so she could reach easier. It felt very unusual for him to be treated in this way, he had no memory of it ever happening before.

"That feels really good." he whispered.

"It's supposed to." she changed her attentions to his chest. "You certainly are hairy, are you sure your mother didn't have a thing for a gorilla?"

"I have no memory of my father, he died before I was old enough, so I can't really say, though people do say that he was an ordinary man, and a good one. I found no one with a bad word to say about him."

"Did anyone mention how hairy he was?" She laughed, slowly taking one of him arms, and washing it from the shoulder to the hand, in slow smooth movements. She reached across for his left arm, and started working on that one, his right hand was now stuck with no where to go, so he rested it on her soft thigh, the sight of her breasts so close made him want to reach out and touch them, but he made do with gently stroking her leg. When she had finished his arm she turned around and started on his feet, he enjoyed the view of her behind so much he just had to reach out and touch it, gently he stroked her buttocks, moving his hand in slow circular motions. She worked slowly up his legs, her hip resting against his, when she got as far as his knees, he sat up a little and ran his hand slowly up her spine, feeling every little bump along the way. He softy stroked her neck, she leaned back into his hand, she liked the feeling of his hand on her neck and shoulders, his masculine excitement was now obvious, poking its head out of the water and twitching with every motion of her hands. As she worked up his thighs the twitching became more noticeable, and his breathing a little ragged, she hitched her body towards him, and raised her self slightly. He ran his hand slowly down her back, and over her hip, down her thigh, his mind was subsumed in the sensual pleasure of the warm water and her attentive touch. He moaned softly as her hands reached the top of his thighs, his body lifted involuntarily towards her. Gently she grasped his swollen member and washed it with both hands, the movement was more than he could bear, with a sudden thrust his passion was spent in a small fountain. His body shuddered with the aftermath, gradually settling down, it was minutes before he could speak, and all that time she just lay alongside him.

"Was that good?" she asked once his breathing had slowed to a reasonable rate.

"It was certainly a pleasure, but how can I decide if it was good, I have nothing to judge it against?"

"You mean you've never done this before?" her voice raised in utter disbelief.

"Not exactly. I've always been alone before." his voice a guilty whisper.

"Well, you've had your pleasure, now I want some."

"Again you are not in the best of hands, I have no experience at all of this sort of thing, it is seriously frowned upon in our order. You'll have to help me, tell me what to do, I am a quick learner."

"What is the rush, we have all night."

"I need some sleep, I have a large responsibility tomorrow."

"Have no fear, you'll sleep, and sleep like a baby. But first give me your hand." She laid on her back and pulled him towards her, so that he was propped up on his right arm, leaving his left for her to do with as she would. She guided his hand to her breast, and rubbed herself softly with his callused palm, he enjoyed the feeling of her hardening nipple, and moved his hand over to the other breast, looking at the nipple standing proud from the small but firm breast, he had an irresistible urge to suckle on it. So sucking gently on it he kept it hard while his hand worked the other one. She pushed her chest up towards his mouth, gasping as he sucked harder. Taking his hand again she guided it slowly downwards, across her flat belly, and down the soft fur of her womanly mound. He felt the soft coarseness of her hair, and teased it gently, pulling on it softly, twisting it into rising twirls that curled back on themselves as soon as they were released. Sucking firmly on her left nipple, he reached down further still, until he found the top of her opening, and there was a small bump, as he touched it her body arched upwards against his hand, and she moaned loudly.

"Oh. That feels so good." she whispered. "Gently."

He rubbed his fingers softly around the small bump, until she was almost writhing with the intensity of the sensation, then he reached down and cupped the whole of her mound in his hand, rubbing the heel slowly from side to side, and pressing inwards with his fingers. She grabbed his hand and forced it harder into her body, pushing his fingers inside, moving them in and out, quicker and quicker until she let forth and strangled scream, that came out more as a gurgling noise deep in her throat, her body pitched and rolled, creating waves that washed from side to side of the bath, almost escaping from the confines of the tub. Slowly she settled down into the water, breathing in ragged gasps, resting her head on his shoulder, her eyes closed, and her body limp.

"Was that all right?" he whispered.

"Are you sure you've never done this sort of thing before?"

"Never."

"For a man with no experience, you are doing just fine. There is still much to learn though."

"Isn't that always the case, for everything a man learns ten new things can now be learned."

"Well I wouldn't say ten, but there are a few things you can learn before morning. Is this water getting a little cold?"

"I really hadn't noticed, a little distracted you know?"

"It's getting cold." With this statement she jumped to her feet, and stepped out of the tub, reaching the fireplace in one dripping stride she pulled down on the hot water lever, only this time she wasn't in any way gentle with it, the pipes gurgled merrily and steaming water came rushing out of the delivery sluice, almost threatening to overflow before it got to the bath. Gorgana watched the water running from her hair, it flowed smoothly down her back, and into the crevice of her buttocks, where it disappeared from view, only to reappear as a puddle between her feet, he barely noticed the temperature of the water around his feet rising as his eyes focused on her breast moving slightly to the pace of her breathing, suddenly she yanked the lever upwards and returned to the bath, she jumped over the edge and splashed into the water, scattering droplets all over the room, she dropped to his side with a huge sigh and a laugh, stirring the water with her feet to equalise the temperature.

"That's better." She said, smiling at Gorgana. He smiled back, his mind taken over by the colour of her eyes, a deep hazel, almost violet. She lean towards him, and closing her eyes, she kissed him, a light touch of the lips, he returned the kiss in a similar fashion, then he kissed her harder, pressing his lips upon hers almost fiercely. She grabbed his head and pulled him towards her, kissing him harder than ever, her tongue forcing its way between his lips and exploring his mouth. He opened his mouth to let her in, and wondered at the feelings engendered by this action. She moved above him and straddled his body, kissing him all the time, not wanting to let go for a single moment, her weight settled slowly onto him. He felt her soft mound pressing against his pelvic bone, moving slowly with a gently grinding action, he was amazed by the fact that his own body was able to respond so eagerly to her touch, in only moments he was hard and ready for her again. She felt his erection between her legs and reached down to grasp it. She rubbed it against her buttocks as she pressed herself against its root, slowly sliding up and down. His hands were busy holding onto her breasts, stroking and fondling them, rolling the nipples until they were almost as hard as he was. Slowly she raised herself, and after a moment of careful positioning, she sank downwards again, this time with him firmly inside her. He moaned at the sensation that filled his body and mind, this was something he had never experienced before, a total feeling that absorbed his entire being. Rocking slowly backwards and forwards she brought herself to a rapid climax, the pulsations of which did the same to Gorgana, with a savage thrust he emptied himself into her. She crashed to his chest and lay briefly, breathing hard, before she rolled off him. Again she rested with her head on his shoulder, her eyes closed, and her body quivering, the ripples in the water slowly spreading to the edge and bouncing back to mix themselves in total confusion.

"How did that feel?" asked Carin.

"That was wonderful. Is it always like this?"

"Not always, but it should always be a good thing, it should be a pleasure for both, not just for one."

"I think I understand, and I also understand why it is forbidden to our priests."

"Why?"

"Because it is too good, too much of a distraction, it certainly saps the energy, I haven't been this tired for a very long time. No, priests shouldn't be exposed to this sort of temptation."

"You would probably be surprised by the number that have."

"What do you mean?"

"This is a primal urge in man, not something that can be denied, very few men can go through life without at least trying it once. Usually when they are young, because that is when the need is the strongest."

"Are you saying that most of the priesthood have broken the rules as I just have?"

"I'd judge it to be about three out of every four, many only the once, and then they understand the nature of the thing, and use the resistance as proof of their own power over themselves. Others will hunt it out at every occasion that they can, without being caught of course. And the rest take up every shade in between. The ones that don't try it have no idea what it is, or its power over people, they only know what they read in books, and that can never give the whole truth, because this thing is from the time before words, before language, and before thought."

"It could be that you are right, but I think the figure is more like four out of five, just thinking of my own group here in this place, I am only certain of one man. This morning I was certain of almost all of them, but now I have doubts, how have you done this to me?"

"I haven't done anything to you, we did it together." she laughed, and sat up in the water, with a few quick flicks of her hands she washed herself quickly and stood. "The water is getting cold again." she said. "Let's go somewhere else and continue our discussion." She stepped over him and out of the tub, taking a large towel down from a peg on the wall she started to dry herself, he quickly followed suit. As soon as he stepped out of the bath, she reached in and removed the large disc that was blocking the drain, and the water started to rush out with a loud gurgling.

"Where does the water go?" he asked.

"Into a large tank that empties into a small stream that runs down the back of the brewery, waste water is carried away in the stream, a bath full like this gives it a good flushing out, helps to keep it clean, stops it getting too smelly."

"Good idea. There seem to be many of those here, far more than I am used to seeing in such a small place."

"We do have a few bright people, and we look after them."

"How do you mean, do the thinkers get to sit around all day just thinking while everyone else sees to their needs?"

"No. We allow them to keep on thinking whatever thoughts they like, we don't restrict their ideas in any way, there are no thoughts that aren't allowed in our village. Can you say the same for yours?"

"No. Some things are unthinkable, and I suppose restrictive. Where do you intend for us to continue our discussion?"

"I have a room above the tavern, it is small but cosy, it will have a fire burning by now, and there may even be another jug of beer in it, seeing as this one is almost empty."

"Somehow I do have a bit of a thirst at the moment, I can't exactly think why." He laughed. She joined the laughter and held his hand briefly, staring into his eyes. She stepped forwards and kissed him, he felt her body pressed against his, he put his arm around her waist and pulled her against him, the heat of contact set his pulse to racing again. Reaching behind her back, she took his hand and pulled if from around her waist, stepping out of his grasp she held that hand and draped her towel across her shoulder. She pulled him gently towards the door. As her free hand took hold of the door handle he stopped and resisted the pull.

"What's wrong?" she asked, softly.

"We can't go out there."

"Why not?"

"We're not dressed."

"And?"

"People might see us?"

"And?"

"It's wrong."

"Why?"

"It just is."

"Now you see what I mean about restrictive thinking. You have been taught that nakedness is wrong, bad, wicked, and therefore forbidden, like so many other things."

"I suppose, but what if children see."

"Children find out soon enough, and nakedness in itself is not wrong, it is how people react to it that can be wrong."

"If you say so."

"Right. Shall we?" She pulled gently on his hand, he reached down and picked up his towel, and draped it much as she had, but with more care. She smiled, opened the door, and stepped out into the courtyard. To his great relief there was no one about, only the moon and the stars witnessed his nearly naked walk across the yard, and up the exterior staircase to the first floor. In through the door, and along a dimly lit, and very narrow corridor. She opened a door and light came flooding out to spill across the corridor, stepping inside she occluded the light for an instant, then turned to witness his entrance. She took him in her arms and kissed him.

"Now that wasn't too bad was it?" She asked, closing the door.

"I suppose not, but there was no one to see us." He said, taking in the room with a sweeping glance, it contained little more than a bed, a small cupboard, that doubled as a table, and a fire. There were two jugs, two mugs, and a fairly large basin on the table. She went over and poured beer into the two mugs, carelessly dropping her towel on the floor, she turned towards him, her naked glory revealed in the soft light of the lamp above the bed, she handed him a mug.

"No one that you could see." she said softly, smiling.

"What do you mean by that?"

"I think that there was probably someone watching and probably very close, but they'd not show themselves unless they thought they were needed."

"I still don't understand."

"Any one in the tavern tonight, knows what we have been doing, because they know me. But they don't know you, so they wont trust you, I would put gold on Paulo at least being somewhere close enough to protect me if you chose to get violent."

"You think I could do that?"

"No, not now, but some people don't take it too well when their beliefs get challenged, some respond in an exceptionally violent manner."

"So, you took quite a risk being here tonight with me. Why take such a risk?"

"I read people very well, I could tell that you are a thinker, an intelligent man, and one having a little trouble with his life at the moment, you are not the sort of man to attack a woman."

"What do you mean, trouble with my life?"

"It is plain to see for anyone with a talent that you are having some problems with your chosen life, your reactions to your fellows are just a touch too slow and forced, you respond as you think they expect you to, not as you should respond, you are showing them someone who is no longer real, not real nor true to you."

"How can you see all this, do you see into peoples minds, like some sort of witch?"

"The mere fact that you make that sort of accusation confirms that I have seen truly, I see how people feel, I don't read thoughts, only reactions, and you react far more truthfully to me than you do to them."

She stepped in close and put her arms around his neck, she kissed him thoroughly, long and deep, his reaction was more powerful than before, he responded in a way he didn't expect, thrusting his tongue into her mouth and exploring it, feeling her teeth, and her tongue, tasting her and drinking of her. She broke away and sat upon the bed, patting the coverlet with one hand as an invitation for him to sit beside her.

"Now that is real honesty. A reaction from the heart. Truth." She sipped her beer while he thought about it.

"You are right in more ways than you can know. I have begun to question my choice of joining the priesthood, long before today. Not true. It's not that long before today, it's only a matter of a few days, though it seems like a lifetime, and every time I open my mouth I tell a lie."

"Do you lie to them or to yourself?"

"Some of both. I can't help but lie to them, they wouldn't understand the way I feel, but I fear that I lie to myself as well." He took a large draft of beer, almost finishing his mug in one, the warmth in his throat did little to thaw the chill in his heart. He sat next to her on the bed, not actually touching but close enough for the heat of her skin to be sensed by his own naked thigh, his towel as forgotten as hers.

"What have they done to make you feel this way?" she asked draping her arm across his shoulders, and leaning against him, her right breast resting warmly against his arm.

"I joined the priesthood to learn, and now these people would destroy something unique, something unheard of, something unknown, just because it stands in their way."

"What is this something?" she whispered, tension obvious in her voice.

"Not your village." he said, his eyes finding hers and seeing fear. "Not your village, we found something strange in the mountain, a rock that had a mind, a simple and slow mind, but a mind none the less, and Worandana decided to destroy it, just because it was in his way, he would have if I hadn't saved some of it, it is much reduced but it still has some small consciousness, with luck I will be able to return and study it after all this is done."

"This sort of thing I important to you?"

"Very. I joined the priesthood so I could learn things, things that can't be learned anywhere else, now, they just destroy."

"So what will you do about this?"

"I have no idea."

"They'll catch you out, you know that, sooner or later you will speak without thinking, probably when you are tired, or surprised. Then, what will they do?"

"They will most likely kill me."

"That would be a sad day."

"Why would you say that?"

"You are good man, any day a good man dies is a sad day, sad for the world, there just aren't enough good men in the world."

"How can I be a good man, some of the people I am with want to burn your entire village down as a place of heretics, they want you all hanging from trees, as an example to others, an example that happiness can only be found in the following of Zandaar, to be happy any other way means death."

"But you won't let that happen will you?"

"I'll do everything I can to stop it, but what can I do, I am only a follower?"

"I am certain that you are going to do something really spectacular, I don't know why, but that is what I feel, you are going to amaze them all."

"How can you say something like that?"

"Why shouldn't I say what I want, or what I feel? You have a strength inside you that the others cannot even hope to match. The only limits on you are the ones that you impose yourself."

"How do you mean?"

"All you have to do is believe in yourself, and you can achieve anything you wish, anything that you can believe, that you can do."

"And what do you wish?"

"I am happy with my life, and I wish it to continue, that is all, I am a simple country girl in a simple country village."

"You are anything but that. You are intelligent, you are a thinker, easily as sharp as Paulo, who I think is still close enough."

"Probably. He's young, but he'll make a good husband, once I've shaped him a little." she whispered, leaning close to his ear. Gorgana laughed out loud, wondering about the young man, who obviously cared a great deal about Carin, and had to be within earshot of their earlier activities. How could a youngster stand to listen to the woman he loves making love to another man? 'Making love.' He thought. 'Not something I even thought to happen to me, but it has, and I have to deal with it.' He looked into Carin's eyes, seeing something that was definitely not love, nor hate, it was something else. 'Why has she done this with me, not to me, I was more than willing, even desperate. Why me?'

"Why me?" he asked, his voice low and gentle. Her eyes opened wide as if surprised.

"Why do you think?"

"Easy target alone in a bar."

"Alone because your friends had left you so, a man with a story to tell, and a pain to reveal. Not easy by any means, but certainly worth a chance."

"A chance for what?"

"A chance to learn something, and perhaps to teach something." Her eyes were wide and focused tightly on his, this was a moment of decision, that was clear to him.

"Have you learned something?"

"Yes."

"Have you taught something?"

"Have I?"

"Perhaps." He fell backwards onto the bed, being careful not to spill any of his beer. "This is a situation I haven't been trained for, it is difficult for me."

"Something new. How long since something new happened to you?" She looked down at him, smiling a small and innocent smile.

"New. Everything is new on this trip. Or perhaps a variation on something old, but something truly new. No, not really, you are certainly something new, and unexpected." She reached down and put her mug on the floor, then she leaned slowly towards him, until her face was just above his, she paused for a moment or two, and then reached down and kissed him, he responded his tongue urgent in her mouth, seeking and searching for whatever it could find. His breath came faster as the kiss went on, suddenly she broke away, a cheeky smile on her wet lips, she kissed him again, this time on the chin, then on the throat, tickling his adam's apple with her tongue, then further down, running her tongue across his collarbone, and slowly down to his left nipple, through the coarse hairs on his chest. As she circled his nipple and suckled it he stroked the back of her neck, and her shoulders, making her shiver as if with cold, he kept his touch as light as he could, like the feel of spider silk. She moved onto the bed so she was on all fours, kneeling across his body, she trailed her tongue across his chest to the other nipple, and circled it until it was as hard as the left one, moving slowly she turned so her breast was over his mouth, he reached up and took it, sucking hard teasing the nipple with his tongue. He bit gently until she gasped with excitement. His free hand reached across and fondled the curve of her buttock, stroking her thigh, reaching round the curve of her leg, towards the centre of her womanlyness. She move slowly down his body, kissing him every inch on the way, probing his navel with her hot tongue, causing a momentary giggle, which was instantly suppressed. He gently probed her opening, feeling the dampness of her, her breath caught as he slowly pushed two fingers inside. She trailed her tongue through the coarseness of his pubic hair, until she found the base of his penis, she kissed the shaft, taking as much of it as she could in her mouth, she traced a line all the way to the tip and back, watching his back arch as she did, he moaned as she retraced the line back down again, she turned round slowly until she was in a position to move her knee across to the other side of his head, then she was straddling his head, she lowered herself onto him, so that he could taste her, he licked all around her mound and the folds of her lips, she sucked hard on his penis, taking as much as she could into her mouth. She wriggled her hips until he was licking and sucking at her clitoris, when he sucked it hard she let out a strangled scream, muffled by his presence in her mouth. She worked his shaft with one hand while licking all around the head of his penis, a second time she clenched in orgasm and ground her body against his face, the salty lubricant squeezed out and smearing his jaw, running down his neck and into the bed covers. Faster she worked him until he could take no more, and he exploded in her mouth, hot and salty, and sort of musky. She slumped on top of him, quivering with release. After a moment or two she rolled off and turned around, she kissed him firmly, he tasted the salt of himself in her kiss, and he held her close. They didn't speak for along time, just rested in each others arms, warm and comfortable, as the sweat of their exertions cooled on their bodies he realised that he would have to go, he couldn't stay here, far too many questions would be asked. The decision made all he had to do was implement it, but that was harder than he had imagined, he didn't want to move, he was cooling quickly, but he didn't want to disturb Carin, he could tell from her breathing that she was almost asleep.

"You'd better get into your bed, or you'll get cold." he finally whispered.

"You mean that you are not going to stay?"

"I can't, there will be far too many questions asked now, if I was to stay all night, it would be impossible."

"I understand." she muttered, crawling into her bed, and holding onto him for a little while longer.

"I shall never forget you, or this night." he said, knowing that he was unlikely to see her again. She said nothing just turned over and went to sleep. Without a moments thought, or even a glance at his towel, he went out of the room and along the corridor, out into the yard, he stood at the top of the stairs and briefly stared at the stars and the moon, smiling he went down the stairs and crossed the yard, into the bath house. He dressed slowly, as if he really didn't want to, being dressed in black again seemed to signify the end of something that he wanted to continue, but dress he did.

Feeling somewhat sombre to match his clothing he left the bathhouse, and walked slowly around the tavern, the moon was casting enough light to see by, but only just, the shadows around the walls were the most intense black, even darker than the caves. Once he was clear of the building the green in front of him showed as an expanse of silver marred only by the intrusion of the lightning stone, a black bar that rose from the sea of silver, like some battered tooth. Slowly he approached the upraised darkness, knowing that in tomorrows light he was going to be tapping this thing, draining it of all its power. When he arrived at the stone he placed both hands on it, and sank to the ground, the cold damp of the grass made him a little uncomfortable, but he was un-concerned. Gradually he tuned his mind to the resonance of the stone, feeling for its power, trying to find a trigger, he tweaked it and prodded it with his mind, trying to find some way to open it up, but it was stubbornly quiet, he didn't want to fail in front of his friends, but if he had to use force to open this, then there would be problems, a flood of power that would be very difficult to control, it would need to be channelled in a hurry, so a target would be needed, something close, no something far away. 'I wonder if I can channel the power into the sword?' He thought. 'It's certainly far enough away, there would be almost no possibility of a backwash, but it would be hard to send so far.' Pushing these thoughts from his mind, he concentrated on the rock, trying to focus on its slow pulsating cycle, every time he thought he had tuned in, it suddenly skipped a beat and changed its cycle, and he lost it again. After a few attempts with the same result he broke away.

"What in all the hells do you want?" he muttered beating the stone with his hands.

"That is simple." said a voice from behind him. He turned round quickly and there was an old woman, wrapped in a heavy shawl.

"Who are you?" he asked

"I am Anya. You are?"

"I am called Gorgana. What is it that this stone wants, please tell me?"

"I'll show you. If you'll step aside." He moved away, she slowly approached the stone, she placed both hands on the flattened top briefly, then took a knife from a pocket of her shawl. Slowly, with great care she used the knife, first on one palm, then the other, shallow cuts that bled quite profusely. Gently she placed both hands on the top of the stone again. There was a moment of tension then a sudden surge of electricity, she appeared to light up from the inside, awash with a hot white light, the energy suffused her whole body then gradually subsided. As she stepped back from the stone her shawl fell open to reveal that she was wearing nothing underneath it. Gorgana noticed the differences between her elderly body and Carin's youthful figure, but it was the light in Anya's eyes that attracted his attention, they seemed to scan the green like bright and tightly focused lamps, they caught his and held them, gradually the light in them faded.

"How do you feel?" he asked.

"I feel wonderful, I come here regularly, the energy gives me a lift that can last for days, sometimes even weeks."

"But it could be doing you harm."

"No, I'm fine, I am fitter and healthier than anyone else in my family, and I am the oldest."

"Have you told any of them about your visits here?"

"No, my grandmother told me, well she showed me, and made certain that I told no one."

"Have you ever noticed any changes in the strength of the energy?"

"No, it doesn't seem to matter how often I come here, the power if always the same, and I don't take much of it anyway."

"Have you any advice for me when I have to try it.?"

"Only one thing, keep enough power when you break the link to heal the cuts in your hands, otherwise you'll just have to wait for them to heal as normal."

"You use this for healing?"

"Yes, but I have found that like my grandmother I can only heal myself. It would be good to be able to heal others, but I cant."

"Is that why your grandmother showed it to you, she needed help to get here?"

"Yes, she was very ill, she couldn't even cut herself properly, I had to do that for her, it took some persuading that first time I can tell you."

"But it made her well?"

"Oh yes. It took a few visits, but she was fit and well inside a week, some people said it was magic, that she was a witch, another reason I have kept quiet about it."

"I think I will give it a little try tonight." said Gorgana. Anya solemnly passed him her knife saying. "Make the cuts shallow, that way they heal easier."

"You speak of healing yourself, is this an easy thing?"

"In some ways yes, for cuts and obvious injuries it is easy, but for something more complex on the inside it is much more difficult, though I feel it is only a lack of understanding that limits the healing power."

"Is it possible to heal another person?"

"It is, but the problem again is the same, it is easy to know where you hurt, but to fix another's hurt is hard, because you don't know exactly where it is. I have tried a time or two, but always in the most dire of circumstances. People have an aversion to being covered in another's blood, and the blood is essential, it is part of the nature of the power."

"Well I am about to give this power a little try, will you stand by and help me if I need it?"

"Of course, young man, can't have one of you dying on our green, now can we?"

"I suppose that would cause some problems for you."

He took the knife in his right hand and started towards his left with the blade, which was more like a razor than a knife.

"No." Said Anya. "Cut the right hand first, it is easier to hold the knife in a slippery right hand than a slippery left one." Gorgana nodded and swapped hands. He was surprised by the ease with which the knife cut through the flesh of his palm, it went a little deeper that he liked, not that any of this was really likeable. He passed the bloodied knife to Anya, she carefully wiped the handle on the edge of her shawl, then put the knife in a pocket. Gorgana rubbed his hands together to ensure that the blood was evenly distributed, he glanced at Anya, she nodded for him to proceed. Gingerly he placed first one hand then the other on the top of the stone. He felt a strange twist deep inside him, like something had just grasped his soul, then a flood of energy, like the opening of a flower blossom, it grew and burst, and grew and expanded, it was forcing his consciousness outwards, making him feel bigger than his physical form.

"Shut it down, it will try and fill you with all its power, and that will certainly kill you, close the connection, it will be hard, but you must do it." Using the flower analogy he made the flower shrink back as if night was coming and it was time to sleep, once the flower was only a small bud, the power it was releasing was manageable, he could feel it pouring into him, his tiredness was gone, hunger erased, the buzzing of beer in his head evaporated, he felt hot and alive in a way he never had before. Even in the darkness of the night he could see everything around him, he could smell the green grass, and the horses, even the slight tang of yeast from the brewery. He felt the coarse cloth of his robe rubbing against his skin, and the clumsiness of the shoes on his feet. Reaching out with his mind as he would on a search, he scanned the whole valley in a moment, seeing the hot points of light that were people, and animals. Reaching south he searched for the sword and the man with it on his back, he was burning energy very quickly in this search, and the further he reached the more he burned, he could feel his hands getting hotter and he pulled more power from the stone, he didn't want to open the flower any more, the flood would have burned him, he definitely needed something to channel all this power. Pulling his mind back to himself, he started to shut the flower completely, only remembering at the last moment to hold onto enough power to heal himself. Thinking a clearly as he could about the cuts in his hands, he focus on the edges of them, and wielding a soft white fire he healed the cuts. When the fire was extinguished his hands were whole, the blood gone, and only the tiniest of lines to show that he had even been injured at all.

"What in all the gods were you doing?" demanded Anya.

"I was looking for someone and something, why?"

"You were throwing beams of light all around, bringing daylight to the whole town, I was expecting that damned cockerel in the tavern to start his racket any moment. How do you feel?"

"I feel great, the best I have ever felt, is it always like this for you?"

"Sometimes, but I don't use as much of the power as you do, I only help myself with it."

"Perhaps there is something about using the power for non-selfish reasons."

"I see!" she snapped.

"Sorry that didn't come out exactly as I intended, I merely meant that using the power for something outside yourself, not just for your self. It is hard to project the power outside, but then it is something that I am used to. By all the gods I feel good." His eyes strayed to her nakedness, and lingered for a while, she seemed unconcerned about her condition, so he didn't think it was his place to point it out to her, anyway he found the sight of her a little exciting.

"I always feel really good, sort of warm and I don't know comfortable, it's very nice anyway."

"I'll agree with that, how long have you been coming to this stone and doing this?"

"Since I was about thirty years old, I helped my grandmother to come here and heal herself, since then, I come when ever I feel the need. Sometimes it can be a month between visits, sometimes days."

"So how long have you been using the power from the stone?"

"I don't exactly know, about forty years I think."

"So that makes you seventy years old."

"Yes, I'm seventy four in the summer."

"You don't look anything like that old, I'd say you look at the most fifty."

"Why thank you kind sir, you don't look so old yourself." She gave a little twirl that caused her shawl to swing completely open, and Gorgana got an even better look at her body, her drooping breasts, and her small sagging belly, both of which bore the scars of childbirth, her dimpled buttocks, and knobbly knees. He found it more than a little disturbing that these sights actually excited his body in the same way it had responded to Carin, even though this woman could easily have children older than him. 'Children, no grandchildren!' He thought trying to drive any thoughts of passion from his mind. He stepped towards her and swept her into his arms, pressing her naked body against the coarse cloth of his robe, he kissed urgently, her mouth responded in exactly the same manner, until she backed away, slowly she leaned away from him and placed her hands on his chest, gently she pushed him away. He was surprised by the panting of his breath, and the urgency of his need.

"No young man. This is wrong and we both know it, this is a symptom of the power, this is one of the things it does, I have noticed it myself many times, it will pass quite quickly, and then you would find yourself in a situation that you would find extremely embarrassing." She stepped away from him as soon as his hands released her, though she made no effort to cover herself.

"It is a very powerful feeling at the moment. It is hard to resist. I want you so much, I just cannot understand how this can happen, have you any idea who built this place originally?"

"It has always been here, it has always been the same, but over my lifetime I have felt it getting stronger and stronger, more and more it wants to fill one with power, you felt it didn't you?"

"It did seem to give some pressure, once the link was opened."

"Yes, sometimes it is reluctant to open the gate, but always the power comes flooding once the gate is open."

"Yes, it is control of that flood that is going to be really hard thing to accomplish, I am going to have to be very careful with that."

"What do you mean?"

"Tomorrow I am going to open that gate, and take far more power than I took tonight."

"What do you intend?"

"You know of our cause?"

"Everyone knows that the Zandaars allow no other god, and they convert people with the sword."

"But you have no god here."

"And the Zandaars hate that even more than having one that is not Zandaar, somehow it challenges them, people with a god have merely made the wrong choice, people without one have made a choice that Zandaar just cannot understand, nor allow to exist."

"You fear for your lives?"

"If not our lives then our way of life, you and yours cannot allow us to continue."

"I have come to like this place, I find it to be an interesting culture to study, I shall make others see it that way, your way of life will be safe from our interference."

"We shall see, but what will you do with all the power you are going to take?"

"I am going to find the man and the sword we are looking for and bring him here."

"Can this magic be performed?"

"I believe so, with enough power, it should be possible, but not easy."

"And what do you intend to do with this man?"

"We shall take him to Zandaar, let our god judge him."

"Then you will kill him?"

"No, if Zandaar wishes him to live then he will live."

"Have you met this man?"

"No."

"He is a good man, he cares for his friends, as he cared for his family, before your kind destroyed them all. He carries a deep hatred for you. And a dark power."

"What do you mean?"

"The power from the stone makes people happy, strong, loving, I know I have been using it for more years than any others. The power he carries is hard, sharp, it revels in pain, it is not something I ever want to feel again."

"You felt his power?"

"He brushed past me in the tavern, he didn't even notice me, but I felt that sword of his, it has a hunger, a hunger for blood. If you bring that power here, when the gate to the lightning stone is open, he will tap it's power, and change it, he will take it unto himself, and then what will you do?"

"I will have control of the gate, he'll not be able to take that from me."

"He wont even think of it, but the sword will, all the time it was here it was feeding on heat, sucking the heat out of the fires, and out of the ground, I came here when they were sleeping, the lightning stone was hiding, its power was so low that I could barely feel it."

"Why would it be hiding? We found it with no problem."

"You are probably more sensitive, you've had more practise dealing with this sort of thing."

"No one has ever accused me of being sensitive before." Gorgana laughed, she shook her head slowly then joined in the laughter. He moved towards her and took her hand gently. He looked down into her eyes, her smile subsided, as she reached forwards to kiss him. At the last instant she turned away.

"No." she muttered. "Please don't bring the man and the sword here, many will certainly die if you do, you have to find some other way to bring him to what you call justice."

"Have you an idea?" he asked hoping she would look up at him again.

"No. Have you?"

"I really shouldn't even think about any other ideas, I have a specific instruction to bring him here."

"If he comes here, then he will awaken all the might of the stone and turn it loose, you and yours will all die, more people here will die, there has to be another way. Perhaps you could talk to him, deflect him from his cause, even mislead him, and finally betray him." She whispered these words, moving closer to him and looking up into his eyes. The temptation was too obvious for him too react, he knew she was trying to influence his decision with thoughts of the flesh, but he didn't want to resist her.

"To talk to him I would have to be close to him, I would have to go to their group. He would kill me on sight."

"If he lets you speak one word, then he will give the chance to speak ten, with ten words, you will earn a hundred, and with a hundred words you could sell him the whole world wrapped up in a bow."

"How do you know this?"

"He is a good man, and so under all that black, are you. You will be able to convince him, and perhaps even come to control him. What would you earn if you brought him before your god, and made him hand over the sword willingly?"

"That would be a victory beyond imagining, this is what Kevana is hoping will redeem his actions."

"Then if you manage to perform this feat, glory should be yours, perhaps a position of power, or a seat beside your god, who can tell what the future holds for a man that achieves the impossible?"

"A seat on the council, that would be the minimum reward for such an action. But would I want it? All those dreary meetings and council sessions, I cant imagine anything more boring."

"But you would be in the centre of your gods power, you could change things from the inside, make it better."

"The last person who tried to make things better, was burned alive, as a heretic. I'd not like to die that way."

"You are too intelligent to be caught out like that, you have already learned from his mistakes."

"The council comes up with new heresies every day. The man who burned was guilty of the heresy of wearing some colour other than black on a certain holy day, he was wearing black, but his undergarment was a little old, and many times washed, it had faded from the deepest of black, and in the strong sunlight it was decreed by the whole council to be dark brown, therefore not black, therefore heresy, and look in the yard we have a nice bonfire ready to go and sturdy stake in the middle of it. He was found guilty of heresy and killed within the hour, his real sin, he wanted to give more autonomy to the priests in outlying areas, where the rules of Zandaar have almost no bearing on the life of the ordinary people. He threatened their power bases and so they killed him. I have no wish to be a part of that."

"You don't think you would survive very long in that place?"

"I would live for as long as it would take to arrange a believable accident, say ten days."

"Then you must find another answer. You can be assured that your masters will know very soon what has transpired for you in this village tonight. No, I do not mean that I will tell them, but you will, by some subtle change in your behaviour, they will know, and most likely make things difficult for you here."

"What other answer can there be? Either he comes here, or I go there."

"You could fail completely, then how would they guess what could have been?"

"No. They would know, our minds will be close enough for them to sense if I was trying anything other than my uttermost."

"You could miss the target and bring another one here."

"That is a possibility, there is one in their group, one who has serious potential for becoming a tool for Worandana, he has made reference to it."

"That would be Crathen, he has eyes for the woman, but she doesn't even see him."

"What of the woman?"

"Do not bring her here. She would kill until none stood between her and the man, and if she is here, then he is coming, and filled with an anger that not even a god could face. Do not bring her here."

"Good. I will bring Crathen."

"Will he know that you chose him deliberately?"

"Not very likely, he is a peasant."

"As am I?" her raised eyebrows spoke more than her voice.

"I did not mean it that way, he is ignorant, no one could accuse you of that, even if you are so very old." he laughed, she paused for a moment then joined the jollity.

"Either way that still leaves you here just waiting to be discovered, what will you do?"

"Once they have Crathen they will leave here in a serious hurry, on the trail of that sword, perhaps if I am injured enough by my efforts they will leave me behind."

"Is that likely?"

He thought for a few moments. "No. Worandana will want to use the power of the stone to heal me, then he will know that I am not as injured as I appear."

"That sounds like another heresy to me."

"Certainly, but we are getting somewhere. All I need is the final part of the puzzle."

"How about the first part of the puzzle again?"

"Meaning?"

"You go there, Crathen comes here, and no one has any idea what happened."

"I am still stuck trying to survive the anger of the man."

"That is a thing that you can do, you have come to him, a strange act indeed, he'll just have to find out why."

"You seem very confident in both of our abilities."

"I told you, you are both good men, he driven by grief and you by something else, but neither of you is inherently evil."

"Perhaps you are right, I shall have to give it some serious thought." He sat down on the grass with his back to the stone. She sat next to him. Taking his hand in hers.

"You do not have a lot of time for thinking, the eastern sky will start to lighten very soon, the night is almost gone."

He looked towards the east, but saw no sign of the change, but he was in no doubt that she was right. 'I should get some sleep.' He thought.

"Why don't I feel tired?" he asked.

"It is the stone, sometimes I don't sleep for a few days, and don't have any of the usual problems associated with insomnia. Enjoy it."

"But I need to sleep, to get all these crazy ideas fixed in my head."

"Then close your eyes and pretend you are asleep. That will work just as well."

"But I will still be awake, and thinking."

"Close your eyes, and relax your mind, that is all you need. Trust me."

"I think I have already trusted you too much."

"That may be the case, but it is too late to do anything about that now."

He closed his eyes, and slowed his breathing, trying to achieve a state of total relaxation, then her head rested against his shoulder, her slow breathing a steady sound by his ear, her small hand pulled his inside her shawl and rested both on her thigh. He matched his breathing to hers, though it was difficult because she was breathing far faster than he would have normally. Perhaps it was the extra oxygen of his accelerated breathing, or the hypnotic sound of hers, whichever he was asleep in moments.

CHAPTER THIRTY SEVEN

"Gorgana!" The shout crashed through the pleasant warmth of his dream, and dragged his consciousness back to reality. Before he bothered to open his eyes he felt Anya stirring alongside him.

"Gorgana. What in all the hells are you doing?" The voice shouted again. Gorgana turned towards Anya before opening his eyes, she squeezed his hand as he looked into her eyes, the apology was there for him to see, but he knew it would never be in her voice when there were others around.

"Kirukana." he said without turning. "Find an elsewhere to perform your dawn observances."

"What have to been doing, lying with this old woman?"

"The sad thing Anya, is that he has absolutely no idea. Kirukana go somewhere else, I suggest you try downwind of the pigpens, that way the stink of your self-righteousness wont upset the pigs before breakfast."

"I think it's time I started making breakfast for my family." she said softly. "Why don't you come for some? I'll introduce you to my husband and children, the youngest only that is, the older ones have families of their own to take care of."

"I would like that." said Gorgana. "But I think I have a few things to sort out first, so I'll be along in a little while."

"That will be just fine, it'll take a while to prepare anyway, I am usually awake long before now." Slowly she rose to her feet, and looked down at Gorgana, a gentle smile on her lips.

"Woman." shouted Kirukana. "Cover yourself, have you no modesty?"

Anya tipped her head backwards and laughed to the sky, with a swirl of her arms she gathered her shawl, and then placed both hands on her hips, the shawl trapped between her arms and her body. She stared Kirukana straight in the eye, cocked her hips to one side.

"If I should be modest then surely to protect my modesty you should look away, but you don't, do you? You keep on staring at my naked body. Despite all the praying and all the preaching there is still a man under all that black." She turned to Gorgana. "Not man as would apply to you, perhaps more a boy by comparison." With a toss of her hair she turned away, and strutted across the green towards her home. Her hips swinging suggestively from side to side. Gorgana watched her for a moment, noticing the slight sag of her buttocks as she moved away from them, he turned to Kirukana, and laughed at the look on total entrancement on his face, he was utterly hypnotised by the motion of those white globes as they swayed in their passage across the green. Gorgana laughed so hard he rolled on the grass, until he finally managed to distract Kirukana from the target of his observations.

"What are you laughing at? There is nothing funny here." snapped Kirukana.

"Wrong again. One day you will actually say something that is right, if you live long enough."

"Why is everyone threatening me these days?"

"I don't threaten you. I merely state a fact. Your mouth is going to get you in serious trouble and without friends like me to look after you, then you will die. Now that you have woken me up, why don't you go and do the same for Worandana and Kevana, I have something important to tell them, but I don't want to be the one that disturbs their rest."

"I have something to tell them as well. You shouldn't be with a woman, it is forbidden."

"Of course it is, now stop being a fool and let's go talk to Worandana." Gorgana climbed wearily to his feet and started walking towards their tents. Kirukana couldn't take his eyes from the spot where Anya had been lying, then he suddenly realised that Gorgana was going to get there first and ran on ahead.

Gorgana shook his head slowly, wondering how a man such as Kirukana could get to be so stupid and yet come so far in the priesthood, intelligence was something that was prized, but there were the odd few who managed to progress without it. 'It must be that they have something else. Probably relatives in the council, or something.' Slowly he walked into camp, he mind on many things, he could hear Kirukana's excited voice, but couldn't be bothered listening to what he was saying. He sat by the fire and accepted a cup of hot soup from Fabrana.

"I think you are in the crap." whispered Fabrana.

"I'll deal with it and he'll look even more of a fool than he usually does."

Fabrana merely nodded, leaving the younger man to his own thoughts.

Worandana came out of his tent, with a grinning Kirukana in tow.

"Gorgana. Is it true what Kirukana says?" he asked, his voice still rough from having been so rudely awakened.

"Of course it is, of course it is." said Kirukana. Gorgana looked at the excited younger monk. "And I don't believe that Kirukana would recognise the truth if it bit him on his ample ass." Fabrana chocked somewhere in the background.

"He says he found you lying with a naked woman and you were asleep in each others arms."

"She wasn't naked."

"She was as near as makes no difference naked!" snapped Kirukana.

"She was not naked, and we were asleep, side by side."

"See. He admits it!" said Kirukana.

"Kirukana. Be silent!" said Worandana. "We are trying to establish what has happened, one more word from you and it will be your last." He turned to Gorgana.

"Did any act of impropriety occur between you and this woman?"

"No it did not. More by resistance from her than from me, that I have to admit. She showed me how to access the power of the stone, she showed me it's secret. I drew on it's power and it was immense. It is a power for good, once the flush of power was gone, we sat with our backs to the stone and fell asleep. Her name is Anya and she has invited me to share breakfast with her and her family, she says that her grandchildren will be with their parents, only her youngest now lives with her."

"You are saying this woman is a grandmother?"

"So she says, and judging by the way the power of that stone made me feel, I wouldn't be in the least surprised. She has been tapping its power since she was thirty, and she says she is seventy four years old this summer."

Kirukana coughed but said nothing, though it was obvious he had something to say. Worandana looked at him for a long moment. "Speak." he said.

"Again he lies, she can't have been more than forty years old."

"Well you certainly got a good enough look at her, you had more than enough time to count the stretch marks on her belly, I thought that is what you were doing." said Gorgana.

"I wasn't staring, I was shocked to see her naked like that."

"So shocked that your head and eyes couldn't move." laughed Gorgana.

"Enough!" snapped Worandana. "Do you think she would mind another guest for breakfast?"

"I am sure she would be glad to have breakfast with someone more her own age than me." said Gorgana.

"What is the secret of this stone?" asked Worandana.

"Much the same as the one in the cave, it needs blood to open the path to the power."

"How is this blood shed?"

"Anya and I both cut our hands and rubbed the blood into the top of the stone, she said to hold onto a little of the power, to heal the cuts, it worked fine, I can hardly tell that I have been injured."

"Good. I would talk with this lady, we shall go and have breakfast with her."

"But what about his sin?" demanded Kirukana.

"What sin?"

"I found him asleep with a woman, is that not enough?"

"That in itself is no sin, he has explained the situation, and I accept his explanation, if you cannot accept it then I suggest you take the matter up with a higher authority."

"In this ass end of the world there is no higher authority, and you know that."

"I am a little surprised that you knew it, but I'll put that down to you actually beginning to learn something of the world."

"Perhaps I didn't explain clearly enough for him." said Gorgana.

"Would you care to try again, but keep it simple." said Worandana.

"When I used the power of the stone I tried to find the sword and the thief, I failed because I couldn't control the power the stone was giving. When I let the power go, and healed myself I felt so good, I just wanted to share that with someone, and she was there, she looked warm and inviting, soft and loving, at that moment I wanted her more than anything in the world, but she stopped me. It seems this reaction is part of the power of the stone, she knew that I would regret my actions in the morning and she didn't want me to be hurt, so she pushed me away. By her actions was my honour protected, a rare woman indeed."

"I still don't believe you." snapped Kirukana, turning away.

"An interesting story definitely." said Worandana, taking Gorgana by the arm and leading him out of the camp, across the green, towards the stone.

"He said sin." whispered Gorgana.

"He did."

"Since when? I know relations between priests and women have been frowned on for some years, but I wasn't aware it had been classified as a sin."

"The more extreme members of the council think of it as such, but I believe those to be the ones that like little boys, if you know what I mean."

"I think I do, I seem to recall from an old record that priests used to be allowed to marry. Is that true?"

"Yes it is, there was a time many years ago when most priests were indeed married, but then it was decided that priests shouldn't be distracted by thoughts of fleshly things, so marriage was frowned on, then banned. Though priests are men after all, so a certain amount of latitude was allowed, but that has been eroded in more recent times, now it seems that almost any relationship with a woman is a sin."

"But relationships with little boys are fine?"

"So it seems."

"Sometimes." said Gorgana. "I think the world is going slowly mad."

"Slowly?"

"Perhaps not slowly."

"Have you any idea where the woman lives?"

"None at all. But she did come this way after Kirukana had disturbed our sleep."

"I am sure that someone will know where she lives." said Worandana as they walked between two houses onto the track that followed the wall of the village, they looked both ways along the track.

"I think I know where she lives." said Gorgana, pointing to a house just up the track from where they were standing.

"Why that one?" asked Worandana.

"It looks in slightly better condition than the others and there are two huge dogs lying on the porch, I believe we have seen those dogs before."

"I think we have, and you think that the owner of those dogs is her son?"

"Who else?"

As they approached the porch the dogs looked up, but didn't move, at least not until the door opened. A young man stepped out, the dogs leapt to their feet, and went to greet him.

"Paulo." said Gorgana.

"Good morning." said Paulo. "Are you the one that kept my mother out all night?"

"I am afraid that I am. She has invited me to breakfast, I hope we are not too late?"

"No. I have mine as I travel, it is important to get an early start, otherwise the cattle get restless, they like to be moving as soon as the sun is up."

"That is good, would you care to introduce us?"

Paulo looked over his shoulder and shouted through the open door. "Mama, your guests are here."

"I'll be right there." Was the reply from inside the house.

"She is just seeing to Papa's breakfast, she'll not be long, I must be off. You will be nice, wont you?" Said Paulo, for some reason the tone of his voice, or some signal the priests didn't see caused both dogs to growl most alarmingly.

"I assure you, we mean no one here any harm at all." said Worandana.

"I hope so." Paulo stepped down from the porch and the dogs followed him, Anya came to the door and smiled at Gorgana, then looked at the other man.

"Who are you?" she asked.

"I am called Worandana, I am one of the leaders of our mission. May we come in and talk?"

"Of course, I was only expecting one, but I can cook for two with no real effort." She stepped aside and waved them in. Gorgana walked in first, the room seemed take up all the floor space of the entire house, the centre of the room held a round fireplace, with a healthy blaze going, a hood above took the smoke upwards and presumably out through the roof. Sitting in a chair near to the fire was an old man, he barely moved as they came in, as if he hadn't noticed them, to their left was a large dinning table, to their right was a group of more comfortable chairs and a small bed against the wall. In front of them was a kitchen area and a stairway that lead to the upper floor. Anya closed the door, and walked over to the man in the chair.

"We have guests for breakfast." She said to him gently. "These are Gorgana and Worandana, visiting priests. Isn't that nice?" The old man made no response. Turning to the priests,

"This is Porto, he is my husband, he's not as lively as he used to be, but he is still my husband." The last almost a challenge.

"We are pleased to meet you sir." said Worandana, getting no more response than Anya had, he looked a question at her.

"He's old. I think his mind went with his teeth, but he is my husband, he provided for me for so many years, it is only right that I help him when he is so much in need."

"How old is he?"

"He's nearly seventy years, but they have been hard on him. Come let's go into the kitchen and talk while I cook." She turned and walked smoothly into the kitchen area, taking a huge piece meat from a hook she carved six thick slices of bacon, and dropped them into a large pan, with some chopped mushrooms and some butter, she went back to the fire and placed the pan in a cradle that had been designed for it. Returning to the kitchen she poured some steaming liquid from a pot into three cups.

"Tea?" She asked. "There is honey if you like it sweet."

"That would be nice." Said Worandana. "You have of course guessed why I am here."

"You want to find out about the power of the lightning stone, don't you?"

"And other things."

"The world has many things to teach, for those who are willing to learn."

"I agree. You seem considerably younger than your husband, but I am told you are actually older."

"I am, four years older, but I haven't had as hard a life as he has."

"The power of the stone helped you?"

"Definitely, it keeps a person healthy, and with good health it is easier to live."

"I agree, I myself am old, nearly as old as your husband, but I struggle through."

"Don't lie to me, you may be nearly as old as my husband, but you don't struggle through this life, you have younger men to support you." She nodded at Gorgana.

"It is true that the younger men can be a great help, but they also cause a deal of heart ache, one worries for their purity of purpose."

"A mother worries much the same for her children, they can be a serious burden."

"We have met one of yours, Paulo, an impressive young man."

"Expressive you mean?"

"Oh, that too, in so many ways."

"He's a good boy, but perhaps a little too intelligent for his own good, if you know what I mean?"

"I think I do, his mouth is going to get him into trouble one day."

"Don't we all do that?" Anya went over to the fire and turned the bacon, and gave the mushrooms a quick stir, taking a loaf from its wooden box she started to cut thick slices of bread, these she buttered with a deft touch. She gathered some wooden platters from a cupboard and laid then out, each with a knife and fork. She looked at both of the monks, and smiled, then went to the fire, returning with the pan, the bacon and mushrooms were divided amongst the three plates in a moment, and two slices of bread dropped on top of each.

"Help yourselves gentleman, I don't do waitress service, I think we'll eat at the table, it just doesn't get the use it used to when the children were all here." She selected a plate for herself and crossed the room, pausing momentarily to stroke the cheek of the old man in the chair, she moved with an easy grace that belied her years. The three sat at the table, the scuffling of chairs seemed to animate Porto for an instant, but he settled back into his blank staring into the fire.

"This bacon is very good." Said Worandana.

"Yes. It's from last years batch, we had a very good year, and had plenty of salt to help with the curing, it's the salt that gives the best flavour, it seems that the blacksmith has done quite well recently, so we should have some salt to cure this years bacon."

"Yes. I believe he drives a very hard bargain, or perhaps my associate is a little profligate with my funds."

"You had someone else spending your money, then you are more foolish that you look." she laughed.

"I was busy with something else at the time."

"You were busy with the stone."

"Yes. How long have you been using the stone?"

"About forty years, after my first two children, but before Paulo was born."

"You must have been nearly sixty years old when Paulo was born."

"Yes, very late indeed, many people couldn't believe that I had even managed to get pregnant, yet alone carried him to full term, and given birth to a healthy boy, it did cause a few problems, some of which have affected Paulo adversely, but he grows stronger all the time. He was a little small to start with, but he was strong and fed well. But I had to switch him to cows milk fairly early, mine dried up."

"Didn't the power of the stone help with that?"

"The stone can heal, but it is necessary to know what the problem is, for a sixty year old woman to have her milk dry up, isn't a problem as such, it's just nature imposing her limits."

"Do you think you could still get pregnant?" asked Worandana.

"That is something I don't want to test, for many reasons, I am too old is the first, if I were pregnant, then everyone in the village would know that I have broken my oath to my husband, everyone knows that he is totally incapable, I couldn't bring that sort of shame on him or me."

"Would you test it if he were to die?"

"I don't know, I am still too old, but the power of the stone can certainly fill a person with the most powerful of lusts, can't it?" she looked at Gorgana.

"I was indeed overflowing with lust, until you pushed me away."

"I swore to him," she glanced over at her husband sitting peacefully in his chair, "that I'd not take another lover while he was still breathing. I am true to my word."

"What do you do with the power you take from the stone?" asked Worandana.

"I take the power into myself and cure the minor irritations and infirmities, the ones that slowly accumulate into the decline that is old age. I have over the years been able to hold a small charge of the power within myself, even after the healing is all finished, sometimes this will last me for days or months, it just gives me a lift to know it is there if I need it."

"Can you put this energy to any use, I mean any use outside yourself?" asked Worandana.

"I have never thought of doing anything like that, other than healing, I usually use it when I am tired, or to help me perform some strenuous task, like getting water from the well, then the power is useful, it gives my old muscles that bit of help that they need from time to time."

"But you don't project the power out of your body?"

"I have only done that to heal, and then only when in direct contact with the stone, that way there is plenty of power available, and it takes a lot to work on someone else."

"Who else have you worked on?"

"Only my grandmother who showed me the way, and my mother who really wanted nothing to do with the power, they are both gone now."

"What of your husband?"

"I may be able to make his body better, but his mind is gone, most days he doesn't even know who he is."

"That must be very hard on you."

"It is, but it is a burden I have chosen to carry, I'll not shirk it now that it has become arduous."

"You are a good woman, though I believe that your neighbours may feel differently?"

"They can feel how they like, but none will speak out against me."

"Do you know what we intend to do?"

"Gorgana has told me some of your purpose, you wish to bring a man and a thing here, that will be a serious test on whoever it entrusted with the task."

"Gorgana is the one who will perform this feat."

"And feat it will be, there are some real risks involved in this you know."

"Yes we know, we are no strangers to the uses of power."

"If he fails with all that power to hand, then it must go somewhere, there will be a blast that could level the whole village, you would risk this?"

"It is a small risk, we are having a tool created to guide the energy where we need it to go, and if that fails then it can be used to channel the power to a place where it can do no harm, there may be a little local flooding, but that will be all."

"Flooding?"

"I think so, if there is a need to dissipate any large amount of power, there is nothing better than melting a few miles of snow, and looking at the peaks of the mountains hereabouts there is no shortage of snow to melt, holding the channel open and dumping energy into the snow, until we have control again, is a relatively easy thing." said Worandana.

"Then you do it." said Gorgana.

"You have the experience, I do not, you will perform this task to the best of your ability, and today that damned sword will be here."

"I shall try, but you must be aware that there is a possibility of failure."

"I am aware, but you must push that thought from your mind, the mere presence of the thought in your mind can precipitate such a failure."

"I am fully aware of that, I shall try my utmost to perform my task to the best of my ability."

"How would you feel about an interested spectator?" asked Anya.

"I would welcome your presence, but that is not my choice to make." said Gorgana, turning meaningfully to Worandana

"If you appear to get too involved with us, it could harm your standing amongst your friends." said Worandana.

"You have no idea the harm done to my standing in the eyes of my friends when my youngest son was born, after that I can ride out any storm they can produce."

"It is likely that there are going to be deaths involved."

"If you must kill this man, I would prefer it if you took him outside the village first."

"I am sure that could be arranged, though I don't believe he will be willing, we can hope that the dislocation will leave him momentarily stunned, so that we can disarm him, and restrain him. Perhaps the power of the stone could even do that for us?"

"I don't think it is going to be happy with that sort of thing." said Anya. "It has always been used for good, never to do harm."

"Who can tell what it has been used for before you came along, my dear?" said Worandana.

"If you try to force it along a path it doesn't wish to follow there could be a backlash, and a fatal one."

"I am sure that Gorgana here can deal with anything of that nature."

"When will all this occur?" asked Anya.

"I am not sure, we are waiting for the blacksmith to complete his task, I would say that this sort of thing is always best at sundown, or thereabouts, we should be ready by then." Worandana pushed his chair back from the table and stood. "Well, thank you for a lovely breakfast, and for sharing your knowledge with us, this has been a most interesting morning, but we have much to do."

"I am glad that I could help." said Anya getting up. Worandana looked at Gorgana, who appeared firmly stuck in his seat.

"You go on ahead I'll catch you up." he said, not looking up from his plate.

Worandana walked slowly to the door escorted by Anya, at the door he turned and saw Gorgana staring resolutely into his plate.

"Goodbye, my dear. I hope you will come to the stone later to witness Gorgana's success."

"I most surely shall." Worandana walked slowly through the door, she closed it almost on his heels. She walked over to the table and took Gorgana's hand, perching on the edge of the table.

"He doesn't care if this task kills you, so long as you are successful."

"I did notice that, I am now more sure than ever, I will make a switch but I will not bring that man and that sword in amongst the good people of this village. My brothers will leave this place unharmed and empty handed, of that you can be certain."

"I am glad."

"You should come to watch, the energy needed to move two things is enormous, it will be something spectacular to see."

"I shall come, but I don't think I'll be too close, there is bound to be some loose energy flying around, no matter how good your focus is."

"I understand." he muttered. "We shall never meet again, you know that?"

"Yes." she whispered, leaning towards him.

"Thank you for all your help, you have changed my life. I'll probably not see her, so can you thank Carin for me."

"Of course I will, she is a good girl."

Slowly Gorgana leaned towards Anya, and kissed her softly on the lips, her response was urgent for a moment, then she pulled away.

Gorgana stood and held her hand for a moment, then left, he had no more words to say, goodbye would have stuck in his throat, he knew that he had to do, and that he was almost certain never to come this way again. Once he was away from the houses he strode purposefully across the green, trying to catch up with Worandana, who looked like he was struggling with the mere act of walking. Worandana was almost level with the stone when Gorgana caught up.

"Sorry about that." he said.

"What was so urgent that you had speak to her alone?"

"We weren't alone, her husband was there, and I had to thank her for her help last night. It really didn't seem appropriate to do that with you there."

"Perhaps, any last advice from her?"

"Yes. She said don't do it, someone is going to be killed, and she didn't want that on her conscience."

"Are you still going to do it?"

"Of course, no one else has as good a chance, I am the best choice for this job, anyone else is much more likely to fail."

"I agree, you have the experience. Do you have the will?"

"Yes. I can do this, given the power in that stone, and a tool to guide it, I can reach out with the energy and drag the man back, it's not going to be easy, but I can do it."

"Only if you have the will."

"I can focus a tight enough beam to bring a man back, and that is what I will do, I really love a challenge like this."

"Yes, but is not just some intellectual task, it could be dangerous, very dangerous."

"I know, it helps to focus, the risk is in itself a good thing."

"Kirukana is going to be a problem."

"He has his uses, this I understand, but if he starts to inhibit things he'll have to be taken out of the circle."

"That would cause some serious instability."

"I'll be at the stone, you will have to control the circle, if he starts to work against me, then things will go badly for us all."

"Have no fear, I will control him, even if I have to end his life to do it." muttered Worandana, the emotion showing in the reduced level of his voice.

"If the circle collapses or the stone gets beyond my control, then we could all die."

"This I understand, probably better than you."

"You have witnessed this first hand?"

"I was in a circle that was destroyed from within."

"How did that happen?"

"That is one of the reasons that women are forbidden to us."

"You'll have to explain, I am not understanding you at all."

"Let us sit by the stone and I'll tell you all about it." Together that sat with their backs to the stone, their senses feeling the power emanating from it.

"It was more years ago than I care to think about." began Worandana. "I was a young man, I know that you youngsters doubt that I was ever young, but I was. Our group had been sent to a small fishing village on the southern shore, there were tales of an enormous sea devil that was eating fishermen and boats, our leader, whose name totally slips my mind, he was a man of little imagination, but he had a certain raw power about him. Our leader talked to the witnesses and piecing together their descriptions of the devil, decided it was some form of sea creature that was just out of it's normal place and needed a prod to get it moving back to its home. His problem was that he didn't believe the people when they told him of the beast, he refused to believe that anything could be that big, he didn't understand that these fishermen can tell the size and variety of a school of fish from a single fin shown for an instant above the water, they judge distance and size very well. Our leader placed us on a cliff top overlooking the bay, a small boat was sent out as bait, it took a demonstration of the power from our circle projected through the leaders staff before anyone could be convinced that they were safe on the water. Out the boat went, the fishermen were throwing their usual baits into the water, gulls were soon flapping around the boat, almost concealing it they were that closely packed on occasion. Suddenly the birds were gone, and the water around the boat went completely flat, a total calm, not a ripple to be seen, at a command the circle was formed, and a energy pulse started to flow around it, growing quickly at first as they do, but the leader kept sending it back round again, never satisfied with the power in it, nor actually have a tangible target for it, we were all straining to add those last little dregs of ourselves to the energy blast that was going to be huge. The beast had surfaced and it was all around the boat, it was four times the size of the boat, with large waving arms and huge yellow eyes. I passed the energy on to the man beside me, straining with the effort of adding just a little more, the man snatched his hand from mine, and from the man on his other side, and formed the bolt in his bare hands and hurled it at a man opposite, the man took the blast in the chest and died instantly, the man beside me was so badly burned that his hands were mere stumps of blackened flesh, he died slowly over a period of a few days, screaming the whole time. The men either side of the blasted man were seriously injured, one is a gibbering wreck still, the other is only fit to tend flowers in a garden, and he still crawls under his bed if there is a loud noise. The two fishermen in the boat, they died too. The sea monster was never seen again, but I couldn't ever claim that it was us that frightened it off. We lost four men, and the village lost two, and the reason for all these deaths, jealousy. Both men loved the same woman, but she only loved one. Since then the hierarchy have been discouraging relationships with women quite intensely, it was sort of accepted before, but now it is most certainly discouraged. So I know what it is like to have a circle of power collapse, I have no wish to be there again."

"I understand."

"Perhaps you do, perhaps you do. Come, let us go and see how the staff is coming along, the smith said that it would be ready today." Gorgana rose first and offered a hand to Worandana, the older man raised his eyebrows before accepting the help.

"Sometimes I think I am getting too old for this." said Worandana.

"Maybe, but what else would you do? Somehow I don't see you sitting in a monastery praying the rest of your life away."

"No, but there are some monasteries in this world with excellent libraries."

"Even so, you wouldn't be content to read about things, you have to be involved in them. Perhaps you should write about the things you have done and seen in your lifetime. Now, that would be a labour of years."

"Especially at the speed that I write. I can pen a reasonably legible letter, but I don't have the patience or the hand for the sort of art that is expected when writing a book. No, I think I'll leave that to the scholars." Worandana laughed.

"Something funny?"

"Yes. I just got a picture of me, scratching away at a parchment, ink all over my hands and my face, and some master engraver throwing his arms up in dismay at the quality of my work."

"You don't see your self like that then?"

"No, you are right, that sort of existence would be just too boring for me, I have to be out and doing, not just reading or writing about it, I have to be making the history that others will write about, perhaps that is a task for Kirukana."

"He has a good hand, I have seen some of his work, but his interpretation of your history would probably not show you in the best of lights, if you know what I mean?"

"I am certain that I would turn out to be only one small step from a demon." They walked into their camp, laughing, Worandana with both hands on his head, fingers pointing upwards, like the horns of a demon. Kevana was approaching from the direction of the smithy, he frowned at the two, but said nothing, wondering briefly if the old man had finally lost his mind.

"Kevana." said Worandana. "What does the smith say about my staff?"

"He has been working on it most of the night, and says it will be ready sometime this afternoon."

"That is good, I feel the need for some serious rest before we try it out."

"There's going to be some sort of test?"

"Not really, this thing cannot be tested, we just have to try it and see if it works, perhaps we will all die in the attempt."

"Have you gone mad?"

"No, this is the nature of these things, it is an unproven magic we attempt. It isn't unusual for people to die trying new things like this."

"Sometimes you frighten me."

"Why? I have total confidence in our ability to take control of all that power, and bend it to our purpose, don't you Gorgana?"

"I shall certainly do everything I can to make this power do what we want it to." answered Gorgana, smiling at Kevana.

"Doesn't it worry you that we could all get killed?"

"No. I worry that I may be killed, but the rest of you can do your own worrying, with one risk, one chance taken, this whole affair could be over, and we could go back to our normal lives. Anyway, we could all be dead tomorrow, or yesterday for that matter. That snake could be living off us for many a month to come, only we killed it before it could kill us. There is chance everywhere, worrying about it, has no effect on the outcome."

"I still worry about this untried magic." said Kevana, turning away, Kirukana came forwards as he walked away.

"What are you going to do about Gorgana?" he demanded, sneering in Gorgana's direction. Worandana shook his head slowly.

"I shall give him a chance, later today, to die for our cause, the same chance I will give to you, though I think his risk will be considerably greater than your own."

"But I found him asleep in the arms of a naked woman!"

"Kirukana, please stop judging everyone by your own standards, I know that you could not have been so close to a woman in the depth of the night without committing some foul act of rape, Gorgana did no such thing. I have met with the woman, she is a devoted and faithful wife, even when her husband is no longer capable of providing for her needs, she has vowed to have no other man while he breathes, and she is doing everything she can to make sure that breathing continues, more I believe than she knows, she supports that crippled old body even though his mind is long fled, I would that some of my acolytes had such devotion. Your groundless accusations sully the name of a good woman."

"Women are inconstant creatures, they have not the strength of mind to hold a vow, not like us men, they make a promise such as she has and next day she's laying on her back like some common whore, laying with him!" He pointed at Gorgana. The tone of Kirukana's voice caused the people in the camp to start moving, the clerics milled around unsure what they should be doing, where the soldiers were making themselves space to move in, and closing in on the action, hands on swords. Gorgana's hand was on the hilt of his knife, still in it's sheath.

"Kirukana!" snapped Worandana. "One more slander against Anya and I myself will kill you. Be apart. Leave here and us. Return at sundown, and beg the chance to prove your self fit for our task." Worandana turned his back on Kirukana, the clerics all followed suit, as did the soldiers, after a quick glance towards Kevana. Kirukana stamped off across the grass, muttering something obviously unpleasant, but inaudible to anyone other than himself, not that any would even have acknowledged his presence. From the corner of his eye Worandana watched him go, in the direction of the tavern. 'I hope he retains enough sense not to get too drunk.' He thought.

"This old man needs some rest. Someone wake me if anything exciting happens." He said to all within ear shot, he patted Gorgana on the arm and retired to his tent, more than a little disturbed by the intensity of Kirukana's feelings, the man had always seemed so level headed in the past. Alverana came over to Gorgana, slowly settling his sword belt into a more comfortable position.

"I've heard of such a punishment, but never seen it used to such effect."

"The situation was approaching violence, that is always a bad thing, especially for a group such as ours, Worandana had to do something to prevent an explosion."

"We soldiers like our explosions, after the shouting, is the pushing, after the pushing is the punching, then a short brawl, some bleeding and some bruising and soon everything is forgotten."

"That is not how it happens with us, after the shouting is the screaming, after the screaming is the silence, the problem doesn't go away, it is never forgotten, it grows in the silence of men's hearts, until one day it gets out again, and if this happens at the wrong moment, say when we are carrying a huge load of power from that stone, then we all die."

"What if he doesn't come back?"

"Even if he comes back, there is no certainty that he will be accepted, Worandana has exercised almost the ultimate sanction, if Kirukana has any qualms about returning he should stay away, if Worandana suspects for one moment that he has returned with the intention of doing us harm, then Worandana will kill him, in a heartbeat. We are going to have a very tense time come sundown."

"I think I prefer the military way."

"But is the winner of the fight always in the right?"

"It's not about the winner, it's about the fight. Any arguments are settled after the fight, while cuts are being stitched and bruises bathed, then the real discussion can start, on many occasions the cause of the fight is actually not the real cause of the problem, but we get things sorted out without people getting killed, normally."

"Normally?"

"Well every once in a while someone will die in one of these discussions, and usually once that has happened the need for further discussion just drifts away."

"You have a strange way of dealing with peoples differences."

"We don't need people to be different, you do. We are soldiers, soldiers of god, but soldiers."

"But there are differences between you."

"Yes, there are leaders, followers, and commanders."

"And which are you?"

"Obviously I am a follower."

"And Kevana is a commander?"

"No. He is a leader there is a difference."

"I don't see any difference, he tells you what to do and you do it. The chain of command is clear in your group, he is first, then you, then perhaps Briana, he seems the best suited to command once you two are gone."

"Sounds like you are planning to remove the two of us."

"No, just thinking about the dynamics of your group, our group would just fall apart without Worandana, there would be so much squabbling over who should be leader that nothing at all would get done. Perhaps it would be better is we 'discussed' things the way you do."

"I think not, you aren't resilient enough for the rough and tumble of our 'discussions', someone would get seriously hurt."

"But I'd really like a chance to give Kirukana a bit of a beating."

"That is the thing, this isn't about personal vendettas, it's about reducing the tension within the group before important decisions are made."

"Could be seen as just an excuse for a brawl."

"Soldiers don't need an excuse for a brawl, we'll sometimes fight over the silliest of things when we are bored, it is boredom that is the real enemy, we have to keep active and fighting is one way of maintaining our readiness for battle. And sometimes it is an excuse to give Petrovana a kicking." laughed Alverana.

"You are a very strange man." laughed Gorgana. "I think I'll get a little rest it has been a hard night for me."

"So I heard."

"Kirukana has no idea what he is talking about."

"Who said I heard it from him?" Gorgana's mouth fell open, his guilt plain upon his face. He glanced around quickly to see who was within earshot.

"Have no fear, I'll not tell anyone, every man is entitled to a little fun now and again, I must say I admire your choice though."

"Somehow I don't feel that I actually had any choice in the matter at all." whispered Gorgana.

"Relax." said Alverana. "We are just two men talking, if you start whispering or looking around furtively, then people will start to listen. A certain young lady came to the well when I was getting water this morning, she asked after you. I told her that you were in a bit of trouble and had been accused of sleeping with Anya. She threw back her head and howled with laughter, saying that there was no way the you would have been capable, she has a lovely smile doesn't she? She walked back to the tavern, I could see her shoulders shaking with laughter as she walked."

"She was wrong. The healing power of that stone, which I felt last night, is such that I was more than capable, I had a serious need, Anya would never have broken her vow to her husband. Mores the pity, I would have enjoyed a little roll in the grass with her."

"Not exactly a priestly sentiment."

"I know, there are occasions when I don't think I'm actually cut out for this sort of life."

"I am sorry, my friend, but you have left it a little late to come to that decision."

"Don't I know it." laughed Gorgana, turning towards his tent.

Alverana returned to his place by the fire, his thoughts turned to Gorgana's words, some of the things he had said rang true for Alverana, there were times when he seriously considered retirement, the thought of his own children running around him, perhaps even grandchildren by this time in his life, something that was never going to happen, it was far too late to start all that. He shook his head and took out his sword, sharpening it always calmed his nerves when he was distracted as he was at the moment. The slow steady sound of the whetstone running from the hilt to the tip of the sword was a sound that tended to irritate so many people, but he found it very soothing. Slowly his thoughts turned to more soldierly things, memories of battles won, fights fought, and temples burned.

"What are you grinning about?" asked Kevana.

"Nothing much, just remembering."

"Well let's go and have another look around this village, for some reason it interests me."

"I can see why you are interested in this place." said Alverana, getting up and putting away his whetstone. Kevana set off towards the main gate.

"What is it then about this place?"

"It is a peaceful place, with some nice people, it is a place we could actually settle down in."

"Settle down?"

"I am certain you know what I mean, we could become part of this community, if they would have us."

"You would want to?"

"I have to be honest to myself, there are times when I wish for a home that is not a barrack room, for a family that is not composed entirely of sweaty men. Occasionally I like to see children playing. These things are all around us here. And we could do some good in this place."

"Somehow I think a few weeks in this place would drive you mad, it would be so boring. No, I'd not give up my life to live here, it would be like being dead."

"No, it would be more like the real life that everyone else knows, those who's lives we disturb in our passing, can't you see that it would be good for us?"

"No I don't. Have you lost the urge to be a soldier?"

"I don't think so, but this latest mission of ours, has certainly given us all many things to think about, we are not just fighting men any more, or hadn't you noticed, there are gods stacking up around us, this thing is far bigger than we know."

"We haven't actually fought anyone yet." snapped Kevana.

"That is what I mean, we are reduced to only five and then we meet up with some clerics, we haven't fought a single person and we are almost wiped out. So far we have had three fights on this mission, and we lost one man only, and that was to that damned bird god. Not a human enemy you notice, but then none of them have been, snow demons, snakes, strange lights in the rocks, but I don't class that as a fight, we haven't even seen the foe, and it seems like for ever since we set out, I remember that departure, do you?"

"I remember."

"You said how proud you were of us all and how great an honour it was for us to be the ones that recover the sword."

"I remember."

"Pride. Honour. We are five out of eight, where is their pride, where is their honour, they died in the cold, and we could do nothing for them, we were hard pressed enough to stay alive ourselves. The one that really surprised me through all this is that damned horse of yours, I was sure that prancing fool was going to die with all the others, but he didn't, look at him he's over there behind the smithy, and yes he's prancing for the attention of the fillies around him. He is unscathed by this mission, but only because he is too stupid to realise just how badly things have gone for us."

"This one has been hard on all of us, especially those still alive, but we are soldiers, and we must carry on until we complete this mission or die in the attempt."

"Somehow it looks like the later is more probable than the former."

"I don't think so, Gorgana has what it takes to finish this thing today, I have felt his power, and he is very good at what he does."

"How do you mean?"

"He is very precise in everything he does, his concentration is exceptional. He'll bring that thief here tonight, of that I am sure."

"We shall all be in it with him, I hope he lives up to your expectations. What about Kirukana?"

"If he causes us any more problems I'll have his head in a heartbeat."

"You better be quick, because I think Worandana or Gorgana will do the same."

"Gorgana wouldn't, he knows that is Worandana's responsibility, he'll let the leader do it, and you are right, they'll both get him before I can even move."

"I worry about these strange magics." said Alverana, very quietly.

"I worry too, but there is nothing we can do about it, Worandana has made his mind up, and Gorgana is determined to try this one."

"Too determined?"

"What do you mean?"

"I don't know really, it just that he felt desperate to do this thing, something in his voice didn't ring too true."

"Do you think this is anything to worry about?"

"Worrying is not my responsibility, that one is yours. I just go where I am told and soldier." laughed Alverana.

"Thank you for that, now will you tell what you mean?"

"I'm not sure what I mean, if I mean anything at all. He just seemed a little impatient to get on with it, it could be that, simply that he wants to get the job done in a hurry."

"Why the hurry?"

"I don't know, perhaps he is as scared of this magic as we are, and just wants to get it done."

"Could be, I suppose, but what else could it be?"

"Don't ask me, if it was Petrovana acting a little strange I might have a chance of working out what is wrong with him, but I have no idea at all what goes on in the minds of these clerics, they are all more than a little strange to me."

"I agree. They are strange but we have to keep an eye on them all."

"But how do we know when they are doing something out of character? Everything they do is strange."

"Did I say it was going to be easy?"

"Nothing is ever easy with you is it?"

"I suppose not."

"Look at that wall. It's pathetic."

"Agreed."

"But it wouldn't take much work to make it useful, some bracing, some of the gaps filling, a step to give the defenders a little height, a few days work and this wall could be twice as effective, and it wouldn't need to look any better from the outside."

"You want to stay here and teach these people how to defend themselves?"

"Would that be a bad choice to make at this time?"

"That would depend entirely on your point of view. Could you desert your friends?"

"If every one decided too leave the priesthood at the same time, then all our friends would be leaving. How many friends do you have who aren't here?"

"Point taken. All my friends are here, but not everyone here is my friend, do you know what I mean?"

"I know, but that isn't necessarily a problem, even none friends could easily go along with the idea of completely disappearing, because that is what it would take, we would have to vanish from the land utterly."

"But we couldn't vanish and be here at the same time, there are people who know we have been here, and others would come here to look for us."

"That is true, we would have to leave until the searchers had given up."

"Searchers that don't actually have to be here to look for us, a competent team could locate either of us from many days travel away, there are after all lots of people who know us very well, they could find us where ever we go."

"Damn, I always forget about that, I'm a simple soldier at heart." Alverana laughed and kicked the wall, a large hole opened in the wall as a plank fell out.

"All this idle speculation is getting us nowhere. In some ways I agree, it would be nice to settle in a place like this, but it is not a thing that is going to happen, now is it?"

"No. But it is nice to dream, if only for a while."

"This is certainly a nice place to be, but we will be leaving soon."

"Yes. And where will we be going?"

"Once I have that damned sword we will be going to Zandaarkoon by the shortest route I can find."

"Then what?"

"I have absolutely no idea, it depends on what Zandaar wants of us."

"So we shall get a command straight from our god?"

"Most probably."

"Some how I feel better if our god is kept at a distance, it feels a little dangerous to have him so close and personal."

"You are afraid of him?"

"Most certainly, he has had whole groups of people killed for the most obscure of reasons."

"I am certain that we will not be amongst those."

"So were they, but as you say we have no real choice in the matter, do we?"

"It is our duty to our god to do as he asked." The two men continued their patrol around the inside of the wall, until they came to one of the steepest sections, there is was clear that the wall wasn't even a token gesture, there was an opening in it that a small man could get through without any effort, a bigger man would have to squeeze a little, or perhaps remove the next plank. While they were looking at the opening a fox poked its nose through then changed it's mind about coming in, they saw a flash of red as it disappeared up the hill outside the wall.

"They really need some help with their wall." Said Alverana.

"Not just the wall, their reception committee, when we arrived." Kevana shook his head. "They wouldn't have put off a small band of outlaws. A party of blank shields would have laughed at them. They need help there too."

"Agreed, perhaps there is something we are missing?"

"Like what? The wall is a joke, and the defence force is worse."

"But nobody comes this way, they live in a place that is nowhere, it isn't on a road to anywhere, and we have only killed one of the obstacles on the path through the mountains, I don't see that opening up into a major road anytime soon, do you?"

"No, we stumbled into this place because we were led here, unless you know it exists then you are unlikely to come this way looking for a town to raid. I think they are fairly safe, so long as only a few know of their existence, but then we now know of it, a heathen godless place, if peaceful."

"I am sure that someone will want to change that, aren't you?"

"Kirukana will certainly want to bring our god to this place, but there is no certainty that he will survive this day, his zealousness has got him into some deep trouble."

"Have you noticed something strange about this place?"

"Everything about this village is strange, to what particular strangeness do you refer?"

"Where is the garbage dump?"

"I haven't seen one, is it important?"

"Not really, but if there was one it would be here, we are at the back of the village, far enough from any of the houses not to bother anyone with the stink, but there is nothing, only a small pile of broken pots. Another thought though, any refuse that is edible goes to the pigs, anything combustible goes on the fires, anything metal is reclaimed by the smith, and the sewage is eventually recycled as fertiliser, this is the garbage dump, these broken pots are all the waste this village produces."

"Again, is this important?"

"Not really, but this place is very efficient. How many towns have we been to that are detectable by their smell from more than a day downwind?"

"Do you remember that tiny little mining village in the southern hills, I forget its name? We were convinced it was just up the valley, for three days we were convinced, then we found it and the stench was so terrible that we only stayed a few hours."

"I remember, and the only way out of that valley was downwind, we rode through the night, damn near killed half the horses trying to get away from the stink."

"Pertovana dived into the river trying to wash the stink off, only the river stank as much as anything else." They both laughed aloud, shared memories of good times, or in this case not so good times.

"This village is much more efficient than that mining town, they waste almost nothing, if fact most of the waste is here in this spot."

"Fine, they are a thrifty people, but how does this help us?"

"It helps us in no way at all, but it helps them enormously, the overall running costs of this village are very low. They need almost nothing from the outside, they have no contact, at least not on a regular basis. This place is almost hidden from the outside world, if a man wanted to disappear, then this a place to do it."

"I thought we had already established that such a thing is impossible, any traitor would be found."

"Yes. Impossible for us, but for any others, then very possible. There could be people here who have prices on their heads in other cities."

"You want to become a freelance bounty hunter, is that it?"

"It could be a way to make a little money on the side, after all we do tend to travel rather a lot."

"But we are not bounty hunters, we are soldiers. Do you have a problem with being a soldier at the moment, you seem to want to leave this profession?"

"It's not that, it's just that a little variety makes the job a bit more interesting. And the money is good."

"How many of our friends have died on this mission? And you want something a little more exciting. Perhaps we should have captured the snake and sold it to some freak show owner, would that have been exciting enough for you?"

"That is not what I mean and you know it. I just think a little variation would help."

"So who is it in this village that is hiding from a previous life?"

"I don't know, it could be almost any of them, that smith has a face I wouldn't trust."

"You have seen his work, he is definitely a smith, and has been all his life."

"But he could still be on the run for some terrible crime or other."

"Or he could just be a simple smith, who completed his apprenticeship, and became a journeyman, who's journey ended here."

"That is a possibility, but he could be on the run."

"As could we all, and fairly soon."

"That isn't very likely though, is it?"

"No, Gorgana will bring the sword to us tonight, and we will be treated royally when I present it to Zandaar. We shall be amongst Zandaar's most favoured."

"I am still not at all sure I like to be that close to god. Bad things can happen to people who are under gods eye, he sees into their minds, who can control every thought? One slip when those eyes are turned your way, and you are dead in a moment. Can't we just send him the sword? Then accept the honours back at our base?"

"The instructions are very clear, the sword must be presented to Zandaar in person, as soon as is possible. The reward isn't actually in the instructions, but for something like this it has to be something really good."

"In my experience, when someone hides something it is for a reason."

"Whoever hid the sword and protected it so well obviously didn't want anyone to use it."

"I wasn't actually thinking of that, but now you mention it, someone didn't want the sword loose in the world, and now it is, perhaps someone had a reason for not wanting Zandaar specifically to get hold of it. No, it was the prize I was thinking of, a simple 'riches beyond the imagination' would have been enough for most people, but for me that would have been a warning. I have a vivid imagination, and anyone who thinks they can match that with gold is offering more money than I wish to earn. To offer a fixed reward would have been too much for some and not enough for others, to keep the reward a secret, now that is a plan, each man will think of the best possible reward for himself and assume that is what he will get, this profession has turned me into a cynical man, I begin to have serious doubts about this mission, I think the prize is secret because no one would actually want it."

"How do you mean?"

"The more I think about it the more I worry. The sword was hidden for a reason, we are sent to recover it, once the protection has been removed, a watcher is set so that we will know as soon as that tree dies, my bet is that the watcher had instructions to carry the sword, we are just his escort. If the watcher was of a higher rank than you he could have given further instructions, couldn't he?"

"Yes, Crandir was a master, of the cleric class, but he certainly outranked me."

"Instructions. Anything specific about the sword?"

"Let me think, the language was a little archaic, and I didn't bring them with me, there was something about the sword being 'unsullied'."

"Unsullied. Not used, not blooded. Well it has almost certainly been that by now, both your search, and Worandana's showed him carrying it on his back, and when we met them in the cave, it was the sword he used to bring down the exit tunnel. So that is one of the conditions of this mission breached. God is not going to be happy with us if we take him the sword."

"We have no choice, but to take him the sword, the only option is death."

"Delivering the sword may also be death."

"So we have nothing to lose."

"I suppose."

"Do you think it is too early for a beer?" asked Kevana, looking at the tavern that was only a few yards away now, their talk having taken round more than half of the wall, though they had actually inspected very little of it.

"You know me, it is never too early for a beer. But Kirukana may be here."

"Then it is his responsibility to stay away from us." Sure enough as they walked onto the veranda they saw a black robed figure sitting alone at a table in one corner, the hooded head lifted, then descended again, the cowl was pulled so far forward that no face was visible. The landlord came bustling out to serve then.

"Good morning gentlemen, what can I get for you today?"

"Just a mug of beer for each of us, if you please."

"I shall be but a moment." True to his word Garath was back in a very short time, and placed two mugs on the table.

"Stunningly quick service, how do you manage it?" asked Kevana.

"Simple, I saw you walking this way and thought that you would be stopping for a beer, seems I was right." laughed the barman.

"What if we had decided it was too early in the morning to start drinking beer?"

"Well if it's too early for you it's not too early for me. I didn't get to be this shape by avoiding beer or food." he laughed slapping his more than ample belly. He sat down on one of the spare stools at their table, it groaned somewhat alarmingly.

"What is wrong with your miserable friend?" he asked nodding his head in the direction of Kirukana.

"There has been a theological disagreement, something to do with the nature of sin, and he has been given a little time to consider his rather extreme and vocal position." whispered Kevana. "Hopefully he will see the error of his ways, I just hope he doesn't get too drunk to think clearly on this wonderful beer."

"He obviously doesn't consider beer drinking a sin."

"Actually he does, but the sin in question today is something far more wicked."

"Can you elucidate?"

Kevana and Alverana exchanged brief glances before Kevana continued.

"I suppose. He has accused Gorgana of laying with Anya, on the green, by the lightning stone. Apparently he found them asleep together this morning."

Garath laughed so hard he almost fell from his stool. Slowly the laughter subsided enough so he could talk.

"She is a little strange, but strangest of all is her absolute devotion to her husband, a mindless cripple though he be, many have tried to bed her, and all have failed. She's older than she looks, but she looks well for a woman twenty years younger than she is. She'll have no man but her husband, not while he lives, and the old bugger shows no intention of dying just yet. How she has kept him alive so long is another mystery. There is no way in the world that Gorgana and Anya have had knowledge of each other, if you know what I mean." Garath had a little smile on his lips as he looked at the two.

"We already know that." said Kevana. "Apparently Gorgana was invited to breakfast, so Worandana went with him. They had breakfast with Anya and her husband, though he said little and eat nothing at all."

"It is both a sad and beautiful tale." said Garath. "He was a vital and strong man once, but the creeping mind sickness took away his memory, now he can't remember anything, but still she loves him. She feeds him, and cleans him as if he were a babe in arms, she is stronger than she looks, both physically and mentally. Despite her age, she would make someone a good wife, even now."

"You would have her?" asked Kevana.

"I have tried, but my horse fell at the first hurdle, and kicked me in the head, I am besotted with the woman, and she doesn't even know I exist." he laughed, stood. "No fool like an old fool, I think I need a beer." He walked slowly inside, his head hanging.

"It seems that everyone in this village knows how Anya feels about her husband." said Alverana.

"It does appear that way, but that said, they do seem to have a loose set of morals in this village, in some places even to attempt to bed a married woman, is a burning at the stake offence, usually for both parties."

"Attitudes are different in every place we go, there can be fewer people more travelled than we, even merchants only go where they know they can sell whatever it is they are carrying, and only buy something when they know where to sell it, their range is much more restricted than ours, so we must meet the entire range of moral attitudes. This is one of the most relaxed places I have been."

"That is certainly one way of putting it."

"We have all heard stories of even wilder places, though haven't we?"

"I once heard of an island in the southern sea, where all the women will simply lay on their backs if man so much as smiles at them, and there are almost no men in this place."

"And I bet some old boy was trying to sell you a map to the place?"

"Funny you should mention that, he was actually after crew for a ship that was going that way."

"You managed to avoid the temptation then?" laughed Alverana.

"It was difficult, but I resisted."

"Blessed be the power of prayer, I wonder how many men fell for that line?"

"Not many, but perhaps he was actually after something else, like my purse."

"That too is a possibility. There are many rogues in this world, one has to aware of them at all times."

"Strange isn't it?"

"What now?" asked Alverana.

"We worry about the morals of people having a little fun, and yet the morals of robbers and bandits are never questioned, when their activities cause far more pain and suffering."

"This is the world we live in, violence is all around, but fun is not allowed."

"It must be getting near to midday by now, I think it's time we had something to eat."

"I agree." said Alverana.

"Service!" shouted Kevana, not quite in his parade ground voice.

"You bellowed sir." said Carin as she came through the door. Alverana laughed.

"I did, my dear. Have you any food to offer hungry travellers?"

"You don't seem to be so much travelling as camped, but I think we can find you something to prevent starvation. There will be pies available in a little while, if that is all right with you gentlemen." she said, smiling at both of them, but mainly at Alverana.

"I am sure that anything prepared by your fair hand will be just fine by us." said Alverana, returning her smiles.

"You are in luck, I'm not cooking today, I have been told that my cooking isn't even fit for the pigs. Garath is making the pies, they'll be ready soon, in the meantime, another beer?"

"Another beer will be fine, I am sure you have other skills, besides being beautiful." said Alvernana.

"I can't cook, I don't sew, I won't have anything at all to do with animals, but they say I will be a good wife to some very lucky man, one day. One day is all he will last." she laughed as she disappeared inside, returning very shortly with two more mugs of beer, she put them on the table, and stood tapping her foot, waiting for the other mugs to be empty. These she took as soon as they hit the rough wooden top of the table.

"She jiggles quite distractingly when she is tapping that foot." said Alverana.

"I noticed." replied Kevana.

"Still, no reason to rush good beer." laughed Alverana.

"Indeed." Kevana joined the laughter with his own.

"I think she could be right." whispered Alverana.

"What do you mean?"

"I am sure she has the sort of skill that would kill a man on his wedding night."

"But he'd die with a grin on his face."

"And a coffin that wont shut." They both laughed loudly at the pictures this comment put into their minds. Carin came out carrying two plates, each with a pie and some potatoes, all covered with a rich brown gravy.

"Are you two laughing at me, because if you are, then you shall be wearing these pies."

"No, my dear." said Alverana. "We are laughing at the demise of your poor husband."

"I'm not married, I thought I made that quite clear."

"You did, you did. But your husband is sure to die on his wedding night, with a big stupid grin on his face, and jealous looks from every other man in the vicinity."

"You think I'm stupid enough to marry a man who can't take the pace. Rest assured, as soon as I find a man worthy, I'll marry him, whether he likes it or no." She dropped the plates on the table, causing only a minor spillage of gravy, it was too rich to go very far. She placed her fists on her hips. "Care to step up to the mark, priest?" she snapped.

"Er." Alverana looked to Kevana for assistance, only to see his friend lean away from the table with both hands in the air and huge grin on his face. "Sorry, my dear. Religious holidays, vows of celibacy, any number of things mean that I can never accept your challenge, but mainly the fact that in some ways I am a very small man. Please forgive me and my useless friend, we meant no harm, nor slight upon your character." Alverana's abject apology caused Carin to throw back her head and laugh to the sky. With a swirl she spun around and dropped onto the stool next to Alverana. She leant towards him, giving him and excellent view of the contents of her shirt, which was open a fair way. She placed her hand on his leg, he froze, then stared at Kevana, a look of terror on his face, again Kevana raised his hands. She slid her hand up his leg until she was forced to laugh even louder.

"Fear will do that to a man." said Alverana, hoping to recover something from the situation. Only more laughter, from both Carin, and Kevana. Slowly she stood and patted Alverana on the head before returning into the tavern.

"She is a strange and wonderful girl." said Kevana.

"That she is, but she is so frightening, I've never met another that is anything like her."

"What, despite all our travels?"

"Yes. She is unique, one of a kind. And the day she chooses a husband all men bar one can breathe a huge sigh of relief. The one will be lucky if he can breathe at all."

"I am certain that she will keep him happy."

"Without a doubt." Alverana plunged a fork into his pie, and was greeted by a wonderful smell, lamb, carrots, onions, and gravy oozed slowly out. "Smells good." he said, then put a piece of the meat into his mouth. "Tastes great, the man that cooked this could make someone a good wife, and after what Carin just did to me, I think that wife could be me."

"I didn't know you were that way inclined?" muttered Kevana.

"I'm not but that girl frightens me."

"Why?"

"Because she is the sort of girl who can make a man break any vow he has ever made, and for what? One night of pleasure."

"Tempted?"

"More than I would like to admit, but definitely tempted."

"But she's young enough to be your daughter." Kevana smiled.

"What difference does that make? And she's old enough to know better."

"I've never seen you so rattled by anyone in my life."

"It's women, they do that sort of thing to me, at least some of them do. That one especially."

"I know you, I know your past, you've had your share of, er, dalliances. Why does this one frighten you?"

"I think it's because she is so certain of herself, she's so confident. But beautiful none the less."

"And does she know It?"

"Agreed, but the food is great. I wonder how he does all this, something else strange about this place."

"Stop it."

"What?"

"There is no way in hell that we are going to settle down in this place, to stop even thinking about it."

"Yes boss." laughed Alverana, filling his mouth with more of the rich contents of the pie.

"You are a bad man." said Kevana.

"No. That is your job." laughed Alverana.

"Right, once we've finished here, we'll return to camp, I think things have been getting a little lax in the last few days, we need a serious training session, after all I don't want you all getting fat on this rich food and beer."

"See what I mean, bad man. I agree, we've been more than a little lazy in the implementation of training schedules recently, probably something to do with spending most of our days fighting for our lives."

"Exactly, I think a hard warm up session then a fencing contest."

"Fine, that should take up most of the afternoon, without taxing mental focus too much. A good plan, I like it, but still a bad man."

"Someone has to be. You can do all the arranging."

"Even better, that way it looks like my idea, and I get all the bad feeling."

"I think you said it, boss, that was the word."

"Thanks, boss!"

"No problem, if we can get some of those damned clerics involved, they may just learn a thing or two, something useful that will keep them alive."

"Or get them killed."

"I see that as no way to lose."

"Bad man. But it might just help them to stay alive in a combat situation."

"How?"

"They may just find out how much they don't know and decide that playing dead is the best way to stay alive." Alverana laughed.

"Playing is better than being."

"I'll agree with that, but can they learn something as complex as lying down?"

"We'll find out this afternoon, you'll have to teach them."

"Great, another impossible task. You really like handing those out, don't you?"

"Just one of the joys of being boss."

"Thanks, I'll do what I can but don't expect too much of those clerics, their training is seriously lacking in certain areas."

"It is time they started."

"What if Worandana wants us to learn some of their arts?"

"Then you, my friend, are in deep trouble." Kevana laughed.

"But we can't afford that sort of thing ahead of tonight's expected work."

"But tomorrow night could be entirely different."

"That's right, look on the bright side."

"What, don't you think you can beat them in a contest of magic?"

"You know me, and I know you, neither of us could beat the lowest of them, in that sort of contest. But on this mission anything in the magical realm is unlikely to require us all in an individual capacity, it's going to be group action, isn't it?"

"Most likely, but who can predict the future, many things can change in a moment, a sword fight could switch to a magical battle in an instant, would you be ready for that?"

"Probably not, but then it is very unlikely, that any cleric could concentrate on spell casting with a sword in his guts."

"Unless he was behind some tree, or somewhere out of sight." Kevana nodded his head in the direction of Kirukana.

"Then Briana is going to have to put an arrow through his head, that'd should sort him out."

"True. Let's get this finished here, then we can get on, there is still much to do today."

They both emptied their plates in short order, and Kevana shouted of Carin.

"Thank you, my dear, the food was excellent and the beer better, please send our thanks to the chef."

"That I shall. Another beer?"

"No thank you, we still have things to do, and a clear head is most definitely indicated, a couple more of those and I'll not be fit for anything."

"Fine. Until later then." She scooped up the plates and mugs and carried them inside, her hips swinging provocatively, both men were momentarily hypnotised by the swaying of her skirt.

With a sigh Kevana got up from the table and left the veranda, without even a glance at Kirukana, who was still sitting in the corner, staring at the table top. Alverana followed as they walked slowly across the green, the sun had passed its peak but the day was warming nicely, they paused by the lightening stone, and stared briefly at the dark stains on the top, knowing that these were bloodstains made them both shiver a little inside.

"More than a bit macabre." said Kevana.

"And later we are going to add to these, with more of our own."

"No. Only Gorgana will be giving blood to this thing, the rest of us will be concentrating on controlling the power, and channelling it through the staff. Gorgana will make the power do what we want it to. It is going to be hard on us all, but it will be worth it."

"I certainly hope so." muttered Alverana, saying a silent prayer to Zandaar.

They walked into the camp and everyone was sitting around on the grass, Petrovana was laying on his back staring up at the clouds rushing by on the high wind from the mountains.

"Attention everyone!" shouted Alverana. Almost all those present looked in his direction. "I said Attention!!" The emphasis on the last word had all the soldiers scrambling to their feet. "Better." He continued in a loud voice. "Someone has decided that we are all getting fat and lazy, I didn't agree with him at the time, but now I see that he was indeed right, lax and lazy. All are invited to an exercise class, and a small fencing competition, this in not the sort of invitation that can be refused. You have a little time to dress for the occasion then we will begin. And that includes you Kevana!"

In fact there was only one man who was exempt from the exercise, on the grounds of his age. All the men returned from their respective tents dressed more suitable for the routines that they knew were awaiting them, each was dressed in light trousers and tight fitting shirts, all black of course. Even as designated instructor Alverana was not exempt from the exercises, he put them through a punishing set of warm up exercises and a few short sprints, followed by a slow run around the entire green, many of the towns folk turned out to watch the strange behaviour. Carin sat on the wall of the veranda of the tavern, laughing until she fell off, at the priests puffing and panting as they staggered past.

"Well." said Alverana, when they had all finally returned to camp. "You are indeed a sorry bunch. You spend too much time letting horses do all the work. We shall have to do something about that in the coming days, in the mean time, you get a short rest before the fencing contest starts." Alverana went into his tent to get the necessary equipment for the competition, and to have a quick drink, he knew that he would struggle with dehydration before the fencing was finished. He returned to the camp fire and called them all for the fencing, each man had to take a numbered token from a cloth bag.

"Kevana. Do you think Worandana would like to take part in the fencing, we are only seven which is a very bad number for someone?" asked Alverana.

"Ask him." was the reply.

"Worandana." called Alverana through the entrance of the old man's tent. "Would you care to join our little fencing competition, just to make up the numbers you understand?"

"You insolent young pup!" snapped the voice from inside. "Just to make up the numbers indeed, I could whip you any day when I was younger, now I can still teach you a thing or two." Worandana pulled the tent open and joined the others.

"There is only one token left in the bag, so it must be yours." Said Alverana.

"You put eight tokens in the bag even though you only had seven competitors?" asked Worandana.

"I suppose I did hope for eight." smiled Alverana.

"Rogue." whispered Worandana.

"The rules." said Alverana, mainly for the clerics, because the others knew how these competitions worked. "First to two points, unless a clear kill is agreed by the spectators. The winner of each match goes on to the next round. Final is first to five points, or two kills. Any questions?"

"Who is the judge?" asked Apostana.

"Me, who else?" said Alverana.

"But you are taking part in the competition?"

"Are you accusing me of bias?"

"Well, no I suppose not."

"Good idea, you can easily lose your first bout with that sort of attitude."

"That's not really fair, is it?"

"Isn't life a bitch?" laughed Alverana. "First up, who drew number one and two?"

Briana and Apostana stepped forwards. Alverana gave Apostana the choice of swords, he picked the one on the left and Briana took the other one.

"These swords have large buttons on the tips and blunt edges. Please gentlemen, no strikes to the head, a sufficiently powerful lunge will break the button and make a hole clean through your opponent, and result is instant disqualification from the competition. Do you understand the rules?" Both men nodded and took up positions, they placed the swords on the baton that Alverana held at shoulder height, when the baton dropped the match was on. Nothing happened at all for a few moments, then Briana feinted on a high line and lunged low to Apostana's abdomen, only find the bigger man had moved his left and slashed at the exposed right leg.

"Point." called Alverana. "Point to Apostana, Briana you over extended on the lunge without first being sure the opponent had fallen for the highline feint." Then he stepped between them and raised his baton again. With a snap of the baton the game was on again. This time the two combatants were a little more cautious to start with, for some time they each made no attempt to strike a body, they concentrated on each others swords, then Briana stepped forwards and slashed at Apostana's legs, Apostana's parry of the stroke was perfect, but Briana changed target mid sweep, he stopped the arm, and turned the wrist angling the sword upwards, the point of the sword curved inwards and struck Apostana in the chest.

"Point." called Alverana. "A good parry, Apostana, but with these flexible swords you have to be ready for the tip to move, which is what Briana did, he has the experience with this weapon." Again the baton came up and both swords were place upon it. A snap of the baton and the game was on. Apostana decided on all out attack, he slashed at Briana continuously, causing the soldier to back up, defensively blocking each attack. Apostana's foot slipped on the grass, his attack faltered and Briana countered with a series of slashing attacks, first left then right, high then low, after three repetitions of the sequence Apostana responded to the attack automatically, even when the attack didn't come, Apostana blocked a low cut to the left only to find Briana's sword pressed against his heart.

"Kill." called Alverana. "Again it was experience that told, Briana trained you in a few breaths, and he could tell that he had done it, on the second time through his cycle your blocks were coming before the attacks, so he knew that he had you. Who's next, three and four?"

Fabrana and Petrovana both stepped forwards.

"This has to be a fix." said Petrovana.

"What are you complaining about?" asked Fabrana.

"Why do I always get you in these sort of things?"

"Lucky I guess."

"Some luck."

"Enough." said Alverana, knowing that these two could argue forever. He offered the swords, the men chose without another word. They took their positions and waited for Alverana to raise the baton, which he did in a moment or two. With a snap of the wrist the match was on. This time the sword play was fast and furious, so quick that most people couldn't even see what was happening, suddenly Petrovana stepped backwards and called. "Point."

"Who to?" asked Apostana.

"Point to Fabrana." said Alverana, "Good strike, a cut to the leg, Petrovana you were off balance, footwork as usual. You really need to concentrate on your feet more."

"That is easy for you to say." muttered Petrovana. The two faced each other again, the baton fell. The swords moved with subtle motions of the wrist, the arms stayed almost still, but the tips of the swords wove a complex pattern in the afternoon sun, slowly people of the village were gathering for the display of martial arts. It took some time and both men were sweating before Alverana called "Point to Petrovana."

"Why?" asked Apostana.

"Did you not see it?" asked Alverana.

"No."

"He caught me on the sword arm, just above the elbow." said Fabrana. "I know." He looked at Alverana. "His wrist was faster and smoother than mine, he spun his sword in a spiral and I stepped forwards at the wrong time. A good point to Petrovana." Fabrana saluted his opponent and took up his 'on guard' position. Petrovana stepped up and waited for Alverana to raise his baton, snap and the game was on. This time the men seemed to be even more cautious than before, neither wanting to commit the error that would give away the winning point, Petrovana stood absolutely still, never once did he move his feet, he deliberately let Fabrana do all the running around, knowing that Fabrana would eventually get tired and make the mistake. Every time Fabrana came in to attack Petrovana parried and blocked but refused to move, Fabrana was getting very obviously tired, until the mistake happened, Fabrana came in to slash at Petrovana's legs and stumbled, as he fell forwards Petrovana lunged forwards, and impaled himself on Fabrana's sword.

"Kill to Fabrana." shouted Alverana, as Fabrana's sword had taken Petrovana right in the centre of his chest. Fabrana jumped to his feet, suddenly looking far less tired than he had, he was breathing hard and sweating profusely, but no where near the limit of his endurance.

"You tricked me!" shouted Petrovana, rubbing his chest where the sword had struck.

"You were trying to tire me out, standing like a statue."

"A good trick." said Alverana. "Any trick that works is good, but something like that only works very occasionally, you would have been wide open if he hadn't just lunged like that."

"I know." said Fabrana. "But he always rushes in when he thinks he has won, this time he ran onto my sword."

"A dirty trick." muttered Petrovana.

"And not a trick that can be used anywhere other than a fencing match, try that sort of thing out here in the wilds and someone is going to stick a knife in your back while you are playing with your opponent." Alverana turned to the rest. "If you find yourself struggling to kill an opponent don't be too proud to call for one of your friends to stick a knife in his back, because you can be sure he is looking for one of his friends to do it to you."

"No one ever fights with us anyway. This whole thing is pointless." said Petrovana.

"Petrovana." said Kevana, in an exceptionally quiet voice, almost a whisper. "Don't let me have to say this again. The people we are chasing have in their party a wizard of some power and soldiers of some skill. Your magical skills are nothing compared to Granger, he did after all best me. You can only hope that your skill with a sword will keep you alive, and that you can actually get close enough to use that sword. They could have a skilled archer or two."

Petrovana looked at the ground but said nothing more.

"Who's next?" shouted Kevana, stepping forwards.

"Looks like it's me." said Gorgana, walking up to take one of the swords. Even though he knew he was going to be beaten Gorgana decided to put up some sort of fight, he attacked hard from the moment the baton dropped, he tried every trick he had learned, but to absolutely no avail, Kevana caught his every thrust, and blocked his every cut. Many times Kevana had a chance to finish the fight but on each occasion he chose not to, until Alverana suddenly shouted. "Break." The two combatants stepped away from each other.

"Kevana." snapped Alverana. "Stop playing games, the next time I see you pass up a chance to kill this man I will disqualify you. Do you understand?"

"I understand, but he was doing so well, and trying so hard, I couldn't bring myself to embarrass him."

"Please." answered Gorgana. "Embarrass away."

Alverana restarted the bout, and it was over in a moment, Kevana parried Gorgana's cut to the head and lunged straight for his opponents heart, stopping as the tip of the sword touched his chest.

"Freeze." yelled Alverana. Both men stopped exactly where they were. "Right." continued Alverana. "Everyone pay attention, even though this is a friendly fencing match Kevana cannot help but try to kill people. His sword has touched Gorgana's chest, but there is still enough flex in his elbow and wrist to thrust that sword straight through the body. If you come up against a real fencing champion, you will find that he has been trained only to touch the target, if you want to take advantage of this, make sure you kill him on the first try, you probably wont get a second one. Thank you gentlemen, you can move now."

"Glad to be of such assistance." muttered Gorgana.

"Sorry." said Alverana, "Gorgana you were completely out classed, Kevana could have beaten you at any single moment of that fight, however you have some considerable skill for a man in your profession, with a little work you could get to be very good." He turned to Worandana. "Looks like it's you and me old man."

"I'll old man you!" Worandana made his choice of the swords that Alverana presented. Alverana tossed the baton casually to Kevana saying. "Your turn to oversee, make sure there is no favouritism here."

"I shall be as scrupulous as you would be."

"I may as well give up then." laughed Alverana, turning slowly towards Worandana, he saluted and stood ready, waiting on Kevana. It was as Worandana was waiting for Kevana to raise the baton that he suddenly realised just how big a man Alverana was. 'How can he be that big and I haven't noticed?' He thought, then remembered that Alverana never stands close to anyone, always is softly spoken, and appears to walk with a slight stoop, all these thing together tend to hide his true size. 'I am glad this is only a game, I would hate to have to face him in the heat of battle.'

Kevana raised the baton, and both swords rested briefly on it. The baton dropped and nothing happened, both men stood perfectly still, staring intently into each others eyes, neither wanting to make the first attack. The tableau held for a moment that seemed to reach out to infinity, both men locked in a battle of wills, if not yet of swords. Then it happened, a piece of wood in the campfire cracked and spat sparks noisily up into the air, one man blinked, the other lunged forwards, swords clashed, a foot stamped, a sword tapped on a head, and three voices called as one, "Point." This sound caused the ones looking at the sparks from the fire to finally look back to see the men returning to their respective starting positions.

"Damn!" shouted Apostana. "What happened? I missed it."

"Someone who should have taken a kill, took a point instead. Can you explain that?" asked Kevana, staring straight at Alverana.

"Well." shrugged Alverana. "It was a trick far worse than any that Fabrana could ever use, and the old man didn't deserve to be completely out of the competition over a trick like that."

"Will someone tell me what happened?" Demanded Apostana.

"Well." said Worandana. "When the log on the fire cracked everyone looked towards the fire, this big brute blinked his eyes, as if he was going to turn towards the fire, I tried to take advantage of that moment of inattention, only he had lied to me, he was more than ready for my lunge, a simple parry, a step to the side and a tap on the head with the flat of his sword. I was so far off balance, that he could easily have finished it there and then."

"Enough chatter, this is going to take all day if we don't push along." Said Kevana, he nodded the two combatants into position and raised his baton again. This time the initial action was fast and furious, Worandana pressing hard and close, slashing broad cuts, and then pinpoint lunges, nothing got him anywhere close to his target, until Alverana caught a root with his toe, and staggered, the moment of imbalance was enough for Worandana to get inside his defences and push the point of his sword against Alverana's chest.

"Kill." shouted both Kevana and Alverana. Alverana bowed to Worandana, and took his sword from him.

"Well fought." he said. "You are surprisingly fast for such an old man."

"Why thank you, you arrogant pup." laughed Worandana.

"Right." shouted Alverana. "We have only four men left, let's have four tokens in the bag, and decide on partners again."

"That is not the way it is usually done." said Petrovana.

"Nothing wrong with a little change now and again, is there?" asked Alverana.

"I suppose not. It matters nothing to me, I'm already out after all."

Lots were drawn again.

"Who's first up?" asked Alverana. Worandana and Briana stepped forwards.

"Right. You two can sit down for a while, only fair that the one who has just fought gets a little rest. Kevana, Fabrana to the mark please."

"Don't I need a little rest?" asked Kevana.

"No." Was all the answer he got.

"He may not, but I certainly do." muttered Fabrana, as he took hold of one of the swords, leaving the other for Kevana.

It was obvious from the moment the baton dropped that Fabrana had no chance, or intention of winning this bout, Kevana tagged him on his sword arm for a point in almost no time at all.

"That was dreadful." said Alverana. "A five year old could have stopped that attack, or at least seen it coming. If you don't try harder I shall have to find something really dirty for you to do. How would you like digging latrines for the rest of this mission?"

"That's not fair. You know I don't stand a chance against Kevana."

"But you should at least try, on the battle field it is your life you are fighting for, here it is more difficult, but you have to try."

The next round went a little better, but with the same result, Kevana caught Fabrana totally out of position and moving the wrong way, in recovering Fabrana managed to block the original attack, but was so far off balance that he could do nothing about the lunge to his chest.

"Better." said Alverana. "Still he managed to twist you around until you were out of position, watch out for that sort of thing. A good kill though. Are you rested enough? Old man." He turned to Worandana.

"More than rested enough to beat you again."

"It's not me you have to beat, it is Briana. Gentlemen, if you please."

They both came forward, Briana let Worandana have first choice of the swords. Briana was left with the one that had been in Fabrana's hand. Carefully he dried the hilt with his shirt, once he was satisfied that it shouldn't turn in his grip he assumed the position in front of Alverana. The first point seemed to go on for a long time, at least to the competitors. Briana decided to use his height and weight as best he could, with a circular block he forced Worandana into a bind, that raised both sword hands high in the air, chest to chest, Briana was leaning down on the smaller and lighter man. Each man was trying to put the other off balance, before Alverana could call for a break Worandana placed his left hand on Briana's chest and pushed him hard away, as he stepped backwards, in a flash of the separation both Alverana and Kevana called "Point."

The combatants pointed their swords at the grass and awaited the decision.

"Point to Worandana." said Kevana. "A cut to the chest."

"Point to Briana." Was Alverana's reply. "A cut to the sword arm. Neither point scores. En guard gentlemen." He lifted the baton, and waited for them to come to order.

"This could go on for ever." muttered Worandana.

"Only if you let it." said Alverana.

The fight was on again with a rush of action, Worandana pressing hard, but still keeping some distance between himself and Briana, Worandana glanced down at Briana's feet, Briana responded with a high backhand cut to the shoulder, Worandana merely swayed beyond the reach of the blade and followed in behind it, forcing Briana to turn and defend. Again Worandana glanced downwards, this time Briana tried a straight lunge, Worandana again forced him to turn and defend. Briana began to feel that something was going on, but he had no idea exactly what it was. Again Worandana glanced down at the ground, this time Briana did nothing just waited. Worandana looked him in the eyes and smiled. For some reason he couldn't quite understand Briana felt like a rat caught in the gaze of a viper. Suddenly Worandana stepped backwards and threw his sword up into the air, involuntarily Briana's eyes followed the sword, as it arched upwards, then it vanished against the glare of the sun, when it dropped into Worandana's hand Briana was blind, a blind man has no place in a fencing match.

"Kill." Called Alverana. Briana felt the pressure of a sword point against his chest.

"Has someone called today dirty tricks day?" asked Petrovana, in utter disgust.

"Where did you see that done?" asked Alverana.

"No where."

"Do you know why he has never seen it done?" asked Kevana.

"Do tell."

"Because it has never been done, It is a campfire tale, told by a young soldier, more years ago than I care to remember."

"You told this tale."

"I did, and it was a complete fabrication from beginning to end, this old fool just made it real."

"You mean that no one has ever thrown their sword up into the sun to win a fight before?" Demanded Worandana.

"Not to my knowledge."

"Well it sounded good, the way you told it, suddenly, I'm not so sure."

"Be assured it wont work against me."

"I wouldn't have even thought of trying it against you, but Briana is younger, and so may not have heard the tale."

"Well That makes it you and me old friend, do you want a moments rest before we carry on?"

"A little rest can't hurt, can it?" Worandana walked over to the camp fire and dipped himself a cup of water from a bucket that was there, as he straightened up he saw Garin the smith walking towards the camp, with a staff in his hand.

"Hail Garin. Do you bring us good tidings?"

"Hello. I bring you a staff strengthened with thunder metal. As you requested. I believe that you haven't paid me anything like enough money for it, but the price was agreed, if I had the chance to make another one I would, it is without a doubt, the prettiest piece I have ever made." With more than a little reverence he handed the staff to Worandana. Who hefted it from hand to hand, spun it slowly around its midpoint, it made a soft whooshing sound as it turned over in his hands. Worandana tossed it up into the air and caught it one handed.

"It is a fine piece of work indeed. Not too much heavier than it was, but much stronger. It should be more than capable of the task we have in mind for it."

"It was very hard to make, the thunder metal had to be drawn into wires, and six wires are fastened to a metal end piece, then intertwined along the staff, everywhere they cross, they are joined, but without burning the wood, a task and a half in itself. I am happy with the work I have done."

"So am I, if it will carry the load that I expect it to try, then I will be more than happy, if it holds together for a few seconds It will be enough. Many thanks, master smith." Worandana bowed deeply, the staff held parallel to the ground.

"Thank you, sir. I think I'll go and get some sleep, I got precious little last night." Garin turned and walked slowly back towards the smithy, a few times he turned and glanced at the staff, he was sad to see it go, he had put so much effort into it. Worandana returned to the group of men and handed the staff to Gorgana.

"You better get a feel for this, your life will depend on it tonight." Gorgana took it, and inspected it carefully.

"It's not as heavy as I thought it would be, and I can't work out how he has joined the wires together."

"Will it be able to carry the load?" asked Worandana.

"No one knows that. We will find out later, no one has ever tried to handle that much power in one blast."

"Are you worried?"

"Stupid question. There are so many things that can go wrong, and for most of those the only important measurement is the number of corpses left, and I get the minimum to be one."

"You can back out, this can never be considered an order, the risks are too high."

"If I do that, then someone else will try, and they will fail, again a minimum body count of one."

"But the one wouldn't be you."

"Not relevant. This task is best suited for me, no one else stand the smallest chance of getting it right."

"Not getting a little large in the head, are you?"

"No one else has any real experience with moving things through space. By all the hells!"

"Something suddenly wrong?" demanded Worandana.

"Something I just remembered, moving through space." Corgana dropped cross legged to the ground, with the staff across his lap.

"Please explain." said Worandana softly settling to the grass beside him.

"The last time I tried this I was moving something small across a room. Today I shall be moving a man across a lot of distance. That has brought something extra to think about."

"I still don't understand."

"To flip this stone from me to you." He said picking up a pebble the size of a gold piece. "I can do that with the energy in my thumb. To toss it as far as Alverana I'd have to use the whole arm. To hit the lightning stone in the middle of the green I would struggle, someone else might be able to reach it."

"So it takes considerably more power to move a man than a stone, but you will have that power."

"If I could throw this pebble as far as the tavern, what would happen?"

"The stone would reach the tavern."

"And destroy itself in collision with the wall."

"Now I see. You will have to control the power to slow him down before he gets here."

"Easy, if I know where he is and how fast he is going. And there is another thing."

"What other thing now?" snapped Worandana.

"You know when you are walking through the city on a windy day there are places where the wind is so strong that it makes the act of breathing very difficult."

"I have experienced that sort of thing, but as I get older I worry more about be blown off my feet than suffocating in a strong wind."

"This is no wind we are talking about, this man is going to be coming towards us as fast as his body can be dragged through the air. I'll be pulling him here, and the air is going to be the force I am working against."

"So you will have to control the force accurately."

"Without the information I need to exercise that control, no that cannot ever work, he'll arrive here dead."

"Is there some other way?"

"There might be. I need to check one of my books."

"Do that, I have a fencing match to finish." Worandana rose and went over to Alverana. Gorgana went slowly to his tent, taking the staff with him.

"Are you rested enough?" asked Alverana.

"As much as will make no difference now, I have something else on my mind, but this fencing thing has to be done first, so let's get on with it, shall we?"

"As you will." He waved Kevana forwards, and offered Worandana the choice of swords. Choices were made and both men stood ready, Alverana raised the baton.

"First to three points or two kills." Both nodded and Worandana held his hand up over his eyes, so that he could check the position of the sun, it was getting considerably lower in the sky.

"If your sword leaves your hand I'll gut you." whispered Kevana, his eyes laughing as he spoke. Worandana smiled as he assumed the en guard position. The first flurry of attack and counter attack was so fast that no one other than the combatants themselves was even sure who was attacking and who was defending, back and forth they fought on the green, sometimes turning one way sometimes the other, switching directions in an entirely random manner. Suddenly as if some agreement had been met, though no words were spoken, both men disengaged. They stood panting for breath.

"If there was a point there, I didn't see it." said Alverana. Neither responded with anything other than a hand signal, Briana went to the bucket and brought both a drink.

Worandana drank his then tossed the cup back to Briana, Kevana drank only half, and poured the rest down the front of his shirt. Alverana stepped forward with a raised baton, and they took up the battle again. There was no slowing of the action, if anything the paced picked up a little, the patterns of the attacks became more and more complex, as each man tried everything he knew, Worandana was moving more and more onto the defensive, his knowledge of fencing techniques was far less than Kevana's. Worandana was moving backwards when Kevana made his first real attack, a pattern of slashes that started low and alternated with high line strikes, until Woandana fell for the feint and blocked a highline attack that turned into a low lunge, a very positive hit to the thigh.

"Point." called Alverana. "A good combination attack, the pattern was more complex than the one used by Briana, but just as effective."

The two men faced each other again, and set to the match with a will, the flashing of the swords in the gradually falling sun was hypnotic, Kevana was forcing Worandana to turn to his left, every time an opening appeared he would lunge for the exposed left shoulder, forcing the turn. Worandana was ever watchful for an expected change, even to the point of deliberately exposing the shoulder by letting it come slightly forward. On the fourth attempt Kevana went for the bait, striking at the shoulder he found that Worandana's blade was suddenly pressed against his sword arm.

"Point." called Alverana. "Perhaps even a kill, if you had slashed that strike it could have taken the whole hand off, and that is almost always a kill. Kevana you were clumsy, you took the bait and paid the price. That makes it all square, one point each."

The baton was raised and fell, the match continued. It was such a balanced fight that neither man could make any impression on the defences of the other. Worandana suddenly stepped back, and in a moment switched hands. Attacking again with the sword now in the wrong hand, Kevana's defences suddenly started to look more than a little shaky, three times Worandana nearly scored, but each time Kevana made a desperate move, a block that left him wide open, but moving away always managed to keep him safe. The last one of these attempts to escape caused Kevana to slip and gave Worandana an opening, a short arm lunge at the chest.

"Kill." called Alverana.

"I have never seen you use a sword in the left hand before." Said Kevana. "I know you write with the left hand, but never fencing."

"A few years ago I found a sword master who was left handed, so I took some lessons with him, so I learned how to fence properly with the left hand. I think I'm quite good as well."

"You are a kill in front. Which is not something I would have put any money on!"

"Live and learn."

"Let's see if I can teach you a thing or two." Kevana moved to the centre and raised his sword. With a gentle smile Worandana followed suit, both men looked to Alverana to raise the baton.

"Have you gentlemen decided which hand you are fencing with?"

"My sword is currently in my right hand." said Kevana. "And mine in the left." said Worandana.

"But it sounds like neither of you is willing to commit to the constancy of this situation." Both just smiled and said nothing further. The baton fell and they went at it with a will, Kevana was the first to switch hands, Worandana was a little surprised, he had never seen Kevana fight left handed either, after a series of lunges that Kevana parried easily Worandana switched to the right hand, and a sequence of slashing cuts to both upper and lower body, these had Kevana dancing from side to side, until he followed one cut through and slashed backhanded at Worandana's exposed neck, turning the blade at the last instant so it hit the shoulder instead.

"Kill." called Alverana. "That makes you even on kills. Next kill takes the match, but a moment or two to rest first." He waved at Briana indicating that water was again required. Both fencers drank the entire contents of the cups this time and looked around, there was quite a crowd gathered, drawn by the sound of steel, none were too close, but they were not certainly watching the contest. Looking at some of the discussions going on around the green, Worandana was almost certain that wagers were being placed on the outcome. 'I wonder if anyone is betting on me.' He thought.

"Ready gentlemen?" asked Alverana.

Both returned to the centre, each raised his sword in salute to the other then the match was on again in earnest. Both these men were the best in their respective professions, neither was used to being beaten, each was desperate to win this most simple of entertainments, not only the complexity of the swordplay increased, the speed doubled, the power behind each cut and lunge doubled, the intensity on the faces was plain for all to see, through the glittering cascade of steel that appeared to encase them. Alverana was watching closely, hoping that it would be over soon, he disliked the look in the eyes of both men, then he noticed a cool breeze, on a windless afternoon, standing in full sunlight, where did that sudden cooling come from. Slowly he reached behind himself, and down to his discarded robe, his hand fell to the hilt of his own sword, with a single motion he lifted the long, two handed broadsword and brought it flashing down between the two fencers.

"Break!" He yelled as one of the lighter blades broke against his sword. The shock was enough to stop the two, both stared somewhat bemused at Alverana, both breathing so hard that talking was impossible.

"What is wrong?" asked Briana.

"This was supposed to be a friendly training exercise, one of them was storing power, pulling heat from the air. I felt the cold, now the heat of the sun returns. I think we should call that a draw."

"I don't understand." said Briana.

"One of these two was storing energy, to use in some magical fashion."

"How could they? Their concentration was totally on the swordplay."

"I thought so too, but the chilling of the air was such an obvious sign that something was happening."

"Could it have been someone else?"

"It wasn't me." muttered Kevana.

"Nor me." answered Worandana.

"Was it one of these peasants?" demanded Alverana, waving a hand at the audience. "Someone of skill and power was setting something in motion."

"Was the cold like a soft breeze on the skin?" asked Fabrana.

"No." snapped Alverana. "It was a deep cold, like it was trying to suck the very life out of my bones."

"I have felt such a thing once before." whispered Fabrana, staring a little guiltily at Kevana.

"When?" asked Kevana.

"It was a few years ago, we were part of a detachment sent to defend a town from raiders, I can't even remember the name of the place. After two days of attacks the raiders managed to break through one of our walls, we rushed to the breach and tried to stop too many of them getting in, I was fighting shoulder to shoulder with Kevana, and suddenly on a day when people were sweating blood I was so cold I thought I had died. The sun seemed to lose some of its brightness, but there wasn't a cloud in the sky. Then Kevana screamed and ran straight at the gap in the wall, every one of the enemy fell before him, he reached the wall and stood in the breach, screaming and killing. Those on the inside were trying to get out, and those on the outside were trying to get in, anyone that came within range of his sword died, there were no exceptions. I swear that I saw one man die when Kevana cut off his head, the man was standing beyond the reach of Kevana's sword, it reached out through empty air and took his head. When the enemy turned and ran the bodies were waist deep around Kevana. Once they had gone Kevana collapsed. He says he remembers nothing of the incident at all. But the cold came first."

"Such a berserker rage is not unusual, especially in a trained soldier, one who sees the day going badly for his friends, then they are capable of extraordinary feats." said Briana.

"This was no simple berserker rage, I have seen that many times, this was something much more." muttered Fabrana.

"I have been told of the incident many times." said Kevana. "But I still have no idea what happened, I remember running towards the breach in the wall, I was calling men with me, but then nothing, until I was awakened inside the barracks. I was dreadfully tired."

"You have no idea how hard it was to get someone to help me move you inside." said Fabrana. "None would approach, there were mutterings of demons and such. It was only when the garrison commander came forwards and demanded that the walls be repaired, that things started to happen. Some of those locals would have cut your throat and piled you with the dead, and mine too."

"Why?"

"You killed friend and foe that day, only those out of reach of your blade had any prospect of safety."

"You think I could have done that sort of thing again, over a simple fencing competition?"

"Perhaps." said Alverana. Kevana snapped a savage look at his old friend.

"Perhaps, there is never anything simple for you when you have a sword in your hand, you take it seriously."

"How else can a soldier take sword play, life depends on it."

"Play is the important word here, today it should have been instructional, informative, educational, not lethal. A dead man has nothing more to learn."

"But I,"

"Enough." interrupted Alverana. "A draw is declared, and now is the time to rest, we all have a task ahead of us for this evening. A light meal will be prepared soon, and there will be no sneaking off to the tavern for a tankard of beer or two." Alverana turned his back before anyone could say anything further, he returned the practise swords to his pack wondering if the smith had the skill to fix the shattered one before they left. Kevana sank slowly to the grass, and sat staring downwards, not wanting to catch anyone's eye, he was feeling a little strange about this whole incident, the tales of his berserk attacks always disturbed him, but Fabrana's hushed report of that particular occurrence, this gave him some concern. As a younger man, such an attribute was a good thing for a soldier, but for a man with responsibilities to a group, it is definitely not a good thing. A leader must have control of himself before he can control others. 'Am I really in control of myself?' He thought, picking a blade of grass and rolling it between his fingers. The fresh smell of greenery filled his nostrils but the darkness of his thoughts were not dispelled in any way. 'I feel like I am in control, perhaps there is some way I can find a way to stop this happening. I need help with this, from one of these clerics, maybe Gorgana can help me. He will be busy resting, I'll ask him tomorrow.' The decision made he felt better. He got to his feet slowly, suddenly feeling very tired. He looked round at the last of the locals gradually returning to whatever tasks they had left to watch the fencing. Somewhat at a loss as to what he should be doing he decided to check on the horses. As he approached the corral his horse came strutting toward him, throwing it's head in the air, and shaking it's mane.

Kevana cuffed it gently on the nose as it's head came across the top rail of the fence.

"You are such a show off sometimes." He muttered, thinking 'You must get that from me, perhaps that is what I was doing during the match, showing off. I was struggling to beat an old man, and my brain decided to step the game up one more level. Now that is a frightening thought I could have killed all my friends, in a single moment of madness.' He took hold of the horses bridle and pulled it's head down until he was staring to it's large brown eyes.

"When you show off all that happens is you look stupid, when I show off people die." The horse pointed two large ears at the man, as if he understood what was being said.

"You are fooling no one but yourself." laughed Kevana, releasing the horse, who shied away from the sound. Kevana was not surprised by this, the laugh had certainly had a desperate sound about it. He leant on the rail, and watched the horse as it stepped sideways, shaking its head again, ears flicking nervously from one direction to another. The horse faced the man, stood absolutely still for a moment, then stamped his front right hoof, and returned to utter stillness.

"Alverana." said Kevana. "The horse sees you, and I heard no one so it must be you."

"Indeed. Old friend."

"Well?"

"I don't understand how it is that I have never witnessed one of these rages, we have been in some really desperate situations, many have died, but you have never gone berserker. Why?"

"An interesting question, and one to which I have no answer."

"There has to be some answer."

"Perhaps things don't seem desperate enough for some reason."

"What reason?"

"I don't know."

"Fabrana has witnessed one of these incidents, who else in our group?"

"I don't know!" Kevana snapped. "I have no memory of the one that Fabrana saw, so presumably have no memory of the others, if there have been others."

"Fabrana says you woke up with no memory of how you got to bed."

"For a man with a taste for drink like mine, that is not such a rare occurrence."

"But there are times when you haven't been drinking."

"A few, but no other reports of massacring friends."

"So, that is a good thing. I still don't understand why I have never felt this power in you before."

"The world is a strange place. It could be that when you are around I am less stressed by the situations we get into. Looking back I don't think we have ever been in a battle where there was almost no chance of surviving. The time when Fabrana was there, we were in a real mess, if that breach wasn't sealed, then everyone would have been dead. Someone had to do something, it turned out to be me."

"Explain the witness who saw a man lose his head when outside the reach of your sword?"

"How can I explain it, I have no memory?"

"You know the battle lore better than any man I know, theorise for me."

"I don't know. When we go into battle the sword becomes an extension of the arm that wields it. Perhaps in the berserker state the sword becomes an extension of the mind, no longer bound by its physical size."

"A nice theory, how do we test it?"

"I have no idea, I don't know how to trigger the berserker state, if that is the right thing to call it. And I wouldn't want to do it with friends around me. There is another possibility."

"Go on."

"It didn't happen. The man staggered away from the sword then fell, that is more likely than the sword reaching out."

"The impression from Fabrana is that he saw the stroke that killed the man."

"Why was Fabrana so far away?"

"Stop changing the subject, could be he was dealing with an enemy and was slow in following you, in this case it saved his life.

It still doesn't tell us how we can use this, or when your friends should run away."

"There is the cold, you felt it. Now you know the warning sign, if the weather suddenly turns chilly, hit the ground."

"That could be the only warning we are going to get, I did recognise the power build up. But did you not notice anything, anything at all?"

"No, well not really. I felt somehow a little out of touch, sort of dreaming but not. It's very difficult to put into words."

"Dislocated and slipping further away."

"That's probably as close as words can get."

"An induced trance, the conscious mind separating itself from something it doesn't want to know about, while leaving all the learned battle skills intact, even adding at least one new one."

"That's it, but I don't like being so out of control, there is no way I am going to try and enter this state, so there can be no experimenting." Kevana turned back to the corral, indicating that this was his final word on the subject.

"I understand. But we will all have to be aware of this strange skill of yours."

"It has harmed no one in years, the last time was probably the one we are talking about, since then I only have two memories of waking up in a strange place and sober. Neither of these had any sort of battle involved."

"Can you be sure?"

"Of course not, I have no memory. Though I cant imagine this sort of berserker state that would trigger and leave me with no injuries at all, on both occasions I woke up without a single drop of blood on me, none of mine and none of anyone else's."

"Let's talk about the last occasion. Go over it all for me."

"I woke up in my bed, no, on my bed, fully dressed."

"What had you been doing before this?"

"I was on a mission that should have gone to someone of a much lower status than me, it was a simple message delivery, but the lord in question wanted to be certain the message got to the recipient without interception, and I was not popular with the garrison commander at the time, I had just beaten him in a fencing match. So I got this mission, six days each way, but only if you kill a horse every day."

"So how long did it take you?"

"I arrived at the destination city, more a large town than city, in nine days, with my horse still alive, this one here."

"And what happened?"

"I delivered the message, the baron said to me that I should come back in the morning for a reply, he needed time to think. I went to the garrison commander and got quarters assigned to me. Then I went out looking for a beer or two, you know what it is like, strange town, strange people, find a bar, get drunk."

"I have heard that soldiers do that sort of thing." laughed Alverana.

"Well I went to several bars that night, not one of them had beer worth drinking, in the last one I tried, it was behind the abattoir, not the best of places as you can imagine, the beer was, if not the worst I had ever tasted, it was close. At this point I gave up, in addition beer wasn't sold by the mug, but by the jug. I had a whole jug of beer that wasn't fit for washing a horses arse. Luckily for me I was wearing my waterproof cape, and the jug had a very flat top, I was so surprised when I ran my hand across the jug, I couldn't believe my luck. I put a corner of the cape across the top of the jug, then turned it upside down and placed is on the bar. There were no leaks visible so I yanked the cape out and left the jug upside down on the bar, almost full. I walked away thinking that this is going to make a real mess for anyone who tries to move it. I walked out of the bar, somehow I made a mistake and left by the back door, I ended up in a dark alley. I remember thinking 'Where the hell am I?' I looked both ways up the alley, then I woke up on my bed."

"You woke up. Were you tired?"

"Not really."

"Tired like a good work out?"

"Perhaps, my sword arm was a little stiff, like a heavy fencing match."

Alverana nodded.

"What happened in the morning?" asked Alverana.

"Well, nothing special."

"What happened?"

"The garrison commander said that the guard had been called out in the night, there had been a fight between two of the local gangs of thieves, one gang had most of its members killed in an alley behind a bar."

"Near the abattoir?"

"Yes actually, it was near the abattoir."

"The bar you had been in?"

"I don't know."

"Did you ask?"

"I didn't want to know."

"So you suspected something?"

"I suppose, but nothing serious."

"What did the watch commander have to say about the incident?"

"He said that it looked like there had been a fight between the two biggest of the local gangs, but only the members of one of the gangs where actually injured, well not injured, they were all dead."

"This was unusual?"

"Definitely, normally there would be a few injured, maybe one or two dead, not a whole group dead."

"Survivors?"

"None. All dead."

"Perhaps they chanced upon you when you left the inn, in the alley, they surprised you and you killed them all."

"I don't see how, I don't know how many there were but they were more than a few. How could I kill all those and not get even one scratch."

"This berserker state of yours seems to reach beyond the bounds of the ordinary."

"So you are saying I killed all those thieves without one of them scratching me, and without one of them getting away?"

"So it would seem, but it could be that they met with an entirely different fate, something that you had nothing to do with. That is unimportant, how were you feeling when you left the bar?"

"I don't know, depressed and bored."

"Distracted?"

"Oh, definitely that."

"You came out of the wrong door, into an alley, and didn't notice that a gang of thieves was having their weekly meeting there, that is about as distracted as you can get."

"I certainly don't remember seeing them."

"If they had seen you what would they have seen?"

"I don't know. Just a man wearing black."

"Hooded?"

"Naturally."

"To most thieves you would have looked like an old man, easy prey, bash him on the head and empty his purse, they wouldn't see many of our kind in that sort of place. Only your berserker state took over before they could cause you any injury at all."

"You think that is what happened?"

"It could be, but we can never know, no witnesses."

"I would hate to leave no witnesses when I was amongst my friends."

"I would hate that as well, I would be one of the dead. Even I can't parry a sword that doesn't exist."

"I'll watch out for the feeling of distraction, or dislocation, and you look out for sudden changes in temperature. We'll be fine."

"Somehow I can't believe the thieves got that much warning."

"They didn't deserve any warning, they were not giving any after all."

"Perhaps."

"We need to stop worrying about this, and get some rest, we have a heavy task to perform in a few hours, looking at the sun, not that many hours, we need to get ourselves focused before we start."

"Right." Alverana turned and slowly walked away, his head bent deep in thought.

'I don't understand how this berserker thing hasn't come to light before now.' Thought Kevana. 'How many times had this happened?' Thinking back he came to a total of perhaps five occasions when he had woken without the usual hangover and no memory of getting to bed. 'Fabrana said that I had collapsed on the spot as soon as the battle was won. These other occasions I managed to get to a safe bed before I collapsed. Why? Could it be something to do with the scale of the thing, the one that Fabrana witnessed was a full scale war, the dead were hip deep all around me. The others perhaps only skirmishes, not something that needs a great deal of energy. So why was I stacking energy today, one simple cleric, an easy target for a berserker, why would it take so much energy to beat him? Unless the berserker inside knew how much power he would have needed to beat the old man.' These thoughts did nothing help calm Kevana, he leant on the rail watching the horses in the coral, his own horse had found a nice heavy rock and was striking huge sparks with it's new shoes.

"Oi." Shouted the man. "Don't you wear those shoes out, they were worth more than you." The horse merely glanced at him, then went back to striking sparks. Kevana shook his head and walked away. The camp was completely quiet when he walked up to the fire, which was so quiet as to be almost completely out, Kevana threw a small log and some dried horse droppings on the fire. Just enough to keep it going for a few more hours. He stared into the smoke curling slowly upwards, the swirling patterns reminded him of his own thoughts, spiralling and confused, reaching for the heavens, only to be dissipated before they get there. 'Stop it.' He thought to himself. 'This way lies depression, madness and perhaps even a killing rage.' He turned towards the sun, which was almost touching the mountains, still bright and yellow, not the huge red ball that appears on the plains or at sea. 'Now is the time for things to start.' He thought climbing to his feet, as he stood he saw walking out of the sunlight a hooded figure in black. Slowly the figure came into the camp, looking for a certain person to talk to. Worandana came out of his tent, once more clad in his most formal of black attire.

"Have you something to say?" he demanded of the figure.

"Yes master." answered Kirukana, falling to his knees, head bowed. "I may have been hasty in my words, I may have been wrong, but I acted as I believe was right at the time, you pointed out the error of my thinking but I didn't listen, for that I am deeply regretful. I wish only to continue to serve our god in the best way that I can."

"How can I be sure that you will obey me in the future? You chose not to listen to me this morning, what has changed?"

"I have had a lot of time to think about this, I think that my own temptations have coloured my judgement, it is the vow of chastity that has caused me the most difficulty in my service of Zandaar. It is the needs of the flesh that distract me the most, sometimes to complete absorption. I find it hard to believe that other men are not as I am. Please, master, forgive my failings, and let me serve as I should."

"I can only let you serve as I wish, if that is not how you think you should serve, then this situation will arise again, and the outcome will not be the same. Do you understand?"

"I truly understand, I will endeavour to perform as you want me to."

"Good. I think you understand, but you must yet prove to me by your own actions that you do."

"I know, and thank you, master." Kirukana bowed slowly until his forehead touched the ground, then he rose slowly, coming to his feet in one single motion. Bowed again and turned away. The whole camp breathed a huge sigh of relief. Fabrana nudged Petrovana and whispered. "Vow of chastity?"

"Yes."

"Serious?"

"The clerics sometimes take it seriously, the soldiers tend not to."

"Oh, that's alright then, I was a little worried there." Fabrana turned away smiling hugely. Kevana, having heard their exchange walked over to Worandana and spoke softly to him.

"Do you really take the vow of chastity that seriously?"

"For some people it is important. For a man like Kirukana it is vital, any momentary distraction of his thinking can destroy more than just himself. And he is one that is terribly distracted by women."

"Then it is good that he takes his vow seriously, just so long as you don't expect some of the others to be the same."

"I am fully aware that the military arm apply far less diligence to certain of our obligations than the secular arm, I don't normally hold it against them, unless it affects effectiveness."

"Trust me, none of mine are affected by this sort of thing, for most of them 'camp followers' are all they need."

"I cannot afford any distractions, not even something as 'simple' as that."

"I can see that, your work is more mental where ours is generally quite physical, it is difficult to be physically distracted when taking part in physical activity."

"Exactly. We have a serious mental task to perform, I suggest we get about it before all the light is gone." Worandana turned towards the tents. "Gorgana." he called. "Are you ready?"

"I am as ready as I will ever be." Came the reply as Gorgana crawled out of his tent, looking somewhat fat in his best black robe.

"How is this going to work?" Asked Worandana.

"I think we should build a large power charge in the circle as normal, then feed it to me just as I open the power to the stone with my blood. Then I target the sword, and bring it and the man here."

"That sounds just too simple." said Worandana.

"It sounds simple but the drain is going to be immense, I have to focus everything through the staff, I have to snatch a large weight and move it through a lot of space, and stop it before it gets here, simple it sounds, but it definitely isn't."

"So if all this works, then we have to close the path to the stone and stop our own power without actually managing to kill anyone."

"And." interrupted Kevana. "At least one of us has to be in fit state to capture the thief and our sword."

"That could be a problem." said Worandana. "We are usually totally exhausted after an attempt such as this. Suggestions?"

"One man could stay out of the circle, and be ready to hit the thief with a stun charge as soon as he arrives." said Kevana.

"Good idea." replied Worandana. "Who?"

"Kirukana."

"Excellent." laughed Worandana. "Give him a vital role and keep him out of the really dangerous part. I'll tell him." Worandana walk slowly away to give Kirukana the good news.

"Everyone gather round." shouted Kevana in his best parade ground voice. He waited a short time for the people to approach. "The plan is, normal circle to build a charge, then we hit Gorgana with the charge as he opens the stone, once that energy flow is established we send anything we have to support Gorgana, he must not fail. Once the thief has been brought here, then we must close down the energy channels. Gorgana will take care of most of that, but we must support him while he does. Kirukana will take no part until the last moments, the thief is going to be confused for a few moments, but he is likely to be aggressive, and we will be in no condition to defend ourselves, Kirukana will stun him as soon as the opportunity presents itself. Everyone clear?"

There were no questions asked, so they all started towards the stone, Gorgana seemed to be deep in thought, staring hard at the ground, avoiding the eyes of all his friends. Gorgana moved slowly towards the stone as the circle formed around it, he carefully balanced the staff on the top of the stone, and took a small knife from the pocket of his robe, a knife he had spent considerable time sharpening for this one task. He looked up to see the sun sinking slowly behind the mountains, the shadows rushing towards him, looking over his shoulder he saw Kirukana standing outside the circle, waiting to take part, almost directly across the green, in front of him, on the edge of the grassed area, stood a lone figure, a woman, though he couldn't actually see who it was he knew that Anya was watching over him, and somehow this comforted him. The circle was formed, he knew that they were waiting for him, he went over in his mind exactly what he had to do, his main worry was the Worandana would know enough of the original intent to notice that he was actually going to do something different, the change could be seen, and Worandana could stop him before the task was completed, the power set loose at that time could easily kill them all. 'Worandana will hesitate, once the power from the stone is running, he will hesitate, and that will give me the time I need to finish my task.' He thought, almost prayed. Turning towards Worandana he gave the slightest of nods, enough to start the power building in the circle of men. Feeling the tension rise in the circle he slowly carved a shallow cut across the palm of each hand, the pain caused a slight twitch of his face, but no one could see it, hidden deep in the recess of his hood. He smeared his blood on the staff, in the places he was going to grip it, then let some fall onto the top of the stone, adding new red to the blackened stains already there. He built the picture of a flower in his mind, a huge blossom, tightly closed, green and yellow. He nodded again and the power from the circle flooded his mind, almost as if it fed the flower in there, causing it to open, slowly at first then more rapidly, the power of the stone rose up inside him, he forced it into the staff, feeling the heat of It, and the incredible strength of it. Holding it in place, building the charge, until he was screaming silently with the pain and the heat, he formed the instructions in his mind, a human voice was just too small a thing to accomplish this feat, a grey swirl formed around him, and his thought reached out for the sword, riding on the power of the stone he found it in a moment, the intervening distance meant almost nothing, now he paused, only for an instant, and a second swirling grey vortex formed, this one in the vicinity of the sword and it's bearer. But this wasn't the man he wanted, groping almost blindly he felt around for the mind that he needed, he was looking for hate, not the blazing hatred of the sword bearer, but something altogether smaller, and darker, the vortex followed his groping mind, until he found the one he was seeking, then in a flash the vortex enveloped the man. With both trapped inside the twin vortices Gorgana released the last part of the spell, and with a huge surge from the stone switched places. Once the transfer was complete he could no longer control the power from the stone, and there was no power coming to support him, he fell face first onto the ground, and into a black pit of unconsciousness.

Crathen stood in front of the stone, a column of brilliant light streaming upwards hurt his eyes, but only for a moment

Kirukana's stun spell took away any conscious thought. The circle of monks fell into complete disarray, their power spent and now without any target, they fell. The light from the stone seemed to be searching for something, it set fire to a tree top at the edge of the green, then moved away a rippling column of multicoloured energy, Kirukana watched it for a moment or two, but had no idea what to do. He tried to rouse Worandana with no success, then noticed that a woman was running towards the stone, he moved to stop her.

"Get out of my way." She screamed. "The power has to be stopped or it will kill everyone around here." She pushed him out of the way and snatched her knife from her skirt, she slashed her hands while still running to the stone, she dropped the knife and rolled to the ground as the power came questing towards her, then she was on her feet again, the power tore a burning swathe through the grass she had been lying on, as she reached the stone and placed both hands on it in the place the power flowed from. A scream was torn from her lips and her entire body appeared to catch fire, not the yellow flames that are part of a normal fire, but white flames the blazed outwards in all directions. Kirukana started to drag his friends away from the blazing woman, he felt the heat on his face, and saw smoke rising from his robe. As he touched Alverana the big man woke and rolled uncertainly to his feet, together they pulled the rest out of danger.

"We have to help her." Said Alverana.

"How? She's the one that knows this power the best, and she's stopped screaming now, perhaps she has it under control."

Kevana was the next to come to his senses, he groaned and sat up, looking round.

"Where is the thief?" He asked, his voice ragged and feeble.

"Over there." Alverana waved an arm in the general direction of Crathen. "But he's not the one we want."

"How do you know?"

"His sword is nothing special."

"Where is Gorgana? How can he have missed? With all that power, how can he have missed?"

"There is another story, he's not here at all." The blaze of light that was Anya slowly began to dim, it shrank until is was human shaped, and then woman shape, then it appeared to vanish inside her skin, briefly she was illuminated from the inside by a deep red light, that gradually faded, until she was standing naked beside the stone with both hands resting on the top. Slowly she turned towards them, she appeared to be completely unharmed, though she didn't have a single hair on her body anywhere.

"You fools really know how to make a mess of everything, don't you?"

"So it would appear." said Kevana. "Are you hurt? Can we help you?"

"I was hurt, the power was running so hot it burned a large part of me, but as you can see I have healed it all."

"Kirukana. Give the lady your robe, before she starts to get cold." Kirukana balked at this command.

"Now, Kirukana." snapped Kevana. As the man started to undress he turned back to Anya. "How is that you are naked and without hair?"

"The clothing all burned when I took hold of the power, and the hair with it, hair is dead and cannot be healed, it will grow again." She took the robe from the monk and threw it around her shoulders, wrapping it around herself, it was far too big, but would certainly keep the chill of evening out.

"Did you see what happened? We were sort of caught up it all."

"Yes. I saw."

"Please tell us."

"Simply put, Gorgana found the man he was looking for and changed places with him, in doing so he lost control of the stone, he almost set it free. I stopped it."

"You are saying that he has gone over to our enemies?"

"No. He has gone over to your enemies, he doesn't see them as his enemies, he felt that you would soon turn against him anyway."

"He told you this?"

"Yes. We had a long talk after I showed him the secret of the stone. He thought that by bringing the man and the sword here he would set off a battle in our village. Many would have been killed, that he wouldn't do."

"So he has turned traitor. I shall deal harshly with him when I catch him."

"He was aware there would be a price to pay for his actions today, but he is willing to pay, you would have considered him a traitor whether he stayed or went."

"I thank you for your help today, if we decide to try this again would you be willing to help us again?"

"I wasn't helping you, I was helping my village, if that power gets loose, then the whole place is likely to be destroyed."

"I understand. Thank you anyway, I am sorry that your clothes got burned."

"They are of no consequence, only the lives of my friends are important, and you threaten them."

"If we decide not to attempt the power of the stone again we shall be leaving in the morning."

"That would be the best all round."

Kevana bowed slightly and turned away, she turned without another word and returned to her house. Anya was feeling particularly good in the gathering gloom, there was a spring in her step, and a song in her heart, she had never tapped so much power from the stone, nor come away from it with so much still inside her. She had a specific intention in mind for this power, she was going to get her husband back, or die in the attempt.

Kevana went to where Worandana was sitting on the grass, the blast had hit the old man especially hard, he was still unable to stand, so Kevana sat beside him.

"Gorgana has gone over to the thieves." Kevana said.

"I know, and he has taken most of his books with him, and the staff."

"That is why he looked so fat, his robe was full of books."

"He must have planned this for a while."

"Not really, only a day at the most. I think he hatched this plan last night when he was talking to Anya. He didn't want to start a battle in this village."

"Without the staff there is no way we can channel enough power to reach him and get him back, without his books we have no way of knowing how to do it even." Worandana shook his head slowly.

"But we know his pattern, we can reach him, read him, and perhaps even destroy him." spat Kevana.

"Perhaps, but he knows this. He may have thought of some form of defence."

"What defence can there be?"

"He must think there is a way."

"What can he do? We have known him a long time, we know the very pattern of his mind, with that he cannot escape."

"If we know him so well, how is it that we didn't know he was feeling so threatened by us that he was forced to change sides?"

"We can't know what he was thinking, but he can't change the basic pattern of his mind, can he?"

"Tomorrow, when we are rested, we will find that out."

"In the meantime, we have a prisoner to interrogate." Kevana got up and went to were Crathen was being held, his hands and feet were bound and linked to each other with a very short length of rope. He was unable to move, so Kevana prodded him with one foot, just to get his attention.

"Who are you?"

"Crathen. Release me at once, send me back, she is in danger."

"No, no, and who is in danger?"

"Jayanne, she is in danger, he means to hurt her."

"Who is the leader of your group?"

"Send me back!"

"Who is the leader of your group?" Kevana emphasised the question with a swift kick to the ribs, not hard enough to break anything, but enough to show that he meant to have his questions answered.

"Namdarin, he leads, most of the time, though Jangor also leads."

"Namdarin has a strange sword, one with a black stone in the pommel?"

"Yes, he has a sword, and a bow, and a stupid white horse. Send me back!"

"We can't send you back, the man that brought you here went to where ever you came from, he took with him the knowledge. Jangor, who is he?"

"A soldier, probably not officer grade, but competent none the less."

"Jayanne?"

"She's the only woman in the group, red haired, and beautiful."

"Who else? Granger?"

"Yes the old wizard, he's very powerful, but not very strong, not physically at least."

"I know him, he beat me once. Who else?"

"Just some ex-soldiers, four of them, friends of Jangor."

"Who else?"

"A new man, just arrived, huge man, called Brank, I don't know anything about him, only met him the once."

"Where are they going?"

"I don't know."

"Where are they going?" This time Alverana put his boot on Crathens wrist and pressed down hard enough for the bones to grind slowly against one another.

"I don't know, they don't know, the bird god told them of an ancient elvish weapon they could use to defeat Zandaar, a mindstone, or something." Alverana released the pressure on Crathen's wrists.

"You talked to the bird god, and he told you how to defeat Zandaar?"

"He was more than a little obscure, but he did say that Namdarin would need the mindstone, but there was some talk of ending all life, I was confused by it all."

"How many people did you lose?"

"What do you mean?"

"When we met the bird it cost us one man, how many did you lose?"

"None. Kern knew how to talk to the bird, he summoned it."

"So this Kern is a servant of the bird god?"

"I don't think so, perhaps an ex-servant."

"So where are they going?"

"I don't know, they went into a city to find something out, but I don't know if they were successful, they had only just got back when you snatched me away. I need to get back there, Jayanne is in danger."

"I certainly intend on catching up with your friends. They have stolen something that belongs to Zandaar."

"If you are talking about Namdarin's sword I think you will find it belongs to Xeron, not Zandaar."

"We were sent to collect the sword and take it back to Zandaar, and that is what we will do."

"I need to come with you, I want to help Jayanne."

"We have seen inside your mind, you are filled with jealousy, I had intended to use that to our advantage, but Gorgana has put an end to that plan, what use can you be to us?"

"I know exactly where they are right now, I can take you straight to them."

"I can find them in a moment, that sword cannot hide from us, I need to know where they will be in a few days, so that I can catch up."

"They think I am a friend, I could be a useful hostage, when you do catch up."

"That is true, but Gorgana could poison their minds against you, he has seen into your heart, once he tells them this they will not think so well of you."

"They won't believe him, he is almost certainly dead, Namdarin would have killed him the instant he saw him."

"He is not dead, one of us would have felt it." Kevana snapped a quick look at Worandana.

"He is still alive." said Worandana.

"How soon before we can change that?"

"We need rest, no chance before the morning, we are too drained."

"What about that?" he glanced at the stone.

"Gorgana was the only one who used it, he was the only one attuned to it, I wouldn't want to chance that not for a while, perhaps a day or two, that stone needs to settle down a little as well, can't you feel it, it is close to eruption all on it's own."

"I do sense its disquiet." said Kevana, turning away for a few moments.

"You live." he said to Crathen. "For now. If you prove false you will die in a heartbeat, if you are useful you will stay alive. Alvernana, put him in Gorgana's tent, relax his bonds a little. Everyone else, rest. At day break I want that traitors mind burned to a crisp." Everyone started moving towards their tents. Kevana touched Worandana on the shoulder as he walked past, and nodded towards the stone. The two walked that way together.

"Can we do that to one of our own?" asked Kevana as soon as the others were out of earshot.

"Oh, we can certainly do it, but should we?"

"What do you mean? He has turned against us."

"Has he? He has gone over to the enemy, but is this just a ploy, a ruse to help us catch them?"

"You knew him best, would he have done such a thing?"

"Yes, but I think he would have consulted us first."

"So you think he has turned traitor?"

"I am not completely sure, it could be that he realised that he couldn't just pull the man and the sword here, and decided to swap places instead."

"Then why swap with the wrong man?"

"Survival, he has swapped a minor member of their group for a minor member of ours, he should be able to talk his way into staying alive, and then feed us the information we need to catch up."

"How will we know if that is his plan?"

"Perhaps we can talk to him tomorrow, before we fry his mind?"

"Fine, you talk to him first, then we kill him if he is a traitor. Could he lie to you with his mind?"

"Almost no one can lie with their mind, it is just too complicated a task, too many things can give you away, he will have to tell us the truth, but if he has gone over to them, then he will just not talk to us at all."

"Then he will die. We can still track the sword, we both need some rest." Kevana turned away leaving the older man to his thoughts.

ABOUT THE AUTHOR

My name is Michael Porter, some call me Roaddog. Formal training for writing, I have exactly none, I did start reading early, generally before breakfast, I actually learned to read before I started school, many thanks to mother for all the hours she put in. Of course this wasn't popular with the school at that time, some fool had just introduced an new learning system, some sort of phonetic garbage. When asked "Why should children have to learn English twice?" They had no answer. I didn't bother with that phonetic junk, they had to get some old books out of storage for me to read. Yes a trouble maker from the start. I was only at that particular school for one year, but before I left I had read every book they had, well, all the ones that were spelled properly. This pattern continued through every school I attended, grammar school was no different, they had a huge library, which I read in less than three years. Much to the despair of my teachers reading didn't help me in my English lessons, spelling, punctuation, these things aren't important it's the story that counts. I'm sorry Miss Boll, Cider with Rosie is boring, I'm not reading it. David Eddings, now he's good. I'm making no friends amongst the English department here. English exams were obviously interesting, mock 'O' level I scored a massive -30%. This was in the days before students got credit for just being there. The scoring system was simple, you start with 100 points, for every spelling, punctuation or grammatical error a point is deducted, it seems that in only four pages of writing I managed an impressive 130 errors. The real 'O' level was unclassified. No real surprise there. I managed to pass on the second attempt, but only by twisting the proposed essay title, and plagiarising large chunks of the sci-fi novel I was currently reading. Enough ancient history.

For those that don't know me I'm getting along in years, I'd be approaching retirement if the government didn't keep moving the goalposts. I've been writing this story for many years, but only got around to publishing it recently due to pressure from she who must be obeyed. I started this mammoth project after reading a particularly dreadful fantasy novel. I decided that even I could write something better than that. I noticed that most books of the genre were lacking in real violence and proper sex, so this series is definitely for a more adult audience. I'm hoping to have the complete set finished before the end of 2018, I have a day job that takes up a lot of my time, I also have an evening job as sound and lighting engineer for a local rock band, which eats a big chunk of my weekends, so time for writing is somewhat restricted. I'll try to get Doom finished on schedule, as there are a couple more projects in the pipe.

For me reading and writing is all about the story.
Enjoy.

Printed in Great Britain
by Amazon